Steve Mosby lives and works in Leeds. His novels have been translated widely and longlisted for the Theakstons Crime Novel of the Year Award and CWA Dagger in the Library.

You can discover more about the author at www.theleftroom.co.uk

I KNOW WHO DID IT

Charlie Matheson died two years ago in a car accident. So who is the woman who looks scarily like her, claiming to be back from the dead? Detective Mark Nelson is called to investigate and hear her terrifying account of what she's been through . . . Every year Detective David Groves receives a birthday card for his son — even though he was murdered years ago. The tragedy took everything from him, apart from his belief in the law, despite the killers never having been found. This year, though, the card bears a different message: *I know who did it*. Uncovering the facts will lead Nelson and Groves on a dark journey to a place where justice is a game, and punishments are severe. In order to get to the truth, first they'll have to go through hell . . .

Books by Steve Mosby
Published by Ulverscroft:

CRY FOR HELP
STILL BLEEDING
BLACK FLOWERS
THE NIGHTMARE PLACE

STEVE MOSBY

I KNOW WHO DID IT

Complete and Unabridged

CHARNWOOD
Leicester

First published in Great Britain in 2015 by
Orion Books
an imprint of
The Orion Publishing Group Ltd, London

First Charnwood Edition
published 2016
by arrangement with
The Orion Publishing Group Ltd
An Hachette UK Company, London

*A catalogue record for this book is available
from the British Library.*

ISBN 978–1–4448–2928–0

Published by
F. A. Thorpe (Publishing)
Anstey, Leicestershire

Set by Words & Graphics Ltd.
Anstey, Leicestershire
Printed and bound in Great Britain by
T. J. International Ltd., Padstow, Cornwall

This book is printed on acid-free paper

To Lynn and Zack

Acknowledgements

Many thanks to my agent, Carolyn Whitaker, and to everybody at Orion who helped make this novel a reality — especially Genevieve Pegg, Laura Gerrard and Jane Selley. Huge thanks also to the people who helped and encouraged me along the way, with special nods to Luca and Merilyn for their comments and support. Finally, thanks to Lynn and Zack for putting up with me while I was working on this book, and to whom it is dedicated, as always, with love.

Groves

The boy in the pit

It was nearly midnight when they finally took David Groves out to the woods. On the surface, he was very calm. Afterwards he would remember that more clearly than anything else that happened. He would remember thinking: *It must seem strange to them, how calm I am.*

They drove north along the ring road that circled the city. Traffic was sparse at this time of night, and became more so the further they went. To the south, this same road fed tributaries into housing estates and shopping centres, and was always packed with vehicles, but the northern fringe of the city was decaying, and there was little worth driving to here. The industrial estates they passed on the left were mostly abandoned and dead. Many of the factory roofs had fallen in without anyone noticing or caring.

And there were the woods, of course. They stretched away to the right of the vehicle, dark and impenetrable. There were occasional footpaths into them, but none went in more than a half-mile or so before curling back out again. Every year, a few people, strangers to the city for the most part, got lost by venturing off trail. Many of the old wells and mineshafts were overgrown and not marked on official maps, and it was strangely easy to lose your bearings out

1

there, as though the area had its own magnetic field that began disrupting your mental compass. The woods were sprawling, dangerous territory.

That was where they were going.

Groves stared out of the car window as the trees flashed past. The distant mountains were pitch-black peaks against the night sky, and the stars stood out above: a bright spill of dust and diamonds. You couldn't see them in the city centre, but there was less artificial light this far north. The heavens only ever appear obliquely, he thought; they disappear when we shine our torches at them. And that was certainly the approach he'd been forced to take towards his own faith of late.

He looked away again.

There were three of them in the car. Groves was in the back by himself, his body rocking passively with the movement of the vehicle. The occasional street lights they passed under filled the car with a quick sweep of orange light before leaving them in darkness again. It was raining slightly, and the wipers squeaked intermittently, but otherwise they drove in silence. None of them had made any attempt at conversation. It would have been impossible to talk about where they were going, and why, but any other topic would have been trivial — an insult, almost — so it was safer to stay quiet, and to pretend that the silence was dignified rather than awkward. But the longer the journey went on, the more it felt as though the air in the vehicle was under pressure, growing so tight that the windows might eventually shatter from the force of it.

He wondered what the officers in front were thinking.

I can't imagine what he must be going through, perhaps.

I wouldn't be able to do this.

He actually didn't know if he could. But then someone had to, didn't they, and in this case it could hardly be Caroline. Even if it could wait, it felt as though it was his duty to do this as soon as possible. Obviously Groves wasn't attached to the investigation himself, but this little trip was a professional favour he'd not had to fight hard to receive. DCI Reeves had expressed concern, asking him twice if he was sure, but the look on Groves' face had been enough. However hard it was going to be, it was the right thing to do, and Groves was universally regarded as a man who always did the right thing. Everybody knew he was a good man. There had been no further questions after that.

The driver slowed and indicated, and they pulled into a lay-by. There were two police vans here, dark, lumpy shapes with the overhanging branches pushed sideways across their roofs. A single officer guarded the entrance to the footpath. The headlights turned his jacket a bright lemon yellow in the seconds before they clicked off.

'We're here,' the driver said.

'Thank you.'

It was a shock to him how strong his voice sounded, almost as though it belonged to someone else, and he wondered again what the other officers were thinking.

3

It must seem strange to them, he thought, *how calm I am.*

Perhaps they thought he was being brave and stoical in the circumstances, or that he was gathering strength and resolve to face the horrors ahead. But he didn't feel strong or brave, and if the last two years had taught him anything, it was that an appearance of calm was meaningless. Calm told you nothing at all about what might happen next. Before it exploded, a bomb was calm.

★ ★ ★

Because of the rain, a tent had been constructed in the woods. It was bright white, illuminated by the spotlights positioned awkwardly between the trees, and seemed to hang over the clearing like a ghost. Groves knew that the tent was simply to protect the integrity of the crime scene rather than out of respect for what had been found here, but still, he was glad.

Respect did come into it, though. As he arrived, stepping into the small, brightly lit clearing, the officers and SOCOs present all fell silent, but every single one of them met his eye, the ones he knew nodding in solidarity. The message was clear. *We are your brothers and sisters*, they were telling him. *Although we can't imagine your loss, we are doing everything we can, and we will try to do more.*

In the centre, beneath the tent, the ground had been disturbed: leaves pushed carefully to the edges; soil scraped away and bagged for future analysis. The result was a small pit below the apex of the tent, a few feet deep.

To reach this place, Groves had needed to walk almost a mile through the pitch-black woods, along marked routes at first, and then down barely worn makeshift footpaths. The officers accompanying him had swept their torches back and forth over the ground. He had barely looked. And yet now that he was here, he found himself hesitating. Even though the ground was clear of physical dangers, it was almost impossible to move forward.

Please help me, God.

He forced himself, the other officers moving back, allowing him space. A few twigs crunched underfoot, the sound soft in the night. The contents of the pit revealed themselves by increments. When he could see everything that was there, it took a few more seconds before the sight resolved into something his mind could process.

A sudden memory. He and Caroline had never succeeded in establishing a bedtime for Jamie, and at the age of nearly three, the little boy had still kept his own hours. It hurt them both too much to hear the sound of him suffering if they left him in his cot. Neither of them could face controlled crying, especially when they spent so much of the time alone together controlling their own. So they had given up. Every night Jamie would eventually lie down on the settee, say *Night night, Mummy and Daddy*, and half an hour later one of them would carry his snuffling, sleeping weight up to the bedroom. The little boy always went to sleep on his side, hands clasped in front of his slightly open mouth, feet crossed at the ankle, soft blond hair swept back behind his ear.

The absolute peace on his face had often stunned Groves. A child drifting off to sleep. Everything else was worthwhile; the day had been won.

The boy in the pit appeared to be lying in that exact same position, and it was that, more than anything else, that brought the first shock of recognition — and then the clothes, of course. The baggy blue jeans. The remaining shreds of that orange T-shirt with the purple shark on it. He remembered Caroline holding that and another one up on the morning Jamie had gone missing. *Shark? Or monkey?* She'd repeated the questions, asking them quicker and quicker, moving the T-shirts backwards and forwards, until Jamie collapsed into giggles. *Shark, Mummy! Shark!*

A few strands of his hair remained, swept back in that achingly familiar way, but as dirty and wiry now as the roots in the ground around him. The small skull was grey and cracked, like an old light bulb stained by smoke. There was a kind of peace here, yes, but it was an emptiness.

The rain pattered on the tent above.

Groves stared down at the remains.

He wasn't calm, he realised. The reality was that he was totally outside himself — that in fact he had barely been in his body the whole afternoon. Since the phone call, he might as well have been hovering above himself, watching his

6

own thoughts and movements without feeling a thing. Right now, he came back into himself — into this moment, here in the woods — with a *thump* as solid as the heartbeat after the one that skips.

He looked at what else was in the pit, buried alongside the body of the little boy. A toy, slightly to one side. Even more than the clothes, the hair and the position, it was the sight of the toy that finally sealed it.

Winnie-the-Pooh. The soil had dulled the colour, but it was still immediately familiar. That stuffed Pooh toy had been Jamie's favourite thing in the world. Every morning in his cot he gave it a cuddle, and it rarely left his hand afterwards until he fell asleep with it hugged close to his small chest on the settee.

'Yes.'

Nobody in the clearing replied. His voice didn't sound as strong as it had back at the car. In the silence that followed, he could hear the rain on the canvas above, slow and steady as drumming fingers, and then, finally, Detective David Groves tried again.

'Yes,' he said. 'This is my son.'

Part One

And when their Mother was said to have passed over, They were brought before Her in Heaven. And She bid Them sit with Her, and They listened with wonder as She told Them secrets of life and death, and of the true nature of good and evil, and of how the dead are never truly gone, and of ways the dead may remain with us still.

Extract from the Cane Hill bible

Mark

A horrible truth

I'm happy now. My life is a good one. But if you were to excavate it, you would find something terrible in the foundations.

It feels strange to look back on what happened from the present day. It all felt so intense at the time — each sight and sound vivid and indelible; every emotion sharp and heightened — and I'd never have believed there'd come a day when I would forget. When I would have a new life in a different place. A job with a respected team in the police. A relationship with a woman I love more than I can say. Back then, it would have been impossible to imagine it could ever feel as distant from me as it does now.

I was on a backpacking holiday when it happened, with a different woman. My girlfriend at the time. One evening Lise and I pitched our tent at a small campsite on the coast, and then we went down to the beach and swam together in the sea. The setting sun was a beautiful sight, lowering itself towards the water and filling the horizon in front of us with a spread of orange flame. I can imagine our shadows, cast back over the beach as we ran down to the edge of the surf, and the soft sand pushing against our feet.

There was nobody else around; we had the beach entirely to ourselves. Which seemed like a blessing at the time. We were young and in love, after all, and couldn't keep our hands off each other. We went into the sea and floated out a little way, buoyed by the slight waves. When we were pushed together by the current, we embraced and kissed. When it pulled us apart again, we linked hands and allowed our lower bodies to swing slowly up to the surface, then lay on our backs and kicked our toes out, watching the sunlight turn the water into burning pearls. It was beautiful.

I wasn't a strong swimmer and wanted to stay within my depth, so I kept reaching down with my feet to find the seabed, feeling the silt between my toes. It gave me a sense of security. But then at one point I tried to touch down and the bottom wasn't there any more. The water went over my nose, unexpectedly, and I came back up again coughing. I craned my neck to look back towards the shore; it suddenly looked a lot further away than it should have done.

Just relax, Lise told me. I can't remember the exact words, but it was something like that. She could tell I was nervous, but at that point she was still calm. *Let's head back in.*

I nodded, and we both struck out for shore. I probably swam a little harder than I needed to. Even though there was no immediate danger, I felt out of control and I wanted that reassuring feeling of ground beneath my feet once more. A minute later, half exhausted, I looked up at the beach again, and it was further away than before.

Treading water for a moment, I could feel the sea pulling gently at me. Lise was a little way off to the side by then, and I could see that she wasn't calm any more. That frightened me more than anything, because she was a much better swimmer than me. She never panicked about anything.

Scream, she told me.

I did — we both did — but the noise was small and didn't go anywhere, and there would have been nobody around to hear it if it had. I struck off again, clawing at the water now. In a single moment, it felt like the sea around me had changed from settled and serene to choppy and dangerous. It happened as quickly as the sun can sometimes pass behind a cloud. I heard Lise scream, some distance away from me now, and then a wave knocked me under. I came up coughing and choking. The beach ahead was smeared by the water in my eyes, and appeared to be above me somehow, as unreachable as the top of a cliff face. Then I was pushed under again.

Somehow I kept swimming. I understood very clearly that I was going to die, and it felt ridiculous and unfair. I'd never been a strong swimmer, but now something animalistic and primal took over, and every time my body flagged, I found strength from somewhere. I kept swimming. There was nothing more to it than that. Some time later — surely no more than a minute — I realised my feet could touch the bottom again, and then I found myself stumbling out of the sea, my body waterlogged with exhaustion. For a moment, I couldn't understand that I was alive. But I was. I made it out of the sea that evening, and Lise did not.

The last image I have of her is from the beach, standing at the edge of the water and shouting out to her. *Swim! Breathe! It's going to be okay!* I remember her face screaming back at me for help, just before she disappeared amongst the black waves, and then I never saw her again.

For a long time afterwards, it felt like I'd died that evening too. I remember that the days that followed were as dark as the nights, and that the grief and sadness were physical sensations — literally *there* in my chest, like a muscular pain that couldn't be relieved by stretching into a new position. I ached from the absence of her in a way that seemed impossible to bear. My life had received an injury that didn't feel survivable. And yet I kept living. Because that's what happens.

Over time, it got easier. Knowing what Lise would have wanted for me, I eventually took my life by the scruff of the neck and applied for a new job — a new start — on the other side of the country. I mourned, but I also tidied away. After a time, I met somebody new and fell in love with them. I gradually put distance between the *now* and the *then*, until what had hurt so badly had finally scarred over, and pressing on it produced little aside from the dullest throb. I built a new life, and it's a happy one. Somehow I had kept swimming.

But there is a horrible truth underlying that, and a question I avoid asking myself. The truth is this: Lise died, and my life changed irrevocably and awfully. But in the end, not all of those changes were for the worse. My happy life now is a structure built on the foundations of that tragedy, and to remove it would remove me. As much as I loved her back then, if I were given an impossible opportunity to wind the clock back — to have Lise survive that evening and my life now to become something else entirely — would I take it?

Impossible, of course, which makes the question easy to set aside. In the end, whatever the junctions open to it, your life can only ever follow one track. You can't turn back time, and the people who are taken from you are gone for ever.

That was what I thought, anyway. But that was before a woman called Charlie Matheson came back from the dead.

Charlie

What had been done to her face

Constable Tom Wilson was driving at a leisurely pace down Town Street when he found her.

He was heading back to the department from a routine domestic call-out: a couple rowing. Today, like the days before it, had been far too hot, and he found the temperature always seemed to bring out the worst in some people. They burned, and they got hot and angry and difficult. The pavements outside every pub he passed were teeming with groups of men, many of them already red-chested and drunk. He didn't envy their partners. He certainly didn't envy the evening shifts.

Wilson checked his watch as he idled along. An hour left of his own shift, barring further incidents, and although he knew that anything could happen, in his head he was already counting down the minutes. A cold beer in the garden. That would do it, he thought — a few drops of peace to dilute the day. He drove along steadily, the window down and his arm resting on the sill, already tasting it.

And then he saw the crowd.

It was more a gathering, really — several people clustered together outside a grocer's up ahead on the right — but he could tell immediately from their body language that something was wrong. They were all focused on the same spot, some of them leaning forward, and one man was crouched right down as though talking to someone on the ground.

Wilson imagined an old lady, fallen down. If so, it was likely that someone had already called an ambulance, but still. He indicated, then pulled in and parked up directly opposite.

As he waited for a break in the traffic, a couple of people in the small crowd turned and saw him, and looked grateful as he finally trotted across the road. A uniform always gave reassurance. In Wilson's experience, and despite the events of this hot afternoon, most people were generally good, and when someone was in distress in public, they rallied round to help. But it was always a little tentative, a little *I don't know quite what to do*, as though the person they wanted to help was a bird that had fallen out of a nest, and they weren't sure whether they were allowed to touch it or not.

'Right then,' he said. 'What's going on?'

It was an elderly woman nearest him who answered. 'I don't know. She was coming along, and then she just sat down. The way she was walking, I could tell that something wasn't right.'

A man behind them said, 'I've just phoned for an ambulance.'

'Good. Can everyone move back, please? Thank you.'

They did as they were told, revealing a woman sitting on the ground outside the shop. She was half leaning against a rack of fruit, head bowed so that a tumble of curly brown hair obscured

17

her face. Her knees were raised in front of her, with both arms wrapped around her shins, hugging them. Even without being able to see her face, it was obvious that she was much younger than he'd been expecting.

Wilson crouched down in front of her.

'Miss?'

The woman didn't react to him in any way. She was dressed strangely, he noticed then: her trousers and short-sleeved blouse were both a brilliant, uniform white. Her bare forearms were thin and pale, a barely distinguishable shade from her clothes. His gaze moved over the criss-crossing scars there. There were so many, and while some looked old, others appeared to have been inflicted much more recently. With that and the outfit . . . he wondered, was she a patient somewhere? There was nowhere nearby that he could think of.

'Miss?' he said again. 'Are you okay?'

Again there was no response. She was gripping her legs so hard that her knuckles seemed to be coming through the skin. And breathing very rapidly, he realised, as though trying to control a panic attack.

Give her room.

Wilson stood back up and turned to the woman who'd answered him first.

'Where did she come from?'

'Down that way.' She gestured further along Town Street, in the direction of the field at the far end. 'I knew something was wrong with her. I could just *tell*. She seemed a bit out of it. I think she might be drunk.'

18

'And what happened? She collapsed?'

'She reached here and stopped, and then she just . . . sat down.'

'Okay.'

Wilson didn't think the woman on the ground was drunk. You could almost always smell it on anyone bad enough to be found in a state like this. Whatever they'd been drinking, the alcohol itself seeped out of their pores. And this woman didn't smell of booze. Breathing in now, he caught the mixed smell of the fruit stall beside them, and the slightest hint of antiseptic, but nothing more.

'Nobody knows her?' he asked the gathered crowd. 'None of you have seen her round here before?'

Blank faces, a few shakes of the head.

'All right.' He crouched back down again. 'Miss? Can you hear me? My name's Tom. I'm a policeman. It's going to be okay, I promise. Can you tell me your name?'

That got him the faintest of replies.

'Sorry, could you say that again?'

'Charlie.'

'Okay. Hello, Charlie.'

'Matheson. That's my name. Charlie Matheson.'

'That's really good,' he said. 'Now — '

'There was an accident,' she said suddenly. 'There was a terrible accident. And I don't know where I am! I don't understand. Where is this?'

He started to answer, but the woman suddenly tilted her head back and looked at him. The people around him receded into the distance, and the noise of the traffic behind disappeared underwater.

19

For a moment, Wilson couldn't say anything. All he could do was look at the woman. Just crouch there in front of her, staring in horror at what had been done to her face.

Mark

Back from the dead

Of course, I didn't know any of that as I woke up the next day. In fact I didn't know very much at all. As I lay in that vague state between sleep and consciousness, my eyes still shut scrupulously tight, my thoughts were grey and heavy and distinctly unusual: disjointed jigsaw pieces that, when assembled, I thought would not make for a pleasant picture. I was dimly aware that moving too much would be a bad idea, but at that point I hadn't quite remembered why.

You're massively hung-over, Mark.

Oh yes. That was it.

'Coffee for you.'

I felt pressure against the side of my leg as Sasha perched on the bed beside me. She clicked her fingers above my face.

'Come on, Mark. Wakey wakey.'

'Ugh.'

'Is that really all you can manage?'

'It seems so.'

I heard the tap as she put the cup down on the bedside table. A moment later, I risked opening my eyes. The room seemed oddly angled. As I stared up at the lightshade for a few seconds, it began moving gradually away to one side. My hangover appeared to be slowly stirring the bedroom.

'Something has happened to my head.'

'Indeed.' Sasha patted one of my legs with exaggerated sympathy. Then she stood up. 'You can't say I didn't warn you.'

'You warned me insufficiently.'

'I warned you extensively. But hey, you're a grown man.'

I turned my head slightly to look at her. She was standing at the side of the bed, peering down at me with her head tilted to one side and a slight smile on her face. Her bright blonde ponytail hung over the shoulder of her uniform, contrasting with the black there.

We were both police. I was a detective, and spent most of my time behind a desk in my office, or at a table in an interrogation suite, or occasionally outside, organising door-to-doors; I wore a suit to work. My fiancée, on the other hand, was a sergeant in the department's door team. Sasha was one of the officers who got called in when we needed a door opened and didn't want to knock. It was tough work, even if she shrugged off anything I ever said along those lines, and she dressed accordingly. The body armour was in the boot of her car, but she was already half suited up this morning. I glanced down at the various weapons and implements pouched in what I insisted on calling her utility belt.

'You look like a superhero,' I said.

'Which I am.'

'Which you are. Yes.' I sat up, and everything swam slightly. 'Oh my God. Thanks for the coffee.'

'No worries. And it's only just after eight. You've got time for a few more.'

'Just after eight? I have the morning off, you know.'

'I know. But I took the executive decision that coffee would be better for you than sleep.' She reached down and ruffled my hair affectionately. 'Plus, you know, I thought you'd want to say goodbye before I left. You didn't *quite* manage to say good night last night.'

I tried to remember coming to bed, and couldn't.

'Ah, yes. Sorry.'

'I survived.' She ruffled my hair again, then stepped away. 'Anyway, I've got to go. Early knock. But you have a good day, Detective Nelson, and I'll see you tonight.'

I sipped the coffee. 'Take care.'

That got me a sarcastic look. 'I think you should worry more about yourself.' She patted the utility belt. 'And anyway. Superhero, remember? I love you.'

'I love you too. And I'm sorry again. Deeply sorry.'

'Ah, drink your coffee.'

I did as I was told. Although it might help my head a little, it wasn't going to do much for the niggling sense of guilt I was feeling. As I heard the front door close and lock, my mind drifted back to last night, and I winced at the blurry memories on display there.

We'd held the party in the back room of a bar near the department, and the place had been rammed with cops. Our mutual colleagues had been mingling, some of them somewhat awkwardly. There had been celebration banners, and a handful of piss-taking speeches, one of them from Sasha herself. Thank God I'd resisted attempting one; I think I genuinely had been considering it at one point. Beyond that, I couldn't recall much of what I'd said, or who specifically I'd said it to. I had a sense that might be for the best.

Way to go, Mark, I thought.

Royally drunk. In the circumstances, Sasha had been much kinder to me than I deserved. I finished my coffee and then lay back down on the bed and rested my forearm over my eyes.

Way to go, I thought again. *Hell of an engagement party.*

★ ★ ★

By ten o'clock, I was fed and watered enough to attempt a shower. As I did, I also tried to think.

I'm an interview man by trade, although that's somewhat by accident. Before I joined the police, I did a degree in psychology, followed by a PhD in behavioural psychology. When I started, I'd had visions of becoming a criminal profiler, studying crime scenes and reeling off illuminating impressions of the offender like some kind of magician. My studies had put paid to that ambition fairly quickly: it just doesn't work like that in real life. While you can always see traces of an individual and his past in the crimes he commits, I learned early on that most offender profiles are about as reliable and useful as a horoscope.

24

Even so, my studies left me with a taste for the subject, and I discovered that I was good at talking to people. I liked figuring out what made them tick, and what I needed to say to get the information I wanted. After my postgrad, I joined the police as a grunt pool officer, specialising mostly in door-to-doors; after Lise died, I transferred across the country to my current assignment here. And I was good at what I did. I enjoyed analysing people.

Much harder to analyse yourself, of course.

What had I been thinking, for example, getting that drunk? From memory, it hadn't been *happy* drunk either. Christ, it had been my engagement party, and yet to everyone there it must have looked like I was drowning my sorrows.

How must Sasha feel about that?

The hot water spattered my chest as I rubbed a foam of soap into my face.

Sasha knew what had happened to Lise, of course. Which meant she also knew that if Lise hadn't drowned, we would probably have got married, and I would never have moved to the city at all. Sasha and I wouldn't ever have met, never mind fallen in love. It was probably a difficult subject for her to think about, and yet she'd never given the impression of being bothered by it; she'd simply accepted that I had baggage, and trusted me to carry it. And I'd repaid that by spending our engagement party getting drunk, acting as though it wasn't a celebration so much as a fucking wake.

But why? I still occasionally thought about what had happened, of course, but the memories were numb now. For a while, there had been a recurring nightmare — the soft sand of a beach; the flat expanse of an empty sea stretching out in front of me — but not for months now. As far as I could remember, Lise hadn't been on my mind at all last night.

Thinking about her now, though, I felt a knot in my chest.

Ridiculous.

I washed my hair, spitting away the water that ran over my face, then turned off the shower. I loved Sasha with all my heart, and I wanted to marry her. So yes, it was ridiculous. But the sensation was there. I remembered the look on Sasha's face this morning — smiling, kind, but also slightly inquisitive and unsure — and realised that for some reason I didn't even understand myself, I'd fucked things up. Just a little, perhaps, but still. Not great.

I towelled myself dry roughly, angry with myself.

You can make it up to her.

I could, and I would. By eleven o'clock, another coffee on the go, I was feeling almost human again. But below the surface, I was still worried that I could hear the plaintive rush of that faraway sea. And the knot in my chest remained.

★　★　★

I arrived at work for midday.

Even after a year and a half in the city, the new department building still seemed alien to me.

That was strange on one level, as I'd only spent a couple of weeks in the old premises before the team moved. Then again, that brief period had been taken up by an intense investigation, so perhaps it was understandable that the events of those first few days had imprinted the old place so firmly on my mind.

It had been a ramshackle, run-down building, with our small team crammed into an office barely large enough to contain us. The new department was different in every way: sleek and gleaming from the outside, all glass and steel, while the interior was lavish and spacious. Everything was state-of-the-art and scrupulously maintained: newly painted white walls and ceilings; plush carpets underfoot; even fake potted plants by the lifts and abstract art hanging on the walls. The corridors smelled of the tree-shaped air-fresheners that were plugged in at various points along the skirting boards. Pine or something.

'Good afternoon.'

I greeted the camera at reception as breezily as I could manage. The facial recognition system behind it hesitated long enough for me to wonder exactly how rough I still looked, and to feel slightly judged, before the red light by the door handle turned green and there was a gentle click.

Unlike in the old place, my team and I had a small suite of offices all to ourselves. I made my way up to the third floor, then through the door that led to our corridor.

My office was first, but I wandered past to

check who else was in. Greg Martin, our IT specialist, was clearly out somewhere, because his door was closed and locked. Even though people were hardly likely to go snooping, and there wouldn't be much to see if they did, Greg liked to maintain the illusion that the security of his work was paramount. From his manner, you would imagine that gaining access to his office could allow a potential hacker to bring down the whole department.

It was in sharp contrast to Simon Duncan's thoroughly cavalier open-door policy. Simon was our forensics liaison; although frequently absent, he barely ever closed his door, never mind locked it. His room was empty too, the computer humming away oblivious on the desk. The walls were bare, aside from a calendar that hadn't been changed since February. Simon was a climber, and he'd settled on a photograph of a mountain range. He'd told me a while back, in his usual arch and dismissive way, that he'd found a picture he liked and left it at that. He didn't need a piece of paper to remind him what day it was.

Past the operations room, I saw that Pete Dwyer's door was slightly ajar, and as I approached, I could hear the gentle clack of his typing. Slow and steady. A two-finger typist, Pete. He was a genial bear of a man who seemed perpetually baffled by the changing technology around him. The impression he often gave was of a man standing in place, looking this way and that in confusion, unable to keep up with what was happening. My boss.

I tapped on the door, pushing it a little wider. 'Afternoon, Pete.'

'Mark.' He looked up from the screen and his face creased into a grin, wrinkles forming around eyes that seemed to shrink back into his face. 'You look like death.'

'I actually wasn't sure the computer downstairs was going to let me in.'

'It probably thought you were a vagrant. Come in. How's your head, young man?'

'It's been worse.' I closed the door behind me. 'Not often, mind you.'

'I'm not surprised. You were knocking them back last night. A machine. Do you remember the conversation we had?'

I winced. No, I couldn't. And while the team was generally fairly relaxed, Pete was still my boss.

'Not as such.'

'Not as such. It was actually about you knocking them back, and how your head was going to be this morning. And let me tell you, you were having none of it. You're a bit more argumentative out of work, aren't you?'

A memory of it started to come back: Pete asking me, with much the same amusement with which he was looking at me now, if I was *sure* everything was all right — making it funny, but also not funny at the same time. He had two teenage girls at home, and was used to being fatherly. For similar reasons, he was presumably also used to having his concerns brushed aside. I dimly remembered doing the latter, before drawing him into an embrace and slapping his

29

back in a drunken approximation of friendship.

'I'm also a lot more affectionate,' I said.

He laughed.

'You and Sasha get home safe?'

'So I'm told.'

'And everything's okay?'

'She's still talking to me. She even made me coffee before she left.'

'You know you don't deserve her.' Pete settled back in his chair. 'She's far too forgiving.'

'That's true.'

'And that means it falls to me to punish you for your drunken transgressions. Not that I wasn't going to anyway. What have you got on at the moment?'

I shrugged. 'There's some stuff I need to prepare for court but no date set. It's nothing that can't wait.'

'Good.' He reached over the desk, holding out a file. 'Have a look at this for me, will you?'

I took it: a slim brown folder with some printouts inside. Everything we dealt with was accessible online from the department's intranet, but rather than supply a case number, Pete had gone old-school and pulled out a hard copy. I flicked through the details and frowned.

'Accident report,' I said. 'Charlotte Matheson.'

'Uh-huh. Fatality.'

'From two years ago. Car crash, just off the ring road. No suspicious circumstances. Case closed.' I looked up. 'Which is very sad, of course, but what do you want me to do about it?'

'No idea.' Pete sounded even more cheerful now. 'But take it and have a read anyway. Then get yourself to the hospital.'

'I'm not that hung-over.'

He laughed again.

'A young woman was picked up on Town Street. Yesterday, late afternoon. She was obviously in distress, and apparently she'd suffered some injuries to her face. I'm not sure what. When she was taken to hospital, she gave her name as Charlotte Matheson.'

'This Charlotte Matheson?'

'Uh-huh. Along with the same address, personal details, everything. Apparently she's adamant. She is Charlotte Matheson.'

I looked down at the file, then back up at Pete.

'And you want me to . . . ?'

'Go and interview her, of course.'

'Why?'

'To establish if there's any validity to her story.'

'That she came back from the dead?'

We both knew exactly how much validity there would be to her story. *It falls to me to punish you for your drunken transgressions* indeed. I shook my head carefully, and Pete laughed again.

'Happy engagement, Mark.'

Mark

She knows all the details

On arrival at the hospital, I faced a long and torturous journey through the building in an attempt to locate the Baines Wing, where the woman calling herself Charlotte Matheson was being looked after.

As I wandered half lost along seemingly identical corridors, searching for clues on the signs hanging down overhead, it began to feel like a mythical destination. After returning to what appeared to be the same junction I'd just left, I toyed with the idea of scrawling chalk arrows on the floor. It also didn't help matters that the walls were a particularly sickly shade of green. The bright sunshine on the drive over here had caused my receding hangover to return with a vengeance.

My contact was a Dr Fredericks, and after eventually signing in at the Baines Wing reception, I was directed to a waiting area. There was nobody else there, which was fortunate, as it was claustrophobically small, with cheap black chairs lining the walls around a low table. There was a spread of tatty magazines, a couple of books. I sat down and breathed slowly and steadily. The air in here tasted warm and recycled, and the back of my head thudded in time with my heartbeat, like an angry neighbour hammering on a wall in protest.

On the drive over, I'd decided I was a little pissed off with Pete for sending me on this adventure. I'd scanned enough of the file to know that Charlotte Matheson was most certainly dead. Whoever the woman here was, it was someone else. Establishing *who* she was didn't seem like a fantastic use of my time and experience, and Pete knew it. It was hardly likely to be a criminal matter. On top of that, if this woman turned out to be seriously disturbed, there were also ethical considerations to bear in mind. Call me high-minded, but I prefer to see the people I interview as people, rather than the butt of an office joke.

'Detective Nelson?'

I looked up to see a man I presumed was Dr Fredericks. He was old and tall, and dressed in a brown suit. Looming over me and looking down, he inclined his head curiously.

'Are you okay?'

'No,' I said. 'Not really, no.'

'Right. There's a water cooler round that corner.'

'Thank you.'

I poured myself a cup from the ice-cold nozzle, drained it, then got myself a second and wandered back round. By the time I'd returned, Fredericks had taken a seat in the corner of the waiting area, balancing his clipboard awkwardly on his knees. His legs were so long that the size of the area was even more of a problem for him than it was for me.

'Join me,' he said. 'You're going to want to sit down.'

'Okay.' I sat across from him, eager to get this over with. 'I know a little about why I'm supposed to be here. A woman was picked up yesterday and gave her name as Charlotte Matheson. That's right, isn't it?'

'Yes. This is Charlotte Matheson's file.' Fredericks showed me the bundle of sheets on the clipboard, separated out with paper clips. 'Her older records. According to this, we've treated her a number of times in the past.'

I held up the folder I'd brought with me.

'According to mine, Charlotte Matheson died two years ago.'

Fredericks nodded. 'According to ours too.'

'We're in accordance, then. So it's a different Charlotte Matheson.'

'That's the thing. Obviously it *is* — or else she has a different name altogether. But she certainly believes that she is *this* Charlotte Matheson. She's given us the correct birth date, home address, everything.'

'She's confused?'

'Yes, she's certainly confused. And in fact she was dressed very oddly when she came in: a white gown and trousers. It looked at first as though she was a patient somewhere.'

'That would make sense.'

'The problem is, if that's the case, I don't know where. There are no identifying marks on the fabric, and it isn't standard-issue clothing from any hospital I'm familiar with. Plus, I've made enquiries. None of the facilities nearby have a patient missing.'

I sipped the water, taking all this in.

'Presumably you've confronted her with the fact that she can't be who she claims to be? On the grounds that Charlotte Matheson is dead?'

Fredericks shook his head. 'I don't follow.'

'I'm well aware that you need to wear kid gloves here, at least to an extent, but I'm asking if you've explained to her that she can't really be this person, because this person is dead?'

'Oh. I see what you mean. No, we haven't done that. We don't need to; that's not a matter of contention.'

I finished off my water.

'It's me that doesn't follow now.'

'Yes, I'm sorry. Perhaps I've not been clear enough. The woman we're treating knows that Charlotte Matheson was killed in a car crash, and yet still maintains that's who she is. Hang on.' Fredericks pulled a couple of sheets from his file and scanned through them. 'I told her that the Charlotte Matheson she is claiming to be has been dead for two years, and she replied: 'Yes, I know I have.' She was disorientated when she first arrived, but we went through all this a number of times.'

'She thinks she's dead?'

'It seems that way. She's very confused, and not sure what's happening right now. There appears to be some memory loss. But she's adamant that she *did* die in a car crash. She told the officer who found her that she'd been in an accident, and that it had killed her. She knows all the details.'

I wanted another cup of water.

'What about the injuries?' I said. 'My superior

told me that she'd experienced some kind of damage to her face.'

Fredericks looked awkward at that. He replaced the paper in his sheaf of records and then stood up, indicating that I should do the same.

'Yes,' he said. 'That's really why I got in touch with the police in the first place. I think you're going to need to see those for yourself.'

Groves

A man carved out of black wood

I know who did it.

David Groves put the card down on the kitchen counter. The post always arrived early to his house, and the day that would have been his son Jamie's sixth birthday was no exception.

It was not yet eight o'clock, but the kitchen caught the morning sun, and the light hung in the air now, divided into fuzzy slices by the half-turned slats on the blind. It was homely, he always thought; you could film a commercial for bread in here, or butter. The whole downstairs was open-plan, and the furnishings were old and wooden, giving it a farmhouse feel.

After Jamie had gone missing, and his break-up with Caroline, Groves had looked around several properties, but had fallen in love with this place the moment he stepped inside. It reminded him of a cat, curled up comfortably in a sunbeam. Every morning the cottage woke up slowly: pipes clanking half-heartedly; eyelashes of dust turning lazily in the air.

He poured another cup of coffee — strong and black — from the glass bulb jug, then turned his attention back to the birthday card, and the message written inside

I know who did it.

That was all, with blank space above and

37

below. Handwritten, like the envelope it had come in: neat lines of black biro that were presumably a deliberate attempt to hide the sender's identity. It was addressed not to David Groves, but to Jamie himself.

At least there was only one this year.

That was something. Jamie's birthday was always when the freaks came out. For a while, he'd wondered about that. Nobody could say for certain when Jamie had died, so they were unable to attack him on that date, but why not the date of the abduction itself? Eventually, of course, he had figured it out. It was because it would hurt more on his son's birthday. The date commemorated Jamie's birth and the two full milestones he had managed to reach before being taken. It reminded Groves that there should have been so many more, and that there never would be.

You should be celebrating, the freaks were saying. *But we are instead.*

In previous years there had been phone calls — silent, until the caller finally worked up the nerve to say something quick and vicious and then hang up — but it was mostly letters. Taunting. Confessing. Explaining to Groves in graphic detail all the things that had been done to his son before he died.

Groves didn't believe any of them were genuine. It was just ghouls and cowards — people with something missing inside them. But still: they got under his skin. One year, someone had concluded a letter by writing: *I'm coming to see you tonight. Be ready.* That

38

evening, Groves had turned off all the lights, left the front door ajar and waited in the lounge. He'd stayed awake the whole night, willing something to happen. Of course nothing had — and deep down, he'd known it wouldn't. But he'd waited anyway. If he received the same message now, he was sure he would wait up again.

He read this year's card once more.

I know who did it.

The coffee was bitter and strong. He put the card back in the envelope and shut it away in a kitchen drawer. Later on, he'd store it upstairs with all the others, but out of sight would do for now, so Caroline didn't see it when she came round later. Even though they were divorced, they always spent Jamie's birthday together.

He put the cup down, then began gathering his things, getting ready for work.

The message stayed with him, though. Only one this year, perhaps, but it had brought a couple of fresh turns of the knife with it. Addressing it to Jamie himself was a new development. And instead of dangling his son's murder in front of him, just out of reach, the message offered up the murderers instead. *I know who did it*, the sender was saying. *But I'm not telling.* It was as though they knew that some days the idea of finding the people responsible was all that got him out of bed and kept him going. It was a new angle from which to hit a downed man, and Groves realised that the blow had landed.

Well played.

He pulled on his suit jacket. Not for the first time, he imagined what he would do if he ever found himself face to face with his son's killers. The scenario had played out in his head on countless occasions. Every atom in his body would want to hurt them as badly as they must have hurt Jamie, and then put a bullet in their heads. And yet he knew what would really happen.

Rather than doing any of that, he would arrest them.

Unlike his ex-wife, Groves had retained his religious faith in the aftermath of Jamie's abduction and murder. If anything, in fact, it had deepened, albeit changed, perhaps in a similar way to a marriage that had survived an affair. He clung to it. He had to believe that God had a plan, and that however abhorrent his son's death was, it somehow fitted into that. It was not his position to deliver the punishment that awaited the killers in the next world, only to apply the law in this one. And in some strange way, it felt as though doing anything else would be a betrayal of Jamie — of his little boy's innocence and goodness. An act like that would sully his son's memory as well as taint his own soul. After everything else they'd done, Groves was determined not to let these people do that as well.

That was also why he was going to work today, in spite of the date. Once, he had been a husband, a father, a man of faith and a policeman; now, those last two were all he had left, and they were intertwined in him. He was a good man. He did the right thing. It was all he had now to define him.

Happy birthday, Jamie, Groves thought as he left the cottage, locking the door behind him, the card forgotten for now.

I wish I could give you a cuddle.

I miss you so much.

★ ★ ★

First call of the day.

Carnegie Avenue ran along the edge of the Larkton estate. The buildings were all but indistinguishable grey-faced blocks of bobbled concrete, and the burned house stood out amongst its neighbours like a rotten tooth. The fire had gutted it so badly that the entire structure had half collapsed. First charred by the flames, then sodden by the fire hoses, it was now smouldering in the morning sun.

There were two fire engines parked out front — idle now, their lights off — and the street was crammed with locals, who had presumably emerged in the early hours to rubberneck the flames. They stood in groups, sharing gossip or conspiracy theories, or just shaking their heads in disbelief at the remains of their former neighbour's property.

'Out of the way, you fucking rats.'

Sean Robertson, Groves' partner, steered the car in slowly behind the nearest fire engine, forcing a cluster of teenagers to amble on to the pavement. They slouched and smirked, taking their time. In the passenger seat beside Sean,

41

Groves thought his partner was going to blare the horn, but instead Sean just grinned through the windscreen at them, nodding sarcastically.

'Yeah, yeah, yeah. Jesus wept.'

'Just kids,' Groves said. 'Doing kid things.'

'Zero respect.' Sean cricked on the handbrake. 'You know what they say? No such thing as a bad dog, only a bad owner. Someone ought to arrest the parents. Not that half of these little bastards know who their fathers are.'

Groves smiled. They'd been partners for years, and had long ago fallen into familiar roles and routines, Sean's generally consisting of this kind of exaggerated outrage and disgust at the state of society. It was all for show. In reality, he would have given any of these kids not only his ear but his time if they'd needed or wanted it. Assuming nobody was around to see it, anyway. Sean always reminded Groves of the Charles Bukowski poem about the tough writer with the soft little bluebird he only took out when nobody was around to see.

They got out and headed over to the scene. Closer to, Groves could smell the mulch of the scorched and soaked building. The windows had been punched out by the heat and the stone walls had browned like half-burned newspaper. One corner of the roof had fallen in slightly. It must have been an absolute inferno before the fire crews arrived. The air above the house still shimmered with the residual heat.

'Robertson and Groves.' Sean showed one of the firemen his ID. They were partners — equal rank — but today he was taking the lead. Sean

42

hadn't mentioned Jamie, and probably wouldn't, but he knew the date, and this was his way of quietly taking some of the pressure off Groves. 'Your commander about?'

'There.'

The commander was an old guy with small, wet eyes and an enormous grey moustache that protruded from beneath his visor. The moustache rolled back and forth as he filled them in, like it was chewing on the words. It was always strange, attending a fire scene as police. Groves was used to being in charge of a situation, but they were second fiddle here, and would only be allowed into the property if and when the commander said so. In reality, their presence was a formality; it was only in case anything came of it later, which rarely happened with house fires. But there was a body inside, so they had to show their faces at ground level just in case the investigation was one of those rare examples that grew more floors.

'You can't go upstairs,' the commander said. 'I'm not being pissy. You literally can't; the stairs are gone. But straight through the remains of that front door yonder — that's your lounge in there.'

'That's where the resident is?' Sean said.

'Unless he's moved, yeah. Which I doubt. Coroner's on his way.'

Groves looked at the house again.

'Hell of a blaze,' he said. 'What are your thoughts?'

The commander shrugged. 'That's for the team to say, and then maybe you guys. There are no suspect containers aside from all the bottles. My guess? Well, you'll see the remains of the ashtray by the settee.'

'Cigarette?'

'Yeah, I'd imagine so. Guy's drunk and sleepy, and he drifts off with a dangler. You know what these builds are like.'

Groves nodded. Most of the houses on the estate were old council homes, sold off cheap to people who then rented them out to people who then rented them out again. Old, threadbare furniture; dodgy electrics; and God only knew what stuffed in the wall cavities. Most of them wouldn't have passed a safety check twenty years ago, never mind today. If that was what this fire came down to, it might still be a criminal investigation, but not one for them. They were only here for the resident.

'Okay.' He turned to Sean. 'Shall we?'

'Let's.'

They stepped through the open doorway into the remains of the front room. The smell hit Groves first: a foul waft of old meat and rust, like opening the oven in an abandoned house. The back window was completely gone, allowing an angle of sunlight in. Everything it touched looked either scorched black or shattered. In the far corner, water was still drizzling down from the remains of the ceiling, pattering on the broken eggshell of a television. What was left of the carpet squelched beneath Groves' feet. Looking down, he saw dirty grey foam bubbling up around his shoes.

The dead man was on the remains of the

settee — or inside it, to be more precise. The fabric had burned away, leaving a rusted skeletal frame with a spread of thick black ash congealing underneath. The man himself was bent double, with his backside on the floor and both legs poking over the front of the settee, the rest of him contorted awkwardly within the frame. If he had been alive, it would have looked for all the world like a moment of slapstick, as though he'd sat on a collapsing deckchair.

He was very obviously not alive, though. You could still tell the body had once been a real, living person, but only just. A patch of skin and scorched hair remained on the scalp, and a single shoe was recognisable on one foot, the melted plastic hanging down in stalactites. Beneath the body, mixed with the ash, the melted flesh had hardened in greasy pools. The man himself might as well have been carved from black wood. The mouth was little more than a gaping hole.

Groves stared down at the remains for a moment, struck as always by the distance between the living and the dead. The spark that just went: a beat of time in which everything changed. What had once been a man now resembled a snuffed-out candle.

'Sir?' Sean clicked his fingers above the figure in the settee. 'Can you hear me, sir?'

'There's the ashtray.' Groves gestured with his foot to a chunky glass bowl near the corner of the settee, then looked around. There were shards of glass and broken cups by the walls, some of the shapes still recognisable. 'Bottles everywhere too. I'm guessing he passed out rather than fell asleep.'

'No wonder it's so hard to wake him up.' Sean stepped back and sniffed. 'Am I imagining that stink of booze in the air?'

'Yes.'

'Even so, I'm thinking the commander called it right.'

'Me too.'

Groves took another look round, puzzled by the lack of furnishings. Aside from the broken television, the settee and the bottles, the room was bare. It must have been a sparse existence. He imagined the man, drunk enough to pass out with the television flickering in the corner, the cigarette falling from his hand. A sad image.

'Been and seen,' Sean said. 'Happy?'

Groves leaned closer, peering at what was left of the dead man's face. The blackened cheek-bones looked strange.

'Have a look,' he said.

Sean did so, inclining his head.

'What am I looking at?'

'I don't know.' Groves gestured at a thin ridge across the man's cheek. 'Something cut into the bone?'

'Old scar, maybe. Like Action Man.'

'There's more than one.'

'Eh. Leave it to the coroner for now.'

They walked back to the doorway, Groves still wondering about the cuts in the bone — but Sean was right. He took a last glance behind him, at what was left of the man's legs pointing out from the settee. Utterly still.

'Not how I'd like to go,' he said.

'It's not like we get to choose, David. Besides, look at the guy. Seems pretty comfortable to me. Chances are the lucky bastard didn't even wake up.'

That was true: when the fire caught, the smoke probably killed the man before he even surfaced. So yes, it could have been worse. At one fire scene, early on in his career, he'd found the remains of an old lady curled up at the base of a walk-in wardrobe. He couldn't imagine the fear and confusion and pain she must have gone through.

Even so, part of him thought that when it came to it, he personally would want the chance to at least fight to stay alive. That he'd want to feel *something* for as long as possible, even if it was only pain. To cling on and not go gently — all the way to the bitter end.

But then Groves thought about Jamie. And he figured that if he didn't feel that way, he'd have given up on the world a long time ago.

Mark

Charlie Matheson

As I walked into the room, the woman claiming to be Charlotte Matheson was lying on her side, facing away from me. The bed took up most of the space, with just enough room for small anonymous cabinets on either side of the headboard, and a plastic chair near the door.

She had the covers pulled up to her shoulders, so that all I could really see of her at first was a mass of brown curly hair — and that only barely. On the other side of the bed, the blinds had been drawn on the window, and the overhead light had been dimmed right down. In the gloom, and without being able to see her face, I couldn't even be sure if she was awake.

'Excuse me.' I closed the door. 'I'm with the police. I'm Detective Mark Nelson.'

For a moment, the woman didn't respond. Then she nodded slowly, rolled on to her back and hitched herself up into a sitting position. The covers bunched around her waist, revealing the hospital gown she was wearing. I presumed the doctors would have kept the clothes she'd been found in. It was possible we'd need to examine them. Unlikely, but possible.

Her hair was hanging forward over her face, but she pulled it back, tucking it behind her shoulders, revealing her face in the process.

The sight of the cuts there stopped whatever I was about to say next.

Her face was almost entirely covered in them. There were whorls around her eyes, and lines and patterns of scarring across her forehead and nose. A complex web of cuts swirled down her cheeks, all the way to her jawline, before joining together in a single passage across the cleft of her chin. As far as I could tell, staring at her, the injuries were perfectly symmetrical.

Amidst all that, her eyes seemed unusually bright in the dimness of the room, as though they were catching a light source unavailable to the fixtures and fittings. But they also looked bleary and confused. Scared. I supposed that was fairly understandable.

I sat down on the chair, and her gaze stayed on me, the way a cat might watch a nearby stranger, ready to bolt for safety. Then I switched on the camera that was attached to my lapel. It had been departmental policy for years now that all field interviews were recorded, the footage beaming straight to a secure cloud and then logged into the relevant file, immediately accessible to any other officers working on the case. Not that there were any on this one, nor were there likely to be.

'How are you feeling?' I said.

'Better than yesterday, thank you.' Her voice was soft, but there was a surprising amount of resolve there. While still wary of me, she was also quiet and to the point. 'It was a difficult transition, but I think I'm getting there slowly.'

A difficult transition. If she was referring to

her supposed return from the dead, it seemed a strangely formal way of describing it.

'What are you looking at?' she said.

There didn't seem to be any point in denying the obvious.

'Your face. Your scars.'

'Yes. I am marked.'

Again she sounded matter-of-fact about it.

'You are marked,' I said. 'Yes. What happened to you?'

'Do you like them?'

'I don't know.' I wondered what the right answer was. 'They're a little too elaborate for my taste, if I'm honest. They're very detailed, though, aren't they? I imagine they must have hurt.'

'Yes, they did.' The memory seemed to make her sad, then her expression brightened slightly. 'But it was like childbirth. It hurts, but very quickly afterwards you forget how much. And you end up with something that makes it all worthwhile.'

I nodded sympathetically, even though I didn't think the two things were remotely similar. After childbirth, you ended up with a baby, a child you loved, whereas this woman was scarred for life. Whenever people saw her, they would always draw breath and look twice. She would forever be asking *What are you looking at?* while already knowing the answer.

And yet, as extensive as it was, I realised that there was something oddly beautiful about the scarification. Perhaps it was the sheer intricacy of it. There was clearly a careful design to the

50

damage that had been done.

I said, 'I wouldn't want them myself.'

'It doesn't matter what you want. One day you'll have them too. That's how it works.'

'How what works, Charlotte?'

'Charlie. Not Charlotte.'

'Okay.' A small detail, perhaps, but it was obviously important to her, and since the question of identity was underpinning all this, I was happy to go along with it. 'How what works, Charlie?'

She shook her head, as though I couldn't possibly understand. I thought about her choice of words. *It doesn't matter what you want.*

'Did you do them yourself?'

'No, of course not.' She pressed her palm to her forehead and the scarring wrinkled as she contorted her face. 'I can't remember it all properly. Anyway, I don't want to talk about them any more. Not right now.'

I very much wanted to talk about them, but there was a hint of distress there, and I needed her to stay with me.

'All right, then. Let's start at the beginning instead. You told the doctor your name was Charlie Matheson. Is that right?'

'Yes. Nobody believes me, but I'm really not sure what else I'm supposed to say, or what everyone wants to hear. I'm Charlie Matheson. I'm twenty-eight years old and I live at 68 Petrie Crescent. My husband's name is Paul. Paul Carlisle.'

The mention of her supposed husband's name caused a look of upset to cross her face, as

51

though she had just remembered something painful to her. But then she blinked it away and shook her head.

'I've been through all this a hundred times already.'

'I know. And you say you were in an accident.'

'Yes. Everything else is a blur right now, but I remember the accident like it was yesterday. I was driving on the ring road. It was late, and I was going too fast. There was a corner, and the wheels locked. I lost control. The car went over the embankment.'

This was good. These were all details I could check — see what she was right about and work out how she might have known about it.

'And then?'

'I didn't have my seat belt on. *So stupid.* I remember thinking that — and then that the airbag would save me, but it didn't. I went through the windscreen.'

'You remember that?'

'Yes. I didn't die right away. Not long. But I was on the grass for a while. Flickering in and out. There were voices, angels, I think, but they kept fading and coming back. And then . . . I died.'

'Two years ago.'

'Yes. According to the doctors.'

'And you've been dead ever since.'

'Yes,' she said. 'Of course.'

I leaned back.

The thing was, she sounded so reasonable, and yet it was obviously a crazy thing for a person to believe. I found myself looking at the scars again. Hard as it was to imagine, it wasn't impossible that she had done them to herself — and if something's possible, you can work backwards from that. The kind of person who would do that to themselves, what kind of story would they tell you, and how would they present themselves? This kind of story, I decided, and probably very much like this. Confused. Vulnerable. On the verge of being angry.

Thanks again, Pete.

At the same time, the cuts bothered me. Someone else had done them to her, she claimed, and I could hardly ignore that. While the whole thing seemed an utter waste of time, and almost certainly would be, I had a duty to pursue it at least a little further.

So I suppressed the sigh I wanted to give.

'I believe *something* happened to you. And I want to understand what.'

'Everything's hazy right now.'

'Well . . . let's see about that.' I thought about it. 'Do you remember what happened yesterday, before you were found?'

'I was in an ambulance.'

'No, before that.'

'I mean I was in *another* ambulance, before the one that brought me here. A kind of ambulance, anyway. It was white — really white — and there was a man with me.'

'Can you describe him?'

'Not really. He's old. He's some kind of doctor.'

'You've seen him before?'

'Yes.' She hesitated. 'I think so.'

'And what was he doing in the ambulance? Did he speak to you?'

'Yes, but I can't remember what he said.' She frowned at that. 'And I need to, because it's important. I was awake for a bit, and he was trying to tell me things. But I must have gone back to sleep again.'

Drugged? I wondered — but then realised I was taking the story at face value. There probably never was an ambulance or a man. Nevertheless, I presumed the doctors would have done blood tests, and even though they wouldn't necessarily be conclusive, I reminded myself to ask Fredericks about it on the way out.

'The next thing I remember is lying in a field. I was on my back, and I could feel the damp grass around me — it was overgrown enough to be taller than me lying down. There were birds singing, and the sky hurt my eyes. It wasn't too bad at that point, but it was still too much. I knew it was going to be too much.'

'Too much?'

'The detail. The *everything*.'

I looked around, understanding now why the room around us was so dimly lit.

'Because it's dark where I've been,' she said. 'I remember that much about it. Everything's very dark when you're dead. Being back wasn't so bad at first when I was lying there in the field, but as soon as I stood up, it got worse. When I walked for a bit.'

'How long did you walk for?'

'I don't know. Maybe ten minutes? It's hard for me to judge. Not long. I came to the road, and the cars . . . I walked a little way along, but it was all yammering at me.'

She cupped her hands over her ears now, wincing, as though even the memory of all that noise and static was difficult for her.

'I couldn't carry on. I sat down. People started talking to me, and I just wanted it all to stop, to go away. I could only cling to a couple of things. I knew who I was. I knew what I needed to say. Some of it, anyway.' She looked worried by that. 'I need to remember.'

My head throbbed suddenly. I took a sip of the water I'd brought in with me, but it tasted warm and metallic now, and it didn't help. Something had clearly happened to this woman, but that didn't mean that anything about the story she was telling me was true. I was trying to think about the man, the ambulance — at least two people involved, then, as there would have to be a driver — but then this woman wasn't Charlotte Matheson, and she hadn't died in a car crash two years ago. Since everything else she was telling me was built on those shaky foundations, there was no point assuming that any other part of the structure was solid.

'You don't believe me,' she said.

'I want to help you,' I said. 'I want to understand.'

'No, you think I'm crazy.'

'Charlotte — '

'*Charlie*,' she spat at me. 'I'm Charlie Matheson. Get my fucking *name* right.'

And there it was — the outburst of anger. I'd interviewed numerous people with psychological

problems over the years, and the flare-up immediately ticked every single box on my internal list
of warning signs. I'd seen this behaviour a hundred times before.

Yes, I thought. You're right, whoever you are.
I do think you're crazy.

'Okay, Charlie.' I stood up. 'I think we're done
here for the moment.'

'I lived at 68 Petrie Crescent with my husband
Paul. We married on the third of February, in a
church in Hardcastle. I kept my maiden name.
We went on honeymoon to Italy. We spent a
week each in Venice, Florence and Rome.'

I opened the door.

'I'll see what I can do.'

'I want to see Paul. I *need* to see Paul.'

'I'll see what I can do.'

As I stepped out into the corridor and closed
the door behind me, I took a deep breath.

Thank you again, Pete.

Thank you very much indeed.

Mark

The accident report

Back at the car, my hangover kicked in harder. The afternoon sun was coming through the windscreen at a painful angle, right into my eyes.

Through the windscreen.

Just like Charlotte Matheson. The real one, at least.

There was a bottle of water and a half-used strip of paracetamol capsules in the glove compartment. I fumbled for both. Then I flipped the sun visor down and logged into the department's computer system on my tablet.

I swiped through to the search screen. While it was nice of Pete to give me the paper files, I found technology easier to deal with. The connection was fast, and a minute later I'd downloaded the entire file on the real Charlotte Matheson's accident. I transferred it to the current case file, then scanned through the details.

They seemed basically to fit with what she'd told me. There had been a car accident, late at night on the ring road to the north. The weather had been bad, and it looked as though she'd lost control on one of the corners and gone over an embankment and down the far side. Bang. She hadn't been wearing a seat belt for some reason, but there had been no obvious suspicious circumstances.

I didn't have my seat belt on ... I went through the windscreen.

So she was right about that.

I didn't die right away. Not long. But I was on the grass for a while. Flickering in and out.

That part didn't fit. The real Charlotte Matheson had been dead when the police and ambulance crews arrived on the scene. There were photographs on file showing the car lit up from within, angled up from the tree it had struck. One headlight was still working, a splay of light revealing spits of rain and the body further down the embankment. Matheson had gone through the windscreen, which had done catastrophic damage to her head and upper body. One photograph showed the blood over the bonnet and on the grass. Another, illuminated further by torchlight, revealed a muddy swirl of hair, and injuries to her head that resembled a shotgun blast. She would have died instantly. No flickering in and out for the real Charlotte.

The file contained no photographs of her in life, but the post-mortem shots had been included. Her body, even more brightly lit in the autopsy suite, was a vivid sight. The head was crumpled in and partly flattened, with a jagged split bisecting the face, so that the bruised eyes looked like split plums lying eight inches apart. The glass had torn off swathes of skin — a world away from the careful scars of the woman in the hospital — and there was a wound to one shoulder so deep that the arm had been nearly severed.

For very obvious reasons, this was *not* the woman in the hospital. But at first glance there was a definite similarity in body type and age, and from what I could tell, the hair, brown and curly, was identical. In life, Charlotte Matheson would have at least slightly resembled the woman I'd just talked to.

What about ID?

The damage was so extensive that I very much doubted they'd have run with a viewing. Swiping through, that turned out to be the case. The husband, Paul Carlisle, had identified her clothing and belongings. The victim had credit cards in Charlotte Matheson's name, Charlotte was missing, and it was her vehicle. That had been enough for a formal ID.

The only odd note in the file was a question over her whereabouts that day. Reading the details, I frowned. Matheson had called in sick to work, yet her husband claimed she had left that morning as usual. It had never been established where she had been instead, or why she had been driving along the ring road at that time of night.

Was that important? Probably not. At the time, it would likely have been a question that was acceptable to leave unanswered. For the police, at least, not everything can or has to be explained; while it was a mystery, it was not one that would have mattered much to us. The circumstances of her death were clearly accidental, and ultimately, that was all we had needed to know at the time.

I wondered about it now, of course, but that was simply because of present circumstances. A woman had just told me a strange story connected to this accident, so it was understandable that a weird detail in the file would seem suddenly intriguing and important. But in reality, there was no obvious connection at all between the two things.

So what was happening here?

I leaned back in the seat, rubbing my eyes.

There were two obvious explanations I could think of. The first, and to my mind least likely, was that she was telling the truth — that she really was Charlotte Matheson, and the police had made a mistake with the ID on the body. It wasn't completely impossible, but it meant that an unidentified woman had been driving Matheson's car that night, dressed in her clothes and carrying her possessions, all for reasons unknown, and that the real Charlotte had been somewhere else for the last two years, the whole world believing she was dead.

But aside from how unlikely all that was, it wasn't even the entirety of the woman's story. *I went through the windscreen*, she'd told me. She claimed to remember dying at the scene. Which really *was* impossible.

The second explanation — the most likely — was that she was crazy. I decided that, actually, I was fairly satisfied with that one. As sad as it was, in due course her real identity would be established; there would be a hospital that Fredericks hadn't checked, or else a concerned relative would come forward. Given the extent of her scarring, it should hardly prove too difficult to establish her real identity. Case closed.

Except . . .

Why Charlotte Matheson?

Despite myself, the question nagged at me. This woman certainly looked like her, and she knew many of the details of what had happened. She knew about Charlotte's life. I could understand somebody being traumatised and confused, and I could understand someone lying . . . but why *this* lie in particular? Why choose Charlotte Matheson?

There was only one possible answer I could think of. She must have known her. She might have been a close friend who had been deeply affected by Matheson's death, or perhaps someone associated with the family somehow. Thinking about it more, in fact, I decided that had to be the case. No matter how confused and crazy you are, if you're giving out information, then you have to have got it from somewhere.

So there was at least one more thing I could do.

I swiped back through the file until I found Charlotte Matheson's address: 68 Petrie Crescent, just as she'd said. It wasn't going to be an enjoyable conversation to have with her widower, but it might clear things up relatively quickly. *Yes, Paul Carlisle might tell me. She had a batshit-crazy sister.* Something like that, anyway. Case then closed for real.

The paracetamol were beginning to work their magic, and I knew I wouldn't be able to leave it — that it would continue to bother me if I did. Better to sort it out now and have done with the whole fucking thing.

In for a penny, in for a pound.

I started the engine.

Mark

Paul Carlisle

After Lise drowned, I moved all the way across the country. Maybe that was an extreme reaction. I know that everyone has their own way of coping with tragedy, and so it shouldn't have surprised me that Paul Carlisle still lived in the house he'd shared with his wife. It did, though. I guess some people can exorcise ghosts from a place more easily than others.

It took half an hour to drive from the hospital to Carlisle's house, which was in a pleasant little suburb towards the eastern edge of the city. A mile or so further on, you were in the country-side proper, but you could already smell it from here.

With the window down, my arm resting on the sill, I drove past the two pubs at the centre of the village. The larger one had a sprawling car park, where a travelling fairground had set up, with miniature wheels and rides, all candy colours and flashing bulbs. The street around was busy with people enjoying the late-afternoon heat. A small local carnival. As I drove slowly through, I heard children's laughter and the *whoop-whoop* of the stalls, and then the flat bang of the punch-ball machine.

I supposed it was possible Carlisle was here somewhere: he lived just around the corner, towards the end of a side road. I indicated, turning in. If he wasn't home, what was I going to do? Leave it, perhaps. Except I knew that I wouldn't.

I'd been thinking about it on the drive over — justifying the trip to myself. Paul Carlisle was the best option right now for discovering the mystery woman's real identity. Since she was both distinctive and fixated on Charlotte Matheson, it was likely he knew her, or at least had done once.

And of course, there was another reason too. However wild her story, she hadn't committed an actual crime, and while her stay at the hospital was voluntary so far, that situation wouldn't continue indefinitely. Depending on how her story shifted, there was no guarantee she'd be sectioned. It was possible that she'd be out in public in a few days' time.

I want to see Paul.

I need to see Paul.

Petrie Crescent and Paul Carlisle would presumably be her first port of call. Regardless of any light he could shed on the circumstances, I figured that Carlisle at least deserved a heads-up about that in advance.

I parked up outside, behind a van, then walked up the path, knocked on the glass door and waited. A moment later, the curtain at the window beside me twitched slightly, and then a silhouette appeared at the door. Despite the time of day, the man who opened it looked like he'd just got up. He was wearing a dressing gown, and his hair was wild. I guessed he was in his early thirties.

'Paul Carlisle?'

'Yeah.' He scratched the side of his head, ruffling his hair more, then gestured at the window, where something had been stuck to the inside of the glass. 'Sign says no selling.'

I held out my ID. 'I'm police, Mr Carlisle. Detective Mark Nelson. I was hoping to speak to you for a few minutes.'

'Right.' He sounded annoyed. 'What's it about?'

I looked at him for a few seconds. 'Can I come in?'

'I suppose so.'

As I followed him in, I felt myself bristling a little.

Nice attitude, Paul.

The kitchen looked like a bomb had hit it. There were plates piled on the side, a stack of old pizza boxes, a toaster resting in a sea of burned crumbs. The floor was only half tiled with cheap plastic squares, many of which were peeling up, and a line of crumbs and hardened cheese and old garlic skin ran along the base of the counter. I had to edge around a box filled with empty wine bottles gathering dust just behind the door.

'Sorry about the state of the place. We're run off our feet at the moment. Come on through.'

We.

It had been two years since his wife died, and it was hardly surprising that he'd moved on. Even so, I felt a twinge of awkwardness. This was going to be an even more difficult conversation than I'd expected.

Beyond the kitchen, the rest of the downstairs

was open-plan: a double room with bare varnished floorboards. There were whorls of cat hair around the legs of the furniture, and the back of the nearest settee was coated with it; the creature must have been nearly bald. That settee, which divided the room roughly in two, was also covered with a pile of coats. The other settee was pointed at a wall-mounted plasma screen. Carlisle had been watching football. As I followed him over, he picked up a remote and muted the screen.

'Have a seat, if you can find one.'

He sat down on the free settee — or rather, half collapsed in the middle — but made no gesture towards clearing the other for me. I scrunched the coats up a little, perched as best I could and clicked on my camera.

'Before we start, I want to say that this is more of a courtesy call. Although I'm also hoping you might be able to help me with something.'

'Right.' Carlisle massaged his eyes and suppressed a yawn; it really was as though I'd woken him up. His whole manner struck me as odd. A visit from the police usually livens up an ordinary person's day somewhat. At the very least, it flicks the on switch.

'Am I interrupting?'

'No.' He gave a sigh and leaned forward. 'No, sorry. I'm just exhausted. We're not sleeping well at the moment.'

'You live with your girlfriend?'

'Yeah. Fiancée. We're engaged. Not married yet.'

Fast work, I thought. But again, who was I to

judge? It made me think of Sasha, and of course of Lise. I forced myself to stop doing so.

'You used to be married to a woman named Charlotte Matheson. Is that right?'

I had his attention now. He stared at me.

'Yes. Yes, I did.'

'And she died in an accident.'

'A couple of years ago. Yes.'

Each *yes* was accompanied by a blink and made to sound final. I felt sorry for him, because I recognised that particular strategy. When you lose someone, people mention it all the time; even if they don't say it out loud, you know they're thinking about it. They express concern, they ask questions, they offer condolences. It's all meant well, but it can feel like a carousel of attention: each person coming forward not to help you, but to take their turn saying the right thing in the spotlight of your loss. Eventually it becomes easier just to shut it down.

'Yesterday afternoon,' I said, 'a woman was found on Town Street in the north of the city. She was very confused and disorientated, and had suffered some injuries.'

'Okay.'

'She gave her name at the hospital as Charlotte Matheson.'

Carlisle continued to stare at me. I tried to read his expression, to see if there was anything there: shock; surprise; fear. But there was nothing. It was the reaction of a man who hadn't been expecting anything like this, and still didn't fully comprehend what I was saying.

'More specifically, she claims to *be* Charlotte

Matheson. Your wife. This woman named you as her husband and gave us this address as her place of residence.'

'I don't understand.'

'Neither do I. She also claims to remember the accident itself.'

'What is that supposed to mean, *she remembers the accident?*' He glanced at the door in the far corner of the room, then back to me, and almost whispered, 'My wife *died* in that car crash.'

'Yes, I know. I'm sorry. This woman knows all the details of the accident. And she claims that she died in that accident too.'

Again I watched the expression on his face.

Horror dawning now.

'Why would she do that? I just ... I don't ... '

'I know. I really can't say at the moment why she's claiming this. The woman clearly isn't very well. At all. But what she *is* is adamant. So the first thing you have to be aware of is that it's possible she will, at some point, seek you out.'

'What?' The horror was absolute now. 'You can stop her. Can't you?'

No, not really.

'Yes,' I lied. 'Perhaps. It depends on her behaviour. The issue we'd be facing at the moment is that she's not obviously dangerous.'

'She's obviously *deluded.*' Carlisle shook his head. 'What is wrong with her? Why would someone do this? I don't ... '

'Well, that's the other reason I'm here.' I leaned forward. 'The *why*. Obviously this woman is not Charlotte, but there must be a reason why she has fixated on your ex-wife the way she has. So it's possible that you know her in some way, or that Charlotte did.'

'I don't know anybody fucking crazy enough to do this.'

'No, I understand. But like I said, she has some injuries. It's possible this woman has been through some kind of trauma, and that might explain the confusion she's suffering. She might be somebody you knew once.'

'What does she look like?'

A fair bit like Charlotte Matheson.

'The most obvious thing,' I said, 'is that she has some facial scarring.'

'Okay.'

Carlisle looked off to one side, thinking it over. *Trying* for me. Which was immediately disappointing, because it meant he didn't know her — at least not as she was now. He was trying to remember women with facial scars, but if this woman had ever been part of his life, and looked then as she did now, he wouldn't have had to think very hard about it.

'I don't know,' he said.

'That's okay. Aside from that, she does look a little like your wife — similar height and build, similar curly brown hair. Did Charlotte have any extended family who resembled her?'

'No. Only child. There were cousins, I *think*, but not that she ever saw or talked about.'

It was something to explore, maybe, but already I wasn't holding out much hope.

'What about close friends?'

'Not that I know of. She had friends, obviously, but none that looked much like her. Not that I can think of, anyway.' He frowned, then rubbed his forehead with the heel of his palm. 'Christ. No. I don't think so.'

'Okay.' I tried to hide the disappointment from my voice. 'That's fine, Paul, honestly.'

'I have absolutely no idea . . . '

'Do you have a photograph of Charlotte?'

'I — '

But then we both heard a noise on the stairs, and he stopped mid-sentence. Someone was making their way down, very slowly. The wood made careful creaks.

He lowered his voice again. 'I'll see what I can do.'

I nodded conspiratorially. A moment later, the door at the far end of the room opened, and a woman came in. She too was in her early thirties, with short mussed-up blonde hair, and she was also wearing a dressing gown, along with the same look of bleary tiredness as Paul Carlisle. She was clearly very pregnant, her belly swollen out front in an enormous sphere. Nearly full term, I imagined.

I'm just exhausted, I remembered. *We're not sleeping well at the moment.* At the same time, I couldn't help doing the maths in my head. Carlisle's fast work was even speedier than I'd first thought.

She noticed me. 'Oh. Hello?'

'Good afternoon.' I gave what I hoped was a casual smile. 'Sorry to interrupt like this.'

'No, that's okay. What . . . ?'

'Police. Nothing serious, honestly. I was actually just on my way out.' I stood up, turning back to Carlisle. 'I think we're done, Mr Carlisle. Thank you for your time.'

'No problem.' He looked sick. 'If you could just wait outside for a moment . . . ?'

'Yes, of course.'

I kicked my heels slightly down the path and waited, feeling bad for the man but also — perhaps bizarrely — just as sorry now for the woman in the hospital. Thinking back on our conversation, as crazy as it had been, she had seemed genuinely to believe the story she was telling me. If she really did think she was Charlotte Matheson, how was she going to react to the knowledge that her former husband was now not only engaged to someone else, but also expecting a child with her?

Not very well, I imagined.

Carlisle emerged a minute later, pulling his dressing gown around him and holding a pack of cigarettes, a lighter and a piece of paper.

'She just gets upset about all that, you know? My past life.'

'I understand.'

He handed me the paper. I looked at it for a long time. It was a straightforward head-and-shoulders shot: a passport photo, I guessed, that had been blown up in size and printed out. He wouldn't have had time to do that just now, which meant this was something he'd kept, despite all the more obvious ways he'd moved on. People are complicated.

In life, Charlotte Matheson had had an

appealing face, with freckles across her nose and cheeks. She wasn't wearing any make-up for the photograph, but she was smiling slightly, and there was a trace of fire in her eyes. Just looking at her, you could imagine her taking no nonsense from anyone. She stared out of the photograph with an expression that said: *I've got your measure, and you know what? I'm not impressed.*

It was hard to be sure, what with the scarring. But it looked a lot like the woman in the hospital. The eyes especially.

Maybe too much like her.

'Any help?'

'I don't know,' I said honestly. 'But thank you anyway. May I take this? I'll return it, obviously.'

'Of course.'

As I walked down the path, I heard the click of a lighter behind me, and then he said:

'There's something else too.'

'Oh?'

I turned back and saw him blow smoke out of one corner of his mouth.

'You said she gave her name as Charlotte Matheson. The woman in the hospital? So that's definitely a lie.'

'A lie?'

He nodded.

'She would never have done that. With her, it was always *Charlie*. Even on our wedding day in the vows.'

He tapped some ash off the cigarette, and sounded sad and faraway.

'Even then.'

Groves

A little boy and his Bear

By the end of the day, they'd attached a name to the man they'd found in the burned house.

The property had been rented to an Edward Leland a month or so previously. He had a file — minor drugs offences mostly — and the last address they had for him was one he'd shared with his partner, Angela Morris. Former partner, presumably. The coroner had sent through a cursory note — a question mark — about the cuts Groves had seen in the body's cheekbones, but pending the results of an overnight post-mortem, that was that. The end of Edward Leland, and the end of their involvement.

After work, Groves went to pick up Caroline.

His ex-wife didn't live in the most salubrious area of the city: most of it was rows of red-brick terraced houses running down a steep hill. As he drove there, Groves was still thinking about Leland. About how it must have been for him not just to die the way he had, but to *live* that way. An endless, jobless cycle of television and alcohol and sleep, all of it soundtracked by the percussion of kids banging a football against the side of your house. It wasn't how he'd have wanted to live.

Looking around him as he turned in to Caroline's dilapidated street, Groves wondered how far his ex-wife was slipping in that direction herself. Even as she came down the path to meet him, he could tell she'd been drinking already. Trying to dull the painful reality of Jamie's absence.

But then, just as Sean had said earlier, there were a lot of things that people didn't get to choose.

★   ★   ★

One summer day — several years ago now — an eight-year-old girl called Laila Buckingham was playing outside her house in the back garden. It was warm and sunny, and Laila's mother, Amanda, was working in the kitchen, a pan of potatoes bubbling away on the hob. There was background music playing quietly on the stereo, but the patio doors were open, and Amanda was keeping a sporadic eye on her young daughter.

Laila was a happy child, but shy, with few friends, and content to play alone. *She had such a good imagination*, her mother would tell the police later. *She was happy with her own company.* The back garden was fenced off, but not high, and it edged a road, although not a busy one. By all accounts Laila was a clever girl, and could be trusted to be careful. She often played outside. And yet that day there had come a point when Amanda Buckingham had craned her neck to check on her, and Laila was not there any more.

The search for the girl began within ten minutes of her going missing. It was extensive.

As time went on, it was also increasingly fraught, because it was obvious to officers within minutes that she had been taken. Every lead was followed and exhausted, while the local community rallied around the family, with hundreds of volunteers searching recreation grounds, parks, riverbanks and outhouses. Trained rescue teams went methodically through the edges of the woods. Laila seemed to have vanished off the face of the earth.

Groves had been a junior officer back then, and his role in the search was door-to-door interviews. It was painful work, in that it was monotonous and achieved nothing, but he wanted to do it anyway. If he was a tiny cog in a huge machine, he was still determined to play his part in its turning. His son, Jamie, was not quite one year old, and he could barely imagine the pain the Buckinghams must be going through. So he tried not to let the consistently empty and useless witness statements dissuade him. He prayed that Laila would be found, and tried to keep hope.

On the fourth day, he was working the Thornton estate, a few miles from where Laila had disappeared. He had a list of names to get through, and just after eleven o'clock that morning, he knocked on the door of a man called Simon Chadwick.

Chadwick was in his late twenties, and known to the police. He had problems with drugs and antisocial behaviour, and something close to a child's IQ, and he hated the police intensely. It was a combination that made it fairly easy for the wrong elements to take advantage of him. A number of his convictions stemmed from allowing another person to sell drugs from his premises.

Groves wasn't looking forward to the encounter, knowing that the minimum he could expect was some verbal abuse, and when Chadwick answered, the door on a chain, peering out through the gap, he seemed twitchy. Groves' initial suspicion was that there were drugs on the premises, and he wasn't sure what to do about that. Under normal circumstances he would have wanted to take him in. Right then, though, they were at full stretch, and he cared more about finding Laila Buckingham than wasting time and resources on a man like Chadwick.

And then he heard the noise.

It was a sound he would never forget. Muffled but distinct, and immediately obvious what it was: a little girl crying. She was somewhere behind Chadwick, deeper in the house.

They stared at each other for a second. Groves knew that Chadwick lived alone, and Chadwick knew that Groves knew it.

As the man tried to close the door on him, Groves kicked it as hard as he could. It was pure instinct. He wasn't thinking about what would be lawful; he was just suddenly sure that Laila Buckingham was inside that property, and all that mattered to him was getting to her as quickly as possible. And perhaps because he didn't think about it, the kick was a good one. It took the door off one of its hinges, and sent Chadwick sprawling back into the hallway.

And then . . .

Perhaps it was strange, but Groves could never remember much about what happened next. The details remained in his head long enough for him to make a statement from his hospital bed, but afterwards it all faded. He knew the fight with Chadwick had been ferocious, but that he'd managed to subdue him and click the emergency button for backup, and then hang on until it arrived. But these days he had to rely on the report to remind himself, or else the coverage that filled the news over the days that followed.

Hero cop saves missing girl.

He didn't know it at the time, but the single interview he gave contained a line that would come back to haunt him:

It wouldn't have mattered how many of them had been in there at the time.

Because while Groves was doing his best to shun the attentions of the media, Simon Chadwick was telling his own story to the police. He claimed not to have abducted Laila Buckingham, and it turned out he had a solid alibi for the window of time around her disappearance. He also claimed that she had simply been staying with him — that he was 'looking after her' — and that he hadn't laid a hand on her. There were other people, he told the police, and it was their fault. He had just been doing them a favour. He hadn't known. He hadn't understood.

It was obvious, deep down, that he knew more, but there was evidence that his testimony was at least partially true. Although Laila

76

Buckingham could remember little of her abduction and ordeal, she corroborated some of Chadwick's story. And there had been a degree of organisation behind the abduction that Chadwick would have struggled to orchestrate by himself. The implication was that a larger paedophile gang was operating locally.

And yet Chadwick was either unwilling or unable to identify the other people he claimed were involved, and those individuals were never found. Ultimately, Simon Chadwick was the only person ever convicted for his part in the abduction and abuse of Laila Buckingham.

Hero cop saves missing girl.

The report had named David Groves, of course. Whoever the gang were, they would have known who he was. They would perhaps have wanted revenge. And two years afterwards, in almost identical circumstances to Laila's disappearance, Jamie Groves had been taken too.

★   ★   ★

It was a warm evening, so he and Caroline sat out on the small patio at the back of his cottage. It caught the sun in the evening, although the light was already retreating, slinking back across the overgrown garden at an angle. The air was mild, but still felt heavy with the day's heat. A fluttering globe of midges hung by the far hedge, while the birdsong was growing lazy and subdued.

They sat on two white plastic chairs, separated by a matching table on which there was a bottle of white wine, beaded with condensation. They each had a glass, and Caroline had an ashtray as well. She was drinking faster than he was, but he was used to that. On a different day, maybe he'd have said something, but not today. There were more bottles inside. More than they would need.

'How was your day?'

Groves thought of Edward Leland burning to death in his half-empty home. The possible cuts on his face. Whatever had happened to him, he hoped the man was at peace now.

'It could have been worse,' he said. 'You?'

'I didn't go in today.'

'No, of course not.'

That was just one of the many ways they handled Jamie's birthday differently. While Groves did his best to carry on as normal, Caroline, consumed by the loss, dedicated her every waking hour to it. She would have spent today thinking about their son: looking at photos of Jamie; turning his memory over in her head; perhaps even cursing the God that Groves still clung to. But there was no recrimination either way. It was the coping that bonded them, not their differing approaches to it.

He imagined it seemed odd to outsiders that the two of them got along better now than when they had been married. Sean, for one, couldn't understand why Groves always spent the evening of Jamie's birthday with Caroline. But the strange truth was that while Jamie's murder had finally broken them apart, it had also brought them together again. In the past, they'd pecked at each other over trivialities, but after their son

78

was taken, there had been no further arguments. It was as though a switch had been flicked and an unspoken truce called, neither of them seeing the point any more in fighting over patches of ground they both knew didn't matter.

It had also held them in place. For a long time, Jamie had been the only thing keeping them together. Before he went missing, they'd been like planets separately circling the bright sun of his life. When that sun had winked out, it had left a centre of gravity still strong enough to hold them in its orbit. And so round and round they went, even now, unable to escape the power of the loss, the absence, the *emptiness* that had once held the bright light of their little boy. And despite the acrimony and bitterness that had once existed between them, there was nobody else Groves would have wanted to spend his son's birthday with. Apart from Jamie, of course.

As the evening progressed, the two of them made small talk, or sat in comfortable stretches of silence, watching the sun as it moved lower. Both of them, Groves was sure, were thinking of Jamie, who was somehow there with them, yet not.

Jamie had never lived in this cottage, of course, but in Groves' mind's eye, he could easily imagine him here. Running around the garden in front of them, perhaps kicking a ball and swiping the midges away. There was a problem with that image, though, because Groves pictured his son as the same little boy he remembered: innocent and excited and delighted by everything. He could even still hear his laugh in his head: a high-pitched, unguarded squeal of joy that had always made everything better. And yet if Jamie had still been alive now, he would be very different. Older and changed. He would like different things. He would look different. He would laugh differently.

That knowledge brought a familiar flavour of sadness with it. Four years on, and Jamie was already being left behind. A small figure stopped in place, destined now to recede forever into the distance. The nearly-three-year-old boy he imagined running around the garden was frozen in time, as old as he would ever be. When Groves was old and grey, Jamie would still be small. He would never grow any bigger than their memories of him.

He had to believe that one day he would see him again, but it bothered him: when he finally died too, and father and son were reunited in Heaven, would Jamie have aged in the intervening time? If so, he would have grown into a man Groves wouldn't know or recognise, and who in turn would not know him. But the alternative was that he would have remained the same, held in a nascent form, and would find himself running to hug a father who had long become reconciled to his loss. Both options seemed intolerable. Maybe that was why the bereaved often committed suicide soon after their loss, Groves thought. It wasn't just the grief and the heartbreak, but a kind of existential chasing.

He drained his glass of wine, then poured them both a fresh one. Caroline smiled her thanks, but her expression looked far away, and he suspected she was thinking similar things.

As the evening wore on, Jamie began to flit around their snatches of conversation. At first it was difficult to acknowledge him directly, and it wasn't until halfway down the second bottle of wine that Caroline said:

'Have you been to the grave?'

Groves shook his head. 'Maybe tomorrow.'

'I left flowers. And a toy. In case he wants something to play with.'

'That's nice.'

Caroline's behaviour made no sense to him, but he could hardly begrudge her it. Every year she left flowers and a toy. The flowers usually remained, but eventually someone would always take the toy. They were always toys for a younger child, because Jamie would always be the same age. Every year his ex-wife bought a birthday present for that same frozen memory of their boy.

'You'll go tomorrow?' she said.

'Hopefully.' He stood up, collecting his glass and the second empty bottle. 'It's getting cold. We should go inside.'

'Can I . . . ?'

'Yes, you can smoke inside. Today.'

Inside, the dam broke. The way other couples might leaf through a wedding album on an anniversary, they looked through all the photographs of Jamie that Caroline had collected in an album and brought with her. They drank more wine. They talked about him a little more, until finally the barrier disappeared entirely and he became all they talked about. The long, soft blond hair that they'd never had the chance to cut; his favourite books and toys; his little idiosyncrasies. How gentle and lovely he had been.

In such a way, for a while at least, they brought him back to life. But their shared memories were like a stone skipping over the sea of his absence, and no matter how hard you throw it, a stone can't skim for ever.

'I miss him.'

Caroline was sobbing now, clinging to Groves on the settee, and he to her. She was close to passing out by then, while he was drunk but wished he was more so.

'I miss him too. So much. I can't say.'

It seemed to him that Jamie *had* somehow become real now. So real that he might as well have been standing in front of them, fingers moving by his sides, that quizzical expression on his face.

Why are you crying, Mummy and Daddy?

'I just want him back,' Caroline said.

Groves hugged her tightly. 'I do too.'

'I'd give anything. Absolutely anything.'

'I know.' His neck was soaked with her tears, but he just held her, wanting her to be okay, for everything to be different, for Jamie to be here. 'I know.'

He imagined Jamie's ghost walking over and standing in between them, leaning into the embrace, wanting to be a part of it, the way he always had. Wanting to make things better.

Mummy and Daddy, are you happy now?

82

It was too much.

'Come on.'

Groves helped Caroline up to the spare bedroom. He helped her get enough of her clothes off to collapse comfortably into the bed, then pulled the sheet over her. She was asleep in seconds, lying on her side, her breath rattling in her throat.

Then he went back downstairs and drank more wine, and thought about Jamie's grave. It was a decent-sized plot with a large headstone, big enough for an adult. Jamie had been little for his age, and when Groves had seen him dead, he had been diminished even further. Aside from the clothes and the toy, his remains might have been those of a kitten. But while the body sealed beneath the packed, silent earth was small, the space that had been allocated to him was not, so that it always felt as though they'd buried everything Jamie might have been. All the possible men he might have grown into.

The inscription on the headstone read:

> Wherever they go, and whatever happens to them on the way, in that enchanted place on the top of the Forest, a little boy and his Bear will always be playing.

The last words of the Winnie-the-Pooh stories his son had loved so much. Words that signal that even as we move on, into adulthood and beyond, a part of us is always left behind, remaining as it was. We remember it, and perhaps it remembers us back, but however desperately we reach out to each other, our outstretched hands can never touch.

'I love you,' he told the empty front room. 'I love you so much. I miss you more every day.'

And like that hardened writer allowing his bluebird out when nobody was there to see, Groves began to cry.

Mark

When you're dead

After leaving Paul Carlisle's house, I headed back north.

The afternoon light was beginning to dim slightly now, but it seemed warmer than ever. As I drove along the ring road, with the woods in the distance ahead, the fields to my right seemed hazy, as though the air above the grass was dozing off. The trees in the distance there were blurred by the heat rising from the land: vague watercolours, smudged on to the sky.

The road curled steadily west as I drew closer to the woods, until the countryside on the right was replaced by the dark wall of trees that marked the city's unofficial boundary with nature. They were so thick and tall here that it was impossible to tell how far back they went, but I knew they stretched on for miles: a vast sprawl all the way to the mountains.

I grew up a long way from the city, and my childhood memories of woodland were happy, sunlit ones: playing with my friends; climbing trees; hacking paths through the undergrowth. Some woods are safe, I thought, watching the rough trunks and shadows flashing past beside me. Not these ones, though. Driving close to them, it always felt like there was something in there between the trees, watching you.

85

And of course, once upon a time, there had been.

My thoughts inevitably turned to my arrival in the city, a year and a half ago. After Lise's death, I'd taken a huge, hopeful leap career-wise by applying for a post here. I'd revered Detective John Mercer, a legend in the force, for years, and been desperate to join his team. A place as his interview man had opened up, and I'd been both overjoyed and nervous when my application was accepted. And then on my first day here, I'd been drawn into the hunt for a man known as the 50/50 Killer.

I say man, but because the 50/50 Killer wore a devil mask while committing his crimes, and we never fully discovered the real identity of the man behind it, it was easy to think of him as both more and less than that. He abducted couples, tortured them over the course of a single night, and forced one of them to decide which of the two would die. Only one of them ever remained alive at dawn. The survivor was left not only alone, but with the terrible knowledge that their choice had resulted in their partner's murder — that they hadn't cared enough to sacrifice themselves instead. I'd die for you, we tell the ones we love. I couldn't live without you. The 50/50 Killer wanted people to understand that those promises were lies.

I watched out of the side window now as I drove past the place where, on that first day, a young man named Scott had emerged from the trees, tortured and confused. I'd spent the night interviewing him in hospital, while officers combed the woods for his partner, Jodie. And by dawn, despite our best efforts, Detective John Mercer's distinguished career and mental well-being were both in tatters.

The scene receded slowly in the rear-view mirror. I'd slowed down as I reached it, I realised; I accelerated slightly now to compensate, glad to see it disappear. About ten minutes later, I reached the patch of the ring road where Charlie Matheson's accident had taken place.

I pulled in by the side of the embankment on the left and got out of the car. I took a few photographs, although there wasn't much to see: no sign at all of what had happened here two years ago. As I walked up and over the incline, the grass was soft and dry and seemed untouched.

At the top of the embankment, looking down the steep slope beyond, I recognised the landscape from the pictures in the file. It was easy to pick out the lone tree, about thirty metres down, that Matheson's car had crashed into. But again, the land appeared undamaged by the incident, and there were no longer any tracks on the ground to indicate the path the vehicle had taken on its descent.

I took more photographs, but really, there was nothing to distinguish this stretch from any other. Something bad had happened here, I thought, heading back to the car; someone had been lost. At the time, there must surely have been marks and injuries to the land in recognition of that. And yet the grass had grown back, the tree had untwisted and righted itself.

In less than two years, nature had healed those wounds without leaving so much as a scar.

I drove away wishing it could be that easy for people. But then in some ways perhaps it was. Whatever happens, your life goes on, whether you like it or not. Your life is stubborn like that.

I'd die for you.

I couldn't live without you.

Both lies, I thought, remembering standing on the beach all those years ago, helplessly watching my girlfriend drown.

Both lies when it had come to Lise.

★ ★ ★

Sasha was home before me. I found her in the kitchen, chopping onions and garlic, with mince defrosting in the microwave. She'd changed into jeans and a thigh-length white T-shirt, one of my old ones. I walked up and hugged her from behind, pleased when she pressed back against me without hesitation. I kissed her neck and stepped away.

'My turn to cook,' I said.

'I know. I just figured I'd make a start. Oh dear.' She grabbed a sheet of kitchen roll and dabbed at her eyes, turning to face me. 'Bloody onions. Anyway. You look surprisingly okay. You survived, then?'

'Somehow, yeah.'

'Was it because of my special coffee?'

'I think it might well have been. How was your day?'

'Ah, just the usual heroics.' She shrugged,

putting the kitchen roll in the bin. 'What about you? Anything interesting to report?'

'Not really. Pete decided to teach me a lesson by sending me on a wild goose chase. He said you wouldn't punish me for getting drunk, so it fell to him.'

'Ha! I always liked Pete.'

'Yeah, yeah. I'll just get changed, then I'll take over in here.'

'Right you are.'

I hung up my suit upstairs, then threw on some jeans and a T-shirt of my own. *A wild goose chase*, I thought — except it was beginning to seem like it might be something else altogether, even if right now I wasn't sure what. And yet my instinct had been to downplay the day's events to Sasha, to not go into detail. I knew why, as well. I kept remembering the look on Paul Carlisle's face: the horror that a life he'd left behind and moved on from might be rearing its ugly head in the present. And every time I pictured that, the knot in my chest tightened slightly.

Downstairs, I fried up bolognese, and set the pasta boiling.

'Your turn to pick five,' Sasha called through.

'Is it? Okay.'

Once a week, we watched a movie together: turned off the lights and ate dinner on our laps, side by side on the settee. The routine was always the same. One of us would select five DVDs from the shelves, and the other had to choose one from them. We liked very different things. Sasha was a big science-fiction and horror geek, whereas I tended to go more for thrillers and dramas. Whenever it was my turn to pick, I always went for four films I wanted to watch, and one I knew she did. When it was her week to pull out five, the routine reversed itself. Neither of us had ever mentioned this arrangement out loud.

Tonight I selected two horror films instead of one, hoping the unspoken gesture might go some way to make up for my behaviour last night, if that was still needed. I left the pile on the settee while I drained the pasta, and then we ate dinner together watching a horror film called *Pumpkinhead*. Sasha enjoyed it anyway. The things we do for love.

Afterwards, I took the bowls through and washed up, the water hot enough to leave the skin on my hands pink when I was finished.

I was still thinking about the case.

'I'm exhausted.'

I turned to see Sasha leaning against the door frame, yawning.

'Early night for me,' she said. 'You coming?'

I dried my hands and hung up the towel. I knew I should go with her, but the folded sheet of paper Paul Carlisle had given me felt heavy in my pocket.

'I just need to check something,' I said. 'I'll be up in a few minutes.'

'Just a few?'

'Not even that many. Promise.'

She smiled at me. 'Good.'

Back in the front room, I sat down in the dark on the settee and logged into the departmental database on my tablet, then synched the device with the plasma screen on the wall. A few moments later, the television showed a still image of the woman in the hospital. In the gloom, it looked as though she was somehow hanging in the air between the television and the settee.

Then I did what I'd known I was going to have to but had been dreading all the same. I walked across the dark lounge unfolding the piece of paper that Paul Carlisle had given me and held it up beside the television.

There was enough light from the screen to see it clearly. I looked from one image to the other, attempting to mentally erase the scarring on the face of the woman in the hospital. Comparing. Back and forth. Over and over.

It was her.

A little older. A little more gaunt.

But definitely her.

I sat back down, then pressed play on the video clip, and listened half-heartedly while I turned the tablet to split screen and opened a blank document in the right-hand panel.

Provisional timeline
3 August 2013 Charlie Matheson's car crash
28 July 2015 Charlie Matheson (?) reappears

For now, that was all there was to include. Two dates that bookmarked whatever had happened. They were like the dates on a headstone, except they delineated not a life, but a death.

Perhaps.

'It's dark where I've been,' the woman was

saying. 'I remember that much about it. Everything's very dark when you're dead.'

I looked up at the screen. The expression on her face seemed much sadder than I'd recognised at the time.

What happened to you?

My thoughts were interrupted by Sasha calling from the top of the stairs.

'I'm not waiting for ever, you know.'

'Coming.'

I saved the document, then logged out and turned everything off. The woman on the screen disappeared, replaced by darkness.

Enough, I thought.

That was more than enough for tonight.

Part Two

And She told Them that true goodness must always shy from the light. A Man may be good at heart, but many do good in search of reward, and that is selfish and not true goodness. True goodness would face the trials of Hell itself without asking for notice. It is neither bright nor loud and it draws no attention to itself. And She told Them that God therefore seeks out good that wishes not to be sought, and rewards it quietly in kind.

Extract from the Cane Hill bible

Eileen

No such thing as monsters

John Mercer's makeshift office was in the attic at the top of the house. He always worked with the door closed, but Eileen could often hear him typing from the bottom of the stairs. A soft sound. It passed from his fingertips on the computer keyboard, down the legs of the desk, then through the floorboards below.

She stood there now, looking up at the ceiling above, listening to the gentle patter of letters falling like rain on to a tin roof.

The sound made her nervous. But then again, the silences were worse — long stretches of time when she could imagine her husband sitting there reading through his documents, lost in thoughts it would be far better for him to leave behind. She'd gone in there once, when John had been out on some errand, and stared with a kind of vacant horror at the wall charts and noticeboards, all covered with scribbled dates and references. The maps dotted with pins and lines of coloured string. The printouts and photographs taped to the bare plaster, some of them so appalling that Eileen had looked away quickly before the reds and blacks could coalesce into an identifiable image.

She knew what they were, and it frightened her to picture John sitting there staring at them, or through them. Eyes were the windows to the soul, they said, and God knew she'd stared into many that showed no hint of soul at all. But John's eyes she'd always thought were more like doorways, and that if he looked at certain horrors for long enough, some aspect of them would take advantage of that and go inside. He was old now. Old and fragile, and not strong enough to bear such things. Eileen lived with the constant fear that her husband, former Detective John Mercer, might break once again.

So as unnerving as the typing was, she supposed it was better than the alternative. And since she could find the alternative anywhere else in the house, Eileen often found herself standing here at the bottom of the stairs, listening.

He's all right.

He's still fine.

She couldn't stand here for ever, though; there was work to do. The pair of them had savings, but Eileen had become the primary breadwinner following John's departure from the police a year and a half ago. They had been apart for a few months afterwards, before tentatively reconciling. Despite everything that had happened, the shared history stretching behind them had drawn them back together. She still loved him deeply, even if events had altered that love. Thinking back on the broad, strong, capable man she'd fallen in love with, it was painful to see him so reduced now. She had never imagined that, in old age, it would become *her* duty to care for *him*.

She went downstairs. While her husband

worked in the attic, her own office was at the base of the house, in an extension built into the drive on one side. This was where she received her private clients; she specialised in therapy for abuse and violence. It was the flipside to her criminal work, where she would often find herself counselling the men who had perpetrated such offences in the first place. People sometimes thought that must make it harder, but in truth it rarely did. As John had written in his first book, everyone stood at the nexus point of the damage done to them and the damage they themselves caused. It was her job to help untangle that. Even the most apparently evil of the men she had talked to was only a man, whether she saw a soul in his eyes or not. There was no such thing as monsters.

Although sometimes that could be hard to believe.

It was only just after eight o'clock, and her first client wasn't due for another hour, but she set the coffee machine going and settled down in one of the armchairs with a small stack of case files. That afternoon she had one of her prison visits, and she wanted to make sure she was up to speed with the inmates she'd be talking to. The sound of the coffee machine gradually began to fill the heavy silence, and she felt the tightness in her stomach easing slightly . . .

And then someone knocked at the door.

Eileen stared over, noticing the silhouette through the bobbled glass panels. She didn't bother checking her watch; she knew what time it was. It wasn't unheard of for clients to call

97

round unannounced out of hours, and if they were feeling especially distressed and vulnerable she even encouraged them to do so. But there was something about the figure standing there that made her nervous. No obvious reason for it. Of course, she was nervous about a lot of things recently, her concern for John's welfare lending everything an edge.

But still.

'Just a minute,' she called.

The coffee machine clicked off. Eileen placed the case files securely in the cabinet, then walked over to the door and unlocked and opened it.

The heat rushed in; even at this early hour, the day was beginning to bake. And yet it wasn't that that made her take a slight step back. It was the sight of the young man waiting on the doorstep. He was about thirty years old, with neat brown hair swept to one side, wearing a smart suit. A plain but somehow attractive face with a nice smile. Genuine. The sight of him brought the tightness back to her abdomen, and the silence in the house behind her felt suddenly more dangerous than before. She had an urge to go and close the door to the hallway and lock it, to protect John from the man on the doorstep, who was a reminder of the past life that had damaged him so badly.

Instead, she forced a professional smile.

'Mark,' she said.

Mark

Vulnerable people

It had been over a year and a half since I'd seen Eileen Mercer. In the immediate aftermath of the 50/50 Killer case, I'd been responsible for interviewing her about what had taken place at this house on that winter morning. I'd actually spoken to her the day before, when she had phoned the office. At that point, I'd detected a hint of mischief in her voice: a sparkle. Understandably, that had disappeared by the time I sat down with her at her sister's house, but she had still been at least as in control of the interview as I was. Given her background in psychology and therapy, it hadn't surprised me, but even so, in the circumstances, I had been struck by how intelligent and self-possessed she was.

The intervening time had been kind to her. She was in her sixties, slim and elegant, and if anything she actually looked younger now than she had eighteen months ago. But she no longer seemed quite so in control. My arrival had clearly flustered her. As she invited me in and showed me to an armchair, she kept glancing back in the direction of the main house, as though worried that my presence was going to disturb some precarious balance. I had no wish to upset her, and a part of me was sorry that I'd come. But I needed advice.

'Quite a library,' I said, admiring the shelves of books that lined the walls. It was a warm room, managing to feel formal and professional but also immediately comfortable.

Eileen poured us both a coffee.

'Thank you. How are you?' For a second, I thought she was asking about Lise and Sasha, but then she added: 'Things at the department, I mean?'

'We've moved buildings. Apart from that, it's the same as always.' I accepted the cup. 'Thank you.'

'You're welcome.'

Sipping the coffee, I realised that my answer wasn't completely true. While I'd only worked under her husband for a day and a half, it was obvious that the aftermath of the 50/50 Killer investigation had altered the internal dynamics of the team for ever. Pete was in charge now, for one thing, and while he was a good cop, he wasn't a natural leader. He certainly wasn't John Mercer. There were none of the flashes of insight and wild intellectual leaps on which Mercer had built his legendary career, something I thought Pete understood only too well. And while Simon had carried on much as before, Greg's relationship with the pair of them had shifted. He had committed a small betrayal that day, and while it was never explicitly mentioned, it had never been entirely forgotten either.

Eileen sat down in the chair opposite me, a coffee table between us. It was possibly the arrangement she used for her therapy patients.

Perhaps, I thought, I could actually use some of that.

'As the saying goes,' Eileen said, 'this isn't a social call, is it?'

'No. I was hoping for some advice. About a case that's come up.'

She almost glanced behind her again. 'From me?'

'Yes. From you. Obviously, we can arrange a consultation fee.'

'Well, I suppose we can see. But I don't even know if I can help yet. Tell me about the case.'

I told her about the woman who was claiming to be Charlie Matheson, beginning with the circumstances in which she'd been found, then working through the story of the accident and her belief that she had died in the crash. I finished up with my visit to see her husband, Paul Carlisle, and the photograph that had convinced me that the woman in the hospital was telling the truth about her identity. By the end of the account, Eileen was frowning.

'That's quite extraordinary.'

'I agree. I've never heard anything like it.'

'There is something,' she said. 'Cotard's delusion. It's quite rare, and I've never encountered it myself, but sufferers can become convinced that parts of their bodies are missing, even though they aren't. In extreme cases, they believe they're literally dead.'

'That sounds promising.'

'Except, of course, they don't really die. And from what you're telling me, someone actually *did* die in that car crash.'

'That's true.'

'What were your impressions of her?'

I leaned back in the chair. 'Well . . . I didn't get the feeling she was lying to me. Her memory was very confused. But on a basic level, I think she really did believe what she told me.'

'Was she fragile?'

'A little.' I thought about it; that wasn't quite right. 'She looked scared. A bit bewildered and overwhelmed by everything. But there was also anger there, especially towards the end. Frustration.'

'Frustration?'

'That people weren't taking her seriously. And also that she couldn't think clearly.' I recalled what she'd said to me: *I need to remember*. 'She seemed to believe there was something important she had to remember, and it annoyed her that she couldn't.'

'And aside from the story itself, did she appear delusional?'

'No. Apart from the content of what she was telling me, I never got the impression she was delusional. She was angry with me for not believing her, but aside from the scars and the subject matter, she came across as fairly normal.'

'Those are big asides, aren't they?' Eileen said.

'Yes. They are.'

'All right.' She closed her eyes for a moment. 'It's hard to say without interviewing her myself, but it seems to me that there are two basic possibilities you're dealing with here. To my mind, one of them is far more likely than the other. And that's obviously discounting a third explanation altogether.'

'Which is?'

'That she really has come back from the dead.'
I thought of Lise, and replied far too quickly.

'People don't come back from the dead.'

'No.' Eileen gave me the slightest of smiles. 'Of course not. Which leaves the next option: that she's making it up entirely. Lying to you. You don't believe that's the case?'

'No.'

'Which leaves the possibility that she's telling not the truth, but her version of it.'

'What do you mean?'

'When people undergo trauma, it's often hard to face up to it, so they parcel it up, compartmentalise it. Recast it in their heads so it's easier to deal with. Some experiences are simply too painful to face head on. The story she's told you so far, and the things she might tell you as time goes on, may well all be her mind's attempt to make sense of what's happened to her. It would be genuine and honest from her point of view, but not necessarily literally true.'

'Partly true, though?'

'Yes. Not a total fabrication. She thinks she's been dead. So wherever she's been, maybe she was surrounded by religious iconography. I don't know; I'm speculating. But the point is, the story could be an interpretation of something terrible that's happened to her, rather than a literal account of it.'

I thought about it.

'Could you *make* someone believe they were

dead?' I said. 'Because she actually claims to remember going through the windscreen of the car. She's sure that happened.'

'You say she was tortured?'

'She's scarred: lots of cuts to her face. I don't know if she sees it as torture.'

'She might not, but that doesn't mean it wasn't. And in answer to your question, yes, I think it's possible in theory. I've never heard of it happening before, but torture, brainwashing, gaslighting, manipulation . . . yes, of course. You see it in cults, certain oppressive regimes. It's usually used to make people more compliant, but this is just an extension of that really. Same principles, same techniques.'

'It's far more extreme.'

'It is,' Eileen said, 'but given two years, and with enough repetition and mistreatment, I think you could probably make someone believe almost anything you wanted them to. In the end, they would *want* to believe it.'

I nodded, thinking it over.

'Some of the details would correspond to what really happened. So the thing to do would be to get as much information as possible.'

'As carefully as possible.'

'Of course.'

'Because you have to be careful with vulnerable people.'

I nodded again, aware once more of the home beyond her office, and the way she kept glancing in that direction. Was John in there now? Presumably so. But I had no wish to see him, and it was obvious from Eileen's manner that she didn't want whatever peace he'd found since leaving the police to be disturbed.

'Of course,' I said again, then stood up. 'Thank you for the coffee. And the advice.'

'I'm not sure how much help I've been.'

She walked me over to the door. But as I opened it, I realised I was still wondering. That I couldn't quite leave it.

'How is he?' I said.

'He's fine.'

But she said it too quickly, the same way I'd responded after her words had brought a flash memory of Lise to my mind. And it wasn't so different, was it? Here I was, a ghost from her husband's past, threatening the new life — the hard-won peace — that had been established over the past year and a half.

'I'm glad,' I said. 'Thank you again.'

As I stepped out, Eileen seemed to relent slightly.

'He's working on a new book,' she said. 'It's about . . . that man.'

Despite the warmth of the morning sun, I felt a chill at her choice of words. *That man*. I knew who she meant, of course. Even though he was dead and gone, we'd never successfully identified the 50/50 Killer; we had no idea who he was or where he'd come from. He stood anonymously at the focal point of the whirlwind of violence he'd unleashed on the city, and on John Mercer in particular.

And Mercer was working on a book about him? I didn't know what to say. The thought of him revisiting that case — poring over it;

maybe obsessing over it — was unnerving, and I now understood Eileen's unease a little better.

'I don't know if it's healthy,' she said, reading the expression on my face. 'But he's fine right now, and I'll take that. It seems to be what he needs.'

'Well, then. That's good.'

'And for now, he's happy.'

But there was an undercurrent to the way she said that. And another one a moment later, when she closed the door gently but firmly without saying goodbye.

Mark

Mercy

As I sat down for my second interview with Charlie Matheson, I knew I was going to have to approach things very differently from the first.

The advice Eileen had given me remained fresh in my mind: there was no telling how much of Charlie's story Was true. Certainly, she hadn't died in the accident. Beyond that, some parts of her account could be entirely accurate, while others might be fantastical elaborations with only a hint of basis in reality. It was my job to begin to delve into that. And I would need to be gentle with her while I did it.

Because you have to be careful with vulnerable people.

And of course another difference from yesterday was that this time I believed the woman really might be Charlie Matheson.

'Detective,' she said as I sat down in the chair beside the bed.

I switched on the camera on my lapel.

'How are you feeling today, Charlie?'

'Better. Thank you.' She nodded once. 'I'm sorry for my outburst yesterday, just before you left.'

'You don't need to apologise.'

'Oh, but I do. That's really not like me. At all. I don't like losing control, and I was annoyed with myself afterwards. It was just that everything was — *is* — so confusing for me at the moment. This is all so overwhelming.'

'Which is understandable.' I tried to smile reassuringly. 'And for what it's worth, I'm sorry too if it seemed like I wasn't taking you seriously.'

'You believe me now?'

'I believe you're who you say you are.'

'Did you talk to Paul?'

'Yes. He was very upset, as you can imagine.'

'Oh? Not pleased, then?'

'Well . . . it's complicated.'

'I suppose so. How is he?'

'He's engaged.' And just as when I'd spoken to Carlisle yesterday, there didn't seem any point in sugar-coating the facts. 'His new partner is pregnant.'

The look on her face when I said it was heartbreaking, but she only allowed the sadness a fleeting appearance before it was gone again. She knew I'd seen it, though, and after a moment she gave me a flat, empty smile.

'Well. Of course. It has been two fucking years after all, hasn't it?'

Just like the sadness a moment ago, the trace of anger vanished as quickly as it had arrived. She was more in control of herself than yesterday, I thought; where she'd appeared vulnerable and disorientated during that first interview, she seemed much more self-possessed now.

'He always wanted children, Paul.' There was a wry smile at that, then she shook her head. 'And it makes sense that he'd move on, especially with me dead.'

108

'You aren't dead, Charlie. I don't know where you've been for the last two years, but I do know that.'

'I remember dying. In the car crash.'

'Are you really sure about that?'

'Yes.' But I thought she sounded less certain than she had yesterday. 'I remember the car. And I remember going over the embankment.'

'But you must see that you're not dead.' I gestured around the room. 'You're in a hospital. You're flesh and blood, not a ghost. Someone died in that crash, but it wasn't you. I mean, how do *you* make sense of it?'

'I don't know.'

'People don't come back from the dead.' I almost added, *I wish they did, but they don't*, but then I thought of Lise again, and I remembered the look on Paul Carlisle's face yesterday. 'And that's where we have to start from. Something happened to you that night, and something's been happening to you ever since, but you certainly didn't die.'

She considered that.

'So what do *you* think happened to me?'

'I don't know yet,' I admitted. 'I think it's possible that someone's worked very hard to convince you that you died in that accident, and that over time, with everything you've been through, you've come to believe it's true.'

Again she was silent for a moment. I leaned forward.

'Let's forget about the actual accident for now. You told me you lost consciousness afterwards. Can you remember what happened next?'

'Yes.'

'But?'

'I don't want to talk about it.'

I spoke as gently as I could.

'I know you don't. I don't know for sure, but I think a lot of very bad things have happened to you over the last two years, and I understand how difficult it must be to think about them. But it's important, Charlie. Unless you talk to me, there's no way for us to work out where you've been.' I leaned back. 'You were on the embankment. You lost consciousness. What happened when you woke up again? Where were you?'

Charlie looked at me for a long moment, her scarred face blank. Then she seemed to gather strength from inside herself.

'Hell,' she said simply. 'I woke up in Hell.'

★ ★ ★

Hell.

It wasn't, of course — not literally — but as she told me her story, it seemed as good a word as any for the place she described. When she had woken properly after the crash, she told me, she'd found herself in a small room: a cell, effectively. The walls were fashioned out of stone and mud, and the air was damp and clammy. Despite a cooler current that drifted through occasionally, the heat was oppressive. The silence was profound, punctuated only by occasional dripping in the distance, like water dropping into a pool somewhere deep underground, the sound echoing.

110

'There was light,' she said, 'but not much. The door was metal, and it had a hatch in it — a letter box that had been cut out at eye level. Like you see in prison on the TV, except this one was always open. I could look out.'

Not that there was anything to see when she did. It was a thin corridor of some kind, with another stone wall opposite the door. It was illuminated by dim lights in dirty plastic cases, strung along the wall. They were always on.

'There was a television too,' she said.

'A television?'

'Yes. Just a small screen, embedded in one of the walls. There was no control, though — no buttons or anything. It would just come on suddenly, bright and loud, like something snarling at me from the side of the room.'

'And what did it show?'

'The news sometimes. And . . . other things. Things I didn't like to look at. Videos of horrible things. Not the sort of things they'd ever show on normal television.'

She looked awkward, as though she didn't want to talk about what she'd seen, what had been shown to her. Which was fine; from what she'd said, I could imagine. And in my head, taking her story at face value for now, I was beginning to work my way down a checklist. Isolation. Sensory deprivation. Visual and audial disruption. They were the kinds of things that Eileen had mentioned earlier as key components of mind control and brainwashing.

Of course, another obvious one was torture.

'You told me someone cut your face,' I said.

111

She didn't reply, and I had to prompt her.

'Your scars, Charlie. You said someone did that to you. Who was it?'

'I don't want to talk about him.'

A man, then. Hardly unexpected, but it was something.

'Was it the same man who was speaking to you in the ambulance the other day?'

'No, no.' She looked horrified at the idea. 'The man in the ambulance was gentle, kind. Not like . . . the one who did the cutting.'

'Can you describe him, Charlie? The one who wasn't kind?'

She shook her head.

'It's important,' I said.

'I can't.'

The way she said it was final, and propped up in bed now, she looked exhausted. I knew I was going to have to wind the interview up soon and allow her to rest.

But I was also trying to run everything she'd told me through the filter that Eileen had suggested. What was real and what was fantasy here? It was entirely possible that someone really had held Charlie Matheson captive, and that they had tortured her, brainwashed her. I knew from experience that such men existed. But then the type of man who would do that didn't normally let his victims go. And what to make of the story about the ambulance, and the other man — the kind one — who had been talking to her?

Where had she been held?

'How long were you in the ambulance for?' I said. 'Before you woke up on the field?'

'I don't know. I was asleep.'

'But the man was there, you said. The kind man who was telling you things. You must have been awake for some of it.'

'I was drifting. It's hard to remember.' She closed her eyes and pressed her palm to her forehead. 'And I need to. I know that I need to.'

'Were you hungry or thirsty?' I said. 'Did you need the toilet?'

She shook her head, her eyes still closed.

'I ate a meal before we left — sandwiches and an apple. I don't remember much after that. I wasn't hungry or thirsty when I woke up. I'm guessing it was an hour or two. I don't know, but that feels right.'

'Okay.'

Again, it was something, I supposed, but not much. A couple of hours' driving meant she could have been held a hundred miles or more away, which was a hell of a search perimeter. A lot of basements. But it was obvious from her expression that we were done for now.

I stood up.

'Thank you, Charlie. You get some rest and I'll see what I can find out.'

'Mercy,' she said.

Her voice was urgent enough to make me pause in the doorway and look back at her. Her eyes were open now, and she was staring at me with something close to relief.

'Mercy?' I said.

'That's part of what the man was telling me in the ambulance. I remember now. That's what I need. I think he wanted me to ask for mercy.'

113

I took it in.

'He was going to hurt you?'

'No, not him.' She shook her head, as though it made even less sense to her than it did to me. 'He wanted me to ask *you* for mercy.'

Merritt

God's work

'There's nowhere else for them to go,' Jennifer Buckle told him. 'It's no surprise what happens out there on the streets. And so what we do here, as much as we can, is give them a safe space.'

A safe space. He could have laughed: as if there were any such thing. But instead Merritt nodded politely, listening as Jennifer continued to talk about the drop-in centre she ran. It was a place where children could come, she explained. Where they knew they'd be listened to. Where they'd be treated as people, not just a problem for society to overlook. Merritt did his best to pretend that he was the slightest bit interested in what she had to say.

Jennifer was middle-aged, with curly hair that was greying slightly, and she was dressed plainly: a dark floral dress. On the street, most people would have passed her without a second glance. This place too, probably.

Merritt looked around the office as she carried on talking. Due to the scrupulous research he had undertaken, he knew that Jennifer Buckle had dedicated the last two decades of her life to helping others, and that while the surroundings here might be drab and shabby, it was still one of the last volunteer-based youth drop-in centres left in this part of the city. He also knew that she ran the place at the expense not only of her time but, frequently, her own personal finances. The centre had faced closure a number of times in the last two years alone. Each time Jennifer had dug deep and kept it alive.

'A lot of them have such difficult home lives.' She was still talking about the children. 'They have problems I find hard to imagine. I was very lucky, in that I came from a loving home.'

Merritt smiled and nodded again, as though he had come from a loving home too. In truth, he could barely remember it. There had been a lot of water under that bridge.

'They're good kids deep down.' Jennifer smiled fondly. 'And you know what? They behave themselves here. They *know* to. Oh, there can be difficulties, of course, but we treat them with respect, and most of them appreciate that. They're not used to it, the respect and discipline, but they repay it.'

'I completely understand.' Actually, Merritt did like that. Respect and discipline were things he found easier to relate to. 'It must be demanding, though?'

Jennifer looked more serious now. 'It is. Very demanding. We have a handful of volunteers, and they work very hard. But ask any of them and they'll tell you — exactly the same as I'll tell you — that there's nothing more worthwhile.'

'Of course.' It was a spiel he was hearing — a pitch — and while understandable from her point of view, it wasn't necessary. He leaned forward. 'On behalf of my employers, may I ask you a somewhat personal question, Ms Buckle?'

'You may.'

116

'Are you a religious woman?'

She stared back at him for a moment, obviously considering what the right thing to say would be, in terms of what he might want to hear. He wondered what she thought of him. He probably looked a lot harder than she'd been expecting. While he was dressed professionally, in a neat black suit, he knew he still carried the bearing of the soldier he'd once been. At fifty, his body remained bulky and powerful, and he kept his grey hair buzz-cut short. His eyes, he knew, could be intimidating: a cold, clear shade of blue that expressed either hate or nothing. He waited for her answer, attempting to convey the latter, hoping that she would opt for honesty. He was pleased when she did.

'I am not, Mr Merritt, no.'

'That's fine. Neither am I.' He chose his next words carefully. 'With my employers, the situation is more complex. But fundamentally, they believe that people need to work for their own salvation — and for the salvation of others. That is why they're interested in you and the good work you do here. You don't do it for reward. You do it because it's right.'

'Thank you.'

'They'll be pleased to hear that. But before we talk, I was wondering whether you might show me around?'

* * *

The tour was tedious but necessary, because what potential benefactor wouldn't inspect the premises? There had to be at least an illusion of normality to proceedings. Merritt suppressed the yawns as Jennifer Buckle showed him the recreation room, with its battered pool tables and dartboards, the kitchen where they cooked basic food for the children at discounted prices, and then the small courtyard out back with a basketball ring nailed to the wall at a slight angle, the net ragged and dirty.

Tedious.

Merritt's work often provided a stark contrast to his early years. He missed it sometimes — the thrill of it. The challenge. He'd seen combat early and repeatedly, while little more than a boy. Killing men had never bothered him, and the threat of being killed in return hadn't frightened him. As an independent contractor in his thirties, the mercenaries he ended up working alongside would remark upon his coolness, even when he was shot in the abdomen and nearly died. That injury had forced him out of the company, and he'd found even less salubrious ways of making money afterwards. He would probably have continued to do so if an older officer hadn't approached him with an ultimately more intriguing proposition.

Merritt was a capable man. He had contacts. He was trustworthy and discreet. *And without scruples*, the officer had added at the time. If he might be interested, the man knew of work available. It was a unique position. Nothing hardcore: a civilian post in many ways, but one in which his skills and discretion would be called for, and that lack of scruples even more so. A family were in need of community liaison work, research, and somewhat unusual security services. They required a dependable individual who could recruit similar men when necessary, and who could gather detailed information without notice. Privacy would be paramount. The money offered was excellent, and it was unlikely he'd ever be shot at again.

While it was true that Merritt hadn't been particularly scared of the latter, the position had nevertheless appealed. And over the years, the work had turned out to suit him very well indeed. The money was better than promised, and he had come to enjoy moving in circles that a normal man would shy away from: meeting contacts, learning secrets, and making connections that even the police had proved unable to form. And no, he hadn't been shot at — although he had, of course, killed. On occasion, the work even brought a few unique stresses and challenges that kept life interesting. If it meant dealing with these moments of tedium, then so be it.

At the end of the tour, they returned to Jennifer's office, Merritt content now with what he'd seen. It was all make-do: threadbare and on its last legs, and impossible for the volunteers to keep on top of. While Jennifer was clearly a woman who refused to give up, Merritt knew that things were coming to an end for her too. He had researched both her and the centre very carefully before reporting to his employers. Donations and funding here were at an all-time low, and the centre faced closure for real this time. The children who relied on this place for somewhere safe to come would soon arrive at its doors and find them closed.

Merritt sat down.

'I would like to make you an offer,' he said.

There were pens and papers on her desk. He reached across and wrote down a figure, then moved the paper over for her to see. Her face paled in shock.

'I can't possibly accept that much.'

'But you need to,' he said. 'It would help to keep this place open. And perhaps it would also take some pressure off you personally. My employers would be happy for you to use the money as you see fit. I'm sure you'll do the right thing with it.'

'Even so. It's far too generous.'

A charade. A dance. He could do without it; they all accepted in the end.

'Ms Buckle,' he said, again choosing his words with care. It had been one of the hardest things to adapt to over the years, this use of careful language. 'My employers are very private people. They are also very rich, and they wish to do something good with the resources available to them. Over the years, I have facilitated a large number of charitable donations on their behalf. I would very much like to make one to you. You do good work here, Ms Buckle. It should be quietly recognised. It deserves to be.'

Jennifer looked at him for a moment, then down at the figure he'd written on the paper.

'They want to leave a legacy?' she said.

'A legacy.' Merritt smiled, and for the first time in the meeting it was genuine. 'Yes. Exactly that.'

Groves

Angela Morris

'Is this about Eddie?' Angela Morris immediately shook her head. 'What the hell am I talking about? Of course it's about Eddie.'

Groves lowered the ID he was holding out.

'Yes, it is, I'm sorry. Can we come in, please?'

The ex-partner of the burned man they'd found yesterday didn't reply — just turned and headed off inside, leaving the door open behind her. Groves and Sean followed her inside.

It was actually a warmer welcome than he had been anticipating. Angela Morris had no criminal record, but rightly or wrongly, he'd still had certain expectations of the kind of woman who might end up in a long-term relationship with someone like Edward Leland, a man with multiple convictions. So he'd been surprised by Morris the moment she opened the door. The woman was young, pretty and well turned out, with neat sandy-brown hair and subtly applied make-up. She was slim, but it was a build that implied she looked after herself rather than going hungry, or supplementing her intake the way her ex-partner apparently had.

Similarly, the house itself was decent: a well-maintained semi on the far side of the estate Leland had moved to. A nice enough area. From the plush suburbs further east it might look like part of the estate, but from the estate itself it was downright aspirational.

'Through here,' Morris called over her shoulder as they followed her down the hall. 'Coffee?'

'That would be good, thanks.'

They entered the kitchen. Like the hallway, it was spacious and clean, only this room looked like something out of a spaceship: black tiles with a hint of glitter to them, and under-cabinet lighting that covered the counters with a soft blue glow. Groves looked around. Everything was polished and new. At the far end, patio doors led out on to a small but sunny back garden, with a large red barbecue closed over on the deck.

'Nice place,' Sean said.

'Thanks. This is all new. We had it put in last year. *I* did, I mean.'

'Mr Leland didn't contribute?'

Angela Morris gave Sean a slightly sour look at that. 'No, Eddie didn't contribute. He didn't have that kind of money. He paid for the food here and there, and helped out with the bills when he could, which was about all I could ask.' She sniffed. 'How do you take your coffee?'

'Black, please.'

'Me too,' Groves said. 'And I'd just like to say, I'm really sorry for your loss.'

'Thank you.' Morris gave him a curious look. 'You know what? You'd be surprised how many people haven't bothered saying that.'

'No?'

'Here.' She handed over the coffees, then

leaned back against the edge of the sink with her own. 'People know what Eddie was like. The drugs and everything. And they figure that we'd split up anyway, so what would I care? My family had wanted rid of him for years. Everyone I've told has just said, *What a tragedy*, like it's a piece of news or something. They don't expect *me* to be affected at all.'

'People can be like that.'

'You know, I wish I *didn't* bloody care,' she said. 'It would make the whole thing a lot easier.'

'You broke up with him three weeks ago? Is that right?'

'Yeah, about that.'

'How long had you been together?'

'Since forever. Apart from the times he was inside. Childhood sweethearts and all that. He was so lovely when we were younger. You wouldn't have recognised him. Troubled, but lovely.'

She sounded wistful. However conflicted she was, it was clear she had still cared about Leland, or at least felt sad for the person he had once been. It happened like that, though, Groves thought. You loved someone, and when they changed a little, you accommodated it, even if deep down it made it slightly harder to love them. And then, a hundred changes later, you realised you were living with a stranger, and that maybe you were equally strange to them. The initial love between you ended up like some half-forgotten belonging in a room you'd both left a long time ago. By the end of the marriage, that was how it had been between Caroline and him.

'Why did you break up?' he said. 'Was it because of the drugs?'

She hesitated, an expression of pain on her face. Then she shook her head and spoke softly.

'No. They'd been there since the beginning. I never liked it, but I kind of understood. It was always on and off, but he couldn't stay away from them for long. I suppose I just had to accept it really — that it was part of him, however much I hated it. But it didn't made things easy.'

'Was he back on them?'

'I think so. He couldn't afford them, though. He'd lost his job, and he was drunk most of the time instead. That's my fault. He knew I'd have alcohol in the house, but I wouldn't pay for drugs.' She gave a sad laugh. 'That's what it came down to. You try to keep things working, you keep pretending, and that's where you find yourself: I'll pay for your vodka, but not your smack.'

'You can't blame yourself,' Groves said.

'Yes,' she said, 'you can.'

Sean had drained his coffee; now he put the cup down on the side.

'Thanks for that,' he said. 'You know any of the people he hung around with?'

'Probably not as well as you lot do.'

'We need to trace his movements in the days leading up to his death, so anything you can tell us would be helpful.'

She frowned now. 'Why? What's going on?'

'There are some suspicious circumstances,' Sean said. 'We're following them up.'

Suspicious was putting it mildly, of course. They'd both read the pathology report that morning. The condition of Edward Leland's lungs indicated that he'd still been alive when the fire had begun. That would have been consistent with his having fallen asleep, of course, but more troubling were the lines they had seen in his cheekbones. According to the pathologist, they had been caused by an exceedingly sharp blade, one that had cut so deeply as to slice into the bone. There were a great many of them — far more than they'd noticed yesterday. Some time before he died, Edward Leland had had his face carved apart.

'Did Eddie have any visible scarring?' Groves said.

'Scarring?' She thought about it, and that told Groves everything he needed to know. 'Not that I can think of. Nothing obvious.'

'All right. Can you think of anyone who might have wanted to hurt him?'

'How would I know?' She leaned away from the counter, frowning. 'I don't understand what you're asking me.'

The confusion seemed genuine to Groves, but Sean wasn't about to let her off the hook.

'What about you?' he said.

'Me?'

'You. The pair of you had just broken up, after all. Lot of emotion flying around when a relationship falls apart, and when you throw drugs and booze into the mix, it can all turn nasty fairly quickly.'

'I'd never have hurt Eddie.' She seemed

flustered, and again it appeared genuine. 'It wasn't like that. I loved him. I just couldn't deal with it.'

'Deal with what?'

'It doesn't matter any more.'

Sean took a step forward.

'Ms Morris. There's evidence that Edward Leland's death was not accidental. Do you understand what I'm saying to you?'

'Oh God . . . '

'So whatever it is, you really *do* need to tell us.'

Groves moved forward to join Sean, brushing his arm slightly to signal that he wanted to take over again. Angela Morris was staring at the floor and shaking her head in disbelief. She looked horrified — either by what Sean had just told her, or at whatever it was that was running through her mind. He could sense the tension in her. She knew she was going to have to tell them something she really didn't want to.

'Eddie's dead,' Groves told her gently. 'He's not going to care if you talk to us. Especially if it helps us work out what happened to him, and who did it. It's important.'

For a moment, she didn't reply. Then:

'It's why I thought you were here.'

'What do you mean?'

'I thought you must have found something at his house. That he had more of them.'

'More of what?'

'The magazines. The . . . *things*.'

Groves glanced at Sean, who shook his head.

'You mean pornography?'

Morris nodded, but didn't say anything else, just kept looking down at the kitchen floor, her hands trembling around the empty cup she was holding. Groves didn't understand. Why would the pair of them have come to talk to her just because they'd found some ratty magazines at Leland's place?

That was when it clicked.

'These weren't . . . normal pornographic magazines.'

'No,' Morris said quietly. 'They weren't.'

All three of them were silent for a few seconds. And then, before anyone could say anything else, she threw her empty cup across the kitchen.

★   ★   ★

'Here.'

They were standing outside on the back patio. The warm air was solid and heavy around them, and the sun glinted off the domed crimson lid of the barbecue. Angela Morris opened it gingerly, like she was turning over a rock that might have something dangerous underneath. The stink drifted up as the mess inside was revealed. Groves smelled burned paper, old ash, stagnant water.

'Eddie tried to put it out when he got home. But it was too late by then. So he just sat down and started crying.' She pointed. 'Right where you're standing, in fact.'

She stared down at the barbecue with a blank expression on her face, seeming oddly calm now. It had taken Groves and Sean longer than her to recover from the cup incident; it was as though the act had released all the pent-up emotion inside her, and that was that. But it also seemed like a part of her had broken along with it. As she swept up the shattered pieces, she had explained to them what she'd found, her voice a monotone.

It had been hidden away upstairs in a shoebox at the back of the wardrobe, she said. Leland had been out looking for work, but he'd seemed strung out that morning, and she suspected he was using again. That was one of her rules — no drugs in the house. So in his absence, she'd gone through all the possible hiding places, expecting to stumble on the needles and wraps she'd sometimes found in the past. It would cause another argument, but she'd forgiven him on those occasions, and no doubt she would have done so again. But instead she'd found a stash of a different and far more awful kind. One that she had ultimately decided was some distance beyond forgiveness.

The material had been a mixture of professionally produced magazines, photocopied pages stapled into book form, photographs, hand-drawn pictures and printouts from the internet. The majority of it was violently pornographic. The scenes in the magazines looked staged, but some of the miscellaneous printouts were all too clearly real. A great deal of the homemade stuff had involved children. She hadn't looked through everything, Morris said, but the stuff she did see was ugly and unbearable. And it was without doubt a collection. One that had grown over time, and that had been taken out in secret and pored over.

Disgusted, and perhaps not thinking straight, she had taken the whole rotten bundle downstairs and set it alight out here on the patio. Staring down at what was left of it now, she said in that same calm voice:

'The worst thing is that I understood.'

Groves left it to Sean to prompt her.

'You *understood?*'

She took a deep breath. 'As much as you can when you come from a loving home. My parents were good people. *Are* good people. They never even smacked me, never mind anything else. Eddie's . . . weren't like that. Like I said, he was troubled.'

No excuse, Groves thought.

No excuse.

'Was he seeking help?' Sean said. 'Treatment, I mean. If he knew he had this problem.'

'No. Although I think all this' — she gestured at the burned material helplessly — 'was partly his way of doing that. Exposing himself to it, maybe, like some kind of test. Or exploring it as safely as he could, without hurting anyone.'

It always hurts someone. But Groves said nothing. He was remembering his impressions of Edward Leland when they'd left the ruins of his sad little house — that it was no kind of life, sitting there getting so drunk that you forgot you'd lit a cigarette and just fell asleep. Now he imagined Leland drinking to blur the memories and the shame, and maybe even his instincts, under the haze of booze.

'So . . . he cried,' Sean said.

'Yes.' Morris nodded fiercely, as though the reaction might mitigate him somehow. 'He begged me to let him stay. Actually, no, the first thing he did was beg me not to tell anyone. I said I was going to, even though I knew I wouldn't. But there was no way I was going to let him stay. I couldn't bear to have that stuff hidden away in the house, and it *would* have been there if he was. Just hidden away inside him instead. Inside his head.'

Groves looked down at the charred pile of magazines and printouts that rested on the barbecue grille. It was impossible to make out much of what was there. A sheet was angled out halfway up; it looked like the corner of a crudely drawn comic, but most of the detail was lost in the brown curl the fire had made of it.

'He went on about his childhood,' Morris said. 'He promised to get help. The proper kind this time. But he would never have done that. Why would he have changed now, after all these years?'

Why indeed?

'He was always burying it. What happened to him, it got buried beneath the drugs, the alcohol. And then this.' She gestured at the barbecue. 'He spent so much of his life burying things, and it would have been too much to ask, wouldn't it? For him to start digging it all up again.'

Groves eyed the burned material — he refused to think of it as pornography — and realised there was probably no longer any evidence for what Morris was telling them aside from her word. She had destroyed it. He tried imagining himself in her position, and could understand why she had, but he couldn't excuse it. Leland had collected this somehow, and now they had next to no chance of finding out where from or from whom. And she hadn't reported it. If Leland hadn't died, who knew what he might have gone on to do?

He had died, though, and he'd suffered a terrible death: most likely cut to ribbons and then set on fire. Groves tried to tell himself the man hadn't deserved that. That nobody did. And of course, it was true. Leland had deserved to be brought to justice, not the appalling things that had been done to him instead.

He kept telling himself that.

'Ms Morris.' Sean put his hands in his pockets and looked miserable. 'I'm going to need your whereabouts for the day and night of the twenty-ninth of July. Dawn to dawn.'

'That's easy enough. I was at work for most of it. I have two jobs. I probably caught an hour or two of sleep in the middle.'

Groves picked up a rusty pair of tongs and very gently nudged the stack. The crisp edges fluttered into the basin, and the thought came unbidden:

Were you in there, Jamie?

He looked up at Angela Morris. She still seemed detached from what was happening, although it was clear that below the surface she was struggling. She had not meant to do wrong, of that he was sure. But she had. He tried to think of what to say to her. What was the right thing — the kind thing — to do?

'I'm sorry you had to see all this, Ms Morris.'

Sean stared at him for a second, perhaps waiting for more — for an explosion — but that was all Groves had. A moment later, Sean took his hands out of his pockets.

'I'm sorry too, Ms Morris.' The steel in his partner's voice surprised even Groves. 'But I'm going to need you to come with us.'

Mark

The briefing

Early afternoon, and we were gathered in our private operations room. It was large enough to seat twenty officers, but for now there were only the four of us, spread out at different desks. The blinds had been drawn, but one was slightly askew, letting a slice of bright sunlight through on to the carpet. Perhaps the only broken thing in the department so far, I thought.

A large part of the far wall was taken up by a plasma screen. Two photographs, arranged side by side, loomed over us from it: Charlie Matheson, then and now. The image on the left was scanned from the piece of paper Paul Carlisle had given me; Greg had searched through my interview footage for a corresponding angle and extracted a still. With that, and displayed as large as this, it was more obvious than ever. They were the same person.

Pete walked to the front of the room.

'Okay, we've got a lot to get through here.' He ran his hand through his hair, already looking harried. 'Mark will deal with the interviews in a few minutes, but for now, let's start at the beginning. Two years ago. Simon. Talk us through the accident report and post-mortem from back then.'

Simon stood up.

'There's really not very much to tell.' As always, he spoke quickly and precisely, forcing you to pay attention in order to keep up. 'I'm sure you've all read through the file, and there's little more to it than that. There wasn't much in the way of real investigation, because why would there be? I'll run through the photographs of the crime scene, and the ones from the autopsy. I'm aware that we're not sure of the identity of this victim, so I'll still refer to her as Matheson for the time being.'

He talked us through the accident, using his tablet to display a map of the terrain where it had occurred, showing the apparent path of Charlie's vehicle, finishing with the sight that had awaited the first officers to arrive on the scene. The photographs from the file were familiar to me by now, but the blown-up autopsy shots of the unidentified dead woman made the damage to the body even more vivid and horrifying. They seemed to fill the room.

'The cause of death is fairly obvious,' Simon said. 'At least superficially. Certainly nobody could have survived those injuries, and from blood loss at the scene they were judged to be contemporaneous. According to the records, Matheson had been dead for about an hour and a half by the time her remains were transported to hospital.'

Pete frowned. 'Run through the timescale.'

'The accident occurred at roughly eight ten p.m. The body arrived at the hospital at nine thirty-seven. The scene had to be processed, of course: photographed and so on. That took

134

about an hour and a quarter. Officers were on scene within ten minutes of the incident. It all fits with the coroner's initial and secondary estimations.'

Greg held up a pen.

'How do we know it was within ten minutes?'

'The accident was called in,' Simon said. 'Another driver saw it happen. There was a phone call to emergency services immediately afterwards.'

Pete said, 'And the driver?'

'Didn't remain at the scene.' Simon nodded, agreeing that it was a meaningful detail. 'And he was never traced. The call wasn't recorded, of course — or if it was, it's long lost. It was a man; that's the only detail we have. And given the time that's passed, that's all we're likely to find out.'

'Greg?' Pete looked at Greg, who was now rotating back and forth on his chair, holding the pen to his mouth.

'Get me the details and I'll see what I can do.' He sighed. 'But Simon's right. It's two years. I'd take it for granted that any data trail is long gone.'

'Do it anyway. Any CCTV cameras on that stretch of the ring road?'

Greg shrugged. 'I'll find out. But again, it's two years.'

'Yes. I know that.' Pete frowned. 'It's a coincidence, isn't it? The driver should have stopped. That would be your instinct, wouldn't it? Any normal person would. Instead, he phones it in, drives away, and nobody ever thinks to trace him. If we're assuming someone else was involved at the scene — that it was staged — then that's our chief suspect right there. Driving off into the sunset as we speak.'

'Driving off into the sunset two years ago,' Greg said.

Pete ignored him and turned back to Simon.

'Okay. We know someone died, but let's assume for the moment that it's fishy — that it wasn't an accident, and that it was staged somehow. Is that possible?'

Simon pursed his lips, considering it.

'Not my area of expertise, so I couldn't say for sure. But I would guess that yes, in theory, it's possible. Matheson — by which I mean our dead woman — definitely went through the windscreen, but she might already have been unconscious or dead in the driver's seat.' He glanced down at his notes. 'The passenger door was open when the vehicle was found. If someone chose the spot carefully, made the right calculations, they could have sent the car over the embankment and jumped out. If they jammed the accelerator, they could have removed the evidence afterwards. It would be a fairly *daring* manoeuvre, let's say, but not impossible.'

'*Could* she have been unconscious or dead already?'

'The toxicology reports all came back clean: no alcohol; no drugs.' Simon looked at the image of the woman's body on the screen. 'But given the severity of the injuries — I mean, you can see she could easily have been struck on the head beforehand. It could even have been a fatal blow. The crash would have obscured the damage.'

Across the room, Greg clicked the pen against his teeth.

'Like a shotgun blast on a paper cut.'

'Yes,' Simon said. 'Thank you for that evocative image, Greg. Something like that.'

'And the remains were cremated?'

'That's correct.'

'Right.' Pete folded his arms and sighed. 'Let's get a possible name for her, then. Any women missing from around that time? Mark?'

'Not had time yet,' I said. 'I've got Paul Carlisle coming in soon, but I'll do it straight afterwards.'

It would involve a trawl through the archives, but it should be simple enough, especially if I narrowed it down to women matching Charlie's age and basic physical description. And given the cremation, and the time that had passed, it was probably our only real shot at identifying the woman who appeared to have died in Charlie Matheson's place.

'Good,' Pete said. 'Anything else from two years ago to discuss?'

Nobody said anything. I couldn't help noticing how slightly helpless Pete seemed — how the authority of heading an investigation could sometimes appear beyond him, as though he was secretly hoping that someone else would step up and take the lead.

'Okay. Let's move into the present, then. The other end of the case. Greg?'

'Yep.'

Greg stood up quickly, using the pen to tap the tablet he was holding. A second later, the screen on the wall changed to show a map of the area: a satellite image with the roads outlined and named and various landmarks detailed. He zoomed in on the image slightly, and it took a second to resolve, the text flicking up piece by piece. The curl of Town Street, with all the shops named, stretched across the screen before forking into two separate streets towards the top.

Greg scribbled on his tablet, and a cross appeared towards the bottom of the screen on Town Street.

'This is Addison Grocery, where the woman was found,' he said. 'So this is an absolute point in our trace. According to the witness statements from the attending officer — which are second-hand; just what people told him at the scene — she was seen coming from this direction, and she appeared to be drunk or troubled in some way.'

He added a few dashes towards the fork higher up the screen, to represent the direction from which Charlie Matheson had arrived at the scene.

'I've chased up the attending officer. Obviously, at the time he didn't realise there was anything unusual going on, and the upshot is that we don't have any details for those witnesses. Crowd gathered; crowd left. We can advertise, of course.' Greg glanced at me. 'I presume we'll be canvassing anyway?'

I looked at Pete. 'If I can get the money and manpower.'

Pete grunted.

'Anyway.' Greg added another cross towards the top left of the screen, beyond the fork, on a triangular area of greenery. 'Based on the woman's story, this is likely where she woke up. It's a stretch of grassland. Extends to the church over there, and then to these tower blocks on the right. So there are roads on all three sides, and footpaths criss-crossing it. It's a couple of hundred metres each side along the roads, so not huge.'

'CCTV?' Pete said.

'Getting to that.' Greg tapped his tablet and a series of camera icons appeared on the screen. 'As you can see, we've got cameras along both main roads. We're checking those for a two-hour period around the woman's appearance. We've already got her on Town Street, and traced her back from there. Observe. I'll play it forward, obviously.'

He tapped another couple of times and set a video running: a stitched-together patchwork of footage from different CCTV cameras. The first scene showed Charlie emerging from the park dressed in the strange white clothes she'd been found wearing. The footage was relatively dim, and so the clothes stood out: bright and shining; radioactive almost, as though she was being displayed in night vision. She stepped hesitantly on to the pavement out of the shadows cast by the trees behind her. It was a sunny afternoon, but even from a distance you could tell she was shivering, hugging herself slightly.

And it reminded me — immediately and unavoidably — of Lise. Rather than an actual memory, it was an impression of some long-ago morning. Unlike Sasha, Lise had always slept in, and I was usually up before her. I could picture her now, dressed in a long shirt, still half asleep and groggy, walking into our front room as precariously as Charlie Matheson now returned to the world onscreen. Awake but still half dreaming . . .

Stop thinking about her.

I shook my head. Concentrated on the footage.

For a few moments Charlie stood still, looking this way and that. She appeared lost and unsure: searching for a clue as to which way to go, but lacking any criteria with which to decide. Eventually she made her choice and began walking in the direction of the camera. As she approached it, passing gradually underneath it and then disappearing, the distress on her face was clear. She was tottering slightly.

'You can see how disorientated she is,' Greg said.

'Which would fit with what she told me,' I said. 'She said it was an overwhelming experience for her. I think there's a good chance that she'd been drugged in some way.'

'Toxicology?' Pete said.

'Blood tests at the hospital came back clean. But that doesn't necessarily mean anything. They weren't testing for everything at that point. Could easily have left her system, or not been picked up.'

'Right.'

Onscreen, the clip changed to a new angle, showing Charlie, more obviously staggering now, moving on to the end of Town Street. She barely reached the grocer's. As she half collapsed there, beside the trays of fruit and vegetables, the impression I got was that her will to keep moving had finally run out. That she had gone as far as she was able.

I watched as a crowd began to gather around her.

'Okay.' Greg tapped his tablet, and the film paused. 'Like I said, we're running through the footage we've got from around the park, looking for any vehicle that resembles an ambulance. An ice-cream van. Anything. But to reiterate, we've only got coverage on two of the roads. If she was dropped off via the third, we won't get the vehicle.'

'Then something tells me we won't get it,' Simon said. 'Given the level of organisation required to fake a car accident and hold someone hostage for two years, this is not an individual who is likely to fall at the dismount.'

None of us said anything. Because assuming all that, he was quite right.

I was up next. Unlike Simon and Greg, I didn't really need to use the screen; the interviews were on file, and they could watch them at their leisure. But I did click through so that the display returned to the two images of Charlie Matheson's face side by side: one clean and clear and slightly fierce, the other scarred and confused and frightened. Then I talked through the scant details that she'd given so far about her period of incarceration and the time around it, concluding with my general impressions of her.

141

'I don't think she's lying,' I said. 'Whatever actually happened to her, she genuinely believes she's been dead for the last two years. She still claims to remember the accident.'

Pete frowned.

'Is it really possible to convince someone of that?'

'If they've been placed under enough duress, and had the story drilled into them over and over again, then it's possible they would give in and accept it as true. Torture, sensory deprivation, repetition. It all plays a part, and that's what she's been describing to me. Taken as a whole, and carried on for long enough, it would give someone a powerful incentive to go along with what they were being told.'

'What about asking us for mercy?'

'No idea. She didn't know what it meant either. Or else she can't remember.'

'And *why*?' Pete folded his arms. 'Why do all this to someone?'

'Lots of sick people in the world,' Greg said.

It was my turn to ignore him. Instead I explained what Eileen had told me: that the story might touch on the truth without necessarily being entirely accurate; that some of the details might be true, but not the whole.

'If the ambulance story is right, there's at least two people involved: the 'kind' man in the back, and the driver, who could be the one who cut her. For the rest of it, all I'd be prepared to say is that I think it's likely she was abducted by someone, probably held underground somewhere — a basement, perhaps — and the scars speak for themselves. Beyond that . . . *possibly* a religious element, but I wouldn't be confident.' I felt a bit awkward, as though I were attempting a profile. 'I have this on advice, by the way.'

'From who?'

'I talked to Eileen Mercer. I don't have a background in counselling, and I wanted an expert opinion before I went back for a second interview.'

'Eileen,' Pete said. 'Right.'

'Charlie Matheson is vulnerable, possibly delusional. I decided I needed some advice.'

The room was silent for a moment. I could see that the mention of his former boss's wife had rattled Pete a little. He and John had been friends once; I wondered whether they'd even stayed in touch after the events of a year and a half ago. Or perhaps Pete was thinking of all the ways he didn't quite measure up to the shadow Mercer had cast. The rest of us were silent with him. I had no idea what Greg and Simon were thinking. For my part, I was thinking that I probably shouldn't have mentioned it.

Eventually Pete shook his head slightly.

'Okay. We've all got our actions and priorities. We'll resume at five, unless anything changes in the meantime. Let's find out who the original victim was. And where the real Charlie Matheson has been all this time.' He looked up at the plasma screen, talking almost to himself now. 'And let's find out why.'

Mark

The missing

Shortly after the briefing was finished, I got a call through that Paul Carlisle had arrived in reception. I went down to meet him. Despite being dressed in jeans and a jumper now, he somehow looked even more dishevelled than yesterday. They hadn't been sleeping well, he'd told me then, and if anything, it appeared that the situation had worsened. His hair was in disarray, and there were dark rings around his eyes. The man looked haunted. I supposed he was.

'Thanks for coming in, Paul,' I said, when we were safely ensconced in an interview room. I'd got a glass of water for him, but so far he'd left it untouched on the table between us. 'And thank you for this.'

I passed him the piece of paper that he'd given me yesterday: the photograph of his wife.

'I wanted to show you a picture myself. It's of the woman in the hospital. Do you mind?'

It felt polite to ask even if we both knew he didn't really have much of a choice.

'No. Let me see.'

'I should warn you, the injuries she's received might be a little shocking at first glance.'

'It's fine.'

I handed him a printout I'd taken from the

interview footage. It was the image Greg had singled out, where Charlie *now* was holding her head in the same position as Charlie *then*. I thought the resemblance was incontrovertible, but then I hadn't known her two years ago, and I wanted to see the reaction of a man who had.

Despite the apparent bravado, Carlisle took the piece of paper hesitantly. I watched his face as he looked at it, noting his obvious determination to remain impassive. Perhaps he thought there was no way this could really be Charlie, not after everything that had happened, but he seemed set on denying it regardless, as though by pretending this wasn't happening he could somehow make it go away. The realisation that he couldn't hit him immediately. I watched him struggle to control his emotions. Maybe he could keep his expression blank, but there was no way to hide the way the colour drained from his face.

He was silent for a few moments.

'It looks like her,' he said finally. 'But I can't be sure.'

'No? Take your time, Paul, please.'

'I don't need any more time.' He handed the printout back to me. I waited a second before accepting it. 'It looks like her, but it's impossible to tell from a photograph.'

'Would you be prepared to see her in person?'

'No.'

It had been an off-the-cuff idea — I hadn't been planning on taking him to the hospital, not necessarily — but the speed of his reply surprised me.

145

'I know this is hard,' I said.

'Do you? Do you really?'

For a moment I considered saying *actually, yes*, and telling him about Lise, but I stopped myself. It was too personal to divulge, but more to the point, did I really know? Lise hadn't returned from the dead. If she was haunting me now, it was as a memory, and while that might be disruptive in its own way, at least a memory didn't threaten to turn up on your doorstep.

'I know this isn't going away,' I said. 'And I think we both know that the woman in the photograph I just showed you is your wife, Charlie Matheson.'

'You're *telling* me now? You were asking me before. And I'm saying I'm not sure.'

'All right.' There didn't seem any point in pressing it, especially as I couldn't force him to go to the hospital. 'But I want you to understand what I said. This isn't going away, Paul.'

'I know.'

He sounded utterly miserable. While I understood and sympathised, it took me back to what Charlie had said in the interview this morning about his reaction to the news. *Oh? Not pleased, then?* She might as well have said, *The man who I loved, and who loved me, would prefer that I was dead.* And the harsh reality was that that was probably partly true.

As if reading my mind, Carlisle started talking.

'I mourned for her, you know? I grieved. It felt like the heart had been ripped out of my life. At the funeral, I tried to speak — to read a speech — and I couldn't because I was crying so much.'

146

'I understand.'

'And what the fuck was I supposed to do? Do that for ever? I moved on. Jesus, I'm sorry, it feels like I should be sorry, like you're expecting me to be sorry, but what else should I have done?'

'Nobody's blaming you for that, Paul.'

'And now . . . this.'

'I understand,' I said again.

'How? How can this have happened?'

'We don't know yet.'

I ignored his tacit admission that it really was happening. He gestured to his face, moving his hand around to indicate the scars he'd seen. He spoke quietly.

'Why would someone do *that?*'

'We don't know,' I said again. 'And so I have to ask. Paul, can you think of any reason why someone might want to hurt your wife?'

He lowered his hand, looking aghast now.

'God, no.'

He talked a little more about how ridiculous the idea was, and I believed him. On the surface, there was nothing there to go on. I already knew that neither of them had ever been in trouble with the police before. Charlie had been a postgraduate secretary in the sociology department at the university; Carlisle was a manager at a pharmaceutical company. As far as I could tell, they were both above board. Just normal people.

At the same time, the question Pete had asked at the end of the briefing had stayed with me. Never mind for a moment what had happened to Charlie Matheson; *why* had it happened? Not in the specific sense of the perpetrators' motives for

147

putting her through what they had, but the question of why they had targeted *her* in particular? Because it seemed clear that she hadn't been chosen at random. There had to be a reason why, out of all the possible people who could have been abducted, they had singled her out.

But if so, Carlisle didn't seem to know.

'She had no enemies,' he said. 'Ask anyone. She could be quite forthright. She had a temper, you know? But it was more confidence than anything else. Nobody hated her.'

I nodded. *Ask anyone.* Tomorrow I would have people do just that. Friends, colleagues, the lot. But for the moment, I thought Carlisle was telling the truth, at least as far as he knew it.

'There's one more thing,' I said.

'Oh God.' He looked at me with a mixture of exhaustion and anger. 'What?'

'The day of the accident. She left for work as usual in the morning?'

'Yes.'

'But she called in sick.'

'Yes. I know that.'

'And you have no idea where she went that day, or what happened to her?'

'No.'

He leaned back and folded his arms. I wasn't sure I'd ever seen a man look so tired and defeated. For a moment he seemed almost scared. But then he delved into the blackness of that past time, and when he spoke next, I saw a trace of the man who had loved and grieved and mourned.

'I guess none of you cared enough to find out.'

148

Let's find out who the original victim was. And where the real Charlie Matheson has been all this time.

Easier said than done, of course. By the time we reconvened in the operations room at five, we were hardly any further forward than when we'd started.

'It would have been a bit of an ask anyway, after two years,' Greg said, 'but there's no CCTV along the stretch of ring road where the accident took place. More depressingly, the park's also a total bust.'

He'd worked through all the gathered footage and come up with nothing. Plenty of vans, of course, and even two actual ambulances, but none that appeared suspicious or that stopped anywhere nearby. While it was still possible that one of them was our vehicle, Charlie had clearly been dropped off from the road with no camera coverage. It seemed to confirm what Simon had said earlier about the organisation and attention to detail of whoever was behind her abduction and reappearance. They — and I was assuming at least two perpetrators for the moment — weren't about to make a trivial mistake like being caught on film.

Of course, that didn't mean they hadn't been caught at all.

I said, 'I've got two officers working the nearby blocks of flats. Wherever the van stopped, someone would have had to carry her on to the field, and that's the kind of thing people would remember if they saw it.'

'It's also the kind of thing people would have reported at the time,' Pete said.

'True. But it's still our best chance now the CCTV's come back clean. We've also got a placard out for witnesses on the high street. Early days, but we've had nothing back yet from either action.'

I'd also had someone compile a list of all the hospitals within a radius of roughly one hundred miles and begin calling round. Although Dr Fredericks claimed to have checked this, I doubted he'd have cast his net quite so wide, and I was keen to eliminate the possibility that Charlie really had been a patient somewhere all this time, and that the story she'd given us was a total concoction. It wouldn't explain the scars, of course, or the victim found at the original scene, but I wanted to open up every route available to me. Nothing had come down that one so far.

'In terms of the identity of the victim found at the scene of the accident, again I've drawn a blank. I've looked at the missing persons reports from a couple of months around that date. There are a lot.'

A surprisingly high number, in fact, but once I'd filtered for age, sex and physical appearance, there were far fewer to deal with: only three women who might conceivably have been mistaken for Charlie Matheson after receiving such a head injury and being found in such circumstances. But all of them had since been accounted for.

'So either I've not gone back far enough,' I

said, 'or we're looking at a victim who for some reason wasn't reported missing at the time — or at least not until much later. So that's the next stage. Expanding it out along those lines.'

Which would not be easy. The sort of people who could go missing without being reported tended to be the ones who had already dropped off the radar of society: the lower edge of the sex industry; the homeless; immigrants without official records. It wasn't a task I was relishing.

'And Carlisle?'

'Is not happy about the situation,' I said.

Pete grunted. 'That's understandable, I guess. His new partner's pregnant?'

'Yes.'

'Well, the whole thing certainly sucks for him, doesn't it? But at least Charlotte Matheson is still alive, and she's our main responsibility right now. Any idea of motive?'

I shook my head. 'Carlisle's got nothing. And as far as I can tell, there's nothing obvious about either of them. I'll get someone on to their acquaintances tomorrow, get them all talked to. Because there has to be *some* reason that someone chose her.'

'Yes,' Pete said.

'There's something else too. A detail in the file I saw at the time. It niggled at me when I first read it, but I didn't appreciate the significance.'

I told them about the information in the report about Charlie's missing day: that she'd called in sick to work on the morning of her abduction, but according to her husband had left as usual.

151

'Again, Carlisle's got no idea,' I said. 'And at the time, it was just a discrepancy. But obviously, given what we know now, that's important.'

'Absolutely.'

'I'll go back to her tomorrow morning,' I said. I would have to be careful, of course, but that detail could be the key to all of this. 'And I'm going to find out where she really was that day.'

Groves

I've been through hell, sir

The end of the day.

It felt to Groves as though it had gone on for ever. The discovery of the burned material at Angela Morris' house had knocked the energy out of him. At the train station, the concourse was busy with a thrum of people, but the sound of their mingled conversation and rolling suitcases drifted around him, only half heard. He bought coffee and a newspaper, then headed through the barriers, out into the cool waft of air on the platform. His train was waiting on the left, doors open, the interior sickly and yellow in the gloom.

Inside, a handful of other travellers were spread out down the carriage, tops of heads visible above the seat backs. Nobody was talking; there was just the quiet vibration of the engine, low and ready and somehow everywhere at once. Groves wandered a little way down the carriage and found a seat. The table in front of him was covered with an old newspaper, the pages splayed out at weird angles. He scooped them together and pushed them on to the seat opposite, then spread out his own and had a sip of coffee so hot that it set his upper lip singing.

He had his back to the doors, but still, he was suddenly aware of a presence behind him. Some

153

kind of difference in the air quality, perhaps. He turned around in his seat and saw that a man had got on and was now leaning over and talking to a young woman sitting closer to the doors.

The man was probably in his early twenties at most, but looked considerably older. Along with the patchy stubble of a teenager, he had the sallow skin and mussed, lank hair of an addict. He was dressed in faded army fatigues, the green fabric greasy-looking in places, and he had a grey knapsack slung over his shoulder. He was bent over beside the woman, intent on her, his hand circling the air on a scrawny wrist. The woman was doing her best to ignore him: headphones in; staring studiously at the iPad she was holding.

Begging for change, Groves thought. Some of the homeless people did it here — paid for a platform ticket and harangued a captive audience for as long as possible before security staff moved them on. But this man was also just by the doors, and the train was about to leave. It was perfectly possible for him to make a last-minute grab for that iPad, leap off and dart back towards the crowds. Which was what some of the homeless people also did.

Groves stood up and walked down the aisle towards them.

'Everything all right?'

The girl looked up at him a little helplessly, not wanting to say no for fear of provoking the man, but clearly not wanting to say yes either. The expression on her face answered Groves' question as far as he was concerned. The man straightened up and turned to him as he approached.

'Police,' Groves said. 'You shouldn't be on here and you know it.'

He was expecting the standard junkie four-step defiance. When you tried to move people on, they tended to keep a certain distance and say they weren't doing anything wrong; then they demanded an explanation and complained; then they insulted you; finally, when you moved towards them, they ran. But instead of doing any of those things, the young man looked helpless. In fact he looked like he was about to cry.

'I know,' he said. 'Thank God! I'm sorry. Please help me, sir.'

His reaction pulled Groves up short.

'I can't help you, mate, sorry.'

The man took a step away from the woman, holding his hands up. There was a desperate expression on his face, as though this was his last chance and he needed to make Groves understand.

'I just need fifty pence.'

For a second, Groves stared into his eyes. Although watery, they were the exact same clear blue that Jamie's had been, and beneath the grime, his hair was the same length and colour. In fact, up close he looked a lot younger than Groves had first thought — late teens, maybe younger. Too old to be Jamie grown up, of course, but close enough to cause a momentary jolt — for the ridiculous idea *this could be him* to briefly enter his mind.

Groves shook it away.

'Sorry, mate. You need to get off now.'

'Please. It's so important.'

'I can't help you.'

How could fifty pence be so important anyway? It wouldn't help the boy in any realistic way. And yet there was something about the desperation on his face. For whatever reason, he clearly believed that it would make all the difference in the world to him. Maybe it was that, or just the partial resemblance to Jamie, but Groves found himself reaching into his pocket.

As he did so, the young man turned his head slightly and pulled his hair to one side, showing the whole of his face, and Groves stopped.

He hadn't been able to see the side of the boy's head before, but now that he could, it was obvious that he'd been badly injured. It looked like he'd been in a fire of some kind. A patch of his hair had burned away entirely, leaving him with a half-Mohican and gnarled pink skin. His ear was mostly gone, and white burn scars stretched along his jawline, the layers of damage overlapping like fingers of bleached seaweed on a beach.

He said, 'I've been through hell, sir.'

'What's your name?'

'Carl. I've been through hell. You look kind.'

Groves stared at the damage.

'What happened to you, Carl?'

'Burned, sir. Badly burned. I was a prisoner of war.'

That was obviously a lie; it fitted with his clothes, but not his age. The boy let go of his hair, and it fell back over the wound, covering it. Groves was about to say something — challenge him, maybe — but the boy held out a trembling hand.

'You look like a good person. Please help me.'

Groves found a fistful of change in his back pocket, extracted a fifty-pence piece and passed it to him.

'God will be with you,' the boy said quietly. 'Never forget.'

Outside the train, the guard was whistling, and waving above his head with one lazy, overfamiliar arm. The homeless boy held Groves' gaze for a moment, then turned around and stepped calmly off the train. As he did, Groves heard a clatter.

'Wait,' he called.

But the doors shushed closed behind him. Through the bleary plastic window, Groves saw the guard attempt to hurry the boy out of the way, as though he were a pigeon that had fluttered into his path.

Groves moved to the door as the train lurched slightly then juddered off and began crawling away from the platform. He could see the homeless boy standing there, receding. He was staring at Groves, his bright blue eyes following him as the train moved off. The expression on his face was peaceful now. Clear and thankful.

Groves looked down at the grimy floor.

A phone.

The boy had dropped a mobile phone.

Sasha

The photograph

Sasha arrived home before Mark, still annoyed with herself over what had happened that afternoon. The mistake she'd made. It was only a little thing, and nobody else knew about it, but that didn't make any difference. *She* knew, and it had been eating at her ever since.

She dumped her bag down on the settee harder than normal — a pointless little punch at the world that she was glad nobody was around to see — then went through to the kitchen and poured a glass of white wine from the box in the fridge. She leaned on the counter, hands on either side of the glass, and stared down at it.

It hadn't been anything serious. It hadn't really been anything at all. The department was doing its biannual public crackdown on the supply of stolen goods, and Sasha had been involved in one of four coordinated raids across the city. In her case, the team had been helping to search a pub in the centre. The King's Arms was a dive, and the rumour was that it was a hub for shoplifting: customers would literally bring in a list, then sit with a drink while things were stolen to order from the nearby shops.

There had been thirty or so customers in when they'd arrived, and the place had been sealed while they were all searched then allowed to leave one by one. The team had recovered a haul of clothes and handbags, including goods stored in the building's cellar, and made five arrests, including the landlord. A good result.

Sasha had been on the door, taking names and addresses and checking for outstanding warrants on each person as they left. She should have been keeping an eye on the searches too — a secondary precaution — but twenty minutes in, her attention had started to wander. She'd got distracted: stopped paying attention. And at least one person she'd let out, she couldn't be sure afterwards that he'd been searched.

It meant nothing in the grand scheme of things. But you couldn't afford to make mistakes like that, however small. Just because you got away with one didn't mean you'd get away with the next. In her line of work, an officer daydreaming could end with someone badly hurt or worse.

Sasha drank a couple of mouthfuls of wine. It was so cold she felt her breastbone beginning to throb. She put the glass down, then leaned back, closed her eyes and sighed.

Her professionalism mattered to her, and a mistake, however small, was intolerable. She was angry with herself. She shouldn't have been distracted, damn it. But she had been. She still was now.

Still thinking about Mark.

It had surprised her, how quickly she'd fallen for him. Throughout her twenties, she'd hardened up and become guarded with the men she dated. She didn't expect much, and she was generally rewarded with just that. When she was a teenager, her father had told her that when you met *the one*, you just knew, and even then she'd scoffed at the notion. The idea of *the one* was ridiculous in itself. Looking back, the men she'd gone out with had generally been interchangeable. But she couldn't deny that when she'd met Mark, something had clicked immediately, and she'd understood what her father had meant.

Things had seemed relaxed and natural between them from the start. The passion was there, but they fitted together in other ways too. If they hadn't been lovers, they would still have been best friends, which wasn't something she could say in all honesty about her former boyfriends. She had fallen in love with him long before she told him. Rather than being frightening, it had surprised her — again — how strangely *freeing* saying it had felt.

The past couple of weeks, though, things hadn't felt quite the same as they used to. It was difficult to pin down anything in particular. Aside from his behaviour at the engagement party, there was nothing she could point to and say, *That! That thing you just said or did right then! Why are you being like that?* But there had been some kind of change. All relationships settled down after that initial burst of intensity, of course, but she recognised those subtle ebbs and flows, and this was different. One of the things she'd always loved about him had been his ability to talk to her — presumably a benefit of his interview training — and yet it felt now that there was something he wasn't telling her.

Something was going wrong.

He's not happy. Not really.

It felt heartbreaking because it was so very obviously true.

Sasha drank more wine. The engagement seemed to have changed everything. Had it come too soon? She'd certainly never pressed for the proposal — never thought she'd marry anyone, if she was honest — but she'd been genuinely thrilled when he asked. Any last trace of cynicism inside felt like it had melted away as he got down on one knee and completely messed up the speech he'd been preparing to say. He'd probably been more nervous than she had. She'd said yes without thinking, because it had felt so right she hadn't needed to think.

And yet now, barely two weeks later, that had changed.

Now, she thought, it didn't feel right at all.

He was regretting it.

★   ★   ★

Upstairs, Sasha walked round to Mark's side of the bed.

He had a small cabinet there. In the top drawer she knew that he kept important things like documents, passport and chequebook, but also items that held more personal significance. There were ticket stubs from memorable concerts and films and theatre trips, for example, one of which was from their first proper date last year. There was a ring his grandmother had given him when he was a boy. In terms of *them*, there were the small number of birthday and Valentine's cards she'd so far had the chance to give him, along with the little notes and drawings she occasionally left if she was working late. Mark kept everything like that. He was far more sentimental than he sometimes let on.

She opened the drawer.

Nothing explicit had ever been said about the privacy or otherwise of this, but it certainly felt like an invasion, and she was careful to note the arrangement of papers and objects inside so she could leave it exactly as she found it. Would he know how the drawer looked? She wasn't sure, but it was important he didn't know she'd gone looking. And she supposed that was deeply wrong, because healthy couples didn't keep secrets from each other. If you didn't have mutual and unconditional trust, then what did you have?

Nevertheless, she worked carefully through the contents, lifting papers so as not to dislodge them from place, keeping everything in line.

The cards and notes from her were on top. But right at the bottom of the pile, pressed against the base of the drawer, she found a photograph. She slid it out cautiously, allowing the papers to rest back down gently on the space it left.

The sight of it froze something inside her. They'd call it a selfie these days. There were two people in the shot, with Mark on the right and a woman Sasha presumed was Lise leaning against him, her head angled to one side so as to rest on his bare shoulder. There was what looked like a beach behind them, and they were both tanned and wearing sunglasses that partially reflected the sunset behind the camera. They both looked so young and happy, and obviously very much in love.

Is that it, Mark?

Sasha looked at Lise. Her rival in some ways, although not one she'd ever have to compete with. Or at least not directly. Lise had shoulder-length brown hair that had been slightly curled and tousled by the sea and sun. Trying to be objective — and why not, because it was hardly this dead woman's fault, was it — Sasha thought that she had also been very pretty. Beside her, Mark looked happier than she could remember seeing him. Happier than she herself made him, perhaps.

Is that it?

Deep down, do you wish you were still with her, not me?

It was stupid to think like that, but then what other explanation *was* there for his behaviour? *Second best*, she thought. Maybe that was all she could ever be. It left her feeling numb. The worst thing about it was that it didn't mean he didn't love her now. It just meant that she was a decent enough option in a timeline that had skewed irreversibly away from what he really wanted.

And yet he kept the photograph *here*, didn't he? Right beside where he slept. Where *they* slept. She knew that Mark used to have a recurring nightmare of some kind about Lise drowning. It was small wonder, wasn't it? He kept her close enough for his mind to touch each night. As close to him as Sasha.

For a moment, she considered taking the photograph away, destroying it somewhere. An exorcism. *I'm sorry,* she would silently tell Lise. *I'm not glad you're dead; not really. But you are, and you had your life, and now it's time to let us have ours.* She wouldn't, of course, but still: she wondered how long it would take Mark to notice. Would it be one day in the distant future, by which point he might convince himself he'd misplaced it himself, or did he check frequently? She pictured him taking it out and staring at it every day, remembering what he'd lost, comparing it constantly to what he had now. But if that were the case, wouldn't it be on top of the pile? Maybe he never looked at it at all.

Faced with the unknowable, Sasha was aware her mind had a tendency to burrow along the various possibilities until it arrived at the bleakest outcome. She also knew that people often saw her as a bit of a soft touch, like Pete telling Mark it had fallen to him to punish Mark because he had known she wouldn't. That was true, but only to a point. The reality was more that she didn't show any hurt she felt. She had always treated her relationships like rooms. There was a slight emotional danger in being in them at all, and if that risk increased — if there was the slightest hint of hurt to come — she would take a step closer to the door, detaching herself by increments. By the time many of her past relationships ended, she'd been able to step out without feeling a thing, leaving her former partner in the centre of the room, bewildered by

164

how suddenly this apparently soft and forgiving woman had disappeared.

And this hurt. There was no point denying it, and she could hardly be angry at the dead woman in the photo. The solution was an unhappy one, but obvious.

Make sure it doesn't end up hurting more than this.

Yes, she could do that. She was good at that. A step away from Mark. It might not come to leaving entirely — and God, she didn't want it to, not this time — but she would be ready if it did. Especially if it was going to distract her like it had today . . .

A car in the driveway.

Sasha replaced the picture at the bottom of the pile — the right way round — then closed the drawer and made her way downstairs. But as she poured another glass of wine and took it through, there were two images she couldn't get out of her head. How sad Mark had seemed at the engagement party.

How *guilty*.

And how happy he looked in that photograph.

Mark

If they don't let you go

When I got home that night, Sasha was sitting on the settee, a glass of wine on the table in front of her already. Rough day, I guessed. She didn't look up at me as I walked into the room, which also felt like a bad sign.

'Hey there,' I said.

'Hey.'

She was watching the television. Local news. I stared at the screen for a moment, watching officers leading a couple of people out of a pub I vaguely recognised in the city centre. The camera followed them towards a waiting police van.

'Wait, was that you?' I said.

'It was.'

'On the door?'

'We got seconded to Operation Viper for the day.' She still hadn't looked up at me. 'Stolen goods sweep.'

'You're a movie star.' I shrugged my jacket off. 'Any joy?'

'A few arrests. Nothing to write home about.'

'No drama?'

'Of course not.'

'Just asking,' I said.

She was annoyed with me. I wasn't sure why. Things had been lovely last night, and everything had seemed normal between us this morning. I had no idea what I could have done to irritate her in my absence. Even I'm not that annoying.

I nodded at the wine. 'Mind if I join you?'

'Be my guest.'

I went through to the kitchen and poured myself a glass of my own, then sat down on the settee beside her. By now, the news had moved on to something about hospital cuts.

'I was there today,' I said.

'The hospital?'

'Yeah. Interviewing a patient.'

'Some kind of assault?'

'Not exactly. Bit weirder than that.'

'Well, now you've got me interested.' The way Sasha said it, that was only half true. 'Tell all.'

I sipped the wine, hesitating for a moment. It was obvious that the Matheson case mirrored my own life to an extent — or rather, that it casually reflected the difficulty that seemed to have arisen between Sasha and me. Sooner or later we were going to have to talk about that, weren't we? And while it all felt too awkward to delve into directly, perhaps this would give us a roundabout way of addressing it.

So I explained about Charlie Matheson, and the story she was telling us, along with the basics of the investigation. And yes, by the end, it was fairly clear that it was Lise bothering Sasha — or at least that she was worried that Lise was still bothering me. Her face was blank.

'Right,' she said. 'A woman's come back from the dead.'

'In a manner of speaking.'

She was silent for a moment.

'Well, her husband must be pleased.'

I sipped the wine again, remembering Paul Carlisle's reaction this afternoon, and shook my head.

'No, he's pretty upset about it. Understandably, I guess. He's moved on, after all. He's with someone else now, and they've built a new life together. It's about the worst thing that could have happened to him.'

'Awkward.'

I shrugged.

'People move on, don't they?'

Sasha was looking at me, and I supposed it would be a good time — if we *were* going to talk about it directly — to mention Lise. I could try to explain how I wasn't glad she was dead, exactly, but that I'd moved on too. I could say that I loved Sasha very much, and wanted to marry her now at least as much as I had when I'd asked. That I knew something was slightly off between us right now, but it wasn't *that*.

Somehow, though, it all felt too much to say out loud. *People move on.* For now, it would have to be enough.

'Yes,' Sasha said finally. 'I guess they do.'

And to an extent, she seemed satisfied by that. As the evening went on, she opened up a little more, and whatever cold there had been when I arrived home began to thaw. We ate dinner together, then relaxed in front of the television, her legs curled up underneath her and her head resting on my shoulder. There was more wine. There was even some easy laughter.

'I love you,' I said. 'I *really* love you.'

168

She smiled at me. 'I love you just the same.'

It was closing in on bedtime. I was about to suggest an early one when Sasha broke the short silence that had developed.

'You know, I keep thinking about my grandad.'

'Your grandad?'

'Yeah. My real one, I mean. He died when I was young, and I actually don't remember him at all. My gran remarried. He was nice, but I always called him *Gerald*. Because he wasn't my real grandad, you know?'

'Sure.'

'And I remember asking my mum, because she was religious, and that was how I was raised: what would happen when they all got to Heaven? Gran had been with my real grandad for decades, and he'd died, so presumably he was up there waiting for her. But then she'd gone and fallen in love with someone else.'

I smiled. 'There'd be a punch-up at the Pearly Gates.'

'Well, yeah.' Sasha smiled back. 'And my mum couldn't really answer. She said it wouldn't be like that, but she couldn't say why or how. I think that's when I started to not believe. Because it doesn't make any sense, does it?'

'No,' I said. 'Not really.'

'You can only be happy if you let people go. But if they don't let *you* go too, it doesn't work.'

It was my turn to be silent for a moment.

'That's right,' I said.

Sasha shook her head. 'I don't know. I just keep thinking about the woman in the hospital.'

'Charlie Matheson?'

'Yes. The whole thing is insane.'

'I know.'

'I mean, seriously. Are you *sure* it's her?'

'I think so.' I drained the last of the wine in my glass. 'We got a photo from her ex-husband. And while he wouldn't commit totally, I know he believes it too.'

Sasha was quiet for a second.

'He kept a photo of her?'

'Yeah.' I put the glass down and stretched. 'But you're right — it's a strange case. Anyway. I'm worn out. Bedtime?'

More silence. I became aware after the first couple of seconds that, somehow, I'd fucked things up again. Either that, or I'd been far too optimistic about how the evening had gone.

Whatever the explanation, the shutters had come down. Sasha picked up her glass and went through to the kitchen.

'No, I think I might stay up a little,' she said.

'Yeah?'

'Yeah. I'll see you in the morning.'

★ ★ ★

I lay in bed, in the dark, listening to the silence from the front room below, thinking about Lise and Sasha, and Charlie Matheson and Paul Carlisle.

Remembering.

There had been a few hours shortly after what happened when I'd allowed myself to believe that Lise was still alive and would be found. Not at first, I don't think; standing on the beach, mixed in with the panic and fear, I'd already felt a kind of grief. But as the coastguards went out searching, and I sat back at the campsite with a blanket over my shoulders, I'd entered that mindset for a time. She would be fine. She would be found.

Yes: out of sight of the shore, I had allowed myself to believe that. Every few seconds I'd turned my head in the direction of the path over the dunes that led to the beach, expecting to see her walking back up, flanked by lifeguards and similarly draped with a blanket. We'd laugh about it later, I'd thought; time would turn it all into an adventure — a story to tell. Even though the footpath remained empty, I'd kept believing it would happen. She would be fine. She would be found.

The search had been called off overnight, but I'd still somehow managed to convince myself that it would all be okay. The universe had simply made a mistake — a bad one — and it would shortly realise that and rectify it. Even as the days passed, and her body wasn't discovered along the shoreline, I still harboured fantasies of the various ways she might have survived the turbulent ocean. Places she might have come ashore without being discovered. I pictured her wandering, head thick with amnesia. She would be fine. She would be found.

But she wasn't, and she never would be, and I think a part of me had known that from the very last moment I saw her, screaming at me from the water.

Lying in bed now, I wondered how I would

feel if she turned up alive again: if she suddenly returned to my life as though the intervening time had never happened. I would be glad she was alive, of course, but only for her sake. I had changed in the interim, and the two of us would be strangers to each other now. I would still want to be with Sasha. I knew that with as much certainty as I knew anything.

So what was the problem?

Because there was one, and I knew that it was mine. Whenever my thoughts turned to the engagement, I felt that knot of tension inside my chest. Thinking about it right now, in fact, I felt sick — exactly as though I was about to make some kind of mistake, or commit a terrible betrayal, and it was almost too late to prevent it. But . . .

I was interrupted from my thoughts by the sound of my work mobile ringing on the bedside table. I reached across to pick it up.

'Detective Mark Nelson.'

'Hello, Detective Nelson. I'm sorry — I know it's late. It's Dr Fredericks here. From the hospital?'

'Yes, of course,' I said, although I'd actually forgotten I'd given Fredericks my contact number. 'Is Charlie all right?'

Fredericks paused.

'Yes, I think so. She's quite excited, because she's remembered something else, but she's all right. She was adamant that it was very important, and I needed to pass it on to you as soon as possible.'

'She's right to do so.' I sat up in bed. 'What

has she remembered?'

'Something from the van, she says. From when the man was talking to her. Does that make sense?'

'Yes.'

He wanted me to ask you for mercy.

'Her memory is clearer now,' Fredericks said. 'And she tells me that she got it wrong before. Not *mercy*. That's what she says now.'

I closed my eyes, somehow hearing it in my head before Fredericks could say it out loud.

'The man told her to ask for *Mercer*.'

Groves

The phone call

Groves took the phone home with him, wondering about the encounter the whole way. The more he thought about it, the stranger it seemed. There was nothing unusual about most of what had happened, but put together, it felt more and more deliberate. Orchestrated, even.

And yet how could that be possible?

If the homeless boy had been intending to give him the phone, he could easily have just done it. Instead, he'd been harassing the woman, and if Groves hadn't intervened, they would never even have spoken. And why demand change? It felt to Groves as though, if he hadn't given him the money, the man wouldn't have dropped the mobile. But what kind of exchange was that meant to be? The phone was old and battered but presumably still worth more than he had effectively paid for it.

The more he thought about it, the less sense it made.

He didn't recognise the model of phone, but it was a long way from state-of-the-art; the kind of thing they probably didn't even sell any more. It had a pale blue rubber casing, a small numerical keypad and a thin green display that would incorporate two lines of text at most. If you'd wanted to check the internet on it, you'd have been sorely disappointed.

Groves turned it on. The battery was only half full. Given the age of the thing, he'd have to be careful about that, because it seemed unlikely he was going to locate a charger for it any time soon. But he wasn't going to find answers if he didn't look.

The menu system was archaic, and it took a few tries to work out how to scroll down through the options on the tiny screen. He had to prod the bottom of one key carefully, moving through the numbered options one line at a time, then click OK to access that function.

By the time the train was approaching his stop, Groves had managed to ascertain that there were no messages or contacts stored in the phone, and that the call history was completely blank. He used it to call his own mobile, but as it rang, the display simply showed *Caller Unknown*. So that was no use. He put his mobile away, then turned the homeless boy's phone off and used a key to prise away the back. Inside, he found a battery and SIM card. He expected the SIM to have the number written on it, and it had done once. Someone had carefully obliterated the numbers there with black scribbles.

A mystery, then.

He walked home from the station. It was only ten minutes, and the night was still warm. Above him the stars prickled gently, and the trees along the country lane rustled beside him in the slight breeze. Beyond them, the fields were dark, the long grass swaying gently in the shadows. The world was mostly silent, but he had the strange feeling that he was being watched. There was no reason for it — nobody else had got off at his stop, and whenever he glanced around, he was totally alone — but the feeling remained, all the way up the short path to his front door.

Groves turned around. The country lane was illuminated by a street light, which also touched the leaves of the tree at the end of the path. On the other side of the lane there was a dry-stone wall, which separated the road from the sloping field beyond and the black silhouettes of the trees in the far distance. Someone was standing out there.

It wasn't obviously a figure, just a portion of the field that was darker than the rest. A pitch-black space in the shape of a person.

He took a step back towards the road, but even as he did, the illusion disappeared. The breeze moved the grass, and the figure dissolved into what it had been all along: fragments of split shadow that had come together to form a person, then separated again.

He listened. Nothing but the breeze. In the dark, and as nervous as he suddenly felt, it sounded like holding a seashell up to his ear.

Once inside, he locked the door. Then, feeling faintly ridiculous, he checked the whole house. There was no rhyme or reason to it, but he did it anyway. Nobody was there, of course. He noticed that Caroline had made the bed and washed up before she left.

Finally, relaxing somewhat, he turned his attention back to the phone. There was one more thing he could think of doing. Sitting down in the front room with a glass of wine, he turned it on again and called the number for his home phone. He let it ring twice before cancelling it, then walked across the room and picked up the receiver, checking for details of the last incoming call.

'The caller did not leave their number. Please hang up.'

He did.

And then the mobile rang.

Groves stared down at it for a second. The display showed no incoming number. It was the ringtone that threw him.

It was a nursery rhyme: 'Twinkle, Twinkle, Little Star'. The notes tinkled in the front room, bringing with them a flood of mixed memories, happy at first, and then sad. There had been a small toy bunny strapped to the side of Jamie's cot, carrying a suitcase. When you pulled on it, the cable slowly contorted back in again, playing that tune the whole time.

No, no, no.

It was how he often used to wake up in the mornings. He would drift awake to the sound of the tune, and Jamie giggling in the cot beside their bed. The house would fall silent, and then there'd be a gentle crunching sound as Jamie pulled on the bunny's suitcase and the music began again.

He stared at the phone for a moment longer, then pressed the green key to accept the call. The music died and he held it to his ear.

'Hello?'

There was some problem with the reception.

Even though nobody was obviously on the other end, there was a sheen of static over the silence: buzzes and rushes and clicks.

Then words started to come through.

' . . . whatever happens to them on the way . . . '

It sounded like an old radio announcement. The voice was grandiose, like a broadcaster reading from a news script during the war. The crackles and pips reminded Groves of music played on a gramophone.

There was a sudden burst of child's laughter. Full and delirious, and then immediately gone again.

' . . . in that enchanted place on the top of the Forest . . . '

'*Who is this?*' Groves said.

' . . . a little boy and his Bear will always be playing.'

It was only then — as the sound cut dead — that he realised it had been a recording. The line was silent now. But still holding the phone to his ear, he thought he could hear someone breathing softly at the other end of the connection.

'Who is this?' Groves said again.

'God will be with you,' a man's voice said.

And then the line went dead.

Part Three

And She told Them that true evil also shied from the light. A Man may be evil at heart, but that is not sufficient, for many wish evil upon others without action, and how can a Man be evil without performing evil deeds? And yet true evil also endeavours to draw no attention to itself. And She told Them that the Devil therefore seeks out evil that wishes not to be sought, and rewards it by forcing it into the light.

Extract from the Cane Hill bible

Mark

John Mercer

The walls of our incident room were now covered with material relating to the case. There was a list of hospitals and phone numbers, a third of them already struck through; photographs and schematics from the accident two years ago; contact details for the acquaintances of Charlie Matheson and Paul Carlisle, and the scant information gathered from them so far; general notes and queries and scribbles. On the plasma screen, the double image of Charlie Matheson's face, the past and the present, seemed to be staring down at the three of us as we waited anxiously for our guests to arrive.

Greg was leaning against one of the desks, his arms folded and his chin tucked down against his chest; occasionally he sighed loudly to himself. He looked like a man in a hospital waiting dutifully for bad news about a relative he didn't particularly care for. Simon, meanwhile, was perhaps as animated as I'd ever seen him. He kept pacing back and forth, stopping at the window from time to time and lifting a slat in the blinds to peer at the sunny morning outside. Each time he did, it clicked when he let it go, causing Greg to look over in irritation.

'You'll break that.'

'I broke it weeks ago.'

I was sitting at another of the desks, elbows on the surface, hands clasped in front of my mouth. Just waiting. Pete was downstairs. The desk had called up five minutes ago, at which point he'd headed down to welcome our guests and escort them up here. Guests: plural. Given how protective she'd been yesterday morning, it didn't remotely surprise me that Eileen Mercer had insisted upon escorting her husband to the department.

'Taking their time, aren't they?' Greg said.

Simon clicked the blind again.

'Patience,' he said.

But I could tell from his voice that, if not quite as jittery as Greg, Simon was still nervous about seeing our old boss. I'd called the hospital again first thing, and Fredericks had told me that Charlie had reiterated what she'd said last night: the man in the ambulance had told her to ask us for Mercer. If anything, she had been even more strident about it. Was there a policeman here by that name? There wasn't, of course — not any more — but Fredericks said that she was insistent. It was imperative that she speak to Mercer.

The word she'd used in the first interview kept coming back to me. *Need.* I looked up at those images of her now.

Why do you need to talk to Mercer, Charlie?

Whatever the reason, Pete had reluctantly made the call first thing this morning. After the reception I'd received from Eileen, I hadn't been convinced that Mercer would agree to come at all, but Pete had returned to the incident room

182

only a couple of minutes later. Former Detective John Mercer would be here within the hour. Forty minutes later, he'd arrived downstairs, with Eileen at his side.

'Has anyone actually seen him since?' Greg said.

Simon and I didn't answer. It was obvious what he meant by *since*. I knew Greg himself wouldn't have seen Mercer, not after his betrayal on that December day. Out of concern for our former boss's disintegrating mental health, Greg had attempted to have him removed from the case. I had no reason to keep in touch with him, of course: although it was Mercer's reputation that had drawn me to the city, I barely knew the man himself. And I couldn't imagine Simon paying a social call, although to be fair, even after a year and a half here, his private life remained a mystery to me.

'Maybe Pete has,' I suggested. 'They were close, weren't they?'

Simon shook his head. 'I don't think any of us were exactly close to him. Pete was his second, and they worked together for years, but I'm not sure they ever socialised outside of work. Not to my knowledge, anyway. John was in charge, but he was never as relaxed and friendly as Pete is. Of course, that doesn't mean we weren't intensely loyal to him.'

'Because we were,' Greg said.

'Yes.' Simon nodded. 'All of us.'

Under other circumstances, he might have twisted that into something more teasing, more knowing, but right now he sounded sincere.

Whatever Greg had done, he'd done it for the right reasons. And with the man himself on the way, it was clear that even Simon felt it wasn't the time for needling.

Greg was about to say something else, but just then the office door opened, and he bit down on whatever it was.

Pete came in first. He looked more nervous than any of us, but was clearly trying to hide it, wearing a smile that was far too casual for the circumstances. He held the door open for Eileen and Mercer, who followed silently behind him.

I'd seen Eileen yesterday, and the only real change in her now was how much more serious she looked. She did not want to be here, and it clearly troubled her deeply that she was. The reason for that was equally clear when I saw Mercer moving into the room beside her.

I don't know if it's healthy, she'd told me. *But he's fine right now . . . he's happy.*

If that were the case, it was difficult to imagine how he'd look if things were worse. Mercer was so diminished from the man I remembered that I wondered for a moment whether this could really be the same person.

When I'd started here, I'd been surprised by how fragile John Mercer seemed in comparison to the legendary figure in my head, but I'd understood that he was still recovering from the effects of an earlier nervous breakdown. He had looked like a solid, sturdy man who was beginning to feel the inexorable effects of encroaching old age, yet remained active and capable. In the

184

last year and a half, though, those effects had accelerated. Mercer looked elderly and frail — easily ten or fifteen years older than Eileen beside him. His hair was gone, and his face was wrinkled and drawn, skeleton-dark around the eyes. He also seemed much shorter than I remembered, and had lost so much weight that he reminded me of a patient you might see in a hospice. Even his gait was slow and awkward, as though he would be far more comfortable with a cane in his hand. I wasn't sure whether Eileen was keeping so close to his side as an emotional guard, or if she was concerned he might stumble.

He looked around the room, giving us all the same cursory smile, one that went nowhere near his eyes.

'Good morning, everyone.'

'John.'

'Hello again, John. Good to see you.'

'Thank you for coming.'

He nodded to himself, but didn't seem to be listening. Instead, he was looking around the room with a sense of wonder. Despite his physical frailty, there was still some kind of life in his eyes. The smile now was a little more genuine.

'My, my,' he said, taking in the decor. 'Haven't you all moved up in the world? If I'd only been able to hang on a little while longer, I could have experienced such riches too.'

There was no reproach in his voice, but even so, none of us said anything, and Pete looked as awkward as I'd ever seen him. Mercer was still looking around the room, his eyes settling finally on the plasma screen on the wall and the two photographs of Charlie Matheson.

'And this is her, then? The young lady who wants to see me?'

'Yes,' Pete said. 'Would you like a seat, John?'

'I'm fine, but thank you.'

Eileen touched his arm. 'I think we should both have a seat.'

If the intervention offended Mercer, he didn't show it. Instead, he just nodded, acquiescing with apparent grace. When they were both seated, he looked at the screen again.

'Tell me everything.'

Pete glanced at me, so I took over the briefing. Unlike the ones yesterday, this time I didn't go into too much detail. While it was possible Mercer could help us with the investigation, it was important to bear in mind that he was a civilian now. He didn't need to know everything that was happening, and it would have been remiss to share it. But if he was going to talk to Charlie then he needed to understand the basics of the situation, so I took him through the accident itself, the bare bones of the story she'd given us, and the details of her reappearance three days ago. As I finished, it was the former that he remained interested in.

'The accident was on the third of August, two years ago,' he said. 'Which is *after* I returned to work and *before* I left again. But it's certainly not something we would have had anything to do with.'

'No,' I said. Back then, this had been one of the top teams in the department, and they wouldn't have been brought in to deal with a straightforward car accident: a non-criminal matter. 'I've gone through the file in depth, researched everything as much as possible. As far as I can tell, there's nothing that would link Charlie Matheson to us. At the same time, it's possible that the connection isn't with *us*. Because it was *you* she asked for specifically, John.'

He frowned. 'Are you sure? What were her exact words?'

'*Ask for Mercer*. That was something she'd been told to do. It's likely she was drugged, and it was hard for her to remember the message she'd been given. But whoever was holding her, they wanted her to ask for you when she regained consciousness.'

'Why?'

'That's what we're hoping to find out.'

'I don't think I know any Charlotte Matheson.'

'I'm not sure she knows you either. If she did, she would have known to ask for you straight away. To begin with, she thought she was meant to ask us for *mercy*.'

Mercer stared off to one side, his expression blank now. Thinking it over. Trying to work out what it might mean.

'There's another explanation,' Eileen said. 'While this woman might not know John, whoever took her and held her all this time clearly does.'

Her tone implied she didn't like that one bit, and I sympathised. Her husband had already had one breakdown, after half a lifetime spent in the heads of killers, and that was before the 50/50 Killer case had nearly destroyed him for a

187

second time. Whatever peace now lay between them was no doubt as tentative as Mercer's fragile mental state. She didn't want him here at all, and she certainly didn't want to imagine that there might be someone out there who had unfinished business with her husband that they were intent on concluding.

Like it or not, there was no way of getting around it.

'Yes,' I said. 'That's a possibility.'

If Mercer himself was bothered by it, he wasn't showing it; his face remained blank, and he was still staring off to one side. Considering the case, I imagined. Although perhaps he was having the exact same thought as Eileen. I noticed that she had moved her chair slightly closer to him and rested her hand over the back of his.

'And it's definitely her?' he said finally.

'If not, it's her twin.'

'Have you identified the actual victim? The woman who really died in the crash?'

'Not yet. I've gone through missing persons for a couple of months around the date, but haven't found any matches as yet.'

'You need to go further back than that.' Mercer looked at me suddenly, and the intensity in his eyes was alarming. 'Two months isn't good enough at all.'

'I'm going to, yes.'

'You need to go back at least two years. *At least*. Possibly even further. Assuming all this is true, then whoever these individuals are, they've shown they're capable of holding a woman captive for that length of time. There's no reason to think they couldn't have done it before. Every reason, in fact, to imagine that they have.'

'I know. John, we've got this covered.'

And yet actually, I realised, that was only half right. As a team, we'd been so intent on Charlie Matheson, and the unique aspects of her abduction and reappearance, that none of us had got as far as to imagine that there might be others.

Whoever had taken her had done so with care and planning, pulling off both the abduction and the return perfectly. The police at the time had been convinced by the evidence they found at the accident scene, and for two years the world had believed that Charlie Matheson was dead. Controlled and manipulated, she had even come to believe the same thing herself.

It took skill and willpower to achieve that. It also took *practice*. That had always been one of Mercer's guiding principles: that sophisticated criminals rarely arrived fully formed; that crime, like any other activity, required an education, and there would be stumbles and falls along the way. Whoever had taken Charlie Matheson hadn't done so out of the blue. It was likely there had been other victims beforehand. It was possible there had been others since.

'We're checking,' Pete said. He sounded subdued.

'What about the abduction itself?'

'She doesn't remember it,' I said. 'Whoever took her, they managed to convince her she'd actually been in the accident.'

'When she was probably nowhere near it.' Mercer shook his head. 'What was the last known sighting of her?'

I glanced at Pete, but he had folded his arms and walked over to a nearby desk, which he was now looking down at.

'The morning of the third,' I said. 'Her husband reported that she left for work, but she'd called in sick. There's an anomaly in the case file there — her whereabouts for the day are unknown. She doesn't remember. We're going to pursue that today.'

'Right.'

There was a despondency to the way he said it — not a criticism of our lack of progress so much as a realisation that he'd lapsed into old patterns and tried to take hold of the case, then remembered it didn't belong to him. He glanced at Pete, who was still looking away, and then back to me.

'Right. And what is it you want from me?'

I took a deep breath.

'Well, first off, to see if her name meant anything to you. Obviously, it doesn't.'

'No. I would remember.'

'What about Paul Carlisle?'

Mercer thought about it. 'Again, no.'

'Okay. Well, then, I was wondering if you might consider coming with me to the hospital this morning. To talk to her.'

Mercer just stared at me for a second.

'Nothing major,' I said. 'Nothing heavy. But she was told to ask for you. We don't know why. It would be good to figure that out, wouldn't it?'

'I — '

'No,' Eileen said. 'Absolutely not.'

She still had her hand over Mercer's — pressed there tighter than before, either for reassurance, or perhaps to send him a message — but she was looking directly at me.

'Eileen,' I said.

'It's completely out of the question.' She looked at her husband, and then back at me. From her expression, she couldn't believe we were asking Mercer to do this. 'After everything that happened? John isn't a policeman any more, in case you'd forgotten. And for very good reason. If you think I'm going to let him put himself in a place where he could get hurt again, you're mistaken. *Sadly* mistaken.'

I stared back at her, not knowing what to say. On the one hand, I completely understood her reaction. In her shoes, I'd have wanted to keep Mercer as far away from a police investigation as possible. On the other hand, we needed his help. And as unwelcome an intrusion as this might be, just as with Paul Carlisle, it wasn't going to go away. I looked at Mercer instead.

'John,' I said. 'What do you think?'

The whole time Eileen had been talking, Mercer had been sitting beside her with apparent equanimity, his expression giving nothing away. If he was bothered by the way she was speaking on his behalf, making the decision for him, then he wasn't showing it. He sighed to himself now, looked at Eileen and then me.

'My wife is right,' he said. 'I'm sorry.'

'John — '

Eileen had already got to her feet, and was helping Mercer to his.

'We need to go, John.' Beneath the anger and steel in her voice, there was the faintest trace of panic. 'We should never have come in the first place. I told you that. But we did, and you've done everything you can, and now it's time for us to go home.'

Pete said, 'All right, John. We understand.'

'Yes,' Mercer said. At the door, he turned back to us, looking confused now, as though events had moved too fast for him to follow and he was having trouble keeping track. 'I'm sorry. But she's right. I'm sorry.'

And with one last curious glance at the images of Charlie Matheson, he was gone.

Mark

The wearing of sins

When I arrived at the hospital, Charlie Matheson was sitting alone in an enclosed garden to the side of the Baines Wing. I stepped out. There was a stone patio, and beyond it, on the grass, wooden benches. A busy main road was only about fifty metres away, past a stretch of neatly trimmed grass and a fence, but it was partially obscured by a row of trees, reducing the traffic to flashes of colour between the leaves. The noise was audible but bearable.

This trip outside had been Fredericks' idea, apparently. Given Charlie's initial reaction when she'd been found — the sensations that had overwhelmed her — it made sense for her to acclimatise herself to the real world gradually. This was as peaceful an area as any to start that process.

As I reached her, she didn't look up. She was leaning forward slightly on the bench with her hands between her knees, her head bowed a little.

'I think it's going to rain,' she said.

I glanced at the sky. 'Do you?'

'Yes. You can smell it, can't you? And there's a kind of pressure to the air.'

It was clear blue overhead, without a cloud in sight, but I did know what she meant. The day was warmer than yesterday, but it was beginning to feel like the kind of escalating heat that couldn't sustain itself for much longer: a gathering problem that could only be resolved by a thunderstorm.

'You might be right,' I said.

'I like rain.'

'It must have been a while since you've seen it.'

She shook her head. 'It rained in the other place too.'

I frowned at that, because from what she'd told me before, the period of her abduction had been spent in an underground cell. But I filed the thought away for a moment.

'Mercer wouldn't come,' I said.

She looked up immediately, her hair falling backwards. In the sunlight, the scarring on her face appeared fresh and raw, and was newly shocking to see. The injuries stood out so badly that I had to resist the urge to wince at the sight of them.

'Why not?' she said.

I shrugged. 'Why did you want to see him?'

'I don't know.'

'Do you know him?'

'No. I've no idea who he is. I was just told to ask for him. By the man — the doctor in the back of the ambulance.'

'How did you know he was a doctor?'

'I've . . . '

She hesitated, and I knew immediately that she was censoring herself: working out what was safe to say. I was getting the feeling now that there was a lot she wasn't telling me.

'I've seen him before,' she said finally. 'In the place. It was obvious he was a doctor because of what he did there, how he helped me. But he wasn't someone in charge.'

'The man who cut you was in charge?'

She nodded.

'And what was supposed to happen when Mercer came to see you? What were you meant to tell him?'

'I'm not allowed to say.'

'Charlie.' I sat down beside her, fighting back the exasperation I felt. 'You're *allowed* to tell me anything. This man can't hurt you any more. And if you talk to me, we can catch him. We can stop him doing this to anyone else. But I can't do that unless you cooperate with me.'

'It's not as simple as you think.'

She sounded angry, and I told myself to back off slightly. I wouldn't get anywhere if I pressed from this angle, not when she was clearly so adamant. But I couldn't leave her story alone entirely.

'You said it rained in the other place too?'

'Yes. Sometimes.'

'But you were underground, weren't you? It doesn't rain underground.'

More silence. I looked sideways to see that she was staring at me, unsure what to say. I was thinking about Stockholm syndrome: the phenomenon where a captive bonds with the person holding them, becoming loyal, brainwashed — willing to defend them, even. Was that what was happening here? If so, I was woefully underprepared at this precise second to deal with it.

'Talk to me, Charlie,' I said. 'Help me to understand. There's nothing to be afraid of now. Nobody can hurt you here.'

She almost laughed.

'You have no idea what he's capable of. None.'

'The man who cut your face?'

'That's right.'

'Well why don't you tell me? Or is that not allowed either?'

She stared back at me, considering it.

'All right,' she said finally. 'I'll tell you about the Devil.'

★   ★   ★

The story came out in fits and starts, and her self-control began to falter even more as it did. The fear she felt just thinking about the man who had held her captive was obvious.

For the first couple of days after her abduction, as far as it was possible for her to keep track of time, she had been left alone in her cell. When she did sleep, she would wake to find that food had been delivered: simple provisions of bread, fruit and ham on a tray, along with cups of water.

'Always when I was asleep. So he must have been watching me.'

Probably, I thought. Why go to the trouble of abducting someone and keeping them in such circumstances if you weren't going to watch them?

It was on the second or third day that she received a visitor.

'I could smell him before I saw him.' She looked disgusted now, as though she still could. 'There was just this foul stench in the air, as though something had gone bad nearby. Something dead and rotting. And I could hear him too, moving around in the corridor. He took his time. I think he was playing with me.'

Despite the fear she'd felt, she had called out. There had been no reply. A little way back from the door, she'd peered through the hatch, sensing him nearby but still out of sight.

'Then suddenly the smell got worse, and he stepped into view. His eyes wide, right up against the hatch. I jumped back. Screamed.'

'What did he do?'

'He laughed,' she said simply. 'And then he told me that I was dead. That I'd been in an accident, and that I was in Hell for my sins. And he told me that he was the Devil.'

For that first visit, there had apparently been little else, and even regarding subsequent visits, she couldn't tell me much. She had seen him clearly once, she said — looked right at him — but it had made him angry.

'The Devil doesn't like people looking at him,' she said.

So she could only describe him a little. Every time she saw him, he always wore the same thing: a black suit with a white shirt underneath. From the single time she had looked at his face, she knew that he was old — perhaps in his sixties or seventies — and bald, but there was little to distinguish him beyond that.

'He didn't cut me at first,' she said.

'How long was it before it started?'

'A month, perhaps.'

She could only guess; there had been no clear difference between day and night in her cell. But after a period of time during which the man she called the Devil had repeatedly explained the situation to her — that she was dead and in Hell; that she would have to repent for her sins — the torture had begun. Other people were present to restrain her, she claimed, but it was the Devil who did the cutting itself. With a light behind him that cast him in silhouette, he worked slowly and precisely, often standing back to contemplate her illuminated face, as if it were a painting he was working on. He appeared to have a plan for the patterns he was carving into her skin. Each time, when he was finished, the wounds were tended to and cleaned with antiseptic.

'He always used his fingernails,' Charlie said, gesturing to the scars covering her face. 'He never needed a knife.'

Strangely, she seemed calmer now.

'And why did he do it?' I said. 'You said he seemed to have a plan. You had to repent for your sins?'

'Yes. The wearing of sins.' She looked at me. 'Are you a sinner, Mark?'

'Probably.'

'Everybody is. It's nothing to be ashamed of, but it's hard for people to admit. That's the point. In life, we hide our sins and imagine that nobody sees them, nobody knows. We even hide them from ourselves. We think the past is the past, but it isn't. They're always there, aren't they?'

'Yes.'

'And sins have to be made manifest in order for us to be cleansed. It is a form of acknowledgement. Do you see? We must admit our sins and crimes before we can repent. We must wear them.' She gestured at her face. 'One by one.'

I closed my eyes and pinched the bridge of my nose for a second, trying to gather my thoughts. This was an interview; this was what I did. But it was hard to keep track and hold it all in my head and figure out where to go next with the discussion.

'And what sins are you wearing, Charlie?'

'I want to go home.'

I opened my eyes. She was still looking at me, but the expression on her face had become desperately sad.

'I know.'

'Why won't Mercer come? I want to go home.'

'I know,' I said. 'But Paul's moved on. Like I said, he's living with someone else now, and she's pregnant. We'll have to work something out.'

'Not *that* home.'

Her voice was smaller than ever; she knew deep down that she was admitting something terrible. Even so, it took me a heavy moment to process what she was telling me.

'You want to go back there?'

'I was *promised*. After I told this man Mercer

— that was supposed to be the end of it.' She looked up and raised her voice now, as though she wanted the sky to hear. 'Mysterious ways, right? Well I've done everything I can, and now I want to go home. I deserve to go home! I've earned it, haven't I?'

'Charlie — '

'I deserve it, don't I?' She looked back down at me, her eyes almost imploring. 'After everything?'

I didn't know what to say. After everything that had been done to her . . . she wanted to go back there. And for some reason, she wouldn't be allowed to until she'd told Mercer whatever it was she was supposed to. In her head, at least. How would whoever had kept her even *know?*

'You don't deserve what's happened to you,' I said.

'You have no idea.'

The thought I'd had yesterday came back to me again.

'Where *were* you, Charlie, on that last day? Before the accident? You left for work in the morning, but you didn't go.'

She just looked at me.

The frustration finally rose up. I had so many questions I wanted answers to. Where had she been that day? Why had she been told to ask for Mercer, a man she didn't know? And as my gaze moved over the elaborate scarring on her face, I wanted to know why she had been targeted in the first place. In her own words, the cuts had been done to a design. It was a mask of admission; of repentance.

'What sins are you wearing?' I asked again.

And again Charlie stared back at me for a long time, still saying nothing. Then she turned her head away from me.

'That,' she said softly, 'is what I need to tell Mercer.'

Eileen

Sit with me

'It's for the best.'

'Yes,' John said. 'I know.'

Eileen glanced sideways at him as she drove them home. She had never seen her husband look so tired and beaten down. He was half collapsed in the passenger seat now, staring out of the side window without taking in the scenery moving past them. His head lolled slightly, guided by the motion of the vehicle. Even the bright sunshine on his skin somehow made him seem less alive than he should be.

It scared her, what effect today's events might have on him. He was so difficult to read sometimes, and the expression on his face right now was utterly blank. It was easy to imagine he was thinking nothing at all, but she knew that wouldn't be true. There was too much clockwork in that head of his, and it wasn't good for him when it all began clicking and turning. He couldn't cope with the noise it created. She could sense that visiting the department today had started movement off in there. Despite how calm and still he was, Eileen was frightened that the turning in there wouldn't stop, and of what the consequences would be for him. For both of them.

That was why she'd had to leap in. Cut the

meeting dead. For his sake, and for hers.

'We should never have gone,' she said.

'It was important to find out what they wanted.'

'Yes, well. Now we have. But they should have known better, after everything that happened. After they forced you out. It was unfair of them even to ask.'

John sighed. She glanced at him again, but he was still staring out of the window.

'They had no choice.'

'They had every choice,' she said. 'It's not your job to be interviewing witnesses and suspects for them. Not any more.'

'I meant no choice in forcing me out.'

Eileen couldn't think of what to say to that. He was right, of course, and perhaps it had been disingenuous of her to bring it up in the first place: trying to make the department into an enemy so that she could pair up with John against it. The truth was that she'd wanted him out of the police long before it happened, and if they hadn't pushed him, she would have done her damnedest to force him out herself.

'Well,' she said eventually. 'It's for the best.'

Her turn to sigh then. His turn not to reply.

But it *was* for the best — and not simply because of the effect getting involved might have on his mental health. Her heart had broken for him back at the department. For a moment he had seemed to come alive again. When he was advising the team on what they needed to do, she had caught a flash of the man she'd fallen in love with all those years ago: smart and capable, and more animated than she'd seen him in a long time.

And that couldn't last.

Many years ago, Eileen had watched her mother die: a slow, agonising descent into dementia that had left her incoherent by the end. The gradually diminishing figure in the hospital bed she visited might have had her mother's shape and form, but it had none of the content; the woman she had loved so deeply had become all but absent. *It's for the best*, her father had told her. Not that the illness wasn't a bitter and cruel one, he explained, but at least she wasn't aware of it. It was true that there had been a sense of serenity to her, and that the fractured fantasy world she inhabited seemed to bring her some degree of peace. If she laughed often at things that weren't there, what did it matter, so long as she laughed? *It's worse for us*, her father had told Eileen and her sister.

Maybe that was true for the most part, but there were also moments when her mother had been more lucid: when it was clear she recognised her husband and daughters. Eileen would hold her hand, recognising the fear and confusion in the old woman's eyes, and her mother would squeeze back, and Eileen would know that she *knew*. Just for a few minutes, or even seconds, she was being given a fleeting glimpse of the real world. When that happened, she understood what she was losing, what she had already lost, and how much it all meant to her. In those moments, Eileen didn't think it was worse for the rest of the family at all.

Watching John in the department had reminded her of that. He had lived for police work, and it had been taken from him, and she knew he had spent the past year and a half mourning that loss in his own way, acclimatising himself to it. Today had provided a reminder of what he had lost — given him a glimpse of his old life again — and she had watched him seize it as strongly but fleetingly as her mother had gripped her hand all those years ago.

And it wouldn't last. Even if he had stayed on and talked to Charlie Matheson for them, he wouldn't be *involved* — not in the way he wanted or needed to be. The advice he'd tried to give them wasn't advice they needed. And what had Mark told her yesterday when she'd asked how it was in the department these days?

We've moved buildings. Apart from that, it's the same as always.

They didn't need him. When they were finished with him, they would discard him again. Like her mother, he would return to his own world, confused and distressed by the experience, and there'd only be her there to hold his hand then.

When they arrived home, John made his way up to the attic. Eileen followed him to the base of the stairs.

'Where are you going?' she said.

'Just to do some work.'

She watched him climb the stairs, slowly and awkwardly. *How old he looks*, she thought again — but then perhaps she did too. They were both now years older than her mother had been when

205

she began wasting away. Against all odds, they were still together, and Eileen had a sudden realisation that time was drawing to a close for both of them. They were not going to grow old together; they already had. Before too long, John wouldn't be climbing these stairs any more, or else he would be climbing them without her to watch him and worry.

'Don't you think you should rest?' she called up.

'I'm fine. I won't be long.'

Sit with me, she wanted to blurt out. *Let's just sit together for a while.* But of course she would never do that. He was too drawn to his research; too lost in it, for all the comfort it brought him. How would it feel to sit with him, knowing he would rather be elsewhere?

Even worse, what if he said no?

He closed the attic door gently. Eileen stood at the bottom of the stairs for a few minutes, waiting for the sound of his typing to begin; the sound that reassured her he was at least not staring into space, not turning too much over in his head. But it didn't come. And finally, when the silence became unbearable, Eileen made her way back downstairs.

Groves

A man without a face

'So,' Sean said, 'do we think this might be our guy?'

Groves was sitting at his desk in their shared office, with Sean leaning over his shoulder, so close that he could smell the coffee on his partner's breath, and the tang of his aftershave. He was trying to ignore both.

'Yes. I think it might be.'

Groves clicked to replay the snippet of footage he'd extracted from the stack sent over from the CCTV suite. It showed one small event during the last evening of Edward Leland's life. The camera the clip had been taken from was on a post just past the end of a short row of shops, the nearest of which was obscured onscreen by a long stone canopy. The pavement was only partially illuminated. The newsagent's, bookie's and post office had been closed at that time, with only a takeaway and an off-licence open, spreading their light out in skewed rectangles over the tarmac.

He watched as Leland passed along the row and entered the off-licence at the far end. Groves counted. Leland was inside for just under two minutes. When he came out, he walked back the way he had come, in the direction of his house, now carrying a plastic bag.

'Spirits of some kind,' Sean said.

Groves nodded. Provisions for the night, he guessed. Just before Leland reached the end of the row of shops, a figure detached itself from the dark bushes beyond the off-licence and began following him.

'You don't even see him there.' Sean sounded full of wonder. 'Even though I knew to look this time, I still didn't spot him waiting.'

Groves didn't say anything, but it was true that, until the moment he revealed himself, the man might as well have been part of the darkness — or perhaps not even there at all. And yet he must have been standing there the whole time. Waiting. They would need to expand the time frame, of course, to try to find the moment he'd arrived, and hope it gave them a better shot at identifying him.

There was certainly little chance of doing so from this. The man walked purposefully after Leland, but all it was really possible to tell was that he was dressed entirely in dark clothes, carrying some kind of bag over his shoulder. His face was completely obscured; he had a hood up, and kept his head down, turning away from the light where necessary.

'He knew the camera was there,' Groves said.

'Certainly acting like it.'

There was a sense of professionalism to the man that was hard to pin down. It made Groves think of a soldier. Perhaps it was to do with the way he moved, or simply the fact that he managed to stay as dark and obscured as he did. Even when the light hit him, it seemed to reveal less than it should. The way he kept his head turned made him a man without a face.

He's used to moving in darkness, Groves thought.

It was irrational, but it felt true.

He looks like he's never seen unless he wants to be.

Sean leaned away. 'Let's get as good a freeze-frame as we can. Then we shake down Leland's friends. Each and every one. Coffee?'

'Yeah,' Groves said. 'Although I think I've already inhaled a day's worth of caffeine from your breath.'

'You're welcome: you looked like you needed it. Be back in five. Don't start without me.'

'I won't.'

Sean left and closed the door.

You looked like you needed it. Groves certainly felt like he did. After the phone call last night, he had found it difficult to sleep, turning the strange events of the evening over and over in his head in a fruitless attempt to make sense of them, and failing. The scarred homeless boy had given him a phone, and on that phone he'd received a message that related to his dead son. There was no way it could have been a coincidence, and yet he couldn't work out what it meant. Was it a more advanced version of the taunting phone calls and letters? If so, it seemed a bizarre and random form of escalation, and the message itself had not been as hurtful and poisonous as it might have been.

At the same time, he couldn't think what to do about it. He had the phone with him now — a solid pressure he could feel in his trouser pocket — but it wasn't turned on. He was keen to

209

preserve the battery life, and had been only checking for voicemail messages at intervals. Beyond that, he wasn't sure what else he could do. He certainly wasn't going to waste departmental resources attempting to trace the call. For the first couple of years, he'd reported the messages he'd received on Jamie's birthday, dutifully logging them, but nothing had ever come of it, and in the end he'd stopped. There had been a strange kind of relief then, at keeping them to himself. They were personal, and passing them on to the department had always felt a little like he was handing over his responsibility for them: giving them to someone else to deal with. This felt similar. For some reason, when it came to the phone, he was reluctant to talk even to Sean about it.

God will be with you.

He took the mobile out now and turned it on. Waited.

Nothing. He turned it off again.

Despite his promise to Sean, he decided to start without him. For now, he focused his attention on the drugs angle. Edward Leland had been low-level, yes, but it was still possible they'd find something there. When you dealt and used, it was inevitable that you'd meet bad people along the way, and transgressions could easily end up being punished. And if any of those individuals had become familiar with Leland's apparent sexual inclinations, maybe it wouldn't have taken quite so much of a transgression for them to turn on him.

He called up Leland's case file onscreen, with

the list of names that Angela Morris had provided for them scribbled on a notepad on the desk. She'd given a grand total of seven, and had stressed that only a couple of them were dodgy, the others more like casual acquaintances. Not that she'd necessarily know, of course, and they'd work them all anyway. For now, though, Groves wanted to see if there was any correlation there with Leland's criminal record. He scanned through to the list of Leland's convictions.

It made for depressing reading. His first offence had been at the age of thirteen. Drunk and disorderly; public affray; damage to property. He had received a caution. A pattern established itself through his teens, with a further three arrests, until he was sixteen, when drugs entered the picture and he was found in possession of a reasonable quantity of cannabis.

Groves knew the type already, or imagined he did, at least. It brought back memories of some of the kids he'd grown up with: hanging around in the local parks and on street corners; older brothers taking orders and bringing boxes of alcohol. Because his father had been both a policeman and deeply religious, Groves had been excluded from all that, and at the time he'd resented it. Despite his own religious leanings, the things the other kids got up to had somehow felt natural and correct, and they *pulled* at him to the extent that, stuck inside of an evening, he would look out of his bedroom window and sense a centre of gravity trying to drag him out there.

Most teenagers did it, of course, and most

came out the other side okay. But some didn't, and Edward Leland was one. He left school with barely a handful of qualifications and little in the way of an obvious future.

His eighteenth birthday had culminated in his being arrested in possession of a small quantity of heroin. A step-change, that. And from there, it had been a slippery slope with a downhill trajectory. He was arrested for dealing in his early twenties and served six months. More drunk and disorderlies afterwards. A longer stretch for dealing six years ago. Since then, he appeared to have been clean, although Angela Morris thought he had at least been using again at various points during that period.

Her words came back to Groves now.

He was so lovely when we were younger. Troubled, but lovely.

He clicked back through to the beginning of the file. It contained no record of the sexual abuse Morris alleged Leland had suffered as a child. Of course, that didn't mean it hadn't happened. He might have reported it and not been believed, or he might have felt there was nobody he could report it to at all. Both situations were depressingly common.

While it didn't excuse what he had done, and what he had possibly become, it made it difficult for Groves to hate him the way that Sean presumably thought he should. Everybody's life was a story that began without them, and for some people, the constraints of that beginning made it difficult to change the ending. Despite Angela Morris' obvious shortcomings, she didn't seem like a bad person, and she had seen something in Edward Leland. It seemed important to Groves to remember that what he was reading onscreen right now was not the man himself, but a list of the bad things he had done. There would have been a lot more to him than that.

He scrolled back down, intending to click through for greater detail on Leland's convictions, cross-referencing any additional names he found with the list Morris had provided. They'd all need following up. He started with the last conviction, and was busy writing down the names of the three other people arrested alongside Leland when he saw it.

SIMO

He paused, then slowly looked down at his hand.

The tip of the pencil was pressed tight against the paper. Not so hard that it had broken, but enough to leave a concentrated dot of black at the bottom of the O.

He forced himself to finish.

SIMON CHADWICK.

He looked at the screen. The name was right there, as plain as day. Leland's arrest that day for dealing had taken place in Chadwick's flat on the Thornton estate.

Simon Chadwick, the man with the mental age of a child. Who was so easily taken advantage of by the unscrupulous people he came into contact with. Edward Leland had been one of his associates.

Groves checked the date.

It had been just over a year after Leland's arrest at Chadwick's flat that Groves had knocked at that same address and Laila Buckingham had been found, tied up and close to death, in the back bedroom. Another two years until his own son had been taken in turn, presumably by people who had been associated with Chadwick.

People who were interested in children.

People who had never been found.

Groves stared at the screen until it began to feel more like he was staring through it. As though he wasn't in his body any longer.

People like Edward Leland?

For a moment, he was completely still, and then he realised his hand had started to tremble slightly. This was too much of a coincidence after the phone call last night, even though there was no reason to assume that was even connected.

Or maybe it was simply just too much.

What would you do, if you found the people responsible?

Arrest them, he'd always thought. Make them face justice. He remembered Edward Leland's tortured, burned body and tried to feel the sympathy he'd felt previously. It was still there, but he found that he couldn't lock on to it properly now. The emotion felt like a lost child with nobody's hand to hold.

Arrest them.

The thought became urgent. If Leland *was* one of them, perhaps there were others here, amongst his associates.

Perhaps —

The door opened, Sean pushing it with his

214

foot, a cup of coffee in each hand and a pack of crisps between his teeth. Out of instinct, Groves minimised the window. But even as he did, he recognised the guilty impulse that had made him do it, and the realisation tore at him inside. More than anything, he wanted to find the people responsible for Jamie's abduction. But if he had a personal connection to the case, he would have to step aside; he would be *made* to. If anything came to trial, they couldn't risk the appearance of bias or impropriety. He wasn't going to be able to hide from that just by minimising a window.

As Sean put the coffee down beside him, he opened the window again.

'You started without me,' Sean said glumly.

Groves gave him a sad smile. The wrench he felt inside himself was almost impossible to bear, but he was a good man, a good detective, and he knew it was the right thing to do. He tried to tell himself that it was a minor loss in the grand scheme of things. He'd survived larger.

'Yes.' He gestured at the screen. It hurt. It hurt badly. 'And I think you're going to be finishing without me.'

Mark

The Devil

When I got back to the department, I saw there were a few updates from the investigation, but I went straight through to Pete's office to debrief him on my latest interview with Charlie Matheson.

It was a precarious situation to deal with. While she remained a victim, and had clearly been through a great deal, there was no denying that we now had to consider her a far more unreliable witness than before. There was something she wasn't telling us. At least to some extent, she was cooperating with the people we were trying to find.

As I explained all this to Pete, the frown on his face deepened. It reached the point where he almost seemed to be in physical pain at what I was telling him.

'She's been lying to us?'

'No,' I said. 'Not lying. I think everything she's told us so far has been true — or true in her own mind, at least. To begin with, I think she was confused, maybe as a side effect of any drugs they used on her. That's why she asked for mercy at first, rather than Mercer. But she's clearer about things now.'

'And not telling us everything.'

'That's right. She's choosing to tell us what

she's been allowed to tell us by the people who took her. She's terrified of one man in particular. But she also wants to do what she's been told. She wants to go back there.'

'Stockholm syndrome,' Pete said.

'Possibly. I think there's something else, but I don't know what. Regardless, she's not going to tell us anything she's not allowed to, not without Mercer there.'

'And what is she not telling us?'

'The sins that she's wearing.' I explained what Charlie had told me about the reasons behind the scarring. 'It's connected to where she was on the day of her accident. But again, she won't tell anyone but Mercer about it.'

'Christ. I want an officer stationed at the hospital. Don't worry — I'll sort that one out.'

'It gets worse.'

'It can't.'

I took a deep breath and told him about Charlie's brief description of the man who had cut her face. While what had been done to her was horrible enough, it was what she'd called him that bothered me most now.

'She said he was the Devil,' I said. 'That's what the man told her. She was dead and in Hell, and he was the Devil.'

Pete was silent.

Then: 'Shit.'

I nodded. Charlie had been told to ask for Mercer, and there had to be a reason for that — most likely a connection to a past case. The 50/50 Killer had always worn a devil mask during his attacks. Even though the man was dead — killed a year and a half ago — and Charlie had described the Devil as an old man without a mask, there was an obvious connection, although not one either of us wanted to contemplate. The wounds from that case had barely healed. Reopening them was going to hurt. For Mercer, in particular, it could be catastrophic.

'Shit,' Pete said again.

'But then it might not be that. There are some discrepancies there, I think, and I want to look at the case again. At *all* Mercer's cases, in fact.' Pete looked so distracted that I wanted to emphasise the fact. 'Because the 50/50 Killer is dead. The case is closed. It might be something else.'

'So check. That's the priority.'

I nodded. 'I'll get on to it. We already know that Matheson has never crossed paths with us before. But I can work through some of the old cases, see if anything leaps out.'

'Yes.' Pete ran his hand through his hair. 'And then there's the victim at the accident scene. We need to identify her.'

'Priority number two.' I nodded. 'I know.'

★   ★   ★

I confess: I put it off slightly. Back in my office, I worked quickly through the various updates that had arrived in my tray first.

There was a fresh list of hospitals. Two thirds of them were crossed out now, representing the rapidly diminishing possibility that Charlie was simply a missing patient. She wasn't; I knew that deep down.

The door-to-doors at the flats had turned up nothing. Nobody remembered seeing Charlie being dropped off, or the vehicle that might have brought her there. A woman who had been in the crowd at the grocery when she was found had come forward, but couldn't tell us anything useful.

Priority number one, then.

I couldn't put it off any longer. I decided to go crazy, loading up every single investigation Mercer had been involved in for the eight years prior to his departure from the department, and working methodically through them.

There was no obvious connection in any of them. While looking at them collectively, though, it was immediately apparent that one case had dominated the latter years of Mercer's long career. The 50/50 Killer investigation hung suspended through them, like a dirty black branch frozen in clear ice. Its tendrils seemed to touch the other cases: ever present; always active. It was there in the period of absence Mercer had taken from work following his breakdown, and it was there again after his return, eventually providing the bookend that finally destroyed his career.

However unhealthy writing a book about it might be, I understood why it continued to haunt him, and he couldn't let it go.

I scanned through the file.

It was impossible to read it all: with all the forensic reports, interviews, statements, photographs and footage, there were over two thousand separate records in the file. The process reminded me of my first day when, new to the team, I'd needed to familiarise myself with the main details quickly. They came back easily again now. Even after a year and a half, my memories of the investigation remained as sharp as the words on the screen.

I loaded up the section on the murder of a man named Kevin Simpson. On my first day, I'd overslept, and finally met the team at Simpson's house, where he had been found burned to death in his own bathtub. He was the latest — but not the last — victim of the 50/50 Killer. I learned that the murderer spent months following and studying the couples he abducted and tortured. He was patient and methodical, learning the secrets of their relationship so that he could tease out the weaker strands, weathering and cutting them, eventually forcing one of the couple to betray the other.

I opened one of the photographs of the spiderwebs.

A normal person embarking upon such a study of others might have taken notes, keeping pages of details about his targets, but the 50/50 Killer had an entirely different way of visualising the information he gathered. On the wall in Kevin Simpson's study — and, I learned later, the homes of all of his victims — he had drawn an intricate spiderweb pattern. At first glance, the designs all seemed random, and yet many of the lines had small checks over them, as though they had been crossed out, one by one, severing the supporting structure of the web itself. Later, we came to understand that this was how the 50/50

Killer visualised the relationships he tested, and that the checks represented the manipulation and games he inflicted upon the couple. One strand at a time, he dissected and severed the love between them.

I skipped to the end of the file. The 50/50 Killer had died from head injuries just after dawn on 4 December 2013. Those injuries had occurred outside the house of John and Eileen Mercer.

Is this case the connection to him now?

There was no way to be sure. We had never discovered the killer's true identity, and the official investigation had died with him. The only real links between it and Charlie Matheson now were the mention of the Devil and the patience required in both cases, and neither was conclusive. And there was another problem too — the discrepancy I'd mentioned to Pete.

I opened up the provisional timetable I'd started the other night and amended it.

Provisional timeline
3 August 2013 Charlie Matheson's car crash
4 December 2013 Death of the 50/50 Killer
25 July 2015 Charlie Matheson reappears

Charlie had been abducted *before* the 50/50 case had concluded, which meant that whatever was happening here had started before that particular investigation came to such a dramatic end.

I stared at the screen for a little longer, then closed down the timeline and the case files I still

221

had open. For the moment, I didn't know how to pursue it.

The next thing was priority number two — the victim who had died in Charlie Matheson's place on 3 August two years earlier. *You need to go back at least two years*, Mercer had said. *Possibly even further.* I'd go one better than that, I decided, pulling all the missing persons reports since the beginning of 2010, and then beginning to sort and work through the hundreds that arrived on screen.

It was a good job I did. Because hidden way back in the spring of 2010, I found myself staring at the photograph of woman who looked a lot like Charlie Matheson.

A woman who had never been found.

Mark

Things nobody else could see

'The hardest part is not knowing,' Mavis Lawrence said.

'Yes,' I said. 'I understand that.'

She was sitting across from me in an armchair in the front room of her house: a small, fragile figure with her knees pressed together and her body bent slightly forward. Her husband, Harold, was standing beside her, clearly trying to appear strong and full of resolve. Stoical. He was failing slightly on that front, I thought. Dressed in old suit trousers, with his white shirt slightly untucked, he seemed hesitant more than anything, as though he wanted to reach out to his wife but didn't know quite how any more. It looked like Mavis was hunched over something in her lap, a parcel of grief, and he no longer understood how to deal with it.

'Well.' He settled for touching her shoulder gently. 'I think we do know, don't we? Deep down.'

'Not for sure. Not until she's found.'

He took his hand away and walked over to the oak cabinet that rested along one wall of the room. There were trinkets on it — porcelain thimbles and bells; painted plates angled on rests — along with a handful of carefully framed photographs. Some were obviously of their

223

missing daughter, Rebecca.

Mavis looked up at me.

'You *haven't* found her, have you?'

I was struck by the amount of hope in her voice, especially because it was obvious that the answer she wanted to hear was *no*. Her husband had been right: deep down, Mavis knew that the only way her daughter would be found would be dead. Until that day, Rebecca would continue to exist in a kind of quantum state, neither dead nor alive, and Mavis could allow herself to believe.

I chose my words carefully.

'There have been no significant advances in the investigation into your daughter's disappearance. What I can say is that the details surrounding it might have a bearing on a current investigation. At the moment, I'm not at liberty to reveal how.'

'Oh God. You've found someone, haven't you?'

'No,' I said. 'We haven't.'

While not strictly true, I could tell that Mavis was visualising shallow graves in forests, unidentified remains, and that was a world away from what we had.

It made me feel bad for the couple again, because what actual news would I ever be able to bring them? They had both spent the last few years expecting to hear the worst. That would be awful enough, but at least if they had their daughter's body, they could bury her and gain whatever sense of closure that might allow. But if it turned out that Rebecca Lawrence was the young woman who had died in Charlie Matheson's place, they wouldn't even have that. The body had been cremated two years ago, the ashes scattered in a place that would hold no resonance for them. We might never even know for certain if it had been her in that crash, just take a guess at the probability. How could that ever be enough for them? The not knowing would continue for ever. There would always be the slightest of possibilities remaining to fuel the fantasy: to keep them both chained in place, as they were now.

'I know it might be painful,' I said, 'but I was hoping you could talk me through what happened to Rebecca. The day she disappeared. The time beforehand.'

'I . . . I don't like to think about it.'

'I understand.'

Mavis didn't say anything more. After a moment, I looked across the room at Harold, who continued watching his wife for a few seconds before turning to me.

'Let's go through to the kitchen, Detective.'

* ★ *

I sat down at the table in the kitchen, and watched as Harold Lawrence made coffee. My initial impressions of him had been slightly wrong, I thought. His wife might nurse her grief more openly, but that didn't mean he'd abandoned his own. It was there in the stoop of his shoulders and his weary gait: the sense that he was weighed down by things nobody else

225

could see, and he didn't know what else to do except carry them.

'I'm sorry about my wife.' He had his back to me, and I could see his bony shoulder blades against his shirt as he poured our drinks. They were so pronounced that it looked as though he'd once had wings. 'Mavis has good days and bad days.'

'There's nothing to apologise for.'

'Sometimes it's like things used to be. And for a time we can both pretend. But it never lasts. It's always there really. It comes back again. You catch yourself pretending, and then suddenly there it is.'

'I understand.' I hesitated. 'I lost someone once too.'

Harold put my coffee down and looked at me. 'Yes?'

'In different circumstances. She drowned. I always knew she was dead, but her body was never found.'

'Do you ever wonder . . . ?'

'If she might be alive somewhere?' I shook my head. A slight lie, but not really. 'I never believed that. I suppose it's something I could never know for sure, but I always chose to go with the most likely option.'

'Me too. Mavis . . . not so much. Maybe it's a male thing.'

'I don't know.'

'Well. I'm sorry for your loss.'

I smiled sadly. 'It was a long time ago now.'

How do you measure a long time, though? If I put my ear to my memories, I could still hear the sea. But it had become increasingly hard to recall images of Lise herself: her face; her mannerisms; the good times we'd shared. Many of the most important things had faded. Maybe in the end that was how you measured it. Not in months or years, but in the clarity of your memories.

Harold eased himself down opposite me. Despite his thin frame, the chair creaked slightly beneath him. It was a cheap set. While the living room seemed well kept, it was considerably messier in here. I got the feeling that nothing in the house had been replaced in a while, and maybe the stuff back through there had just weathered the years better.

'Thank you for the coffee.'

He nodded, running his hands around his own cup.

'It's interesting what you said,' he told me. 'That you lost someone. It's a strange word. We use it for when people die, but it's not quite right, is it? When you lose something, it implies that you might find it again. That you might get it back.'

'That's true.'

Harold smiled. 'And when you've lost something, it's always in the last place you look. My father used to say that as a joke when I was a boy. But with people, there's never a last place to look, is there? Unless you're a religious man, Detective?'

'I'm not.'

'Neither am I. How could I be religious now? I wouldn't want to meet the God that took my daughter away from me. But I don't expect to find Rebecca again anyway. She's not lost. She's gone for ever.'

'Can you tell me what happened?' Where possible, I always wanted to hear the story from a primary source. 'And about Rebecca in general too, if you don't mind.'

'No, I don't mind.'

He went through it all in detail, and I was glad. Maybe other officers wouldn't have wanted to hear so much about Rebecca herself, preferring to concentrate on the facts of her disappearance, but I wanted a good picture of this young woman. Not just the circumstances, but who she *was*. Because just as I was sure there was a reason why the people behind this had targeted Charlie Matheson, I was betting there would be a reason why they'd chosen Rebecca too. If she'd been held for three whole years before the accident, I doubted very much that her abduction had been simply down to a physical resemblance to Charlie.

For a grieving parent, Harold was remarkably candid about the relationship they'd had with their daughter. Rebecca was lovely when she was younger, he said, but grew distant in her teens, and it was a distance they never really managed to recover. They'd encouraged her quietly, always aware that pushing her in any direction would mean she'd push back in the opposite one.

'Most kids leave the nest eventually,' Harold told me. 'With Becky, it seemed to happen much sooner. In her head, anyway.'

She did fine at school, but had few friends, and those she did connect with were not always the best influence on her. He couldn't remember any names, but it was obvious he hadn't approved. It was the usual teenage stuff, though, and it hadn't affected her too badly; her grades were good enough that she'd secured a place at university to study child psychology. But she'd dropped out in her first year and returned home. After a brief period of soul-searching, she had got a job at a local nursery.

'She was good with kids,' Harold said. 'She seemed happy.'

'Did she stick with that?'

'More or less. She moved around a bit. Different places. But she took courses and got qualifications.' By now, I'd finished my coffee, and his must surely have gone cold, but he continued to sip at it slowly. 'She stayed in the profession. She was working at a nursery when she went missing.'

'Can you remember the name?'

'Cherubs, I think.' He shook his head. 'I'm sorry. It's been such a long time.'

'That's okay.' It would be in the files, I was sure. 'How did she seem in herself? Before she went missing?'

He took a deep breath.

'I don't really know.'

The truth, he explained, was that Rebecca had moved beyond independence by then, to a position where she seemed to be actively pushing her parents away from her life and keeping them at a distance. They spoke on the phone intermittently — once a week at most — and they rarely saw her. Despite their best efforts, they knew little about her life beyond the tiniest parcels of information they managed to extract from her in conversation. They didn't even know if she was seeing someone.

'But she seemed happy.' He shrugged helplessly. 'That's all I can tell you. The last time we spoke, she seemed fine. Same old Becky. Resilient and steadfast. We were never able to wear her down enough to get past the barricades.'

It was his turn to smile sadly at that, looking down at his hands, still encircling the coffee mug. It seemed clear enough to me that in Harold's mind at least, the pair of them had lost Rebecca a long time before she disappeared.

'We always called her on Monday evenings,' he said. 'Mavis did, I mean. It was usually the best time to catch her, and I guess we'd fallen into a kind of routine with it.'

Another element of the arms race between parents and daughter: a kind of truce that they'd all agreed to without speaking it out loud. But on this occasion, the phone rang out. They had tried again later, with the same result.

'We just sent an email at first. Sorry to miss you; hope everything's okay. That kind of thing. And there was no reply, which wasn't like Becky at all; she'd normally manage to send a quick message at least. We did have a spare key for her flat, so on the Saturday, Mavis was getting worried and I drove us over. We knocked — obviously — and there was no answer. So we let ourselves in.'

What they had discovered inside was a

perfectly normal scene. The flat was tidy and well kept, the kitchen was clean, and there were no signs of a disturbance. On a glass coffee table in the front room, they found a note, apparently written by Rebecca. It explained that she was fed up with her current life in the city and wanted to start afresh where nobody knew who she was, severing ties completely with her old life and beginning something new. Perhaps she would be in touch, but she couldn't guarantee it; she needed to find out who she really was, and to do that she needed to leave and be on her own for a time. Possibly for ever. There were also suggestions that she felt stifled by Harold and Mavis and found their attentions oppressive.

'That was the hardest thing to read,' he told me. 'I know it hit Mavis badly. For a long time she felt like she'd driven Becky away. She blamed herself. And I think for a while I blamed Becky for that. It was cruel. Unnecessary. But that was when I still thought the note was genuine.'

Even so, they had still reported their daughter as missing. The police had taken samples of Rebecca's handwriting and concluded that it was likely she really had written the letter. Her bedroom had been left tidy, but clothes had clearly been taken, along with a few other valuables — a laptop; a phone and charger. Basic things. It was discovered that on the Monday, she'd withdrawn almost all the savings from her bank account — a relatively paltry sum of less than two hundred pounds — and that the account hadn't been touched since. Whatever had happened to her, and whether she was alive or dead, Rebecca Lawrence had been off grid ever since that day.

I said, 'You don't think the note was genuine now?'

'Who knows for sure?' Harold shrugged, as though it made no difference any more. 'Maybe it was, and she really did mean to start again somewhere else. But how likely is that? With that much money? How can that be possible?'

I didn't think it was.

'She didn't have friends elsewhere?'

'No. And that was all checked, all gone through.'

'It would certainly be hard for someone to disappear in those circumstances,' I said.

'Exactly. So maybe something happened to her afterwards, and that's why we've not heard from her. But that's not what I think.' He looked down at his hands. 'I think she was forced to write that message. I think someone else took her things, along with her, and withdrew that money. And I think she was dead long before we went to her flat. That's what I think these days, Detective.'

I nodded slowly. In his position, I might well have come to exactly the same tentative conclusions. Of course, assuming Rebecca had been the real victim in the car crash two years ago, that wasn't the case. Whoever had taken her had kept her for three years before she died.

Harold was still looking at me. He looked helpless now.

'What I don't understand,' he said, 'is *why*.'

Outside the house afterwards, I took a deep

breath, trying to work out the repercussions of what had happened to Rebecca Lawrence. My thoughts were interrupted by my mobile buzzing once in my pocket. A text message.

And when I took the phone out and read it, I stopped thinking about Rebecca Lawrence entirely as panic set in.

Sasha was in hospital.

Groves

The homeless boy

Groves figured the odds of finding the homeless boy were pretty good. It seemed a reasonable guess that he was based in the city centre, and he was unlikely to have moved on in the past twenty-four hours. With the burns and scarring, he was distinctive enough that people would remember him. So late afternoon, after checking the phone for messages once more, he set out to find him.

Back at the department, Sean was continuing the investigation into Edward Leland's murder. Groves had already talked to DCI Reeves and removed himself from the case. There were other things for him to do. And yet, after pottering around with them for a while, he had decided on this course of action instead. He might not be able to be involved in the case in his capacity as a detective, but there was nothing to stop him pursuing it from a different angle.

The first place he tried was St John's Crypt.

The Crypt was the basement of the city's main church, which had been converted into a soup kitchen for the homeless. It was run entirely by volunteers, and given that their customers had frequent low-level run-ins with the police, the department had a working relationship with the staff. Groves had personally dropped people off there himself on a few occasions. While a police presence was never exactly welcome, it was always tolerated, and the workers helped them out when they could. Groves was confident that if he could spin his search for the boy named Carl into something positive, someone there would be prepared to talk to him.

He pushed open the heavy oak doors and entered the Crypt, struck immediately by the smell of the steaming pots of vegetable broth on the far counter, and the sweet, sickly aroma of wine and unwashed skin that hung constantly in the air. The sounds echoed: the clattering of metal pans; the sniffs and murmurs. At this time of day, there were only a handful of people in. Two homeless people were seated at the far end, little more than enormous bundles of layered, greasy clothes and wild hair. The guy behind the counter was wiry and middle-aged. Taking in his pale, pockmarked face and the thin streaks of beard, Groves wondered how long he'd been on the working side of the counter rather than queuing up on this side. It often worked that way here.

'Yeah,' the man said. 'I know him. Carl.'

He'd barely even looked at the badge Groves offered. He gave the impression of being some-one who'd seen it all before and didn't much want to see it again.

Groves put his wallet away.

'Are you sure?'

'Yeah, little guy. With the burns down one side of his face?' He gestured vaguely. 'Looks a lot younger than he is. I know him.'

'That sounds right. Do you know his surname?'

'Thompson or something. Timpson maybe.' He shrugged. *Why would it matter to me?* 'Didn't see him around for a while, but the last couple of weeks, he's been back in. What are you looking for him for?'

'There was an assault in town last night. We got it on camera, and it was pretty vicious. Bunch of skinhead types kicking off on someone.' It was the best he'd been able to come up with. 'We picked them up straight away, but we lost the victim. Want to make sure he's all right, first and foremost, but also see if he can help us with the charges.'

That got Groves a suspicious look.

'Doesn't sound much like any police I ever knew.'

'We're not all the same. Has Carl been in today?'

'Nah. He's usually in much later on. Spends the day underground. Evenings, he begs around the station, I think.'

Groves nodded.

'Underground where?'

'The arches below the station.' The man shrugged again. 'Close to his *place of work*, you know?'

★ ★ ★

Back at the car, Groves used his tablet to log in to the police database and search through the files for a Carl Thompson or Timpson. Given his

236

behaviour, he was confident he would be in there somewhere. And there he was, under Thompson.

Groves worked through the file. Carl Thompson had been arrested a number of times. There were drug offences and convictions for shoplifting. On one occasion he'd walked into a Chinese restaurant, eaten a five-course banquet with wine, and only revealed at the end that he had no means of paying for it. He was twenty-three. There was — unsurprisingly — no mention of military service.

Which begged the question: where had he got the scars?

Groves kept searching back. There was a wealth of detail at the beginning of the file covering Carl Thompson's upbringing: a summary prepared by a social worker as mitigation for an offence he'd committed. He'd been taken away from his parents at the age of two, and spent the following years ricocheting from one foster home to another. There were accusations of abuse made against people in a number of the places he'd stayed in, although none of it was proved. Later, Thompson became disruptive at school, and was diagnosed with learning difficulties that were not adequately addressed. By the age of twelve, he had been cautioned several times for drinking and drug use in public places. But it was not those offences that the mitigation had been prepared for.

Groves felt something fall away inside as he read through. When he was thirteen, Thompson had been arrested in the women's changing room of the council swimming pool. The mother of a five-year-old girl had allowed the child to get changed by herself — a treat for her, acting grown-up. Thompson slipped in unnoticed, and was caught by a member of staff masturbating a short distance from the child. He had been crying as he did it.

Because of both his age and the distressed state he was in, he escaped an actual custodial sentence, but was hospitalised for a short time, then referred for counselling upon release. He was placed on the sex offenders register for a period of two years, and lived on licence for that time. He wasn't charged with any further sexual offences, but the file detailed plenty of drug-related offences from his late teens onwards. Nothing for the last year or so, though, which seemed strange. Groves remembered what the man at the soup kitchen had told him: *Didn't see him around for a while.*

So where had he been?

Groves looked away from the screen for a moment, thinking.

He had to check something. There was no reason for it to be there, but for some reason he still expected to find it. He went through Thompson's drugs convictions one by one, the sinking feeling intensifying, until there it was again.

SIMON CHADWICK.

The arrest had been made in similar circumstances to Edward Leland's, except this time the pair had been caught in possession of heroin in a car park.

Oh God.

Very quickly Groves scanned through the rest of Thompson's file. There was no mention of Edward Leland, and he didn't remember seeing Thompson's name on the list he'd started to compile that morning.

But the connection was there. Both Leland and Thompson had — or were at least suspected to have — child-related offences in their history. Both had convictions for drugs. Both were known associates of Simon Chadwick.

What was going on here?

Groves stared at the screen, remembering how Thompson had seemed last night. The scars. How frightened and desperate he'd appeared. The way it had felt like he'd been acting on orders by giving Groves the mobile phone, with its message about his son.

And what he'd said, of course.

I've been through hell, sir.

★   ★   ★

He checked the train station concourse first of all, asking around a few of the staff, but nobody had seen Carl Thompson that day. A couple of the guards recognised him from the description, but he wasn't hanging around the two entrances to the station, or the beer garden out back of the single pub.

So. It was time to head into the arches.

Groves had been down there a few times years back, mostly to deal with shoplifters who had run off and hidden, although he knew the darker stretches were frequented by the homeless and the occasional prostitute and punter. The entrance was below an underpass. You turned right, passed through a cave of small retail units, most of them craft shops and cafés, until finally you reached a warren of walkways and tunnels. They were nominally closed to the public but were easy enough to access via the various missing service doors. Nobody cared.

He made his way between the shops now. In the time since his last visit, many of them had closed and been boarded up. The few places still open were empty; the place was dying, really. It was one of the older areas of the city, where the rails overlaid the river, and the sporadic attempts to commercialise it anew rarely lasted long. There was nobody around to pay him any attention as he reached the far end and walked through an empty doorway into the depths.

A minute or so in, he began to find them: the homeless, camped out in the thin spaces below the dark arches. Some were clustered together in pairs, but most were alone, staking out their hard-fought patches. A few of them had small fires going, made from litter, old newspaper, maybe even the dried-out detritus the river had left at the lower points of the passages. The ones who were awake eyed him silently as he approached them.

'I'm looking for Carl Thompson. The boy with the burns.'

Shrugs, for the most part. One man started singing at him: a booming operatic sound, devoid of words, that echoed after Groves as he walked away. A couple seemed to know who he was talking about, jutting scabbed chins to tell him to keep going. He moved on. The dark passageways were disorientating. Mentally he unfurled a ball of wool behind him.

Out on to a metal walkway. The river was to the side of him now: thundering away beyond a stone wall studded with spitting pipes. As another rumble passed overhead, he thought how strange it was that the homeless lived here. Above, the tracks spread out from the railway station like a frayed grey bow on the land, while all around down here was the sound of the river constantly tumbling past. Everything around them was moving elsewhere, while they were trapped underground at the nexus of it all, squatting and stagnant.

What are you doing here, David?

'I'm looking for Carl Thompson. The boy with the burns.'

Why, though? It was becoming increasingly clear to him that both Thompson and Leland were connected to the abduction of his son — or at least that he was meant to *think* they were. That meant he should turn this over to Sean, just as he had the Leland case, but something kept him moving. He kept remembering the phone call from last night. Memories of Jamie flickered in his head, the little boy running away, forcing him to chase after him. It was his job to do so. His responsibility.

'I'm looking for Carl Thompson. The boy with the burns.'

'Down there.'

The woman's eyes were bleary and sad. She

might have been any age, but he guessed she was about fifty, with lank black hair plastered to her skull and wrinkles everywhere.

'You know him?'

'Down there.' She indicated another service door in the wall, rusted and hanging off its hinges. 'That's his. He'll be there.'

'Thanks.'

Groves felt her gaze following him as he moved away from her towards the old door. There was just enough space to squeeze around the fractured metal, and then he was in another corridor, this one tighter and shorter than the others, with two-metre-deep arches along the right-hand side. The lights here had been placed above the arches, so that the interiors were dark and shadowy. The first two were empty, but it was obvious that someone was lying in the furthest.

As Groves approached, he smelled the remains of Carl Thompson's fire — old ash and burned wood — and then something altogether worse. A cold draught through a vent in the wall was wafting the stench out into the small corridor. He stopped at the edge of the last arch, staring down, then flicked on his torch.

The charred wood and snatches of old paper reminded him of the mess on Angela Morris' barbecue. The ash glittered slightly. And there was Carl Thompson. He was lying dead, with the side of his face in the debris of his fire. *I've been through hell, sir.* If that were true, there was something peaceful about him now. It was as though those long-gone flames had been the most natural place in the world for him to be pressed, finally, to sleep.

Groves stared down at the dead boy for a handful of seconds in which he could hardly breathe. Two people potentially linked to his son's abduction. Two people dead. A phone in his pocket that connected him to Carl Thompson, on which he had received a message about Jamie. Someone making contact. *Involving* him.

What is happening here?

He needed to know. The right thing to do — the sensible thing — was to call this in immediately: turn it over; explain everything. But the weight of the phone in his pocket distracted him. He wanted to take it out now and check for another message, but there would be no signal down here. There *would* be a message, though. *God will be with you.* There was no rational reason for thinking it, but Groves was sure that whoever was behind all this knew he was here and had seen what had been done.

Jamie.

The memory of his little boy had stopped running from him now, and the image burned brightly in his mind: Jamie, standing in the trousers and T-shirt he'd worn on that last morning, squinting in the sun, waving tentatively at his father. Groves wanted so badly to reach into his own thoughts and embrace the boy, and the fact that he couldn't caused an ache deep inside him. While he couldn't leave Thompson lying here dead like this, he also knew he couldn't bring himself to give the phone up.

Not yet.

Back out of the arches, keeping away from any CCTV, Groves checked the mobile. No messages. No voicemail.

There would be soon, though. He was sure of that.

Forgive me, he thought.

He called the Thompson scene in anonymously.

Merritt

The Devil's house

It stood on top of a hill, jutting up from the land like a broken tooth. Merritt had no idea how old it was, but doubted it was Christian in origin. It had been since, of course, but even those days were long past. The interior was a rough cross shape, with just enough space to seat the few isolated people who must have lived nearby in previous centuries. At one side, a staircase led down to an old crypt. It was there that the renovations had been made.

The tunnels had been widened and extended over the years, presumably by similarly recruited independent contractors. Additional rooms and staircases and corridors had been added, some of them reaching all the way to the open air on the far side of the hill. The whole structure had electricity and running water, along with an elaborate system of security cameras and speakers. Merritt parked at the base. Looking at the hill in front of him, it was impossible not to imagine it as a hornets' nest. Sometimes he even imagined he could hear it buzzing.

He walked up the winding path to the arched oak door, which had been left slightly ajar. It creaked as he pushed it further open and stepped inside.

The Devil's house.

As always, it felt far colder in here than it did outside. The stone floor and walls were dusty, and there was an odd rush to the air, as though a breeze was being generated within the walls, a strange kind of spirit.

The door to the cellar was open. Merritt went down the stone staircase, then through another door at the far end of the crypt into the warren of tunnels beyond. The stone gradually gave way to something more organic: a compressed mass of earth and timber and rock. It began to feel to Merritt as though he was moving through the veins of something living. Struts held a makeshift ceiling in place, and the tunnels were illuminated by old lights on the walls, encased in plastic. He'd never been claustrophobic, but the nerves jangled slightly here. While he had been assured it was safe and stable, the tunnel system always felt ramshackle and dangerous.

It wasn't long before he reached the cells. It was difficult to think of them as rooms, as they seemed to grow off the sides of the tunnels like bulbs in the earth, none of their inner edges entirely straight or flat. Some were larger than others, with jagged edges where the earth must have given way, but most were barely large enough to lie comfortably in. The entrances were secured with metal doors, the earth around them reinforced — not that any of the prisoners here were inclined to attempt escape. Within a week of entering this place, most were already too weak and broken to consider it.

Hell wasn't full right now. But even so, several of the cells Merritt passed were occupied.

Peering through the open slots in the doors, he recognised most of the occupants. After all, it was him and his shifting team that had brought them here. Most of them were insane by now. He paid them little attention.

There was one, though, who intrigued him more, and he stopped outside the man's cell now. It was the smallest room of all, and the man inside sat cross-legged against one wall while a television played his sins back at him barely a metre and a half away. The light flickered over his face, which — uniquely down here — was uninjured. Unlike his fellow prisoners, this man hadn't been hurt by the Devil. Not yet. But after all this time alone down here, he was probably as mad as any of them.

Merritt knew what the man had done in real life: why he was here, and what was in store for him. Looking through the hatch at him now, he felt an unfamiliar emotion, one he'd rarely had time for in the past.

He felt genuine pity for the man in the cell.

But that evaporated as he felt a presence a little way down the corridor from him. He turned his head to make sure, registered the dark shape standing metres away, then looked away quickly, down at the ground. He was a loyal employee, and there were rules to follow. The Devil didn't like to be looked at.

Merritt waited as the old man slowly approached. He had never been predisposed to fear, but these encounters in the tight little corridors always gave him a taste of it.

'It's finished,' the old man said.

He was holding something out. Without looking up, Merritt took the piece of paper that was being offered to him.

'Yes, sir.'

But the Devil was already retreating into the darkness. Merritt looked down at the paper, and the designs that had been drawn on it. A map of sins. A severing of ways.

He nodded to himself. He always carried a gun, concealed beneath his suit jacket. It was second nature to him now. Tonight, he was going to need a knife as well.

Mark

The truth of it

Sasha was waiting for me in the hospital reception, and was clearly extremely pissed off with everything that had happened. She almost walked straight past me when I arrived, eager to find the car and get what was to her clearly an embarrassing experience over with as quickly as possible. If she'd had her own car with her, I was sure she'd have driven herself. As it was, I was half surprised she'd contacted me at all, and not just set off stubbornly on foot.

'Absolute bullshit,' she told me as I drove.

'What happened?'

'I don't want to talk about it.'

I glanced to one side. She was resting her head on her hand, leaning against the passenger window, staring straight ahead. Whatever had happened, she was furious with herself.

For my part, I was just glad that, anger aside, she seemed okay. The text message I'd received outside the Lawrences' house had sent my heart racing. Panic had set in immediately. Why was she at the hospital? What the fuck had happened? I knew how dangerous her job could be, and I'd always been afraid that she'd get hurt somehow. Even though she'd been able to text me, I'd automatically assumed the worst. While I still didn't know what had happened, there was at least some relief in the fact that she appeared unharmed. But the adrenalin remained in my system. I pictured having to drive home with an empty passenger seat beside me, and my heart sank.

Thank God you're okay.

Because for a moment there . . .

I fought down the panic and tried to sound casual.

'What was the absolute bullshit, then?'

'Sending me there.' Sasha turned around and glared behind us, even though the hospital was out of sight by now. 'I told my boss I was fine, but blah blah. Possible concussion.' She stared ahead again, still fuming. 'He made me look like an idiot in front of everyone. Know how many other members of the team got sent to the hospital today with possible concussion?'

'No.'

'None. It's hard enough being a woman on that team. There's this constant feeling that you're second best.' She pulled a face, then shook her head. 'It's bad enough without this kind of shit.'

'You're not second best.'

She didn't reply.

I did understand, because I knew how much Sasha's career mattered to her. She prided herself on being good at her job, and she was, but the door teams were macho environments at the best of times, and perhaps even more insular and contained than teams like ours. You needed the respect of your colleagues; they needed to know they could rely on you. I could imagine how much a mistake would bother her.

I turned the steering wheel slightly, trying to keep calm.

'Are you going to tell me what happened?'

'It was nothing.'

'It shouldn't take long, then.'

That got me a glare, one I pretended not to see, but after a few more seconds of silence, she sighed and started talking.

As she'd said, it was nothing really — or at least it should have been: a routine operation targeting premises above a licensed sex shop to the west of the city centre, which it was believed were being used as an illegal brothel by traffickers. Sasha had been one of the first three officers in, clearing rooms as they went. The place was actually on two levels, with a reception room for the clientele on the first floor, and bedrooms on the second. No problems in reception, but Sasha had been the first officer into one of the upstairs bedrooms, where she'd found a girl cowering on the bed. She was barely into her teens, and clearly terrified, and without thinking, Sasha had taken a protective step towards her, wanting her to at least see a woman before the other officers barrelled in. She hadn't been thinking.

'Didn't clear the corner,' she said. 'Stupid mistake. *Rookie* mistake. I didn't realise there was a client in the room.'

A big guy, too, by the sound of things. He'd been waiting against the wall, and after Sasha had stepped into the room, he'd barged her out of the way and tried to head downstairs. The

251

shove had sent her sprawling on to the floor, and she'd banged her head on the wooden edge of the bed.

'I saw stars,' she said. 'For about *three seconds*. That's it. But I hadn't had the chance to get up again before Killingbeck rugby-tackled the guy straight back into the room and saw me sprawled out there.'

She shook her head again. From what she'd said, I wasn't convinced her boss insisting on a hospital check-up had been entirely unreasonable. At the same time, I didn't think the decision to send her to hospital was the real source of her annoyance so much as the embarrassment of making a mistake in the first place. A *rookie* mistake at that. Maybe it hadn't been serious this time, but in the line of work she did, a rookie mistake could get people killed.

We drove home in silence. I kept replaying the scenario in my mind, each time imagining it slightly worse than before. Sasha turning her head at the last moment so it was her temple that struck the bed frame, fracturing her skull; the client coming at her with a knife rather than his shoulder; someone more seriously involved in the operation, perhaps, who was prepared to defend it with a gun. I saw each situation vividly in my head, and in each case desperately wanted to be there to help, but was reduced to observing it passively.

Anything could have happened to her.

Anything still could.

The panic remained, and as we pulled into our drive, it was sharper than ever. She was fine, but she might not have been. That text message had been the most frightening thing I could remember in a long time, and while things hadn't turned out badly, they could have done.

'Well,' I forced myself to say, hoping the anxiety didn't come out in my voice. 'As bad as it was, it could have been worse, couldn't it?'

'Yes. And that's the problem.'

'I know.'

'I got distracted.' She looked at me. 'I got sloppy. And it could have been a lot worse.'

I couldn't read the expression on her face.

'So you have to learn from it,' I said.

Sasha continued to stare at me, thinking about something. Finally she looked away again, nodding to herself. Even though we were sitting as close together as before, it felt like she'd somehow taken a step away from me. I wanted to say something to pull her back, but I couldn't think of the words. *You'll never be second best to me,* I almost said. But given my behaviour recently. I was suddenly scared that she wouldn't believe me.

'You're right,' she said finally. Her tone was flat, empty. 'I can't afford to get distracted again.'

★ ★ ★

That night, for the first time in months, I had the dream again. But tonight it was different.

In the past, despite being a nightmare, there had been nothing overtly horrific about it. I was always just standing on the shoreline, staring out at a calm sea, the sky above speckled with gulls.

The sea was empty. Lise never featured at all, always conspicuous by her absence. The dream was about how she was no longer there.

Tonight, though, it truly was a nightmare. I was still standing on the beach, but the sea in front of me was dark and churning. The rolling waves formed angled lines of froth like the haphazard slices of a razor, and the sky above was heavy with blackening clouds. I was shivering with cold and screaming at the water.

Swim. Swim.

Because I could see her out there, even though the waves were too violent for a clear view. They kept tossing her up, then pushing her down: playing at killing her. But she was there, and somehow I could hear her too. She was screaming for help, but the words were torn apart by the wind, so that all I caught was the fractured sound of someone who knew they were dying.

And so I had to save her, the woman I loved.

I had to go back into the sea.

I stepped forward, up to my shins, but even this close to the shore the current threatened to pull me off my feet, and I froze. *Come on.* Except I couldn't. Only a minute ago, I had been out there, being thrown this way and that by the waves. I had gone under and swallowed water and come up coughing and choking. I had been convinced I was going to die. But I had got to shore, and my body refused to allow me to go back in. I was literally held in place, shaking with fear, reduced to screaming impotently at the sea as it killed my girlfriend.

Breathe, I thought. *Breathe.*

You'll be okay . . .

And then — just for a moment before she disappeared — I caught sight of her face amongst the black waves, and realised that it wasn't Lise out there at all, but Sasha.

I woke with a start, my heart beating hard in my chest, and lay very still for a time, trying to calm myself down. After a few minutes, I rolled carefully on to my side.

Tonight, as much as it had been a dream, it had also been a memory. That was what had happened, after all. I wouldn't have been able to save Lise anyway, as I wasn't a strong swimmer and had made it to the beach more by luck than anything else. Nevertheless, I had still stood there, helpless, and watched Lise drown. I had been too afraid — too weak — even to try. I had failed her.

Sasha was sleeping with her back to me. I watched the covers rising and falling, listening to the soft, slow sound of her breathing. I wanted to put my arm around her and press myself against her, but for some reason I didn't. I was thinking about the panic I'd felt when I'd picked her up from the hospital, and about the way I'd been recently. About the fact that while the wounds from Lise's death might have healed, for a long time they had hurt very badly indeed.

That's what's wrong with me, I thought eventually. *That's the truth of it. It's not that I don't love you. I love you more than anything.*

I'm just terrified of losing you too.

Dr Gordon Peters

Ghosts

Ghosts.

That was what it always made him think of.

Gordon Peters stood in the brightly illuminated bathroom, listening to the silence of the house below him. It was nearly midnight, and all the other lights were out; he was standing in the only pocket of brightness in the whole property. His mind's eye tracked along the dark hallway outside the bathroom, down the stairs to the entrance hall, with its old alarm system on the wall by the front door. It had been there when he bought the property, years ago now, although he had long since given up using it.

He counted the silent seconds. Almost dreading it.

The alarm sounded again. Two quick beeps: one high, the second lower in tone. It was the noise the front door made when someone opened or closed it.

And then silence again.

At some point over the past few years, the alarm had taken on a life of its own. It needed servicing, presumably, but he'd always been too distracted to bother. Easier by far to put up with it than go to the trouble of calling a tradesman in. The bell box on the outside of the house was similarly temperamental, and tended to screech and chatter to itself when the weather got too hot. But the door alarm was more disturbing. Anything could set it off. Sometimes he'd run the hot tap in the kitchen, and when he turned it off the alarm would sound. At other times it seemed to go off entirely randomly, occasionally even in the dead of night, like now.

It was just a glitch, of course, but it always made Peters think of ghosts: as though the sensor wasn't malfunctioning, but registering the passage into the house of people and things invisible to the naked eye. And always *coming in*, he thought to himself. Never leaving again. He had lived by himself for many years now, and yet he hadn't felt alone for a long time. Over time, the house had slowly filled up with ghosts . . .

Another beep. Quick and shrill in the dark house.

There were so many of them to arrive, weren't there? God help him, he had been responsible for more deaths and ruined lives over the years than he could count. Even if for most of them his involvement had been tangential, he knew there was little mitigation he could expect on that level. He remained culpable. From the vantage point of these advanced years, it was difficult to remember how it had all started, or why he had allowed himself to continue. The money, of course. There had been fear. And there had also been *awe*. Those latter feelings had never quite left him. But it was hard to recall now how quickly he'd felt trapped — entwined by the snakes of what was done — and also that, once upon a time, he'd been able to suppress the guilt. Now, it weighed so heavily on him it was hard to bear.

Peters stared at his face in the mirror of the bathroom cabinet, waiting for the alarm to sound again, for another ghost to arrive. You couldn't run forever from the repercussions of what you'd done; they always found you eventually. The light in here was harsh and unforgiving, and Peters could see the shape of his skull. His skin was pale and sweaty. How had he become this old? His whole life seemed to have slipped away behind him in minutes: a walk so familiar you forgot to notice the scenery. His face was wrinkled enough for him to look like one of *them*. The lines might have been drawn by time rather than cut in by hand, but what difference did that make? He could see a sin in each one regardless.

Another beep from downstairs.

There had been good done too, of course, and he tried to concentrate on that. The lives saved in his day job: there had been a handful of those. But lives saved didn't provide a counterbalance to the ones he'd helped to take. The world didn't run on that kind of calculus.

God help me, he thought, still staring into the hollow eyes of his own reflection. And even that was no good. If God existed, He had turned his back on Gordon Peters a long time ago. *Thou shalt not follow false idols.* But he had chosen to follow a different God, a self-made one, and he suspected that one wouldn't help him now either.

He listened, waiting for the next beep to come.

Silence now. Perhaps the house was full for tonight.

Peters' reflection swung away from him as he opened the medicine cabinet, retrieving the items he needed: the needles and packets; the misty plastic tubing. As he prepared the syringe, he knew he was taking too heavy a dose — that his hand had been altogether too heavy recently — but he just tapped the plastic, no longer caring.

To hell with it, he thought, then smiled to himself at the choice of words.

To hell with . . . them.

He pressed the plunger home.

⋆   ⋆   ⋆

When he woke in the middle of the night, Peters thought he must still be dreaming. His mother was standing at the foot of the bed, looking down at him. She was a pale grey figure in the darkness, dressed as he remembered her in childhood, just before she'd died and he'd been taken away, and everything had gone wrong. Before all the hospitals. She was far younger than he was now, and shimmered slightly in the air. The expression on her face was kind and sad.

I'm sorry, she mouthed.

He sat up, frightened now. 'What?'

I'm sorry for . . .

But he couldn't make out the rest from the way her mouth moved, and she seemed to realise it, and stopped. Instead, she reached out to him, with a hand that was only just there. Out of instinct, and a sudden childish desire — *Mum!* — he reached back, but he blinked just as they were about to touch, and she was gone, and he was alone in the room again.

He woke up properly then, his heart hammering in his chest. Too hard. His body, drawn taut and fragile by age and drugs, couldn't handle how fast and hard his heart was beating. The dream still felt real.

If I'm going to die, he thought, *why didn't you wait for me?*

It brought a memory of bitterness and resentment with it: a childhood feeling he hadn't experienced in longer than he could think.

A noise from downstairs.

He listened carefully.

A scratching noise. It was only faint, but the chill came immediately, and he found himself swinging his legs out from under the covers and rising uneasily to his feet. The effects of the drugs remained with him; he made his way around the bed on unsteady legs, pressing his hands against the walls for guidance. When he reached the bedroom door, he stepped out on to the dark landing.

No sound at all now. The drugs were just messing with him. Even so, Peters made his way downstairs, each one creaking slightly under his slender weight. In the entrance hall, he stared at the closed door to the front room. He reached out and rested his hand against the wood, ready to push it open.

Beep.

His heart leapt as the alarm sounded directly

behind him. He whipped round. The front door remained closed, but it felt *fuller* down here than it had a moment ago. The pitch-black air seemed to be coiling, trying to form a shape from the darkness. He turned back to the front-room door, blinking. *Enough.* He pushed it open, stepping inside, flicking the switch on the wall to the right.

And froze.

The man was standing in the centre of the room, dressed in a neat black suit and pointing a silenced gun directly at Peters' face. Peters swallowed, but it didn't quite work.

'Mr Merritt,' he said.

'Gordon.' Merritt nodded. 'Have a seat, please.'

The slightest gesture of the gun, and Peters saw the dining chair that Merritt had brought through into the room. He considered running, but knew it wouldn't make any difference. Even stone-cold sober he wouldn't have stood a chance, never mind as blurry as he was right now. And he was so tired of it all. Hadn't he known this day would come eventually? Like everyone, he'd just deferred thinking about it.

'I messed up,' he said. 'I know. Too big a dose.'

'Have a seat.'

Merritt's eyes were such a pale shade of blue that they seemed to bore into him. Peters did as he was told. Merritt began securing his arms and legs to the wood, then stepped back, considering him.

'You've been too loose for a while now, Gordon.'

'I know.'

'But you've done good work for us in the past. It's been so many years now, hasn't it?'

Peters nodded. 'As long as I can remember. It all catches up with you in the end.'

Merritt looked at him, then shook his head.

'And I don't dislike you. I never have. I have my instructions, but since you and I are the only ones who'll ever know what happens here, I'm going to give you a choice.'

Merritt showed him the piece of paper, with the designs that had been drawn on it. He should have been afraid, he supposed. Perhaps it was the drugs, but instead of fear, he felt almost ready for this. Merritt put the paper on the floor, then pulled out a knife. He held it up beside the gun.

'I can do the cutting before or after.'

It was an act of mercy, Peters realised. If he asked for it, Merritt would put him out of his misery before he started the cutting. If he didn't, he would do so afterwards. Both things would happen regardless, but at least one route would be painless.

Beep.

Peters' gaze flicked to the front-room door. Another ghost coming in. So many now. He deserved each of them and more. He looked back at Merritt, standing in front of him, and thought about the cutting and the killing. Both things would happen regardless. In the end, it was an easy choice to make.

'Do the cutting first,' he said.

Part Four

And They asked Her whether men were born with evil or good in their hearts, and She told Them this was so, but that circumstances would test that, and that the point of each Man's life was to settle the battle within and without himself.

Extract from the Cane Hill bible

Mark

Visualisation

I didn't sleep well after the nightmare, and ended up getting up early, just after five. I drank coffee and paced the kitchen, trying to work out what I was going to say to Sasha. It was obvious I needed to talk to her about what was really bothering me. This worry, this irrational *fear* — it was my problem to deal with. But I needed to at least let her know what was on my mind.

It's not you, it's me.

Clichéd but true.

I want you to know that I really love you.

Better not to rehearse it, though: leave it to the moment, and keep it simple, so as to make it clear that it was really no big deal, and that I was going to sort myself out and stop acting so tense all the time.

Before work. Just mention it.

Hey — I had the dream again last night, but it was different this time, and it got me thinking . . .

I checked my watch. Sasha wouldn't be up for an hour or so yet, and I didn't want to spend my time pacing and over-thinking things before then. So I went through to the front room and turned on my laptop, opening two separate windows.

The first showed a photograph of Rebecca

265

Lawrence. Just as I'd thought when meeting her parents yesterday, there was no way to be certain, and there probably never would be, but the resemblance to Charlie Matheson was uncanny, and the circumstances of her disappearance suspicious. Out of all the unresolved missing person reports I'd found, this was the only serious candidate. I was fairly sure Rebecca was the real victim found at the scene of Charlie's car crash.

Which was frightening.

I flicked to the other window, which had my provisional timeline open in it. Bare bones still — exceedingly thin. But at least I had another date to add into it now.

Provisional timeline
19 June 2010 Rebecca Lawrence reported
    missing (14th?)
3 August 2013 Charlie Matheson's car crash
4 December 2013 Death of the 50/50 Killer
28 July 2015 Charlie Matheson reappears

The 19th was the date that the Lawrences had reported their daughter missing. Because of the note, it had then taken a little longer before the disappearance was properly followed up. The actual date she went missing was likely to be the day her savings were withdrawn, which was the 14th. But what were a few days here and there? The concern I felt was because of the *year*.

Assuming the body at the crash scene had been her, over three years had elapsed since Rebecca Lawrence was abducted. If true, that meant she had been held for even longer than Charlie Matheson had been. We'd already noted the patience and planning of the individuals behind Charlie's kidnapping, but this seemed to indicate another level altogether.

I rubbed my mouth, looking down at the screen, considering it. That was when my mobile rang in my pocket. I took it out and answered the call.

'Mark?' Pete sounded shaken. I could almost picture him running his hand through his hair while he spoke. 'Where are you?'

'I'm at home.' I checked my watch again. No, it really was only just after seven. 'Where are you?'

'Got an address for you. Simon's there right now. Greg and I are up and on our way.'

I clicked my laptop through to the mapping system.

'Shoot.'

'Eighteen Forest Lane.'

When the mapping software found the property, it showed me that the street was situated in a neat little suburb to the west of the city. Nice area. Affluent.

'Fifteen-minute drive,' I said, gathering up my things. 'Depending on traffic. What have we got?'

'A dead man. Face apparently cut up like Charlie Matheson's. But there's more. A lot more.'

When he told me what else they'd found at the property, I was completely silent. For a few moments, it became hard to think.

Talking to Sasha was going to have to wait.

'I'll be there in ten,' I said finally, and hung up.

★ ★ ★

As I approached the address Pete had given me, I saw that there was already a substantial police presence in the street. The end was taped off several houses down from the crime scene, and much further ahead I could see a corresponding barrier at the far end. A few of the residents were out on their doorsteps at the nearest houses, and I was pleased to see officers standing with each of them, ostensibly reassuring them but also doing their best to keep them separated for the moment. Assuming any potential witnesses were willing to cooperate, it was much better to get stories individually, uncontaminated by even a few moments of idle gossip while the police went about the necessarily slow business of dealing with the crime scene itself.

I showed my badge to the officer at the cordon.

'Detective Nelson.'

'Thank you, sir.' He lifted the tape so I could duck under and gestured up the street. 'It's number eighteen, just up — '

'I see it, Officer. Thank you.'

It would have been difficult to miss, the epicentre of all this activity. Number 18 had three police cars parked directly outside, and two vans on the opposite side of the street. There were also two ambulances I could see, the nearest one with its back doors open and people standing around it.

I walked up slowly, trying to get a vague sense of the street. This suburb was mostly residential,

268

and the properties on Forest Lane were prestigious and desirable: detached mini-mansions, their double-barrelled frontages set back from the road behind spacious driveways. The pavements were broad, with well-tended grass verges. The trees there had grown so tall that the uppermost branches met over the centre of the street itself, giving the road a warm, contained feeling. Charlie had been right yesterday — the weather had broken, and it was raining gently. The sound overhead reminded me of the comforting patter on a conservatory roof.

Most of the people I could see outside the houses were middle-aged or older. They looked shell-shocked — afraid, even. Murder was not the kind of thing that happened in areas such as this. It would make the door-to-doors easier. They would be cooperative, I thought; they would want reassurance; they would be respectful of the police. It's not always the case.

I reached the first ambulance. Three paramedics were attending to an elderly woman perched on the edge at the back. She had a blanket draped over her shoulders, and was holding a plastic mask over her mouth and nose.

'Detective Mark Nelson.' I showed the nearest paramedic my identification. 'How are we doing here?'

'We're doing okay. This is Mrs Sheldon, who lives in the next-door property to the scene you're here for. She's the one who discovered the body this morning.'

'Is Mrs Sheldon up to talking?'

The paramedic shook her head. 'Maybe in a

bit. She's had a rough morning. But I can run you through a little.'

The two of us moved over to one side, out of earshot.

'We got the call just after seven,' she said. 'Mrs Sheldon called an ambulance first, police second. Not that we could do much when we arrived. You'll see what I mean when you go inside.'

'Right.'

'She told us she was just out collecting the paper and noticed the door was wide open, said that wasn't like him . . . you get the drift. Something bothered her anyway, so she went round and knocked. No answer. So she goes in, finds him in the living room.'

I glanced over at the woman, who still looked like she was struggling with the shock of what she'd seen. From that description of events, it didn't sound as if she'd have much of immediate importance to tell us. Talking to her could certainly wait a while.

I thanked the paramedic, then approached the house itself. The front door remained open, but the property now cut a very different scene from the one Mrs Sheldon must have encountered first thing. The large garden was half filled with officers and members of Simon's CSI team, and I had to show my ID again before crunching up the gravel drive to the door. It led into a wide, ornate hallway with a staircase in the centre, the oak fittings gleaming. At the top was a half-landing, where a vase of fresh flowers was silhouetted against the window.

She goes in, finds him in the living room.

There was an open doorway to my right, the room there busy with people. I saw Simon, dressed in white scrubs, standing beside a man with a camera, gesturing towards something I couldn't see, his hands forming a frame for it, directing him as to how to take the necessary photographs.

Let's see it, then.

I took a deep mental breath and stepped through the doorway. It was immediately apparent that the man had been murdered, and even though I had known as much already, the sight in front of me was still jolting. The victim was seated in a wooden chair towards one edge of the room. The chair was old but looked sturdy — one from a dining set, I thought — and the man had been bound tightly to it using coils of sharp wire. His head was angled forwards, as though he'd fallen asleep, but it was obvious he was dead from the injuries. While his torso seemed mostly unmarked, the whorls of grey hair on his chest were crusted with the blood that had poured down from above. From what I could see of his face, it had been cut to pieces.

Jesus.

I'd seen bodies before, of course, but rarely encountered savagery on a level like this. I felt a beat of sympathy for poor Mrs Sheldon. No wonder the woman was in shock.

I waited for the man with the camera to take shots from this angle before stepping a little closer, mindful of the blood spatters on the soft carpet around the chair, then crouched down for

271

a better look at the victim's face. In the torn and tattered skin it was just about possible to make out what had been done to him. The cuts weren't random. There were patterns there: curls and loops. It was reminiscent of Charlie Matheson's face, but in an entirely different league. Her injuries, while extensive and elaborate, seemed precise and delicate in comparison to the damage that had been inflicted here. This was an entirely more crude version. A rough and ready first draft.

'Unpleasant, isn't it?'

Simon was standing next to me, his hands casually thrust in his pockets. I stood up.

'I've seen worse.'

'Oh yes. I'm well aware of that.'

Simon glanced behind him. I followed his gaze. A cluster of people, Pete and Greg amongst them, were standing by the fireplace, blocking my view of the wall. I wasn't ready to look at what had been found there. I turned back to Simon instead.

'First impressions?'

'While the injuries themselves are horrific, there's nothing that strikes me as a definitive cause of death. The cuts to his face are extensive but relatively shallow. He's lost a fair bit of blood from them, but not enough to kill him.'

'So . . .'

Simon shrugged. 'So I can't say. You've noticed the track marks on the inside of his arms, of course.'

I hadn't. I looked now and saw the dots and bruising. An addict, then, despite the rich surroundings. I gestured at the wires around his wrists and ankles.

'I can see a few possible obstacles to him shooting up.'

Simon laughed softly. 'Which doesn't mean he didn't overdo things beforehand. Perhaps that's even why he was subdued so effectively, which I'm only saying because I can't see any obvious defensive marks on first inspection. Regardless, his system will have been weakened by it, and he was old. If I was a betting man, which I am resolutely not, I'd put money on a boring old heart attack. Although not boring in the circumstances, I suppose. Not considering what brought it on.'

'Any initial idea of the weapon used?'

'I can't say for sure. Not fingernails, if that's what you're thinking. A knife of some kind, but one with a very thin blade. Even so, the cuts themselves are quite ragged and awkward. There's a significant degree of tearing to the lines.'

'Perhaps the victim was moving his head?'

'You'd imagine he would be.'

'It's a little less *artistic* than what was done to Charlie Matheson.'

'Yes. But similar enough.' Simon looked over at the fireplace again. 'Of course, that's only one of the connections to our current investigation right now. I'm sure you remember your first day, Mark.'

'Very clearly.'

'I thought you might.'

I moved over to the fireplace now.

My first day. Over a year and a half ago now,

of course, and as I'd reminded myself yesterday while scanning through the file, the 50/50 Killer himself was long dead. So when I saw what was above the fireplace, I stopped in my tracks.

Like the injuries to the victim's face set against those inflicted upon Charlie Matheson, it was rough in comparison to the symbol I remembered from that first day, but the similarities were impossible to ignore. Whoever had killed the man behind me had used his blood to paint an elaborate spiderweb on the wall.

Groves

No matter what

The next morning, the heat had peaked and cracked, the weather had broken, and soft rain was pattering down as Groves made his way through the cemetery.

It was early, so it was quiet, and it felt like the rain was something that might be happening only to him. It reminded him of a time when he and Caroline had been on holiday in France. In the hot centre of a day, the sun had retreated behind a cloud and it had snowed. They had stood in an empty village street, looking at each other in disbelief as the flakes drifted down around them, and then they had laughed. It had lasted for thirty seconds at most, and they were the only people around to see it. It had been as though God had revealed a secret, just to them, in a rare moment of playfulness. *Let's never forget this moment*, Caroline had said. He had been so much in love with her back then.

A long time ago now.

Despite the rain, it was still warm. As he walked through the cemetery, he could smell the trees at the sides of the path, the misty drizzle bringing out the scent in the glistening leaves. As it settled on him, it was indistinguishable from the sweat he could feel gathering on his back, his face.

Jamie.

He reached his son's grave. Whatever toy Caroline had left was gone, but the pale flowers remained. They were wilting already, the petals curling up like small, slowly closing hands.

Groves read the inscription there.

A little boy and his Bear . . .

There had been no further messages on the mobile phone, but he'd had most of the night to think it over, and he now had an idea. One possible explanation for what might be happening. And it bothered him — scared him — because it came down to the card he'd received on Jamie's birthday.

I know who did it.

Someone out there had discovered the identities of the gang who had abducted both Laila Buckingham and Jamie Groves, and God knew how many others, and was targeting them. Punishing them.

Who would do such a thing? Groves remembered only too well his own emotions when Jamie had gone missing. He was a good man — or tried to be — but he was only human. In the darker moments, he would have given anything for a chance to tear those people to pieces for what they'd done. He'd waited up that time, hadn't he, with the door unlocked? That evening he hadn't felt very much like a policeman, and he wasn't sure he would have behaved like one if it had come to it.

But a policeman was what he was. He believed in the law and in justice and in doing the right thing; it was an integral part of him. At the same time, he could easily imagine that for another grieving parent, things would look and feel entirely different. That the urge to take the law into their own hands would be very strong indeed.

But that wasn't what frightened him.

I know who did it.

The card had been addressed to Jamie, not to him. When he had received it, he'd thought that was just an extra little dab of torture, but now he wondered if it might be something else altogether: that the sender hadn't seen Groves as being worth corresponding with; that it was a message directed solely to a murdered child. *I know who did it.* And unlike your worthless father, with his faith and his stupid belief in right and wrong, I'm prepared to do something about it. I'll avenge you.

Groves wondered whether a parent of a murdered child might resent a man like him — a policeman who had also lost a child, and whose name was in the papers, and who should have done more to stop these people before they struck again. They might even hate him enough to begin what he now suspected was happening as a sideshow to the killings.

Framing him.

Was that melodramatic? Perhaps. But he doubted he had an alibi for the murders of Edward Leland and Carl Thompson. He was in possession of a phone that had belonged to Thompson. He'd gone looking for Thompson and found him dead, and he hadn't reported it.

In the cold light of a new day, he wanted to

kick himself for that last thing. The thought of Jamie had pulled him on — the urge to have that mobile phone ring again — and it was only when he was home that he'd even considered how many of the people he'd talked to over the course of the day would be able to identify him, however vaguely. He'd realised that, at least in other people's eyes, he had motive. He'd wondered if, just maybe, he had played into someone's hands.

He looked down from the quote on the gravestone to the words inscribed below.

Jamie Groves. Loved and missed.

The rain picked up a little.

You know I loved you, Groves thought. *Don't you?*

Despite everything he'd done, and everything he hadn't, that much was true. Surely it was. Just because he wanted to do the right thing, that didn't mean he hadn't loved his son. So very much. More than he could bear.

Surely Jamie would know that?

And you know I always will, Groves thought, preparing himself once again to do the right thing, the difficult thing, however belatedly. Trusting that this was all happening for a reason, even if his fallible human mind couldn't fathom it.

No matter what.

★ ★ ★

There was no choice but to carry out the interview in one of the standard rooms. It needed to be officially recorded and notated. After all, Groves had confessed to a crime: perverting the course of justice by hiding from the department his role in the discovery of Carl Thompson's body. Although he hadn't been arrested, it was more than possible, DCI Reeves advised him, that charges would be brought. He would certainly be suspended from duty.

Reeves had then shaken his head in disbelief.

'What on earth were you thinking, David?' The DCI hadn't sounded unfriendly, or even angry. 'Were you even thinking?'

He couldn't answer. *Jamie.* That was all he'd been thinking, but he couldn't bring himself to try to explain the ache inside him. In his boss's office, he would have felt weak.

The interview room was tiny: little more than a cupboard. The desk protruded directly from one of the walls, leaving only a metre of space free, and there was hardly room to draw back the chairs on either side of it before they touched the walls behind. The floorboards were bare, and the pale green paint on the walls was flecked and peeling. In one corner of the ceiling a camera was angled down at the desk and chairs. The only other fitting, aside from the bare light bulb humming above him, was the digital recorder bolted to the table by the wall.

They trusted him to wait by himself, at least. Groves kept glancing at the door, wondering if Reeves had stationed someone outside in case he ran, but he didn't think he would have. *Too straight.* That was what they thought of him. He could almost have laughed. He had no idea what

he'd been expecting to happen, but this outcome
— being treated like a criminal — had already
left a bitter taste in his mouth. It felt like he'd
tried to do the right thing and deserved
something better as a result. But then where had
doing the right thing ever got him? What had it
ever achieved?

The door opened.

It was Sean who came in. He was breathing
heavily, and he didn't look at Groves as he shut
the door behind him. The thick sheaf of papers
he was holding whapped down on the table
between them.

'Sean — '

'Don't talk to me for a second, David. Don't
fucking talk.'

Sean sat down opposite him, landing heavily
in the seat, then rested his elbows on the table
and rubbed his eyes. Groves just watched him.
When Sean took his hands away, he could see
the disappointment on his partner's face. He
looked almost heartbroken. Immediately Groves
felt the sensation mirrored inside himself. It was
obvious how badly he'd let his partner down. His
former partner most likely.

'Before we get started,' Sean said, 'I need to
know something.'

'Go on.'

'You didn't do it, did you? Kill these two
people?'

For a second, Groves thought he was joking.

'God, Sean. You know the answer to — '

'Because honestly? If it *was* you, and if
everything Reeves just told me is true, then I'd

understand. I want you to know that I'd completely get it. But if it's true, it's better to admit it now. I'm your friend, and I want to help you, so please don't fuck me around.'

Despite himself, Groves felt a flush of anger.

You, Sean? You of all people?

'I didn't kill them.'

He heard the resentment in his own voice, the sense of betrayal going both ways now. Sean just stared at him for a few seconds, evaluating him.

'You'd better not be lying to me, David.'

'I'm not.'

'But you realise that the focus of the investigation is going to turn your way now, don't you? It has to. You're prepared for that?'

Groves nodded. 'Yes.'

'I hope so. Right. Let's get this shit started then. And let's get it finished.'

He reached out to set the recorder going, and began to run through the preliminaries.

They went through the cases in detail, but out of order, beginning with the specifics of Groves finding Thompson's body. Sean rubbed his jaw, looking even more tired than before.

'Why didn't you report what you'd found?'

'I did.'

'No, you made an anonymous call. Why didn't you report it properly, as an officer? You were on duty after all.'

'Because I had no official reason to be there.' Groves felt helpless. 'I don't know. Something odd is happening, something to do with Jamie, and it felt like I needed to figure out what before I came forward.'

'You say Thompson *gave* you this phone?'

'Yes.'

He knew how it looked. He was in possession of Carl Thompson's phone, and there was only his word that he had received it in the strange manner he claimed. For all anyone else knew, he could have simply taken it off the boy's body.

'Why do you think he did that?'

Because I gave him some change.

That was the truth, as far as he could tell, but it was ridiculous.

'I don't know. It was made to look accidental, but it wasn't. I gave him some money first, and then he deliberately dropped the phone. I went looking for him because I wanted to know why.'

'And you think he was specifically targeting you?'

'Yes. I told you. Someone phoned me on it later. It was obviously a message for me. It wouldn't have made sense to anyone else.'

'What did they say?'

'It was about Jamie. Somebody was reading the inscription from his gravestone. Then they told me that God would be with me.'

'Where is this phone now?'

'It's at my house. In the front room.'

He hadn't brought it with him because he was worried that if he had it in his pocket, he'd feel compelled to keep checking it — that it might have stopped him from reporting what had happened. Relieved of possession, it was easier to distance himself. To surrender it all to the right people.

'Okay. Well, that's something.'

Sean bit his lip slightly. They both knew he shouldn't have said that when the recorder was on — that he needed to remain impartial. Groves realised that for all his anger, his partner was at least partly still on his side.

'Right. Tell me about Simon Chadwick.'

Sean knew it all, of course, but it was necessary to go through it again for the official record.

'Simon Chadwick is in prison,' Groves said, 'for his part in the abduction and imprisonment of a girl called Laila Buckingham. He also had some drug offences on his sheet. Edward Leland and Carl Thompson were both associates of his, way back. They both also appear to have committed child-abuse-related offences. Thompson was charged as a juvenile. It's only suspected in Leland's case.'

'So you found the connection between the two victims — their link to Chadwick — but you didn't report it?'

'I reported it on Leland. That's why I asked to be taken off the case.'

'But not Thompson.'

'No. It was only just before I found him.'

Sean just stared at him then, and the expression on his face was clear enough. *You know how this looks*, he was telling him silently. *This all has to come out eventually, so let's lay it on the table now.*

'All right,' Groves said. 'I didn't report the link with Thompson because of the connection to Jamie.'

His son's name seemed to startle the air in the

interview room, and for a moment they were both silent. By rights, Sean should have clarified the name — asked Groves to confirm who Jamie was — but he didn't, and his voice was quieter when he spoke next.

'And what do you think that connection is?'

'I think someone out there is killing people who were involved in my son's murder. And you *know* what the connection is, Sean. Most of the people who abducted Laila Buckingham were never caught. It's not a huge leap to imagine them doing it again, and again.'

'Not a huge leap, no. But not an established fact either.' Sean sighed. 'You understand that, don't you, David? And there's only the vaguest of circumstantial evidence that Leland or Thompson were ever involved. They were friends with Chadwick. That's it.'

'There's the abuse angle too.'

'Which is all buried in police files. Join-the-dots stuff. Which means that right now, you're the only person with a motive to kill them who knew about that connection. There's not a shred of evidence that anybody else does.'

I know who did it.

'I got a card.'

Groves told him about the birthday card. As he did so, the disappointment on Sean's face became more pronounced.

'So? That doesn't prove anything.'

'Maybe not. But it's *something*.'

'It probably *isn't*, David. And you know it.' Sean leaned back in his chair. 'Where is it now? At your house?'

'Yes. I can get it for you, along with the phone.'

'No, you really can't. I think it's better right now that you don't go anywhere near your house. Give me the keys. I'll get them.'

It rankled, but he was right. 'Okay.'

'Let's talk alibis. Please tell me you've got one?'

'Not for Leland, no; I was at home by myself all night. I don't know when Thompson was killed.'

'PM's scheduled for this afternoon. Jesus Christ. Okay. Run me through your whereabouts before you found the body.'

Groves told him everywhere he'd been — the soup kitchen, the train station — and eventually Sean switched off the recorder and retrieved a consent-to-search form from his folder of papers.

'Honestly, David. I don't know what to think.'

'Neither do I.'

'You really believe someone out there is killing these people and trying to ... *frame* you somehow? None of it makes sense.'

'No. But I can't think of any other explanation right now.'

Groves began filling in details on the form, listing the exact places in his home that Sean was allowed to go through.

It has to be like this, he told himself. *By the book.*

The right thing to do.

Sean took the form off him, along with his house keys.

'Are we done?' Groves said.

285

'We're done.' Sean left him to open the door. At least he was letting him leave by himself rather than escorting him out. 'But David? Don't go too far. And keep your phone on.'

Mark

The centre of the web

Half an hour later, after coordinating the door-to-door team outside, I walked back to my car. Enough time had passed for the media to begin to gather beyond the cordon. I held up a palm at the first reporter to approach me as I reached the vehicle, then tinted the windows dark when I got inside. All else aside, I didn't want them seeing the look on my face.

With the tablet on my lap, I logged into the department's computer system and loaded up the file on the 50/50 Killer.

I already knew I wouldn't find Charlie Matheson or Paul Carlisle's names in the file, but now I had a new one to search for. The dead man in the house up the street appeared to be Gordon Peters, the owner of the property. According to records, he had been a doctor for most of his life, retiring four years ago.

A doctor.

As I ran the search, I wondered if we might have found the mysterious man who had been in the back of Charlie's ambulance. The one she had described as kind.

I suspected we had.

And yet the search came back blank. No obvious connection with the 50/50 case, then. I ran a general check on Peters, and that came back clean too. Never in trouble with the police for so much as a speeding ticket. Apparently, despite the track marks, and the paraphernalia that had been found in the medical cabinet upstairs, Dr Peters had managed to stay off our radar.

I looked up, watching my officers as they moved from house to house, talking to the dead man's neighbours.

No connection in the 50/50 file — but there had to be one somewhere, didn't there? The spiderwebs the killer drew had never been made public, but even if they had, the one on Peters' wall was too similar to be a mere copycat. Anyone who vaguely knew about the webs might have attempted one, but whatever version they came up with would be some distance from the intricacy and eeriness of the real thing. No, I'd seen the originals a year and a half ago, and I recognised one when I saw it now.

Not drawn by the 50/50 Killer himself, though.

That much was certain. The man responsible for the crimes was dead. At the same time, the web back there had been drawn by someone who understood what they meant, and who had seen them before. It hadn't been designed at random, but with careful thought and consideration . . .

Just like Charlie's scars.

The realisation brought my thoughts to a stop for a moment.

Whoever had inflicted those facial injuries on Charlie had also done so with intent and care. Like the spiderwebs, they were not random.

They represented *the wearing of sins*, and everybody's sins are specific to them; everybody has their own unique moral fingerprint. The similarities between the two things were obvious now.

What about Gordon Peters, then? What had his sins been? It was reasonable to assume that his injuries reflected some inner sins of his own, but what? It appeared that he had been a drug addict, and perhaps that would be enough in our perpetrators' eyes to demand punishment. But then, assuming he was the man Charlie had described in the ambulance, and at the place she'd been held, it seemed they'd been happy enough to employ his services in some capacity over the years.

And how many people were we looking for now? From Charlie's story, I'd been assuming at least two — the kind man and the old man who called himself the Devil. She'd also mentioned that others had held her while the Devil did the cutting. How did this murder change things? It was impossible to know, but the organisation behind all this felt larger with every fresh development.

I called up a driving licence photograph of Peters from the files and saved it to the tablet. At least I could show that to Charlie and see if she could confirm the man's identity. Assuming she remembered his face well enough. And that she was *allowed* to tell me, of course.

I called the number for the officer stationed at the hospital.

'Detective Mark Nelson,' I told him. 'Is

Charlie Matheson still there?'

'Yes, sir. Safe and fine.'

'Right. Keep it that way. Nobody in or out. Okay?'

'Understood, sir.'

'And for the moment that means her too.'

'Understood.'

I hung up, then swiped back through on the tablet to the 50/50 file. The killer was dead, yes, but I couldn't get it out of my head. There *was* some connection between him and our present investigation. It was there in the spiderweb, and the connection to Mercer, and it was there in the precise designs of the scarring inflicted on Charlie — the visualisation of something intangible in the form of a complicated pattern. It was there in the Devil.

But it wasn't there in the file . . .

I stared at the screen.

Suddenly thinking: *What* else *isn't there in the file?*

One simple fact. We had no idea who the 50/50 Killer had been. We had a handful of different aliases for him, but no clue as to his real identity. His last two known addresses were listed, but we'd never discovered where he came from before that. Despite the fact that he was dead and his murder spree at an end, the man himself remained a ghost to us, as ephemeral as the devil in the mask he'd worn. He could have been anybody. He could have been nobody.

But of course, he hadn't been. He had been *somebody*.

Because people like him don't simply emerge

out of the ether, their personalities blinking into existence. They're shaped by their environment and their upbringing, just as we all are. A confluence of factors conspires to create them. So what kind of environment might the 50/50 Killer have been moulded by, with his devil mask and spider-webs and hatred of love? What sort of upbringing might he have had? What sort of family?

He came from somewhere.

I put the tablet to one side and took out my phone.

You have to be careful with vulnerable people, Eileen had told me. She was right, of course. But it was late morning, and Eileen would likely be with a patient right now. Mercer himself would probably be working away on his new book, researching the 50/50 Killer and where he had come from. Obsessing over it. And despite his manner in the operations room yesterday, I was wondering if I could tempt him in with a key piece of information about that: a possible move towards an ending for the story that haunted him. I was betting I could.

You have to be careful with . . .

But I was already dialling the house number as I started the car.

Groves

Do you want to see your son again?

Groves wasn't allowed to go home, but he needed to go somewhere. Still seething a little, he sat in his car outside the department for a few minutes, and then, for reasons he was conflicted about, he drove to Caroline's house.

Sean might never have understood why they had remained friends, but it was no mystery to Groves himself. It was similar to the way strangers who had been involved in the same traumatic incident often bonded and formed otherwise unlikely friendships. Damage, especially when it was sudden and incomprehensible, created a powerful glue between people. Despite the divorce, it had remained unspoken between them that if one of them was ever in trouble and needed the other's support, they would have it.

Well, Groves thought. He was in trouble now.

The whole of the drive over, he couldn't get his mind away from what Sean had said. The way his partner had *doubted* him. Even though he'd tried to do the right thing, and always had, they were still suspicious of him, and he had still been relieved of duty. Not that they had much of a choice, he supposed, but still: it angered him. He was going to be investigated now, and that also scared him, because the only real evidence he

292

had for his story was Carl Thompson's mobile phone . . .

God, he thought suddenly.

You don't actually know who *it belonged to.*

He'd just been assuming it belonged to Thompson, which was bad enough in itself, as there might be no proof he hadn't just taken it off the boy's body. But what if it was someone else's?

What if it had been Edward Leland's mobile phone?

The possibility made him go cold inside.

And who knew what else he'd missed? Because he still couldn't get the slightest handle on what was happening here. Why had Thompson given him the phone in the first place? Out of fear, presumably. *I've been through hell, sir.* Groves remembered the boy's scars, and also his absence from recent police files. Was it possible that someone had held him captive, tortured him, convinced him that if he performed this one last task then he'd be set free?

But why frame me?

Again the answer came quickly enough. He was increasingly sure of it. *Because you're a policeman.* He'd saved Laila Buckingham, but not his own son, which gave him two stakes in the investigation. And yet he'd still failed to catch the people responsible. In the intervening time, he thought, someone else had lost a child, and they'd decided that Groves was at least partially to blame. Someone with the will and the means to do what Groves had proved unable to.

I know who did it.

The card again.

Addressed not to the grieving father, clinging to his beliefs, but to the murdered son.

* * *

Caroline's house was in the middle of a long row of red-brick terraces that sloped down a steep hill to the main road at the bottom. Every second house was a storey lower than the one beside it, and the rooftops bristled with cables and antennae, like curls of metal shavings caught in the teeth of a rusty saw blade.

Her gate screeched slightly as he opened it, the old paint rough against his palm.

There was a small garden between the street and the house, but it was paved over and bare. Caroline had always been a fastidious gardener — a natural tidier, in and out of the house — and he suspected that the paving here was a quiet acknowledgement of how much she'd changed. She no longer had the energy to maintain a proper garden, but she preferred to hide that fact altogether, to cover it with concrete, rather than admit it.

He suspected that she'd be at work, but he knocked and waited anyway. No response. He had a spare key for her house, though, just as she had one for his. Opening the door created a *whump*, as though the air inside was being disturbed for the first time in days. It opened directly on to the front room, which was dim and gloomy. The dark-red curtains were closed and the air smelled stale.

'Caroline?'

No response.

Groves flicked on the light switch.

It hadn't been immediately obvious in the gloom, but the place was a tip. There were tangles of clothes on the settee, and the coffee table in the centre of the room was covered with old plates and glasses, along with a teetering pile of unsorted post. Empty vodka bottles were lined up on the floor against the side of one of the armchairs, while in front of it, there was a pint glass smeared with a mist of fingerprints, lipstick at the rim. Dust had collected along the skirting boards.

No wonder the place smelled stale. And now that he saw it, Groves felt guilty for letting himself in, even given the circumstances. This disarray was the opposite of the image Caroline liked to present to the rest of the world, including him. She was still proud, and would be upset to think he'd seen her home in this kind of state. The amount of alcohol, especially, confirmed how badly she was coping these days.

So his first instinct was to turn around and walk back out: to pretend he'd never been here at all. But the sight of the room worried him, and he felt an urge to see how bad things really were. Not that he would ever let her know he'd been in here and seen it like this, but perhaps there would be some more subtle way he could help.

He took the creaking stairs up to the first floor. As he poked his head quickly into each of the rooms, it became increasingly obvious that she hadn't been looking after herself. The bathroom was filthy; the towels draped over the side of the bath stank of old water, and the mat scrunched up against the base of the sink was speckled with green and black mould. The spare room was full of boxes, some of them very old indeed, with the vacuum cleaner half buried at the far end. In the main bedroom, there were more glasses on the table and more clothes strewn carelessly on the floor. Her bed was unmade. The album containing photographs of Jamie was lying close to the pillows. She'd clearly been sleeping next to it.

Groves stared at that for a moment, feeling an immense sadness that was impossible to describe. A sensation of emptiness and loss that was profound, almost spiritual. The feeling that God shouldn't allow decent people to endure such misery.

But there was guilt there too.

I'm sorry, Caroline. I should have noticed.

I should have realised you weren't doing well.

Sean would have said there was no need for the guilt — that it wasn't his responsibility. But Groves had never found it easy to stop caring for someone. Even though he wasn't with Caroline any more, he should still have recognised how quickly she was heading downhill. It seemed the least he could have done; not just for her, but for Jamie as well. She had been Jamie's mother, after all; for his son's memory, he should have looked after her.

And I'm sorry I wasn't there for you either, Jamie.

The grief rose in him, ending with a twist in

his throat. His son had been murdered, and what had he done? Held on to the last vestiges of himself as a police officer, intent on doing the right thing, on bringing the perpetrators to justice. Carrying on as before, ultimately. Trusting that God had His reasons. Right now, Caroline's reactions, from her loss of faith to her disintegration, seemed far healthier and more natural than his own. Perhaps he really hadn't cared as much as he should have done. Perhaps if there was a man murdering these predators in his place, that man was right.

Groves took out his phone as he went downstairs, unsure at that moment exactly what he was planning to do, but needing to talk to Caroline: wanting to apologise to her for everything he had done and everything he had not. He opened the front door, leaning on the frame, and just as he did, the phone buzzed in his hand.

He looked down at it. The screen display read: *Unknown Number.*

Someone at the department, he guessed, although he'd presumed that Sean would be in touch with him first. He answered the call and held the phone to his ear.

'David Groves speaking.'

For a couple of seconds there was silence on the line. And then that familiar tinkling nursery rhyme began. 'Twinkle, Twinkle, Little Star', with scratches and pops in the background. Groves stared out at the street through the rain, looking up and down the hill, wondering if he was being watched.

'Who is this?'

There was no reply, just that scratchy recording, as though the simple tune were coming from a different era, across time itself.

'Tell me who this is!'

Abruptly the music cut out, and the, line was silent again. Except Groves could hear someone breathing softly.

He spoke more quietly now: 'Who are you?'

It was a man's voice that replied. Quiet and calm.

'Mr Groves,' he said. 'Do you want to see your son again?'

For a moment, the world around Groves receded into the distance, and the sound of the rain diminished until it was softer and quieter than even his heartbeat. It felt like he was underwater. *More than anything*, he thought, even though he knew the man's promise was a false one. Even though the only way he'd see Jamie again was in death. *More than anything*. He tried to speak — to say something, anything, in reply — but his voice wouldn't work.

'If you do,' the man said, 'then you need to listen to me very carefully. Because I'm going to tell you how.'

Mark

As though coming back to life

I picked Mercer up at the end of his road.

'Does Pete know you're here?' he asked as we set off.

'Not as such. But I imagine he knows I'll be pursuing the investigation in the best way possible in order to move it forward.'

I wondered what Mercer thought about Pete now, especially after the awkward encounter in the office yesterday. Whether he had any opinion on how Pete was handling the responsibility of leading the team. There had been more than a hint of nostalgia in the way he'd gazed around the new premises: a sense that he missed his old life even though he understood he could never return to it, the way you'd miss someone you'd loved once but could no longer have.

It was also apparent in the way he'd agreed to come with me to the hospital. After I'd told him a little about the new developments in the case, I'd been half expecting to have to cajole him into meeting me. Instead, there had been a few moments of silence, when I could picture him looking around the house, considering. Then he'd quietly told me to meet him at the end of the road. He had been waiting outside when I arrived, the rain pattering gently down around him.

I didn't need to ask whether he'd told Eileen where he was going.

He seemed distracted now: lost in thought. I had broken with strict protocol and allowed him to sit in the passenger seat beside me. I glanced at him and saw that he was sitting very still, staring straight ahead. His hands were pressed down tightly on the pile of paperwork he'd brought with him. It was a hastily assembled patchwork of his notes and research: a fragmented attempt to understand the case that had half destroyed his life and brought his distinguished career to such an ignoble end. On top of it, his hands looked terribly old and weak, the skin papery and thin. He didn't turn to look at me as he spoke.

'How *have* things been?'

'Since . . . ?'

'Since I left.'

'I only worked with you for a day,' I said, 'so I'm not sure how different it is.'

He didn't reply.

I took the turning that would take us on to the ring road.

'Do you miss it?' I said.

Again he didn't reply. But out of the corner of my eye I saw one of his fingers tapping thoughtfully against the top of the pile of papers, the obsessive research with which he'd filled his retirement. It was a stupid question, of course. Detective work had been everything to John Mercer, the basis of his entire life. Just because it had nearly killed him didn't change that.

'Every day.' It was as though he was talking

more to himself than to me. 'But it's in the past now. I know I can't go back.'

It was my turn to be silent. After a moment, he sighed to himself, moving slightly, as though coming back to life.

'Tell me about the man who was found dead today.'

I did, although there still wasn't much to say. Dr Gordon Peters was a drug addict, apparently, although his career record was unblemished. He had worked at a few different places, but for the last couple of decades he'd been employed at the main hospital, precisely where we were heading. There seemed a reasonable possibility that he was the man Charlie had described in the ambulance.

Mercer thought it over.

'And he was scarred the same way Matheson has been?'

'Yes. Although it was done with much less care.' I thought about the weapon used, and the lack of precision. 'Possibly even by someone different.'

'If they're supposed to represent sins, I wonder what Dr Peters had done wrong?'

'Beyond helping to keep a woman prisoner, drug her, manipulate her?' I shook my head. 'Obviously, to whoever's behind this, things like that don't count as sins. I can't decide about the addiction issue.'

'If they were using him all this time, they must have been aware.'

'They?'

'All this would take several people. And

they've obviously used Peters' services before.' He thought about it for a moment. 'But he did a poor job this time with Matheson, didn't he?'

'What do you mean?'

'Whatever sedative he gave her, it seems like it was too much. Perhaps he set everything back slightly. For people as organised and precise as this, maybe a mistake like that would be a sin.'

'Maybe.'

'And his murder is also a sign, of course. Or at least, the spiderweb is. A way to make sure I came to the hospital, so I could hear whatever it is that Matheson is meant to tell me.' He thought about it. 'The web seemed . . . authentic?'

'Yes,' I said. 'Very similar to one of the 50/50 Killer's. Whoever drew it had at least seen one before. It's not the same as the others, obviously, because they were all unique to the couples. But it's no copycat.'

I told him my theory about the scarring serving a similar purpose to the spiderwebs. That they were intricate designs, particular to the individual disfigured by them: their sins visualised in a similar way to the relationships of the couples patiently watched, stalked and attacked by the 50/50 Killer.

'And yet the 50/50 Killer is dead,' Mercer said.

'But we never found out where he came from.'

'No.'

'He had a history,' I said. 'A past. Once upon a time, he must have had a family.'

I saw Mercer tapping his files again.

'I know you've been researching a book about the case,' I prompted. 'What have you found?'

He sighed. 'Bits and pieces. Nothing concrete. Every time I find a thread and follow it, it doesn't go anywhere. A possible rental in one identity here, another there. But no real records. I can't be sure any of it is actually him. I still don't know his real name.'

I nodded to myself. On the one hand, it was ridiculous that a man might appear out of nowhere, his past shrouded in a mist that couldn't be shone through. Everyone leaves a trace. And yet it didn't surprise me that the 50/50 Killer of all people would be someone who had done precisely this. I was increasingly sure that we needed to blow that mist away, though, and that when we found where he had come from, we'd find the place where Charlie had been held all this time.

I took the turning for the hospital.

Mercer stared ahead. 'Do you remember the last time we were here?'

That first day again. I'd spent the early hours of that snowy morning interviewing a man called Scott, teasing out details of a story that would end in tragedy for so many of us.

'Yes,' I said.

I thought about adding that it was very different now. That Charlie was in an entirely different wing of the hospital. That it was morning. That time had passed, and we were here for different reasons. And that this wouldn't necessarily end in the same tragedy that it had back then. But as I pulled in to the car park, it didn't feel like any of that made any difference at all.

Groves

The fire station

In the far north of the city, driving along the ring road, Groves passed the spot where two years earlier he'd walked into the woods and identified his son's body. The memory of that night was visceral, but it was embedded more in his heart than his head: a sudden shiver in his chest, like walking through a cold spot in a supposedly haunted house.

He glanced in the mirror and watched the small parking area recede behind him. It seemed so innocuous and ordinary in the midday light and drizzle.

Do you want to see your son again?

The man on the phone had refused to answer any questions. Instead, he had simply given Groves a series of directions. He was to drive north, skirting the edge of the woods, passing the spot where he had come that night. About a mile further on, he would see a place on his left-hand side. He would know it when he saw it.

Groves watched the counter on the dashboard. Outside the car, there was nothing of interest to see. Just the woods on the right, and a high red-brick wall on the left, its top ringed with coils of old razor wire, which had fallen down the stone in places, like ivy.

What are you doing, David?

He couldn't explain it, even to himself. The sensible thing to do would have been to call Sean and tell him what had happened. And yet even as he'd realised that, he'd started to rationalise himself out of making that decision. What did it prove? It was only his word about the content of the call, and he had a strange feeling that if he did report it, then whatever he was supposed to see here would be gone by the time the police arrived.

But deep down, he knew the real reasons he was heading here on his own. It burned him that he'd tried to do the right thing and it had backfired on him — placed him under suspicion. And he wanted to meet the man behind all this.

He rounded a corner, a mile past the footpath that had led to his son's makeshift grave, and saw it up ahead.

A section of the wall had broken down, falling like steps into what had once been a large opening, big enough for vehicles, and now stretched even wider. Through that, Groves could see an open expanse of tarmac, and what appeared to be an abandoned factory of some kind.

He indicated — force of habit — and drove into what turned out to be an old car park. It was only as he pulled up in front of the crumbling building that he realised it wasn't a factory at all, but the remains of an old fire station.

He stared out through the windscreen, rain pattering down steadily on the glass. He vaguely remembered the place now: the station had closed down years ago, and was little more than a shell now. The main building was in the centre of the area, with two cavernous bay doors open to the elements. Shards of glass littered the tarmac in front. Inside, beyond the brick dust and piles of broken timber, he could see fading graffiti on the walls. A door to one side of the bays, which looked like it led into a reception area, was missing, and the space was half blocked by debris, the plinth above collapsed. Grass had sprouted around the base of the building, and at the far end of the car park, the surrounding undergrowth had encroached metres over the tarmac.

Groves stepped out of the car. Standing still for a second and listening, he heard nothing but the rain. The place had the air of an ancient temple — of work done by long-forgotten human hands that was already being undone and reclaimed by nature.

His footfalls echoed as he stepped into the huge bay. Old wooden beams rested against one wall, charred and thinned in the middle. There were rusted tanks and some trampled-down green sheeting. Up close, he realised that the graffiti he'd seen was desultory and half finished, as though whoever was responsible had realised that nobody would ever see it and had given up partway through. This far out, the place wasn't even a draw for bored kids.

What am I looking for?

There was nothing obvious to see. Groves searched the building as quickly as he could. A side door from the bay led into the broken-down

306

reception area. Pared-down stone steps rose two flights to the top, where an entirely open space stretched across the whole building, interspersed with pillars and, in the far corner, a pole that ran down through a hole in the floor. The walls were covered in dirty tiles, and there was a squared-off area in one corner that turned out to have plumbing for absent toilets. In life, this all might have housed a gym and rec room, but now it was just a waste ground. The windows along one wall were vacant squares. A breeze brought the rain in a little, but nothing stirred; the litter and leaves up here had long since been pressed into corners or blown under dropped beams and settled there.

Nothing.

Groves made his way carefully back outside. What was he meant to see here? It was a mystery. He walked across the front of the bay again, wondering, then made his way down one side and behind the building.

And paused.

From the front, the station had obscured it: a slim three-storey tower, standing some distance away. It had a missing door and empty square gaps for windows, and the brickwork was burned black and sooty from top to bottom.

A practice tower, Groves guessed. He moved across to the doorway, his shoes crunching on the gravel and broken glass, then stepped over the threshold. Inside, there was a ten-foot-square space, with torn maps of fabric scorched to the stone floor, melted at the edges. The air was sour. Even after all this time, he could smell the soot in it.

A blackened staircase led upwards in the near corner, curling around out of sight to the first floor. Groves walked over, looking down. The steps were covered with a thick layer of mulch: ash and dust, moistened slightly by the rain. It had obviously been disturbed recently. The messy footprints suggested a flurry of activity, although the impressions left were impossible to decipher.

He gazed up the stairs. The policeman in him didn't want to disturb the scene — but then he was hardly here as a policeman right now. After a moment's hesitation, keeping his back to one wall, he made his way up the steps, avoiding the other footprints, listening carefully, hearing only the squelch of the mush beneath his feet.

The room on the first floor was silent except for the slight rush of air coming in through the empty window. It was identical to the space below, but the stone steps leading up were at the opposite corner, and the thin, skeletal remains of a settee rested against one wall, its metal wires scorched black. In its parched state, it reminded him of Edward Leland's front room. Once again, there was nothing to see.

One floor to go.

He headed up the stairs, keeping to the side as before.

The tower's final room was at the top of the steps. As Groves reached it and stared at what was there, his heart dropped away, and for a moment he couldn't even move.

This was what he'd been summoned to see.

The second floor contained a replica of a

bedroom. The stone floor was covered with layers of burned foam and charred bedding. Against one wall were the remains of a double bed: just an iron frame with square posts, a blackened web of springs and metal wires strung between them.

And lying on that, the body of a woman.

Mark

Ella

After I showed the officer stationed outside the
Baines Wing my ID, I led Mercer through to
the waiting room, where we found Charlie sitting
with a book. She seemed engrossed, but as we
approached and she recognised our presence,
she closed it and placed it back on the table. I
was used to the sight of the scars by now, so
what I noticed first was the look on her face. She
no longer seemed quite as confused or frightened
as before. If anything, seeing Mercer behind me,
she looked almost triumphant.

I noted the book she'd been reading.

'The Bible, Charlie?' The expression on her
face annoyed me. Stockholm syndrome aside, her
capitulation with her abductors annoyed me too.
A man was dead. 'Must be a bit poignant, surely?
What are you doing, checking for loopholes?'

She ignored me, still looking at Mercer.

'Is this him?'

'Yes.'

I glanced behind me. For his part, Mercer
didn't display any kind of shock at the sight of
her injuries. He stepped forward to stand beside
me, his hands in his pockets, staring down at her
with a look of concentration on his face,
as though she were less a human being than a
problem he needed to solve.

'And you must be Charlie,' he said.

'That's right.'

'Do we know each other, Charlie?'

'No.' She stared back at him. 'I don't know anything about you. All I know is what I need to tell you.'

'So I understand.' He was still squinting down at her. 'No, I don't think we've ever met. Even without the scars, I'm sure I'd remember you.'

'Do you like them?' she said

'No.'

If Charlie was insulted, she didn't show it.

'I like them very much.'

'I don't understand why.' He took his hands out of his pockets and rubbed his jawline thoughtfully. 'If it were me, I imagine I'd hate the man who'd done that to me. The Devil, or whatever you want to call him.'

'Why would anyone hate the Devil?' she said. She picked the bible up again. 'That would be ridiculous. God is all-powerful, remember? It's Him that allows the Devil to do what he does. It's Him that allows evil and lets all the wrong things be done to us.'

'I suppose that's true.'

Mercer sat down across from her, a little awkwardly, as though the movement caused him pain.

'You were right, Mark. Now that I've seen her in the flesh, the scarring is clearly deliberate, isn't it?' He looked her over. 'Designed. There's a specific pattern to it. It reminds me very much of the spiderwebs. It's different, but clearly related somehow.'

'Spiderwebs?' Charlie said.

'Patterns drawn on walls,' I told her. 'We found one this morning in the house of a man who was murdered. We think he's the doctor who helped you. The *kind* one who brought you back.'

She blinked at me, startled by that.

'Here.' I slid my tablet across the table, showing her the photograph of Gordon Peters. She looked down at it, then closed her eyes for a second before looking back up at me.

'It is, isn't it?' I said.

'Why would they . . . ?'

'I guess the Devil moves in mysterious ways. Maybe he doesn't always keep his promises. Why don't we find out?'

Charlie looked down at the photograph again, unsure now what to say or do. The news of Peters' death had clearly unsettled her; she didn't understand the implications, or what it meant for her. And when she looked up a few seconds later, she didn't appear half as triumphant as before.

Mercer was still watching her. Patient. Curious.

'Well?' he said.

She stared at him for a moment, considering. But what choice did she have, ultimately, apart from to see this through to the end?

'I need to tell you about Ella,' she said.

'Who is Ella?' I said.

She looked at me.

'Ella is my daughter.'

★ ★ ★

312

On the day she died — as she continued to put it — Charlie told us she had left the house as normal, but called in sick to work from the car. Neither her husband, Paul Carlisle, nor her employers had known where she was really going that day. At that point, she was eight weeks pregnant, but she hadn't told anyone else, and she had no intention of doing so. She wasn't planning on carrying the baby to term. But she also knew that Paul would be delighted by the news, and that he would try to persuade her to keep the child.

'He always wanted children,' she said.

'And you didn't?'

'God, no.' She relented slightly. 'It's different when they arrive, of course. But Ella wasn't here back then. She wasn't *real*. And the whole thing was an accident. I'd never wanted a child. Paul wouldn't have understood. It had always been one of those things between us. He respected my decision, while it was just theoretical. But I think my having an abortion would have been too much for him.'

'So you kept it secret?'

She bristled at that.

'No. *Secret* implies that someone else had a right to know. That I was *keeping* it from them. But that's not how it was. It was nobody else's business.'

'All right,' Mercer said. 'So you were planning to have an abortion?'

'I had an appointment. I went. But in the end . . . '

'You couldn't go through with it.'

313

'No.' She looked down at her hands, her hair obscuring her scars. 'I don't know why. I remember being annoyed with myself at the time, because it was as though I was being the sort of weak woman I hate. I thought I'd be strong and matter-of-fact when it came to it, but . . . I wasn't. I couldn't do it.'

'You decided to keep the baby?'

'No, I just decided not to do it there and then — I wanted some more time to think. But I didn't know what to do afterwards. It was too early to go home, and I didn't want to turn up at work.'

So she had driven to the north-east of the city, spent some time in a café — she couldn't remember the name — and walked aimlessly around. The afternoon turned to evening and, lost in thought, she found herself late, so set off home in a hurry, or tried to at least. But it was raining, and it was already getting dark, and she was distracted . . .

'And I crashed.'

'You know that's not true,' I said.

She didn't reply. It didn't matter, though. At some point, she'd been intercepted and abducted, and the crash scene had been staged with Rebecca Lawrence. The important thing right now was that I thought she was telling the truth about the pregnancy. The story fitted with the details in the file about her missing day — and also, I remembered, with what she'd told me during the first interview, when she'd been speaking about the scars.

It was like childbirth. It hurts, but very quickly

afterwards you forget how much.

'And your daughter? Ella?'

'Was born seven months later, yes.'

'In the other place?'

'Yes.' She looked down at the tablet. 'That's how I knew the man was a doctor. He was there when Ella was born. He helped to deliver her.'

Both Mercer and I were silent for a few moments. I had no idea what was going through his head. I was thinking that it at least made sense of Charlie's refusal to cooperate with us. Not Stockholm syndrome — or at least not wholly that. She was determined to do what she had been told for another reason entirely.

'Ella is still there?' I said.

'Yes.'

'In Hell?'

'No, no.' Charlie shook her head emphatically. 'Of *course* not. God would never allow that. She was born without sin, so there was no need for her to go through Hell. She went straight to Heaven.'

I hesitated. I wanted to shake my head too.

'Heaven?'

'Yes.' A look of upset appeared on her face, and for once the emotion held. 'But they let me see her quite often. They would take me to the edges of Heaven and let me spend time with her, hold her, play with her. And when I go back, that's where I'll be too. It's what I'll have finally earned.'

'Charlie,' I said. 'Slow down. Tell me about Heaven.'

Her face brightened at that.

'It's lovely.'

She described 'Heaven' as best she could, and it provided a stark contrast with the vision of 'Hell' she'd given. There was a kind of park, she said — a field, with a wood and an orchard. It was silent and peaceful, and even when it rained there was a sense of tranquility and calm. At the centre, there was a large white building, like a cliff face made of chalk. On a few occasions, when visiting her daughter, Charlie had been allowed inside. The rooms were all white, the furnishings new and clean, and the bed sheets soft. Ella had wanted for nothing.

'Who looked after her?' I said.

Again that look of surprise.

'God,' she said. 'Of course.'

And for a moment, I couldn't think of anything to say.

If what she was telling us was true, she was describing something far more extensive than we'd been previously considering. Not just a hell for punishment, but a heaven too. And not necessarily just a single madman, even with accomplices to help him, but more than one. A group — a *cult*, perhaps — with the patience and resources to act over a period of several years.

Beside me, Mercer spoke gently.

'And that's where you're going back to, now that you've told me all this?'

'Yes.'

'But Charlie,' he said, 'how will they even *know?*'

'They're all-powerful.'

I started to answer that no, of course they

weren't — but then they hardly needed to be. You had to go through the main entrance by the car park to reach the Baines Wing. These individuals were well organised. It would hardly be beyond them to have someone watching.

Someone who might still be there now.

I stood up. 'John. We have to go.'

'Wait,' Charlie said. 'I haven't told you yet.'

'Haven't told us what?'

'What I'm supposed to. Ella is part of it, but not everything. I haven't told you about the sins I'm wearing.'

I stared at the scars on her face and realised that no, of course she hadn't. Because how could being pregnant count as a sin? And what was it supposed to mean to Mercer in particular anyway?

'Go on, then,' I said. 'Tell us.'

She took a deep breath, gathering herself.

'My sins,' she said slowly, 'are numerous, but the one I am wearing now is very specific.' Her hand went to her stomach. 'My sin is that I didn't abort my unborn daughter. That I decided to keep her for a second longer than I had to.'

I was losing what little patience I had left.

'Why would that be a sin, Charlie? You said Ella was born without sin. That she was being taken care of in this . . . *Heaven*.'

'Yes. That is true. But it was my sin to keep her back then, because deep down, *I knew*. Before I died, I could pretend I didn't; I could hide the truth from myself. But I've admitted it now. I have worn it. There's no need to deny it any longer.'

'Deny what?'

'That a part of me knew exactly what a monster my husband really was.'

She rubbed her stomach gently, and when she looked up at us, her face was desperately sad.

'That a part of me knew full well what he would do to a child of his own.'

Groves

The last image of him

It didn't look as though the dead woman had been there for very long. She had been laid out like a star, her hands and feet tethered to the four bedposts with wire. Her hands, hanging down from their bindings, somehow reminded Groves of dead birds. Her head was tilted away from him, staring lifelessly towards the open window, where the dim light coming in revealed the extent of the injury to her throat. It looked as though she'd been nearly decapitated by the ferocity of the attack. Blood had crept down the white silk blouse she was wearing.

Groves took a careful step closer to the bed, edging around the base and towards the far side. He wanted to see the woman's face, but at least some of the policeman within him remained. He did his best to move slowly and quietly, just as he often did at crime scenes, almost as though the victim was sleeping and mustn't be disturbed.

The woman's face was familiar, but for a moment he couldn't place where he might have seen her before. Closer to, the other wounds she'd suffered were more obvious: cuts to her arms and body, done straight through the clothes, and several further slices on her face. Someone had drawn on the skin with a knife. A spray of blood from the larger wound had dried

319

on the wall beside her, and a pool on the floor beneath the bed had already congealed.

The same killer.

Clearly it was: the same man who had killed Leland and Thompson. Which implied that this woman, whoever she was, had also been linked to Simon Chadwick and the rest of them. It was possible she had been involved in Jamie's murder. That knowledge should have tempered his reaction to seeing her dead like this. It ought to have made it easier to look at the body, knowing that in some sense she had deserved it. It didn't.

Groves wasn't sure what he was feeling, but there was certainly no pleasure in knowing that this woman had suffered and died. If he felt anything at all right then, it was a profound sense of sadness. Whatever else it might have achieved, what had happened to these people wouldn't bring Jamie back. In spite of the guilt he'd felt earlier, this didn't look anything like justice to him. Suffering and evil could never be cancelled out by more of it.

He crouched down, careful not to touch the bed itself, and peered at the woman's face. Even with what had been done to it, it was easy enough to imagine what she would have looked like in life . . .

He stood up suddenly, taking a panicked step back.

Shit. *Shit.*

He didn't know the woman's name, but he knew where he recognised her from. Back when Jamie had been alive, she had worked at the nursery he'd attended. Laura something. That was her first name. He'd probably never heard her surname.

Groves nodded to himself.

He could almost have laughed.

Stitching me up good and proper, aren't you?

What to do next? There didn't seem any point phoning this scene in. It was the right thing to do, but it would surely damn him. However much Sean might want to believe him, the evidence against him was mounting. He needed to figure out the best way to handle it. He needed a hand of cards to play.

He turned to leave the room. And then froze for the second time.

Do you want to see your son again?

When he'd walked in, he hadn't seen them.

Photographs. Stuck to the wall beside the doorway. There were about twenty of them, and they looked home-made, as though printed out on photographic paper. Each one showed almost the exact same scene: the room behind Groves; a child standing at the foot of the bed.

He took a step closer.

The light in each photograph was subtly different. Some appeared to have been taken in the daytime, while others were illuminated by candle- or torchlight. The girls and boys were of various ages.

This is where they brought them.

This was where they had brought *Jamie*. Groves crouched down, panicking now, peering at the photographs. Laila Buckingham was there. *Oh God*. One by one, he looked, not believing that Jamie could really be here amongst these children, his gaze flicking from photo to photo, and then he stopped looking, because there he was. Everything in the world disappeared. Apart from the photograph, everything went away entirely.

It was strange how calm he felt.

Jamie.

In the photograph, his son was standing by the bed dressed in the blue jeans and orange shark T-shirt Groves could remember so well, the clothes he'd vanished in. His blond hair, never cut, was brushed into a neat parting, and the ends curled up above his small shoulders, as though afraid to touch them. Groves had a sudden, visceral memory of how it had felt to touch his hair. How thin and soft it had been.

Jamie wasn't crying in the photo, but his expression wasn't blank either. Instead, he was looking at the camera with something approaching curiosity. His expression seemed to be saying: *This is strange; what is happening here?* There was certainly no indication that he was scared or hurt — but then he was never easily cowed, never afraid of anything. Every new experience had been treated as an adventure, as though he believed the world couldn't hurt him, because it never had. Until it did.

His cheeks were slightly red. Groves could see the rash just below his eye, and remembered rubbing cream into it the morning before he went missing, while Jamie tried to squirm out of Caroline's embrace. He was exactly as Groves recalled him. A little boy, frozen forever in time.

This is the last image of him.

Groves reached out to touch the photograph, not caring now about fingerprints, not caring about anything. There might be other pictures, of course — later ones that would be unbearable to see — but this was a more recent image than any in Caroline's album, or in their memories.

He took the photograph from the wall. It was tacked on, and came away with a slight snap. He stared down at it again, then stroked his son's face, surprised for a brief second that the paper was cold; he had almost been expecting the warmth that came from touching skin.

He put it in his coat pocket.

Time to leave. He went back downstairs, moving less carefully than before; there didn't seem much point in trying now. He would be tied to the scene eventually, whatever he did, and it felt like the photograph had changed everything. He was going to call this in and deal with the consequences. He didn't care any more.

He walked outside, where the rain had picked up, already taking out his mobile, but he didn't have the chance to make the call. He faltered. *God will be with you,* he remembered, looking around the car park. Looking at the people walking quietly towards him.

Mark

The photographs

As I pulled up at the end of the cul-de-sac, directly outside Paul Carlisle's house, I saw that his front door was slightly ajar. I remembered coming to visit him days ago — pulling up behind the large van that had been parked nearby. The street itself was empty now, dead. I stared at the house for a moment, watching the clouds reflected in the implacable glass of the windows, the windscreen of the car slowly smearing with rain.

'Right,' I told Mercer. 'I'll need you to wait here, John.'

'I understand.'

I pulled out my mobile as I approached the house, dialling Pete's number. Even though the rain was falling harder now, the weather still hadn't broken the heat, and the air was clammy and moist as I made my way up Paul Carlisle's path to the open front door. The house felt ominous, as though someone inside might be standing slightly back from one of the windows, watching me.

I stopped on the doorstep, the phone to my ear. The door was open far enough to give me a view of the kitchen beyond, empty and full of shadow.

'Detective Pete Dwyer.'

'It's Mark.'

I gave him a rundown of the situation: that I'd persuaded Mercer to come to the hospital with me, and what Charlie had told us there. I could hear he was annoyed at me involving Mercer again without his permission, but by the end of the account, he seemed to have decided to let it ride for the moment.

'Carlisle's front door's open,' I said. 'It might be nothing, but I'm going in to check it out. His girlfriend lives here too, and she's pregnant.'

'Right.' Pete sounded firm. 'I'm sending a car, and I'll be over straight away. Don't take any stupid risks, Mark.'

'Don't worry.'

I hung up.

'Mr Carlisle?' I called out, rapping hard on the door. It opened a little wider. 'It's the police, Mr Carlisle. Are you inside? Can you hear me?'

There was no reply, so I pushed the door fully open and stepped into the kitchen. It was even messier than the last time I'd been here, but there was also an atmosphere to the place now that I didn't like. The gloom seemed darker than it should have done.

'Mr Carlisle?'

I moved through to the front room, and immediately stopped in the doorway. The room was empty, but there were obvious signs of a struggle: the coffee table had been knocked out of place, and was now pushed at an angle against the settee, while the television had fallen off the wall. The clothes and newspapers that had been piled on the seats during my last visit were scattered at random across the floor.

Charlie, I thought, *what have you done?*

What have your new-found friends done here?

'Mr Carlisle?'

Again no answer. I stepped into the living room, my heart beating too quickly. Something in the house was making my skin crawl. I wanted nothing more than to back slowly out of the room and return to the car to wait, but I had to make sure that either Carlisle or his partner weren't lying injured somewhere. I made my way carefully across the room to the door at the far corner. Pulling my sleeve down over my hand, I turned the handle, stepping back as I opened it in case anyone was waiting on the other side. Nobody was.

The carpet on the staircase was old and battered, worn through in places, and the landing at the top was illuminated by a single bulb, the lightest place in the house so far.

'Mr Carlisle?'

I was no longer expecting a response, but this time I did hear something — not a reply, but a sound coming from somewhere upstairs. Somebody crying. A woman, whimpering softly to herself.

I took the stairs three at a time.

'It's the police,' I shouted. 'Where are you, please?'

The woman was still crying, and the sound drew me towards the half-closed door of what was obviously the main bedroom. I pushed it open slowly, and saw her straight away: Carlisle's girlfriend, sitting on the floor between a wardrobe and a dressing table, her back against the wall, her arms hugging her swollen stomach. I realised that I didn't even know her name.

'Miss?' I said. 'It's the police. Are you hurt?'

She didn't answer me.

I took out my phone and called for an ambulance. As it dialled, I asked her, 'Is anybody else in the house?'

She shook her head. 'I don't know.'

'How long have you been up here?'

'I don't know.'

She was crying so hard that it was difficult to make out the words.

'What happened?' I said.

'They *took* him. They came in and *took* him.'

The hospital answered. I gave them my police ID.

'I need an ambulance right now at 68 Petrie Crescent. Pregnant woman, possibly injured.'

'On its way, Officer.'

I hung up, then pushed the door wider and stepped into the bedroom.

And faltered for the second time since entering the house.

The woman was sitting across from the bed, which I hadn't been able to see before from the occluded doorway. Now that I was in the room, I could see the spiderweb that had been drawn on the wall above the headboard. It had been done hurriedly in black marker, and the design was different from the one at Gordon Peters' house, but it was just as authentic.

I moved over to the bed, intending to get a better look at the web, perhaps thinking that by staring at it I might gain some insight into the sins Carlisle was supposed to have committed. *A part of me knew full well what he would do to a child of his own.* But as I stepped closer, I realised that the drawing was not the only thing wrong with the room.

There was a box file on the bed. Someone had opened it and emptied the contents over the quilt. My gaze moved over the papers and pamphlets and photographs, and I recognised with disgust what they were.

The papers were mostly photocopies. The one nearest to me had a hand-drawn picture of a naked child on it, sketched in pencil. Others had drawings that were even cruder and more explicit, depicting sexual scenarios between children and grown men and women. Many were almost cartoonish, depicted in seaside postcard style, while others were realistic. The pamphlets I could see appeared to be hand-printed and stapled and old: vile material that used to be passed around by hand long before the advent of the internet. Collectors' items, perhaps. But there were printouts from online as well: stills from what looked like videos; real people in real poses.

And then there were the photographs.

I took another step closer to the bed, not because I wanted to, but because I needed to make sense of what I was seeing. There were perhaps twenty of them in all, lined up in the centre of the bed in rows and columns, like cards for a matching game. Each of them was similar but horrifyingly different. Similar because they all showed a child standing in what appeared to be the same desolate room; horrifying because each child was different — boys and girls, ranging in age from infants to early teens. Each photograph was a memento of what I could only imagine had been an individual case of terrible abuse.

'I didn't know.'

I turned my head to see that the woman was looking up at me. She had seen the poison on the bed too, and the need to disassociate herself from the material transcended whatever pain she was in right now.

'I didn't know. I swear I didn't know.'

I started to say something in reply — I wasn't even sure what — and that was when I felt the movement in the doorway behind me.

Sean

I know who did it

Sean took a deep breath, unlocked David's front door and stepped inside.

It felt strange and wrong to be in his friend's house without him. He'd visited before, of course, so he was familiar with the layout, and over the course of his career he'd done more searches than he could even begin to remember, but this was different. Remembering how beaten down David had looked in the interview room, this felt very much like an invasion. Not to mention that being here like this — in an official capacity, alone — brought it home to him how much trouble David might really be in.

He didn't do it, though.

Sean was quite sure that was true. Whatever was actually going on, he knew David, and trusted him. David was a good man. Over the years, Sean had known his partner tell a small handful of harmless lies, and none of them had come close to being convincing; lying just didn't fit with him. Today, when Sean had asked if he was telling the truth, David had said yes and Sean had believed him. David hadn't killed Leland and Thompson.

But that didn't mean he wasn't in real trouble. At the very least, his career was severely tarnished, and there was a good chance it was over altogether. That worried Sean. Without Jamie, David's career was his life. A policeman wasn't just what he did, but what he *was*.

 And that was really only the bare minimum of damage. If David was right that someone was trying to frame him, then that person had done a pretty good job of it so far. There was nothing to say that wouldn't continue.

Come on then, David.

Prove yourself right.

Sean checked the details on the consent-to-search form, then headed through to the front room of the cottage. The phone was where David had said it would be, on the coffee table in the middle of the room, next to his laptop. It was an old model, and a bit battered and scratched, but it still seemed unlikely that a homeless addict like Carl Thompson would have owned it. *Not impossible, though.*

From David's description of events, someone had persuaded Thompson to pass it on, but only after there had been a test of sorts. David had stepped in to help another passenger, then given Thompson change when he begged for it. David had been a good person, in other words, and the phone was a reward for behaving correctly, doing the right thing.

But why?

Sean's mind wandered. If that was how it had happened, what did that say about the person who was behind this? They wanted to put David through his paces. Have him prove himself. And yet the more he did that — the more entangled he got — the more in trouble he found himself.

If David's theory that this was another grieving parent was right, and they were angry with him as he'd suggested, maybe they were emphasising the fact that he was good, but not good enough.

Maybe. Still didn't make much sense, though.

The temptation to turn the phone on and check through it right now was strong, but Sean resisted. It was better to do everything exactly by the book; that way, when it came to it, the evidence would be untainted. And anyway, he was hardly the techie type. The IT team at the department would examine it carefully, whereas ten to one he'd fuck up and accidentally erase everything. He slapped gloves on and bagged the phone up, placing it in his jacket pocket. According to the search form, David had stored the birthday card upstairs in the bedside table.

Sean made his way up.

As he pushed open the door to the bedroom, whorls of dust danced away across the floor. The bed itself was unmade, and there were clothes tangled up in a pile at the end. A faintly unpleasant aroma in the air. Sean wrinkled his nose, and again felt awkward. The room wasn't in a *disgusting* state, but David wouldn't have wanted him to see it like this. On previous searches they'd done together, Sean had always been quick to crack a joke about the hygiene and living standards of the people involved, and right now, he hoped David knew he'd never really meant any of that.

The table was on the far side of the bed. Aside from a single free-standing wardrobe, it was the only other furniture in the room: a small cabinet, really, with a single door and a drawer. There was a lamp on it, and David's battered bible. Sean didn't bother with the drawer, but opened the door to reveal a pile of cards and paperwork.

Shit, David.

Sean picked the pile out and placed it on the bed carefully. There must have been at least twenty letters. How could people be so cruel? he wondered. What was *wrong* with them?

Even more than that, what had driven David to keep it all right here, beside the bed? It seemed like the hate from a collection like this might leach into your dreams if you slept beside it. And yet apparently David had kept them close, the way someone else might keep something of sentimental value — a photo, maybe, or a postcard or letter from a loved one. It was like he'd *valued* the hate in them. As though they were important to him in some way. Sean didn't understand it.

It was probably worth taking the whole lot. If the guy had written to David once — if it even *was* the guy — then he might have done it before. They could search through the letters for similarities. Maybe there'd even be some detail that would lead them to him.

He pulled out a larger bag to store them all in, but couldn't resist looking at the one on top. The birthday card that David had received. The envelope had been torn raggedly open, but the card had been put back inside. Sean looked at the envelope first. There were no delivery details printed over the stamp, but that didn't necessarily mean it had been hand-delivered; sometimes the post office machines barely left a trace at all. It had been addressed, in clear, characterless black ink, to Jamie Groves.

Bastard.

Sean took the card out carefully, holding it by the edges. The front showed Winnie-the-Pooh playing in a meadow with his friends. The colours were pastel, giving the picture a faded watercolour effect, as though the characters were gradually disappearing from an old photograph. An image from another age, slowly fading.

He opened the card.

For a second, all he could do was stare at what had been written there, in the same neat black handwriting as the envelope.

I know who did it.

That was exactly what David had told him would be there. But David hadn't told him about the lines below that, all clearly written by the same hand.

Their names are Edward Leland, Carl
Thompson and Laura Harrison. I'm so
sorry for what I'm going to do. I hope you
can forgive me. I hope I'll still be able to
remember you smiling at me.

Sean read the words again and again, trying to find some alternative meaning in them. Something different from what they clearly signified. There was none.

'Oh David,' he said.

His hands were shaking slightly as he read the
end of the card.

*I miss you so much, my beautiful little
boy, and I love you more every day.*
  Daddy xxxxx

Mark

David Groves

I turned to see Mercer standing in the bedroom doorway.

'I thought you were going to wait in the car,' I said.

'I was worried you might be in trouble.'

But he wasn't looking at me, or even at the crying woman sitting against the far wall. Instead, his eyes were transfixed on the spiderweb that had been drawn above the bed. The idea that he could have helped me in a physical situation was laughable; I knew full well why he'd come inside. The desire to know. To understand. And I suppose, given everything, I had to allow him that.

'My,' he said. 'That really is the genuine article, isn't it?'

I didn't answer. I wondered how it made him feel to see it there for real — a new one, after all this time. The strange thing was that, staring at the design now, absorbed by it, he seemed less fragile than before, almost as though he was drawing energy from it in some way. As though the sight of it had added some power to whatever internal battery was keeping him going.

'How strange,' he said. 'I can't work out what's happening here. The 50/50 Killer is dead. And yet this . . . this is his work.'

'Because the man came from somewhere.' Now that Mercer was in the room, there didn't seem any point in hiding the evidence on the bed. 'And there's more. Look at these.'

He came and stood beside me, clearly reluctant to tear his gaze away from the web on the wall. He scanned the material half-heartedly.

'I think this might have all belonged to Paul Carlisle,' I said. 'That's clearly what it's meant to imply anyway. And it would fit with what Charlie told us. Whoever these people are, they punish the guilty. What I can't work out is why *now?* Why, take Charlie for not knowing, but leave Paul Carlisle free for the next two years? If this is true, then he was by far the more guilty of the two, and they would have to have known . . . '

I trailed off, because Mercer wasn't listening to me. The half-hearted examination of the papers on the bed had stopped, and he was now staring intently at the photographs lined up in the middle. He'd gone pale.

'John?'

'I've seen these before,' he said.

'Where?'

He closed his eyes. 'Oh God. I think I understand.'

'John, I need you to tell me.'

'The ones I saw were found in an abandoned fire station. There was a woman's body there too.' With his eyes still closed, Mercer pinched his nose, trying to remember. 'Laura Harrison. That was her name. We believed she was part of a paedophile gang, and that the photographs were her souvenirs. A number of other people

337

had been murdered in the days beforehand. A man — a policeman who'd lost his son — had been killing them. It was our case. Just a formality, really, given the evidence, but still ours. *Mine.*'

'John?'

'David Groves,' he said. 'We never found him afterwards.'

Finally Mercer opened his eyes again.

'He went missing two years ago.'

Part Five

And She told Them this world is a playground for God and the Devil, and that life was a battle between good and evil in the hearts of Men, and that when eternity came to a close, those scores would be tallied and the true nature of Man settled for ever. And She told Them that within the heart of each individual Man the larger battle was present, just as the entirety of the tree resides in the seed. And they asked if, between them, They might therefore settle that nature in Their lifespan, and She told Them this was so.

Extract from the Cane Hill bible

Mark

A hell of a guy

'Let me get this straight before we start,' Detective Sean Robertson told me. 'I don't think he did it, and. I never have. I won't help you do anything else to destroy David's reputation.'

Robertson was sitting on the other side of a desk crowded with paperwork and coffee cups, while I was perched on one of the plastic office chairs that had been backed up against the wall when I'd arrived. I'd had to move it myself. It had been quite clear, when I'd called ahead, that Robertson had no interest in talking to me, and no desire whatsoever to rake over the coals of a situation that had burned him so badly.

I tried to remain implacable.

'I'm really not here to destroy his reputation.'

'Yeah, well. It's a bit late for that anyway, isn't it? Your man already did that.'

Mercer, he meant. It didn't matter to Robertson that the investigation into his former partner's conduct had taken place before my time; it was still my team, and even though he was long gone from it, Mercer remained *our man*. He was the one who'd had David Groves charged and convicted *in absentia*. But then, from a cursory scan of the file on my way over, he'd had good reason to.

'You're right,' I conceded. 'David Groves'

reputation was ruined a long time ago. I mean, I've seen the file. Three counts of first-degree murder. At first glance, it looks pretty tight to me too. So whatever the damage done to his reputation, maybe your ex-partner did some of it himself?'

Robertson stared back at me for a moment, his beefy arms folded and resting on a stomach that strained at his shirt. His tie was low and off-centre. With his red cheeks and the stubble that hung around his neck under the chin, I thought he looked more like a seedy reporter than a police detective — the kind of guy you'd see at a crime scene, wrapped in an overcoat and eating a burger out of a bag. Appearances could be deceptive, of course. I knew from his file that he was distinguished and capable, and looking back at him now, I could see that his eyes were sharp, even if the rest of him wasn't.

'Anyway.' I patted the file I'd brought with me. 'I'm actually not here to cause any problems for him. At the time, I can see it looked clear-cut. But things have . . . changed. That's why I'm here.'

'How have things changed?'

'You'll have to trust me on that for now.'

'Oh, will I now?'

'Yes.'

I wasn't just being overcautious about sharing the details of the Matheson investigation. The truth was that I really *didn't* know how things had changed, only that they had. It was now clear that Mercer was connected to our case in two ways: from the 50/50 Killer, and from the two-year-old tying up of the murders supposedly committed by Detective David Groves. As to the links between the two — the web that connected it all together — I could hardly even begin to guess right now. I was hoping that exploring the Groves case might help me, and to get Robertson on side, I decided I needed to throw him a crumb.

'Look,' I said. 'All I can say is that we're pursuing something that maybe . . . casts doubt on the charges back then. Is that enough for now?'

He looked at me, considering. Didn't answer.

I tried a different tack. 'Despite all the evidence at the time, you really never thought Groves was guilty?'

'Not once. He was my partner.'

'There must be more to it than that.' I glanced at the file again. 'Like I said, to an outsider it looks clear-cut. Believe me, I get the loyalty. But you don't strike me as the kind of guy who'd defend someone to the end like that, not without good reason.'

Robertson shook his head. 'You didn't know him.'

'I'm aware of that.'

'All you *do* know, assuming you've even done your fucking job properly, is what's in that file. That's not the whole story.'

He looked away suddenly, clamping down on the anger he still felt. I knew from scanning the file that he'd cooperated with the investigation, but it had also been obvious that he hadn't remotely agreed with its final conclusions. It was equally apparent that he'd pursued the case, here and there, adding brief notes to the file as he went, none of which had come to anything. He was annoyed and frustrated with himself for that, I thought — for failing his friend — and my presence here reminded him of that.

'All right,' I said. 'No, I don't know everything. So how about you take me through the details? Because you never know, do you? If we pool resources, maybe we can help each other out.'

He looked back at me for a moment, still considering.

'Okay,' he said finally. 'Let's see how we go.'

⋆ ⋆ ⋆

My second impression of Robertson had been correct. Despite his dishevelled outward appearance, he proved sharp and incisive, succinctly summarising the case and giving me a far clearer picture of what had happened than the file ever could, even if I'd studied it for hours. It was obvious from the moment we started talking that not only did the case mean a lot to him, but he knew it inside out.

More to the point, he began relaxing with me. As the conversation progressed, it felt more and more as though we were on the same side. Perhaps we were — although I still wasn't sure. Whatever Robertson's own personal doubts, the evidence against David Groves remained compelling, to say the least.

Groves hadn't started out as a killer, that

much was certain. He'd started out as a hero, when eight-year-old Laila Buckingham had been found — badly hurt but alive — chained to a bed in a back room.

'He saved her life,' I said.

'Yes.' Robertson nodded once. 'And nearly died doing it. He would have done the same thing again too. Without hesitation. He was a hell of a guy.'

'I can see that.'

'And that's why he felt so guilty about what happened to Jamie. Not that he ever *regretted* saving Laila Buckingham; David wasn't like that. Even with what happened to Jamie, I don't think he'd have gone back and changed a single thing about what he did.'

'He thought the same people took his son?'

'Yes. To take revenge on him. I think that too.'

At the time, it must have seemed a somewhat far-fetched idea — few gangs would be so bold — but in hindsight there was something to it. The flat had belonged to a man named Simon Chadwick, and the information he had given upon arrest had indicated that a paedophile group was operating locally. They were never caught, and David Groves, the man who had thwarted them, had been paraded through the newspapers as a hero. You could see why he might come to the conclusion that his son had been targeted. More to the point, the photographs in the collection retrieved from Paul Carlisle's house today contained images of both Laila Buckingham and Jamie Groves.

'Have you got kids, Detective Nelson?'

I shook my head.

'Well,' Robertson said, 'let me tell you. A lot of people would probably sympathise with what David's supposed to have done. A lot of people would say he was *right* to have done it.'

'I'm sure that's true.'

'And that would be my position as well. If he had done it, I'd understand. But that's the thing. He *wouldn't* have done it. He wasn't that kind of person.'

'What was he, then?'

'He was a *good* man.' Robertson leaned back. 'Despite everything that happened to him, he still believed in God. Can you imagine that?'

I thought about what Rebecca Lawrence's father, Harold, had said to me. *How could I be religious now? I wouldn't want to meet the God that took my daughter away from me.*

'Not really,' I said.

'But David had real faith. He believed in justice, sure, but not *that* kind of justice. He was a cop through and through. Following the law meant everything to him, and after Jamie died, it was all he had left. If he'd found the people responsible, he'd never have killed them. It just wasn't in his nature.'

We talked through the crimes Groves was supposed to have committed. The first murder he'd been convicted of was that of Edward Leland, who was killed on 30 July 2013, just over two years ago. Leland had been tortured and murdered; Groves had tried to cover up his actions by setting fire to the victim and the house around him. As the investigation progressed, there had been a suggestion that Leland was implicated in child pornography, although no direct evidence was ever found to confirm it.

Leland's laptop was found later in Groves' home. The working theory was that from either the computer, or Leland himself, Groves had managed to extract information that led him to a young homeless man named Carl Thompson. Thompson's remains were discovered in the tunnels under the railway arches; he too had been tortured before being killed. A man matching Groves' description was witnessed leaving the scene shortly before the discovery of the body. Groves later confessed to phoning the report in anonymously, and Thompson's phone was discovered in his house.

'Okay. What about the third victim? The woman in the fire station.'

'Laura Harrison.' Robertson nodded. 'She was a nursery worker.'

'A nursery worker?'

That made me think about Rebecca Lawrence again. She'd worked in a nursery too.

'Yes,' Robertson said. 'Years before, Harrison worked at the nursery that Jamie Groves used to go to, before he was abducted.'

'You think Harrison targeted him?'

'Yes, I think so. She was vetted at the time, obviously, and came back clean. It's impossible to prove it either way, though, now that she's dead.'

'And what about the birthday card?'

'David got them every year, always on what would have been Jamie's birthday. You know what sick fucks some people are. He got that one on the thirtieth.'

'The same day Leland was killed?'

'That's what he told me. But it had been added to since then. He said that when he opened the card, the only thing there was the first line. Like a taunt: *I know who did it.* But when I found it, someone had turned it into a confession, naming the victims.'

I opened the file I'd brought with me, turning to the page close to the end that contained a photograph of the birthday card. The message inside had been written very carefully, and while the handwriting was never conclusively matched to Groves', the implication was obvious. Groves had written the birthday card to his son, apologising for what he was about to do, and then started delivering the boy a special birthday present by killing the people responsible for his murder.

'The thing is,' Robertson said, 'why would David have lied to me about that? Why would he *bother* at that point? He didn't even need to mention the card. No — I think someone got into the house and set the scene.'

'Playing devil's advocate,' I said, aware of how appropriate the phrase was right now, 'that *someone* could have set a better scene.'

'Yeah, but it was good enough. And without David around to defend himself . . . '

Robertson leaned back, the look of frustration on his face allowing me to finish the thought for him. *Without David around, it was left to me. And I wasn't good enough, was I?*

348

Not when he'd come up against Mercer, anyway.

I turned to the last few pages of the report, which dealt with the disappearance of David Groves. His vehicle was discovered, apparently abandoned, on the ring road to the north of the city, with empty bottles of vodka in the passenger footwell. The woods were combed without success, and nobody had seen anything of David Groves since that day. Suicide was the presumption, and certainly the woods contained a multitude of places where a body might lie undiscovered.

The evidence had been compelling back then. On the surface, it remained so now.

'You think Groves was framed?' I said.

Robertson didn't even hesitate. 'Yes. He thought so too. He thought it was maybe another parent — someone else who'd lost a child to the same people — but I don't know if I ever bought that idea.'

'Why not?'

'I don't know. It all felt too organised for that.'

Organised. I nodded to myself. Yes, it did. And everything about the recent case spoke to that too. The planning and execution had spanned years. We were dealing with patient, resourceful individuals, and right now, I was sure we were only seeing a small fraction of their activities. Based on what we knew so far, I imagined they'd be more than capable of framing David Groves. And of course, suicide was only a presumption. His body had never been found.

'I believed him, though.' Robertson turned his

head to look out of the window. From where I was sitting, all I could see was the sky, full of dark grey cloud. 'But I can't work out *why* anyone would do that to him. Because it's true what I told you earlier, you know. I realise you never met him, but it's true.'

'What is?'

'That David Groves was a good man. A decent man.' Robertson turned away from the sky and looked at me again. 'Maybe the best man I've ever known.'

And thinking again about the lack of a body, and the way the people behind this could orchestrate disappearances and fake deaths, I began wondering.

David Groves was a good man.

I began wondering about that use of the past tense.

Groves

Now

There was little past any more.

There was certainly no future. Groves had given up attempting to keep track of time; it had ceased to have any meaning down here. There was just the darkness, the dripping noises, the blaring bursts of television that seemed to come at random. Only the *now*.

You got used to everything eventually, and the *now* no longer caused him the pain it had done back at the beginning, immediately after his death. His grave was just large enough for him to stand in, but not long enough to lie down, so he'd become used to half sleeping in a bent and awkward curl on the hard ground, or else leaning in the corner, trusting the exhaustion to keep him under for a time. The aches in his body remained, but he'd become accustomed to them, so that what had once been extreme discomfort — agony, even — was now only a background hum of pain. The boredom had become normal and everyday. He no longer thought much. Even his dreams, which had been as bright and shocking as the television to start with, had dulled and flattened. However hard the path it has to tread, your life finds a way to continue.

Not life, of course.

Just as there had once been pain, Groves knew

there had also been a time when he had questioned the fact of his suicide — railed and fought against it, even as the Devil had patiently explained it to him, time and time again. Again, that was so distant now as to feel meaningless and alien. How could he ever have doubted it? It was ridiculous. He had killed himself, and now here he was. In Hell. When he tried, he could even remember what had happened, and the memories were as vivid as any from before his death.

I saved a little girl, and so my son was murdered.

I failed to catch his killers, and so someone else did it for me.

They took everything I had left from me.

And there was nothing left to live for.

The words came easily; he had repeated them often enough. Thinking back now, Groves was sure he could remember parking his car by the path that led to the clearing where Jamie's body had been found. In the afternoon light, the rain pattering down, he had retraced the steps that had taken him there on that dark night two years before, and had stood for a while looking down at what had once been a grave and was now simply an anonymous patch of land. There was no sign his boy had ever been buried there.

After a short time, he had moved on, deeper into the woods, ever deeper, until he had found a ravine that was high and isolated enough. He had been completely calm when he jumped. He remembered thinking that. *It would surprise anyone who could see me,* he'd thought, looking up, the individual drops of rain visible against the sky as they fell. *It would seem strange to them, how calm I am.*

He had jumped. And then he had been here. In Hell.

This was his reward. All through life, despite everything that had happened to him, he had kept his faith and tried to be a good man — always trusting that God had a plan, and that the terrible things that happened to him were taking place for a reason. Always attempting to do the right thing. And look how it had turned out for him. The realisation brought a surge of bitterness. One by one, all the things that had ever mattered to him had been taken away, and now he was here, being punished still. His behaviour and his faith — it had all apparently counted for nothing in God's eyes. If he felt anything at all in the darkness now, it was hate.

As if on cue, the television came to life, filling the cell with sharp blue light. Once, Groves would have winced from the contrast, but his eyes barely registered the sudden burst of pain. Now, rather than turning away from it, as he had sometimes done, he sat down cross-legged before it.

It was a recording of a news report. There were a handful of different ones played to him, but this was the most familiar. The red banner at the bottom read: REVENGE MURDERS: COP SUSPECT STILL MISSING. The main screen was taken up by a head-and-shoulders shot of another policeman, standing outside the department building. He was old, his hair receding, and he looked very tired and serious. Groves recognised him, of course. John Mercer was a legend in the force.

'Detective David Groves is currently the main suspect in the murder of three individuals,' Mercer told the off-camera reporter.

The screen split to include three photographs on the right-hand side. Edward Leland, Carl Thompson and Laura Harrison.

Mercer said, 'We are investigating links these individuals may have had to the abduction and murder of Detective Groves' son, Jamie, along with a number of other children. We are currently requesting that anyone who may have information come forward. We are also appealing to David Groves.' He turned to face the camera directly. 'David. Your colleagues and family are extremely concerned for your safety. We urge you to get in contact with us.'

Groves stared at Mercer's face. There wasn't an ounce of compassion or concern in it. The man had already made up his mind, just as they all had. There would have been no chance of fair treatment. If he hadn't been dead already by the time this broadcast aired, there was no way he would have come forward.

The reporter said, 'Can you comment on rumours that Detective Groves' car has been found in the northern area of the city?'

Mercer turned back to the reporter. He was nodding along to the question, but said, 'No, I'm afraid I can't comment on that. All I can repeat is that we remain concerned for Detective Groves' safety and well-being, and ask for him to get in touch with us at the earliest opportunity.'

'And are you looking for anyone else in connection to these deaths?'

Onscreen, Mercer hesitated slightly, and the action gave him away. *Cut and dried*, Groves thought. Already. Despite everything he'd done, and tried to do, they had all immediately decided that he'd done it. Judged him. His deeds, his character — none of that had mattered at all.

'I can't comment on that either, I'm afraid.'

The camera remained on him for a moment, and then the television flicked off, plunging Groves back into darkness again. A ghostly pale blue after-image of Mercer's face hung in the air for a moment, gradually fading.

Groves stood up slowly, his atrophied muscles finding the movement hard. He wondered what he looked like. He hadn't seen himself in . . . well, what did time matter down here in Hell? But he knew his hair was long and matted, his beard overgrown, his body thin and filthy. There was no sunlight here. His skin was probably the colour of teeth.

Not that it mattered.

He became aware that someone was outside his cell door. He could hear them breathing. When he looked towards the slot there, he saw what looked like a pair of eyes peering in at him. That didn't matter either. He was too exhausted to care.

He backed into the corner of the cell and leaned there.

It counted for nothing.

And with that thought echoing through his empty mind, he closed his eyes and slept.

Mark

The long game

Fifteen minutes until the briefing.

Back on our corridor, Pete's door was open, and I could hear him talking quietly to Mercer. I ignored them for now, heading instead into my own office and closing the door. I cleared piles of paperwork from my desk, then checked an update from the hospital.

Paul Carlisle's partner, Jenny Cantrell, remained distressed, and was being cared for under guard. She had managed to give a brief account of events at the house. She had been in the front room with Carlisle when three individuals had appeared in the living room; she had no idea how they'd got in. They were dressed in black, including face masks, and she described them as *feeling* like soldiers, but she hadn't had much of a chance to see before a panicked Carlisle told her to get upstairs.

Cantrell had hidden in the bedroom, where she could hear the sounds of the disturbance below and her partner screaming, and then two of the men had entered the bedroom. One began arranging the material on the bed, while the other worked on the wall. She had sat still throughout, closing her eyes and holding her hands over her ears. When the men left, she had seen what was on the bed and collapsed again in shock.

I put the report down, then spread my various files on the desk and opened up a blank document on my main computer, keeping a tablet to one side of me as well. I wanted all the information at my fingertips, because I needed to make sense of it — to place it into some kind of order and context, even if the ultimate meaning remained unclear. I hit the option for the tablet to feed through to the plasma screen I had mounted on the opposite wall, because I also wanted the details writ large.

I typed in the additional dates from the Groves case.

Provisional timeline

15 March 2008 David Groves rescues Laila Buckingham

14 June 2010 Jamie Groves abducted

19 June 2010 Rebecca Lawrence reported missing (14th?)

8 September 2012 Body of Jamie Groves discovered

30 July 2013 Edward Leland found murdered (home)

1 August 2013 Carl Thompson found murdered (arches)

2 August 2013 Laura Harrison found murdered (fire station); last known sighting of David Groves

3 August 2013 Charlie Matheson's car crash

4 December 2013 Death of the 50/50 Killer

28 July 2015 Charlie Matheson reappears

1 August 2015 Gordon Peters murdered; Paul Carlisle abducted

There were some obvious correlations there.

Start at the beginning, though.

It began with Groves saving Laila Buckingham on 15 March 2008, over seven years ago now. I looked through the initial reports, reading how he'd fought with Simon Chadwick and saved the little girl. She was eight at the time of the abduction. Groves' own son, Jamie, was less than a year old. I knew this additional detail because for some reason the file contained a clipping of a newspaper interview Groves had given shortly afterwards. Perhaps Sean Robertson had included it. The profile of a hero, added in to counter the accusations and evidence that filled the rest of it.

My son's not one yet, Groves was quoted as saying, *but all through the search I kept trying to imagine how it would feel if he was Laila's age and had been taken from me. How I'd do absolutely anything to get him back. And how a child must feel. I prayed for her and tried to keep faith.*

A religious man, just like Sean Robertson had said.

Which hadn't done much for him in the end. Groves believed that in saving Laila Buckingham, he'd crossed paths with an organised gang of paedophiles, and that they'd targeted his son afterwards as an act of revenge. Jamie went missing on 14 June 2010.

His body was found on 8 September 2012, and after over two years missing, it had been far too deteriorated to estimate either a cause or time of death. It was assumed that he had died shortly after his abduction. Since there was no way of telling right now, I decided not to guess, and to concentrate instead on the date of the abduction.

The first connection, then.

14 June 2010 Jamie Groves abducted
19 June 2010 Rebecca Lawrence reported missing (14th?)

The dates didn't match precisely, but the 19th was only when the Lawrences had made the call to the police. It was likely that Rebecca's disappearance had occurred on the 14th, when the money from her account was withdrawn, which meant that they would tally exactly.

And that couldn't be a coincidence.

I rubbed my jawline, trying to work out what it meant.

Like Laura Harrison, Rebecca Lawrence had been a nursery worker. Was it possible she had also been a member of the gang? But if she had been involved in the abduction of Jamie Groves, then it was clear something else had happened that day too. Because that was when Rebecca Lawrence had vanished from the face of the earth.

Fast-forward three years.

30 July 2013 Edward Leland found murdered (home)
1 August 2013 Carl Thompson found murdered (arches)
2 August 2013 Laura Harrison found murdered (fire station); last known sighting of David Groves

These were the three killings that Groves was convicted of *in absentia* — the rest of the alleged paedophile gang. Leland's body was discovered on 30 July in the remains of a house fire believed to have been started in the early hours of that morning. The other killings followed in the handful of days afterwards.

Of course, if Charlie was to be believed, there had been one other member of the gang.

3 August 2013 Charlie Matheson's car crash

The staged accident had occurred the day after Groves' disappearance. Charlie was connected to the paedophile gang in two ways: through her husband, Paul Carlisle, who for some reason had not been targeted at the same time as the others; and through Rebecca Lawrence, who had reappeared in dramatic fashion as her stand-in at the crash scene.

I couldn't make sense of what I was seeing, but looking at it as a whole, it was fairly clear to me that there was no way David Groves had been responsible for most of it. While he could still conceivably have committed the three murders in 2013, it made little sense that he'd abduct Rebecca Lawrence on the day his own son disappeared, and then somehow hold her in captivity for over three years. Not to mention the fact that *three* men had abducted Paul Carlisle today.

So that was two members of the gang he couldn't have dealt with himself. Robertson was convinced he'd been framed for the killings of the other three too, and I was beginning to believe he was right. Someone else — the people behind Charlie Matheson's imprisonment, I suspected — had targeted them all, and in the process framed David Groves.

But why?

From what Charlie had talked about — the Devil in Hell; God in Heaven; a cult of some kind — it made a vague kind of sense to me that they might go after a gang of murderous paedophiles. But Groves had been a good man. A decent man.

And what about you, Charlie?

I looked up at the screen.

28 July 2015 Charlie Matheson reappears

She'd been sent back to deliver a message to Mercer. But that interested me less right now than the timing.

Why *now*?

I stared at the screen again. I'd interviewed Charlie on 29 July, the day after she was found. Not quite a full two years since her abduction, but only a few days out. Was there some kind of resonance there? There had to be, but I couldn't see what it might be. So what about the long game then? These people were highly organised. They had planned this carefully.

Mercer's words from earlier came back to me.

Peters did a poor job this time with Matheson, didn't he?

What he'd suggested about Dr Gordon Peters.

Whatever sedative he gave her, it seems like it

was too much. Perhaps he set everything back slightly. For people as organised and precise as this, maybe that would be a sin.

If Peters had been more careful with his dosages, then Charlie might have remembered to ask for Mercer when I'd first spoken to her. Allowing for some time for her story to unfold, and for arrangements to be made, he might have gone to see her as early as 30 July, two days ago. Which was the anniversary of Edward Leland's murder. But there was nothing special about Leland, was there?

No, I realised.

Not the anniversary of Leland's murder at all.

Jamie Groves' birthday.

He would have been eight years old on 30 July this year. I flicked back through the file on the desk until I found the newspaper interview Groves had given after saving Laila Buckingham. The portrait of a hero. A good man.

I read the quote again.

My son's not one yet, but all through the search I kept trying to imagine how it would feel if he was Laila's age and had been taken from me.

How I'd do absolutely anything to get him back.

Mark

The briefing

'You know what you're asking, don't you?' Pete said. 'You actually do realise what you're suggesting?'

'Yes.'

'And you're serious about this?'

'Absolutely.'

There were five of us in the main operations room. I was standing beneath the plasma screen, which still showed the twin images of Charlie Matheson — from before and after her abduction. Greg and Simon were sitting down. Mercer remained with us for the moment, mainly because of his knowledge of the 50/50 case, but he appeared to be completely ignoring me. He kept pacing back and forth, staring at the various sheets and notes that had been tacked to the walls. Pete was standing up. He had spent the last minute staring at me as I spoke. Now he ran one hand through his ruffled hair and sighed heavily.

'Jesus Christ,' he said.

I understood his unease. I'd just suggested we contact Caroline Evans, the ex-wife of David Groves, and begin formalities for possibly the worst invasion of a bereaved parent's peace I could think of. The exhumation of her murdered son's body.

I turned to Simon. 'What were the autopsy results on Jamie Groves?'

Simon was silent for a moment; the situation seemed to have subdued even him. He consulted the notes he had in front of him.

'The cause of death was undetermined,' he said. 'The body was entirely skeletal.'

'Identification?'

'That was established by the father, David Groves. The boy's body was found in the clothing he was wearing when he disappeared, along with a stuffed toy that belonged to him.'

'Except we know that the people we're looking for are pretty good at staging scenes like that. Substituting one body for another.'

'Mark.' Pete shook his head. 'I'm going to need more.'

Mercer was still wandering the perimeter of the room, looking at the various documents on display. I didn't think he'd been paying the slightest attention to me, but now his voice drifted over.

'He's right, Pete.'

'Right about what?'

'David Groves isn't dead,' I said. 'And I don't think his son is either.'

The silence from that settled in the room for a few seconds.

'Right.' Pete sighed. 'Start at the beginning.'

★ ★ ★

I did.

'Here's what I think.' I clicked through so the

plasma screen showed the timeline I'd developed. 'I think we're looking at two very distinct groups of people at work.'

The first was an organised gang of predatory paedophiles. The membership included Rebecca Lawrence, Edward Leland, Carl Thompson, Laura Harrison, Paul Carlisle and — at least to some extent — Simon Chadwick. Over a period of several years, the group had abducted and abused a number of children of various ages, some of whom it was likely they had also murdered. We'd never identified all the children in the photographs that had been recovered.

'Our second group,' I said, 'amounts to a kind of cult.'

We didn't know how many people were involved, although there were clearly several, with perhaps two at the top — the individuals Charlie Matheson had described as God and the Devil. They weren't *really* those things, of course; they were just men. But the group had been abducting people and subjecting them to their own version of Hell. Bad people who hadn't been caught, and who needed to wear their sins to repent. If Charlie were to be believed, there was even a Heaven of a kind. In their own minds, these people seemed to be creating their own version of the afterlife here on earth.

'We don't know who they are,' I said, 'but we know they have money and patience, and that they've been active and well organised for a long time. There's also evidence that they're connected to the man we knew as the 50/50 Killer — that perhaps this is where he came from. We know the 50/50 Killer was highly organised too, and that he stalked and researched his targets for lengthy periods of time. We know he was religiously motivated, to some extent, and independently wealthy. All that tallies.'

I glanced over at Mercer as I said this, but again, he had his back to me and seemed not to be listening. He was studying the information on the walls as though it was ancient hieroglyphs that he could make sense of if he looked at them for long enough.

Pete was staring at my timeline.

'And the connection?' he said.

'Is that at some point, the second group — this cult — became aware of the first.'

'When? How?'

'I don't know. I'm guessing it was when Laila Buckingham was abducted. I think that was certainly the moment they became aware of David Groves. But we know they have money, resources, determination. They're actively looking for sinners. Maybe they started making connections that we didn't, or following up on things we couldn't. Monitoring people in ways that just aren't open to us. Putting together the pieces.'

'And then?'

'And then the first group targeted Jamie Groves.'

I couldn't be certain about this, but I thought that it had to have been Rebecca Lawrence who stole Jamie away from his garden, and that it was at this point that our second group had intervened. Lawrence had then been held captive

366

until the car crash, when her resemblance to Charlie Matheson had proved useful in making the substitution.

'What makes you so sure Jamie Groves is still alive?'

'Again, I don't know for sure,' I said. 'There are two options that I can see. Lawrence could have killed him herself, but I don't think she would have done that alone, and she was the only member of the gang that went missing that day. I think it's more likely that our *second* group took Jamie — that they decided they wanted him for some reason. Maybe it was a spur-of-the-moment thing at that point. But I think David Groves is the key to all of this now.'

Pete frowned.

'So then they wait three years to deal with the rest of the gang?'

'Five years in total,' I said. 'If we include Paul Carlisle.'

'All right. Why?'

It was a good question, and for now, I only had a partial answer. I looked at the timeline on the screen.

'We know they framed David Groves. And I believe they abducted him too. That would all have taken time to organise. But the dates themselves might be crucial.'

My son's not one yet, but all through the search I kept trying to imagine how it would feel if he was Laila's age and had been taken from me. How I'd do absolutely anything to get him back.

'Laila was eight years old when she was taken.

Jamie Groves would have turned eight two days ago. I believe that something was supposed to happen then — and that Charlie was meant to set it in motion — but it got delayed. And I think it might be some kind of test for David Groves.'

'A test?'

I shook my head. 'We know these people are obsessed with Heaven and Hell, and right and wrong, and Groves was painted in the press as a good man. A religious man. A hero. He said he'd do anything to get his son back. I think maybe they want to see whether that's true.'

'Have him prove his love,' Mercer said.

I didn't reply. Because if that was the case, then once again, the parallels to the 50/50 Killer would be there.

Pete was looking over at his old boss.

'But why ask for John?' he said quietly. 'What's the point?'

'Maybe it's not as complicated as it seems,' I said. 'If this is where the 50/50 Killer came from — his family, let's say — then they would obviously have a grudge against John. Perhaps they just wanted him to understand about David Groves. That he didn't die. That he was wrongly convicted. That he's been held in captivity ever since. That John got it wrong, which means an innocent man — a good man — has been suffering all this time.'

I glanced over at Mercer.

'Maybe they just wanted to rub John's face in that.'

Although Mercer still had his back to me, I could see that he was processing the possibility, and that it hurt him. His head was bowed slightly.

'Yes,' he said.

For a moment, nobody else said anything. Everyone's focus was on Mercer, while he stared at the wall in front of him, or through it. After a few seconds, Pete turned to look at me.

'But we still don't know where this place is?'

'No.'

'So if David Groves really *is* still alive — and if his son is too — then we have no way to get to them?'

I shook my head. 'Our best bet probably is tracking Charlie. She's convinced she'll be taken back there — to Heaven this time, to be reunited with her daughter — so they'd have to collect her at some point. But we don't know when. We don't even know *if.*'

'And we know how careful they've been,' Simon said.

Which was uncomfortable, but true. As things stood, we had no way of tracing these individuals and finding any of the people they were holding captive. It was possible we never would. And whether my theories were accurate or way off the mark, we might never know for sure.

Mercer broke the silence that followed.

'What's this?' he said softly.

'What's what?'

I walked over to where he was standing, and saw he was pointing at one of the sheets tacked to the wall.

'Oh, that's nothing. It's a list of hospitals vaguely in the search area. I wanted to make sure

Charlie Matheson hadn't just wandered off from one.'

'Yes, but why are most of them crossed out?'

'Those are the ones the officers contacted about missing patients.'

'But not all of them are. Look.'

He pointed at one of the names on the list, and then another. There were four in total. Instead of crossing them out, whichever officer had made the calls had scribbled something next to them.

'CD?' Mercer said.

'I'm not sure.' I shook my head. 'Closed down, perhaps. I don't know where they got the list from. Why?'

'Cane Hill Hospital.'

Mercer tapped the paper with the back of his finger, then walked over to one of the desks, leaving me to peer at the line he'd indicated. *Cane Hill Hospital — CD.* The name meant absolutely nothing to me. I looked at Pete, and he shook his head. Him neither.

Mercer was leaning over, working through the file he'd brought with him.

'What are you thinking, John?' I said.

'One of the identities I discovered for the 50/50 Killer. Wait. Here it is.' He pulled out a couple of documents and read from them. 'From a car rental. He gave his name as Nicholas Cane.'

'That's pretty thin, John,' Pete said.

'Isn't it.' Mercer walked back to the wall beside me, then spoke almost idly over his shoulder. 'Greg, can you access the files for Gordon Peters,

370

the doctor who was found murdered this morning?'

Greg hesitated.

'Sure. But I remember the list of hospitals. Peters never worked anywhere called Cane Hill.'

'That's not what I'm asking. Check his *own* medical records.'

'His — '

'His medical records, Greg.' Mercer sounded impatient now, still staring at the list of hospitals. 'Gordon Peters. Can you do that or not?'

Greg looked over at Pete, who stared back at him for a moment, then nodded almost imperceptibly. Greg raised his eyebrows.

'I can try.'

I moved over to a spare desk and set to work on my tablet, putting Cane Hill Hospital into an internet search engine. As the pages loaded, I glanced up. Mercer was still staring at the list of hospitals, his head inclined slightly, as though he was seeing patterns that nobody else could see.

'Got them,' Greg said.

'He stayed at Cane Hill,' Mercer said. 'Didn't he?'

Greg didn't reply.

I looked between them all — Greg, Pete and Mercer — and then back at the tablet in front of me. The search page had loaded, and the top link referenced *Cane Hill Psychiatric Hospital*. I clicked on it and began reading through the information there.

When I looked up again, nobody else in the office had spoken. They all seemed to be in exactly the same position as the last time I'd looked. My heart was beating fast. There was a sense of magic to the air, and now the inside of my chest was glittering with it.

I kept my eyes on Mercer, but he was completely motionless as I spoke. He didn't even seem to register the words.

'I think we've found it,' I said.

Eileen

No such thing as a happy ending

When Eileen heard the front door quietly open, the panic she had been feeling abated slightly. She resisted the urge to get off the settee and rush through to the hallway. Instead, she sipped from the glass of wine she'd poured herself and waited, confident that today John would come to find her, and not vanish upstairs as he so often did.

She heard him bolt and chain the front door, then the gentle sound of him slipping off his shoes. Slow movements. She sipped her wine. A few moments later, the door to the front room opened and he stepped inside.

Eileen wanted to seethe at him — she *was* furious — but she still found herself looking him over with concern, checking for signs that something had gone wrong, and that he was in danger of collapse. Of course, it didn't work like that; any damage done would be more slow-burn, and it would emerge in the days and weeks to come. Nevertheless, she was relieved to see that he seemed like himself — or, at least, the way he'd been recently. His expression was blank, unreadable, and as he walked across the room and stood in front of her, his gait was awkward, but no more so than before.

Thank God.

She took another sip of her wine, then put the glass down.

'Well?'

'You know where I've been today,' he said.

'I have a pretty good idea, yes.' Her heart was beating a little too fast, and she was pleased by the amount of disdain she managed to get into her voice. 'I hope it was worth it.'

He nodded slowly, then put his hands into his trouser pockets and stared down at the floor. In the early evening gloom of the lounge, he struck her as a miserable, grey figure, penitent and subdued. But it also reminded her of his former self. She had often seen him, back when he was well, standing like that, staring down at nothing, lost in thought, his mind turning over some problem in ways other people struggled to follow, viewing it from angles they could never even begin to imagine.

'All right.' She picked up the glass again. 'Tell me.'

And so he did, the whole time just standing there, still not looking at her. He told her what Charlie Matheson had said, what they'd found at Paul Carlisle's house, the way it tied in to the 50/50 Killer investigation.

'Why did they ask for you?' she said.

He shrugged, and for the first time, his expression changed from blank. He looked miserable now. Exhausted.

'I don't matter,' he said. 'It's a coincidence that I'm the one that handled the Groves case. There's something larger going on with that, but releasing Charlie Matheson, having her ask for me . . . I think it was only ever a sideshow. A way of taking a small amount of revenge on me for the 50/50 case. They wanted me to know that I'd failed him. David Groves. That I got it wrong.' The sadness on his face intensified. 'But that's all, I think. In the grand scheme of things, I never really mattered.'

That's not true, she thought.

'Has there been any progress?'

'I think so, yes. I think they've found the place they're looking for.'

'That's good news. It means you can finish your book. Maybe it will even have a happy ending after all.'

He didn't reply, and she could tell she'd hurt him. That was awful, wasn't it? Beneath her. And the words had felt ridiculous even as she'd said them, because what happy ending could there ever be? Certainly not for David Groves, or any of the other people involved. Not for John, either. There was no such thing as a happy ending. Things stopped, or else they were abandoned and left behind, and life continued without them. When this case was closed, the damage it had caused people would continue. Even if John wrote the last word in his book and closed the cover, it wouldn't really seal anything away. You could attempt to draw any line you wanted, but wet ink always seeped down the page.

'When will it be over?' she said.

'I don't know. Soon.'

'And you didn't fancy tagging along?'

'I decided not to,' he said.

'Oh?'

'I couldn't help them. You were right. I was of no use to them. They didn't need me. And I decided I wanted to come home to you.'

Eileen stared at him.

'Did you?'

'Yes.' He looked at her, finally. 'I'm sorry. I thought you deserved that.'

She continued staring at him. The sadness on his face hadn't gone away, and she knew full well that he was lying to her — at least in part. He'd wanted to go, she decided, and they had, predictably and understandably, turned him down. And now he was trying to salvage the situation and make the best of it. Cast it in a flattering light.

Oh John, she thought.

For a moment, she didn't know what to say to him.

And then . . .

'Sit with me,' she said. 'Let's just sit together for a while.'

She held out her hand to him. He stared at it. And then, after a moment, he reached out and took it, and he did.

Cane Hill

We left the department in a convoy.

Pete drove the front vehicle, with me in the passenger seat beside him and Greg sitting behind, working on his computer as we went. Glancing in the side mirror, I could see three vans behind us. Eighteen officers following in our wake.

Under normal circumstances, I would have been glad of their presence. While I had no idea exactly what we would find when we reached Cane Hill, I suspected it would be bad, and I should have been pleased we were going to have as many feet on the ground as we would. But it also made me uneasy. The department's door team had been seconded to join us, which meant that Sasha was in one of those vans. She would be heading into the unknown with us.

Worry about yourself, Mark. She knows what she's doing.

Which was true, but for some reason it didn't help. As we approached the outskirts of the city, I couldn't shake the feeling that something bad was going to happen.

Outside the vehicle, the late afternoon had darkened. It remained stiflingly warm, but there was an edge to the air now, and the sky ahead of us was full of boiling swirls of grey-black cloud. At ground level, everything seemed shadowed and dull, as though evening had already fallen.

'Twenty minutes,' Pete said.

Focus, Mark.

I turned my attention back to the tablet in my lap.

Cane Hill Hospital. When I'd scanned through the history available online back in the office, it had felt obvious that it was the place we were looking for. I read the page again now.

The hospital was situated about ten miles east of the city, a short distance into the woods that stretched across the countryside there. The main building had been constructed in the 1880s, on land belonging to a man named William Cane. Cane had come from a family of rail entrepreneurs. He was very rich, and also well known for his philanthropy. He'd paid for the construction of the psychiatric hospital himself, then run it on a charitable basis. It had never been a large facility. At the height of its use, it accommodated fewer than fifty patients.

The property had passed to his grandson, George, in 1941. George Cane had the top floor of the main building converted and lived there with his wife, Melissa. Their twin sons, Joseph and Jonathan, were born in 1953. Following the war, the lower floors had continued to be used for psychiatric services, principally for traumatised soldiers, but over the decades that followed, the property's use as a hospital began to steadily diminish. The family remained.

The twins were home-schooled by Melissa, who was an intensely religious woman, said to give sermons to the patients in the hospital's chapel. However, there were intimations that her mental health deteriorated over the years, and that the sermons became muddled and unintelligible. An undisclosed event in 1961 resulted in her being cared for by her sons on the top floor of the hospital.

George Cane died in 1969, when the twins would have been sixteen years old, and the hospital closed two years later. Gordon Peters had been one of the last patients, while still a teenager himself. The place seemed to have disappeared from people's memories. It was small and specialised enough, and sufficiently distant from the city proper, that many had forgotten its existence even before its closure.

I checked through again. There was no mention of a Nicholas Cane. No date given for Melissa Cane's death either.

I wondered about that *undisclosed event*, though. Reading between the lines, it suggested a breakdown or even a suicide attempt, after which she had effectively been confined in the hospital. Joseph and Jonathan would have been eight years old when they started looking after her, and so I also wondered what further lessons they might have learned at their disturbed mother's bedside. There was no information about what had happened afterwards. It seemed to be assumed that Cane Hill Hospital had been vacant since its closure, although there was nothing as to what had become of the twins afterwards, or where they had gone. They would be in their early sixties now, so it was more than possible that they, at least, were still alive.

It was even possible, I thought, that they were still there: that they had never left Cane Hill. And that they weren't alone. That for reasons I still couldn't entirely fathom, David Groves was with them too.

* * *

Merritt watched David Groves standing upright in the corner of his small cell. Sleeping, apparently. It amazed him what people could grow accustomed to, even if they didn't have any choice. In his time as a soldier, he'd endured terrible things too, but that had been such a long time ago now that it was hard to recall; his life had been one of relative comfort for years, running security and research and administration here at Cane Hill. And of course, as complicated as things could be, he had at least *chosen* to be a soldier to begin with. Whatever discomforts and agonies he'd suffered all that time ago, on some level he'd deserved them. He'd at least signed up for it.

That wasn't true of David Groves.

Merritt had been involved in everything that had happened to the man, and those connected to him. He had been complicit in destroying his life, framing him and bringing him here two years ago. And just as with the other men and women he'd abducted, he knew exactly what Groves had done to deserve this.

Nothing.

He was simply a good man.

He also knew what lay in store for Groves over

the next few hours. *God help you*, he thought, even though he was no believer, and once again he felt that strange surge of pity.

Guilt, however, was an emotion beyond him.

Merritt had spent the last hour emptying out Hell: working his way methodically through the cells and dragging the occupants into the corridors, and then out into the open air. They had wailed and screeched like animals, but it was done now, and the place was silent.

With one last glance at David Groves — still sleeping — Merritt turned and made his way back through the corridors, heading for daylight, passing open cell after open cell. With the exception of its one remaining prisoner, Hell was now empty.

The rain hit him again as he walked out of the church. Down the hill in front of him, he could see the handful of sinners, naked and chained to the trees. The air and the rain and the last ebbs of gloomy daylight must have been a shock to them. A few more hours of suffering, then. Nothing new to them — not in itself. He walked past them, ignoring the screeching.

As he crossed the clearing, he reached the man in the centre: his latest addition to the collection at the Cane Hill compound. Paul Carlisle was naked, his hands cuffed together in front of him, chained to a post that had been driven into the ground. The man was on his knees in the mud, his head bowed. Merritt could see Carlisle's rain-wet back shuddering, and hear him whispering.

'Please,' he was saying. 'Please.'

Merritt ignored him. He knew what Paul Carlisle had done, him and his group of friends, and he doubted *please* had ever done much to help their victims. Merritt had killed each of the others himself, and his only real regret was that he wouldn't necessarily get to kill Carlisle as well.

At the back of the main hospital building, he spotted Cane, an older man in a black suit, and made his way across. Cane was staring at the clearing and didn't seem to notice Merritt approaching until he was beside him.

'Sir.'

'Mr Merritt.' Cane shook his head. 'Are we ready?'

'Yes, sir.'

'Good. You know what to do next.'

'Yes, sir.'

He felt an urge to add something — he knew what this meant to the man: that Cane saw it as settling the lifelong conflict with his *brother* once and for all — but couldn't find the words. Instead, he moved back down the patio until he reached the boy, who was standing with the baby in his arms. Jamie Groves and Ella Matheson. It only really mattered about removing Jamie from the scene — for now — but Merritt knew he wouldn't allow himself to be separated from the baby. He had been caring for it since its mother had left. Merritt put a hand on the boy's arm.

'What is our Father doing?' Jamie asked. 'Who is that man?'

Merritt did his best to smile.

'Please come with me,' he said.

★ ★ ★

Ten minutes.

'Mark,' Greg said. 'I'm sending you a map through now.'

The notification flashed up on my tablet screen.

'Got it.'

When I opened it, I was greeted by an overhead satellite map of the area we were heading towards. The main road we were on was obvious, curling along the bottom of the screen, with what appeared to be a thin driveway about a kilometre long snaking up through the woods towards the compound itself. The remains of the hospital looked like some abandoned outpost. The grounds were roughly circular, with the main building a grey shape that bisected the area horizontally, the edges lost amongst the green at either side. A second structure, much smaller than the hospital itself, was set further back, closest to the depths of the woods. The land around it seemed slightly shaded and odd.

'The little one,' I said. 'What do you think it is?'

'I don't know,' Greg said. 'It's elevated, though — up on some kind of hill.'

The chapel, I thought, where Melissa Cane had given her sermons. Looking at it onscreen, I thought it seemed older than the main building. While it was impossible to make out any real detail, I had the sensation that I was staring at some ancient structure.

I closed down the map for a moment and

383

began to search online for more information about the grounds, working through variations of *Cane Hill* and *hospital* and *church*. The movement of the car made it hard to type properly, but a few moments later, I was rewarded with a screen full of results. Most were unrelated, but one close to the top of the page was relevant.

'Hang on,' I said. 'I've got something here on an urban exploration site.'

'A what?' Pete said.

'Urban exploration,' Greg said. 'Bunches of people who go looking round abandoned buildings. Housing projects and railways and hospitals and things.'

'Why would anyone do that?'

'They explore. They take photographs.'

'That sounds like the sort of pointless activity you'd know all about.'

I tuned their conversation out as the site finished loading, and then began to read. It was a thread in a forum, only a few pages long, and it was from a few years ago. The initial posts implied that Cane Hill was a little-known but desirable target, and yet the handful of expeditions that had attempted to gain access had met with scant success.

'There's security there,' I said. 'The groups that have tried to get in found a gate on the road in, and some kind of fence that runs off from that into the woods on either side.'

'All the way round?' Pete said.

'It doesn't say. It looks like they tried to follow it a little way into the trees, but the ground got too difficult for them.'

I kept reading.

'Another group tried coming at it from an angle through the woods, but they ran into the fence too. They got a few photos.'

They were clear images, but there wasn't much to see. The fence itself was obvious — a web of mesh running through the trees, topped with haphazard curls of razor wire. One photo showed a smiling man in a hoody and sunglasses standing close to the fence for scale, making it obvious it was at least ten feet high. *Didn't want to get too close*, he'd written.

'They thought it might be electrified,' I said.

'Why would an empty hospital have that kind of security?'

'Exactly.'

There was another photograph, this time of the gate they'd mentioned, shot from a short distance away. The road leading up to it was little more than a dirt track, but the gate looked far more elaborate. It had two iron struts at the sides, with a solid slab of metal between them. There was something that looked like a keypad on one side. A second photograph showed some kind of sensor in the undergrowth, with a grille above it for speaking into.

'They all seem to have given up a while ago,' I said, scanning the last posts in the forum. 'The consensus seems to be that the place isn't abandoned after all, although none of them have any idea what might be going on there.'

Maybe the Cane twins are still there? someone had written. *Hanging out together with their dead mum?*

The reply, the last comment in the thread, read: *I hope not. The thought of the poor bastards living their whole lives alone in the woods like that is too creepy to imagine.*

'Well,' Pete said, 'we're about to find out.'

We'd left the city behind us. To the right, fields sprawled away, dotted with trees and piles of hay bales. To the left, the woods were still with us. As they flashed past, it was impossible to see more than a few metres into them before darkness claimed any real detail.

I looked ahead, at the blackening sky above, just as the first fat bulbs of rain began to fall. They hit the windscreen hard. Within seconds, the storm was all around us. Pete turned on the wipers, smearing the water away, while the road outside suddenly sounded like it was fizzing with electricity.

I glanced into the side mirror. Behind us, the convoy of vehicles had turned on their lights.

'Five minutes,' Pete said.

★　★　★

Perhaps because of the television broadcast, Groves had been dreaming of the three victims he was supposed to have murdered.

Edward Leland.

Carl Thompson.

Laura Harrison.

The dreams were more vivid than he had become used to: bright splashes of colour playing in the blackness behind his closed eyes. He remembered the bodies as he had found them, tortured and burned and cut to pieces, and as he drifted slowly towards consciousness, his mind went further and he imagined that it had been him who had done those things to them. He pictured himself carving at Leland's face, pressing Thompson's head down into the burning campfire, cutting Harrison's throat as he stared into her widening eyes. And why not? For all that trying to be a good, righteous man had achieved for him, he might as well have fucking killed them. God had abandoned him here regardless.

As he woke, he kept his eyes closed and turned the images over and over in his mind. They brought a savage twist of satisfaction with them. Because it had all been their fault, hadn't it? Without them, and the terrible things they had done, everything would have been different. He would never have been condemned to Hell. Tracing things back, he imagined himself still alive, his career intact, his beautiful son growing up . . . perhaps even his marriage to Caroline restored, rebuilt into something they could both have lived with.

He thought about Caroline now. Since his death, he always imagined her in the blue and white spotted dress he remembered her wearing long before Jamie was born, when they had both been so young and the world had seemed full of love and hope. When snow had fallen in the height of summer, and it had felt like God was showing them both a wonderful secret.

And then he heard a faint click from one side of the room — a real sound this time. He opened

387

his eyes and looked at the metal door to his cell. It had swung back very slightly, just an inch or so. It was as though somewhere a button had been pressed, an electronic lock deactivated, and the door's weight had relaxed it backwards.

Groves eased himself away from the wall and took a step closer to it. Nobody came in. It just remained as it was, slightly ajar. Was this some kind of trick? Was he being taunted? He imagined reaching out to push the door wider, only to have it slam back cruelly hard against his fingers. He looked in the direction of the television, almost for guidance, but it remained blank.

He reached out slowly, his body trembling, until his palm rested against the cold metal. Nothing. He stepped forward, pushing with his whole weight, and the door opened wider with a steady screech of metal.

For the first time in two years, and with his heart knocking hard inside his chest, David Groves stepped out of his cell.

Hell

The rain was coming down even harder by the time we reached the entrance to Cane Hill.

As we pulled up on the main road, I heard a rolling grumble in the sky overhead. It was a sound that seemed to want to rumble over and crash like the sea, but instead it just faded away. The undergrowth amongst the trees to the left was nodding swiftly in the downpour, and a trail of water was racing along the edge of the verge, the soil sodden and moist, already beginning to dissolve and flow away under the force of the storm.

The driveway up to the compound was narrow and nondescript: perhaps wide enough for a truck to drive up, but neglected and overgrown at the edges. The ground was ridged and muddy, though. The light-brown soil had been churned up around the roughly parallel lines that marked the passage of countless vehicles. *Something* was still happening here. But if there had ever been a sign for the hospital while it was open, it was long gone now; all that remained was a single rectangle of white plastic, emblazoned with the words PRIVATE PROPERTY — and even that looked to have been left over from a much earlier age. It was tied to the trunk of a tree by the roadside with rusted wire, and hanging at a slight angle, as though it had fallen into the under-growth and been hastily reattached.

Through the sheen of rain, and the darkness from the over-hanging trees, it was difficult to see any great distance along the trail.

'All right.' Pete picked up the radio mic, then spoke louder. 'All right, everyone. Cameras and GPS on. DS Killingbeck?'

The voice came over the radio. 'Here.'

'I want your team to take the lead.'

'Roger that.'

'We might be encountering a metal gate, possibly electrified, some distance along.'

'Not a problem, sir.'

'We go second. Other two vans in behind.'

The team commanders confirmed.

'Right,' Pete said. 'Let's go see if anyone's home.'

He reversed slightly, and a few seconds later Killingbeck's van pulled around us and eased on to the trail. I watched it as it turned in, knowing that Sasha would be in there — that she was part of the team taking the lead — and tried to shake the feeling that she was in danger. It was stupid and irrational: they were far more qualified than us to deal with any obstacles we might encounter. But I could still sense the beginning of the panic in my chest. I fought it down.

Everything will be fine, Mark.

Of course it would.

Pete followed a moment later. I heard the mud squelching beneath the tyres as we set off up the slope, and the sound continued as we rolled steadily forward. Almost immediately, the world

390

grew darker around us as the car was encased by the surrounding trees and foliage. Fronds and branches swiped against the sides. The car undulated as it went. A short distance in front, I could see the red lights of Sasha's van. *Everything will be fine.*

I turned to look out into the trees, but couldn't see far between them. In some places the undergrowth had grown up into a waist-high tangle that would be impossible to make your way through on foot. It was far wilder than the woods closer to the city. These didn't have even that vaguely civilising presence to constrain them.

Greg said, 'Good place for an ambush.'

'You've seen too many films,' Pete said.

'I'm just saying.'

He was right, I thought. We had no real idea what we were driving towards here, only how organised these people had been in the past. Maybe that was partly why I was keeping an eye out to one side, half expecting an attack from the trees, albeit still far more worried about what might happen in front. Despite the sheer number of officers we had with us, I was nervous, as though — even as mob-handed as we were — we still weren't prepared for whatever was to come.

'Any idea where the gate would be?' Greg said.

I shook my head. 'Far enough away from the buildings to keep them out of sight, but it must be fairly close. Big area to fence off otherwise, if it goes all the way round.'

'Slight bend in a bit. That would be a good spot.'

I looked at the tablet, and he was right. The

trail leaned to the right about two thirds of the way up. Less than a minute later, I felt Pete pull the car to a halt. The van in front had stopped.

Pete and I got out, and I was struck immediately by the force of the storm. I pulled the hood of my coat over my head, but it didn't help. My feet fought for purchase on the muddy ground as we made our way around the van, fingers of rain tapping me everywhere.

I recognised the scene from the photograph in the forum: the twin metal struts at either side of the road; the solid slab of metal resting between them; the fence extending into the impenetrable woods. To the right, I saw the buzzer panel mounted on a short pole in the treeline. Two of Killingbeck's team were already crouched around that, the rain bouncing off their helmets, a toolbox by the side of them. Three others were standing by the gate itself, waiting. I couldn't tell which of them was Sasha. They were all concentrating on the job at hand.

As you should be.

Killingbeck flipped up the visor on his helmet as we reached him. The rain spattered off the top.

'Two minutes.' He swivelled at the waist to check. 'Two minutes?'

'Yes, sir,' one of the officers kneeling by the intercom called back. The other had erected a small umbrella over the device and was wiping it down with a cloth, working nimbly even wearing thick gloves.

A moment later, sparks began flashing and flickering through the air like dandelion seeds.

The corridor Groves found himself in was so narrow that the open door almost entirely blocked it off to the right-hand side. He closed it behind him, so that he could see in both directions. The walls were made of old stone and were thick with green moss. Lights in oval plastic cases had been strung along them at head height, wired together with dirty cabling. To his right, the lights were off, and the corridor became lost in darkness only a few metres away from him. To the left, the route was illuminated, and he could see all the way to a turning a short distance ahead.

There was something on the floor there.

No.

The light from above didn't quite touch it, but even in the gloom, Groves recognised it. He stood very still for a moment, staring down the corridor. Somewhere behind him, water dripped and echoed.

He started walking towards the turning.

His legs were weak, and he had to hold a hand against the wall as he approached, his gaze focused entirely on the thing on the floor. The world shook around him. When he reached the corner, he crouched down awkwardly and picked up the soft toy that had been left there.

Eeyore.

He turned it over in his hands, marvelling at the texture, tears prickling his eyes now. For so long, there had only been rough stone to touch. This was the softest thing he could ever remember holding.

He pressed it to his face.

And then, from around the turning to his left, he heard the sound of a child laughing. For a moment, he didn't look up — just kept his face buried against the toy, crying softly — but the laughter was unselfconscious and full of joy. He recognised it, of course. Jamie. The thought that his son might be here in Hell too was intolerable. How could that be possible? Even God couldn't be that hateful, could He? Except Groves was no longer sure about that.

He stood up. The corridor ahead of him was indistinguishable from the one behind, aside from the laughter. He started along it, chasing the sound, moving more urgently now. He needed to find his son.

'I'm coming, Jamie,' he said.

★   ★   ★

The gate was open, and we were all back in our vehicles. If the people at Cane Hill hadn't known we were coming before, they almost certainly would now.

'There's another trail,' Greg said. 'I'm sending through a new close-up.'

I checked my tablet and saw what he meant straight away. The driveway we were on led to the main compound, which the hospital building crossed from one side to the other. Before the drive reached it, however, a thinner trail led off to the right, circling around the edge and entering the top part, closer to the small building on the hill.

'Passable?' Pete said.

'Hard to tell.'

'It will be,' I said. 'The place is still in use. And this trail right here has seen plenty of activity. I think the church, if that's what it is, is key. Charlie talked about being allowed out to see the edges of Heaven. Going by the history of the place, that would be the main building. I bet the sinners are kept beneath the church.'

'Right then,' Pete said. 'When we get there, we'll take that trail, with one van behind us. Other two units keep to this one. Agreed?'

'Yes.'

Killingbeck came on the radio.

'Ready?' he said.

'Ready.'

Pete told him, and the other two commanders, the plan. There were a few seconds while everybody checked their maps.

'Roger that.'

A moment later, Sasha's van started off again in front, and then Pete set our car moving after them. It rocked gently from side to side with the terrain as we passed between the two metal struts, then Pete guided us around the upcoming bend. It wasn't sharp — just enough to hide the trail ahead from anybody peering through the fence back at the gate — but the driveway opened up a little here, as though the trees had moved back a step. In less than a minute, it was wide enough for two vehicles side by side, although our convoy remained in single file.

A minute later, we reached the second trail. The first van continued on. Pete turned to the right, with one van following behind us. As the other two vans disappeared off to one side, I had the sensation of Sasha drifting steadily away from me, our lives bisecting along different paths that would never again converge, and I had a desperate urge to be closer to her. To reach out and pull her back towards me before it was too late.

It will be fine.

The road was easier here, and Pete picked up speed as we went. We curled gradually around, and as we approached the far side of the compound, the land began to slope upwards, the ground disappearing a short distance ahead, replaced by a dark grey arch of sky. Evening had fallen.

'Nearly there,' Greg said.

I checked the tablet. The other two vans would get there first, I thought. Perhaps the officers were already approaching the front of the old hospital. I looked up as we moved over the top of the slope, the trees falling away behind, and then tried to take in the scene that was waiting for us.

I couldn't even begin to make sense of what I was seeing.

'What the hell?' Pete whispered.

★　★　★

Groves found more soft toys as he went. He gathered them up and held them in the crook of his left arm, using his right to steady himself against the stone walls. Jamie's toys. The ones Caroline always left at the grave on his birthday.

Toys intended for the memory of an ageless little boy, frozen in time at the moment of his death. Groves could still hear him laughing now, but however hard he forced himself along, Jamie always seemed to be the same distance ahead, as though he was playing and running away. As though Groves would never catch up with him.

'I'm coming.'

The sound drew him on. Oh God, he sounded so *happy*. Groves had never really thought about his son's laughter before. It had been joyful to hear it, of course, and he could still remember that unexpected first smile, when Jamie had been lying on the changing mat, staring up at him. But he hadn't realised how *familiar* it would be — that the sound of a child's laughter was as unique as a fingerprint.

'I'm coming.'

He staggered along the stone corridors, trying to move faster than his emaciated body would allow him. He stumbled, dropping the toys, then forced himself to gather them again. Eventually he reached a staircase carved out of the stone, spiralling up above him. There was another toy on the bottom step. Winnie-the-Pooh. Too many to carry properly now, and with his son's laughter echoing overhead, Groves allowed the others to tumble to the floor. The Pooh toy would do. It had always been Jamie's favourite.

A boy and his Bear will always be playing . . .

He leaned on the wall for a moment, gathering his strength. And then he began climbing the steps.

It seemed to take an age. Eventually he emerged into what was recognisable as a small church of some kind. There was little light, and it was hard to make out much detail beyond the handful of pews and the dirty stained-glass window above the altar. But he could see the open door at the far end, and the rain slashing down in the gloom outside.

The laughter cut out suddenly, replaced by the hiss and fizz of the weather. Looking up at the corner of the ceiling by the door, Groves could see the speakers it had been coming from.

But he was more astonished by the sight of the open door, because through that, he could see the sky, blackened and bruised with cloud. When he breathed in and smelled fresh air, it took him a moment to realise what it was. His heart almost stopped at the scent of it, and then memories began to pulse through him with every slow beat that followed. Flashes of everything that had been taken from him.

He walked over to the door, resting his hand on the hard corners of the wooden pews as he went.

The sound of the rain grew heavier. It was torrential, and he could feel the icy temperature of it as he stopped at the doorway, peering out. A path led down the hill outside, all the way to a clearing. There was a large building beyond it, painted white. The clearing itself was illuminated by floodlights, and someone was kneeling in the centre of it.

Finally, Groves looked down, noticing the two things that had been left on the floor by the door. He crouched down to reach them. One of the items was a photograph. He picked it up and stared at it. The portrait of Jamie, standing in that filthy room, staring with curiosity at the person who would go on to murder him.

Above him, the speakers crackled slightly. A moment later, a man's voice came out of them, gnarled and rasping and old.

'Edward Leland. Carl Thompson. Laura Harrison.'

Groves stared at the photograph.

'I miss you so much,' he whispered.

'And Paul Carlisle,' the voice said. 'The last of them.'

Groves put the photograph down gently, then looked out through the doorway again. Even kneeling on the floor, he could still see down the sloping path to the floodlit clearing. To the man kneeling there, penitent in the rain.

'The last of them,' the voice said again.

Groves understood. He looked down at the second item that had been left for him.

After a few moments, he picked up the gun, clambered painfully to his feet, and stepped outside into the driving rain.

* * *

Pete stopped the car short of the illuminated clearing. The other van pulled up alongside us.

'Everybody wait,' Pete said into his mic. 'Hang fire. I repeat: hang fire.'

I stared through the windscreen. The rain was so heavy now that the wipers were having trouble slashing it away.

The circular clearing was about twenty metres

in diameter, and brightly lit by four floodlights positioned around the edges, their lamps angled downwards towards the man kneeling in the centre, his arms out in front of him, cuffed at the wrists and tethered to a post in the muddy ground. He was naked, his skin bright white where it wasn't bruised, and his head was resting on his outstretched arms, face pointed down.

For a moment, all I could hear was the rain. But I could see enough of the man to recognise him.

'That's Paul Carlisle,' I said quietly.

He had been abducted and brought here. But in his case, there had been no pretence at faking a death or staging a scene, and he hadn't been confined to a cell underground.

To the right, a pale path wound up a hill towards the church. There was a thatch of trees to the side of it, and I could see people there: five or six of them, naked and bedraggled, their arms chained around the trees, as though embracing the trunks. Their knees and feet were churning the mud into waves. Where I could see faces, they looked shocked and terrified.

'Jesus,' Greg said quietly, leaning between the seats.

'And look over there.' Pete pushed his arm in front of me, pointing in the direction of the large building to our left.

The main building of what had once been Cane Hill Hospital stood four storeys tall. Here at the back, at ground level, there was a patio with an awning above, and as I watched, I saw an old man walking slowly along it. I couldn't see

400

his face, but he was dressed in a neat black suit.

'One of the Cane twins,' I said.

'So where's the other?'

I scanned the treeline, where the people were tied up. They were the damned, I guessed — the occupants of Hell, brought out from beneath the church to witness whatever was taking place here. From what Charlie had told me, Heaven was based in the main building. So if one of the brothers was over there, the other . . .

'Somewhere in the trees, I guess,' I said.

'I think you're right.'

Pete inclined his head towards his mic again, and I could tell he was about to order everybody out. But that was when I saw the figure moving down the path from the church, and I held out my hand.

'Wait. Look.'

This new man was emaciated, his skin hanging off his bones, and he was walking awkwardly, stumbling slightly, as though he hadn't moved as far as this in a long time and was on the verge of collapse. As he staggered into the floodlit clearing, I realised who it was. I'd seen the photo in the file.

'That's David Groves,' I said.

As I watched him limping closer to Paul Carlisle, I noticed the gun he was carrying, and suddenly I understood. Not completely, and not the *why* of it, but the *what*.

David Groves was a good man. A decent man.

Maybe the best man I've ever known.

Without thinking, I opened the car door and stepped out into the rain.

The baby was crying.

Which was bad luck, Merritt thought. But then, what could you do? From his army days, he remembered a soldier raising some ethical dilemma, when the rest of them were all reclined on their bunks. You've rescued a woman and her baby in enemy territory, and you're hiding afterwards, and the baby starts crying. If you don't kill the kid, the soldier told them, the enemy are going to find you and kill you all. If you do, you'll be okay, but you'll have killed a baby. None of them had taken the scenario seriously at the time; they'd all laughed it off. Life didn't work like that. You did what you were told, or what you had to do. Killing the baby wasn't going to help him here, otherwise he would have done it.

'What's happening?' Jamie said.

Merritt looked across the room. The boy was doing his best to soothe Ella, but for once the baby was oblivious to his attentions. It was as though the little girl knew everything was falling apart. Merritt could hear the officers working their way through the rooms on the lower floor. A few shouts. None of his men were here tonight, but there were immigrant workers — carers and the like — who didn't know the full truth of Cane Hill, and who were probably panicking, wondering what the hell was going on. Nothing bad was happening in this room yet, but that would change very shortly. The baby seemed to know that, as though it had some kind of sixth sense.

Merritt checked his gun.

'Don't worry,' he said.

'What's happening outside?' Jamie asked again.

'A test.'

'What kind of test?'

What kind indeed? Merritt heard a clattering next door, and then movement in the corridor outside the room. The door was locked, but that wouldn't stop them. Not for long.

'Take Ella into the centre of the room for me, please.'

Jamie did as he was told, carrying the baby. Merritt moved into the corner of the room, behind the door. When it opened, it would act as a shield. He'd have a chance.

Not a good one, admittedly. When the alarm had first sounded, he hadn't quite believed it. This wasn't meant to be the way things ended here. Whatever he thought about the Cane family deep down, his life here had been a good one, and — again picking his words carefully — he'd wanted them to have the conclusion they desired. He'd immediately done the mental calculations, and figured his chances of escape were slim. He could have run for the woods, but the weather was bad and the terrain on this side of the compound was terrible. He wasn't sure he could reach civilisation, gather his things and get away in time. He had an exit strategy, of course, but it required a twelve-hour head start, and it began with him being able to drive out of here.

It all catches up with you in the end.

He shook his head.

'What kind of test?' Jamie said again.

'The Book of Job,' Merritt said.

Of course, that meant nothing to the boy. A part of Merritt wanted to explain. He wanted to tell the boy that, in a story in a book called the Bible, God had pointed to Job as a righteous man, but had then been challenged by the Devil, who argued that Job's goodness and faith were only due to circumstances — that they came from the abundances God had blessed him with. So God allowed the Devil to torment and torture the righteous Job, taking everything from him apart from his life. All simply in order to test him: a bet between the pair of them to see if, in the end, Job would curse God and relinquish his faith and everything he believed in. A human life reduced to the status of a poker chip.

The door handle rattled twice, then stopped. Merritt said nothing. They wouldn't try again, he knew. The next time, the door would come in. He had enough bullets to take a few of them — maybe buy Cane some time to see the result of his wager. For himself, he wasn't going to prison. That would be intolerable. He would save one bullet: head off to whatever actual afterlife was waiting out there. If there was one, then for him it would be Hell. He knew that for certain. His own heart was entirely settled.

'What does that mean?' Jamie said.

Merritt didn't answer.

The door banged and splintered. He took aim.

*   *   *

The last of them.

Groves couldn't even remember the man's

404

name as he moved across the clearing towards him. What did names matter anyway? He believed what he'd been told. The Devil, at least, had never lied to him.

The world around him was shaking and trembling, but he struggled on, his thigh muscles sore and tight now. The gun in his hand was heavy; hard to keep hold of it. But he did. Moving slowly towards the man.

What did it matter?

The rain soaked his hair and was pouring down his face, pooling in his eye sockets like tears. He blinked it away, then rubbed at his face with the back of his free hand, only for more water to take its place. He was shaking violently, but barely registered the discomfort. As bad as the weather was, and as much of a shock to the skin, it still seemed warmer out here than it had been in the grave.

David, David, David.

Someone was shouting his name.

He ignored it, remaining focused on the man kneeling in front of him now.

The last of them.

The man barely even looked like a human being any more, crouched and folded over like that. He reminded Groves more of cattle: staked up and shivering and ready for slaughter. He recognised the muscles and form of a man, but the sight was almost alien to him now; it barely made sense. With every drop of rain, the thing moaned and shuddered, as though being struck by gunfire rather than water. Even if it *had* once been a man, its actions had long since taken it out of that sphere.

David.

Groves remembered the dream he'd had, and the bitter satisfaction he'd gained from imagining hurting the people who had killed his son. And why shouldn't he? What difference had it ever made, trying to do the right thing? He'd have arrested him once, he dimly remembered. He'd had a belief in justice. Where had that got him? It was a lifetime away now. How naïve he had been.

David!

With the rain hitting him from all sides, Groves pressed the gun into the back of the man's neck. The man tried to duck away, legs kicking in the mud, but Groves raised his hand and pushed the barrel down harder, between the tendons. The man stopped fighting, apparently resigned.

Everybody stand back!

STAND BACK!

Groves put his finger on the trigger. Everything had counted for nothing, and here was the man — the last of them — who had murdered his son, who had taken his world from him and caused all this to happen. The hatred piled up inside him, and he started to pull the trigger.

David! Don't forget who you are!

The gunshot rang out.

And then another: a dull thud.

A third.

Then silence.

Groves stared down at the gun in his hand,

confused by the sounds. The gunshots had been real, and yet his finger was still on the trigger, and the man on the ground was still alive and whimpering. He looked around, the rain splashing over his face, and for the first time he noticed the cars around the clearing, and the young man who was standing at the edge of the light, one foot into the mud. The man who had just been talking to him.

Now, though, that man was looking off towards a large building to one side, with an expression of horror on his face. *That* was where the shots had come from, Groves realised. Something had happened in there. There was shouting coming from that direction now, and when the younger man turned back towards him, he looked terrified.

'David,' he said. 'Please. Don't forget who you are.'

Groves stared at him for a moment, at the panic and desperation on his face. He looked back at the man kneeling before him, then up into the sky, closing his eyes. He held the trigger firm. The rain struck him hard — constant solid taps on his face — and Groves allowed himself to become lost in it for a moment . . .

He opened his eyes, and instead of rain filling the world above him, all he saw was snow: beautiful bright white crystal shapes floating down through the black sky towards him. One of them kissed him coldly on his cheek. Another landed on his forehead. *Let's never forget this moment*, he thought. *Let's not forget who we are right now* . . .

And suddenly, the world *thumped*, and the rain

started up again. Groves stared down at the gun in his hand, still pressed against the neck of the man cowering on the ground, then up at the man standing metres away from him, his hands out now.

'David, *please*.'

'I'm not a killer,' he said.

'I know.'

Groves lowered the gun. Dropped it. He thought of all the things that had been taken from him — his son, his career, his faith — and he stared at the wretched man on the ground before him and whispered:

'You're under arrest.'

And then he closed his eyes again, feeling an inexplicable and giddy flood of love in his heart. He felt the summer sun on his face, as though God Himself was smiling at him.

I love you, Jamie, he thought. *I'm coming now. I've earned it.*

★ ★ ★

Breathe, Sasha thought.

It was like her chest was encased in rock.

Breathe.

'You okay?' Killingbeck said.

'Yes, sir.'

'You did good. We're clear.'

The adrenalin was still coursing through her, the insidious poison of it doing everything to convince her otherwise, but he was right, and she forced herself to nod — acknowledge the simple praise. The man in the corner of the room was lying on his stomach, hands cuffed behind him, gun safely removed from the scene. Officers were attending to him, just as others were to the two children who had been in the centre of the room when Barnes had battered the door down and she had started to step inside.

She could still see it clearly. The boy had been staring at her, his eyes wide in fear and confusion, and something had made her stop just before she cleared the busted door. The boy and the baby were in the middle of the room, just as the young girl had been in the raid yesterday, and that memory had immediately come back to her. *Clear the corner.* Maybe without yesterday she would have attempted that mechanically, but the positioning of the children, the look on the kid's face, had made her think *bait.* She had crouched down low, aiming the Taser as she cleared the door.

The first shot had gone high, just above her head.

The second had been hers. The electricity suddenly running through the man's body had jolted his hand up, and the two quick shots he managed before dropping the gun had blown chunks of plaster from the ceiling.

All over in seconds.

Breathe.

She did, slowly. Then she walked across to the boy and the baby. The baby was screaming, which Sasha figured was fairly understandable, and the boy was doing his best to rock and reassure the child. However frightened he'd been when they had burst in, the kid seemed much calmer now. Almost unnaturally so.

'It'll be okay,' she said.

He didn't seem to acknowledge her words, too intent on soothing the child in his arms. Sasha looked to one side and saw Mark entering the room at the far side. He was moving too quickly — *it's lucky we cleared it*, she thought — but he pulled up short when he saw her standing there, her visor flicked up. In all her years, Sasha didn't think she'd ever seen such relief on someone's face before. She could still feel the whisper of that bullet above her head, and that strange pressure wrapped around her chest — *breathe; just breathe* — and she smiled at him before turning back to the little boy and the baby.

'It's going to be okay,' she said.

Part Six

And in life, She had named Him the Devil,
for He was a wicked child with evil in His
heart. And He had wanted Her to love Him,
but She could not. And in life, She had
named His brother God, for His virtue and
goodness had been apparent. And when He
came to Her in Heaven, She could not be
sure which He was, and on some days She
spat on Him, and on others She loved Him
dearly, just as He had always desired, and so
it came to pass that He became They.

Extract from the Cane Hill bible

Mark

The boy in the pit

Two weeks after the events at Cane Hill, I parked up outside a house in the south of the city.

The curtains were closed in the front-room window, but I saw them move as I walked up the front path, and I didn't need to ring the bell. I was expected, of course; by the time I got to the front door, it was already opening, and I was greeted by an attractive woman in her late thirties. She had shoulder-length brown hair, cut neatly, and was wearing jeans and a mohair jumper. She looked tanned and healthy. Having spoken to Detective Sean Robertson again, I'd been led to believe that Caroline Evans had developed problems with alcohol addiction following her son Jamie's disappearance. If so, there were no obvious signs of it now.

'Detective Nelson?'

'Yes.'

I showed her my ID, and she smiled. It was an odd smile. Hard to work out whether it was happy or not.

'Please come in,' she said.

Ten minutes later, I was sitting in an armchair in Caroline's front room. She sat down on the settee opposite me, next to Jamie, and put her arm around her son. For a moment, he didn't

413

respond to the touch, and the gesture seemed a little awkward, but then he leaned into her slightly. She gave his shoulder a gentle squeeze, then moved her arm away and rested her hands in her lap.

'Hello, Jamie,' I said. 'My name's Mark. I'm a police officer. I was hoping to talk about everything that's happened to you.'

'I know.' He glanced sideways. 'Mum told me.'

'And is that okay with you?'

'Yes.'

He looked up at me, and I was startled by the assurance in his eyes. I remembered the photograph of the boy from the file: the one found in Paul Carlisle's collection. Although over five years had passed since it was taken, the resemblance was clear, and there was that same sense of curiosity and confidence in the way he looked at me now.

In other ways, of course, he had changed. His hair was straw-blond and shoulder-length now, and like his mother's, his face was tanned and freckled. He looked older than his years. Even at eight, his body already seemed lean and strong, as though he'd grown up on a farm, working outside in the sunshine. The only obvious concession to his actual age was the stuffed toy he was clutching tightly in his lap. An old and battered Winnie-the-Pooh.

'Okay,' I said. 'Let's start at the beginning then. Do you remember what happened to you?'

'You mean how I died?'

I saw Caroline flinch slightly at that, but I wasn't surprised by his choice of terminology. It was going to take a long time to deprogramme Jamie of the beliefs that had been instilled in him over the years. His time at Cane Hill represented the majority of his life, and he had been very young when he was taken. Why wouldn't he have come to believe what he had been told there? That was what children did: believe stories. Regardless, it wasn't my job to challenge him about it today.

'Yes. The day you died.'

'I remember Rebecca.' He screwed his face up a little. 'I thought she was good, but she wasn't.'

Rebecca Lawrence, who had vanished on the same day he had.

'She worked at your nursery, didn't she?'

Jamie nodded. 'She was always lovely to us there. Looking after us. She liked to play. That's what I was doing: I was outside in the garden playing, and she parked at the bottom near the road and told me she'd come to pick me up. I was really happy to see her, because it was boring being at home. My dad was out. He and Mum were arguing all the time.'

I glanced at Caroline. Understandably, she looked uncomfortable at that. Bad memories. Guilt. Grief. She reached out to put her hand on her son's leg, but changed her mind at the last moment. I wanted to reassure her. It was highly unlikely that Jamie remembered everything from that age accurately. The chances were that this was a story that had been drilled patiently into him over time. But of course, that didn't mean parts of it weren't true.

'And then what happened?'

'I went with Rebecca. But we didn't go to the nursery.'

'Can you remember where you did go?'

'An old fire station. There was a big tower, and Rebecca told me it was a game — to see how high we could climb, and who would be the quickest. So I raced her to the top, and I won. She took my photograph so I'd be able to remember.'

I was reluctant to ask the next question, but Jamie still seemed perfectly relaxed and at ease.

'And what happened to you then?'

'Something horrible happened.' He frowned, as though he didn't know for sure. 'And I died. But I can't remember, and God told me that I didn't have to.'

'That's fine, Jamie.'

'But I do know that's when they arrived.'

'They?'

His face brightened.

'The angels,' he said.

⋆ ⋆ ⋆

An hour later, after we'd finished talking, Jamie went up to his room, and I spoke to Caroline a little more downstairs.

'He's getting better,' she said. 'Already.'

I nodded. 'On the surface, he seems fine.'

Which was true. But then it was difficult to know how hard the situation really was for him. Throughout our conversation, he'd seemed self-assured, but there had also been a blankness to him. However resilient children might be, it

416

was going to be a long journey back for him, adjusting to real life.

He'd come alive most when talking about Cane Hill. From what he told me, the people there had given him a good life. He'd been looked after and treated well, and had wanted for nothing the whole time. From an earlier physical examination, there was no sign that he'd undergone any harm during his years as a prisoner there, and there was no evidence of torture or mind control. But of course, he had been so young that those things would not have been necessary. And he had been happy. As inexplicable as it might be from the outside, Cane Hill had been his world, and for the most part it had been a good one.

'Do you recognise this man?'

I'd shown him a photograph of the Cane twin we'd arrested at the scene.

Jamie smiled.

'That's God,' he said.

It was the most emotion he showed until the end of the interview, when he had asked me about Ella. Where was she? How was she? Could he see her? The bond between them was obvious. I could only be honest in answer to his questions. Ella was back with her mother, I told him. They were being supported and cared for, just as he was. And yes, perhaps one day he could see her again.

'He didn't recognise me at first.' Caroline looked like she might be about to cry. 'But he does now, I think. It's coming back to him.'

'He was very young when he went missing,' I

said. 'Those early memories must be vague for him.'

'But I think we all know deep down, don't we? I mean, I recognised him straight away, of course, but that's different; he hasn't changed so much. I like to think he does know, in his heart. That I'm his mother. That he *felt* it.'

I smiled. I liked the idea that there was something inside us that was forever connected to those we loved, and that we'd always be able to recognise it, no matter how long the absence between us and no matter how much we changed. I wasn't sure it was true.

'He'll be fine,' I said. 'I'm sure.'

She was silent for a moment.

'They tell me I can't see David.'

'I don't know all the details,' I said. 'But the way I understand things, that's for the best right now. He's been through a lot. He needs time to recover. He needs quiet and care.'

'What about the others?'

The others.

On the evening of our raid, we had found sixteen people at the compound. In addition to Cane himself, there had been six arrests: a man we had subsequently identified as a former soldier named Warren Merritt; and five individuals who had been working illegally at the hospital. We were trying to trace other workers who hadn't been on site at the time. The other ten we'd found that night had been residents. Jamie Groves and Ella Matheson had been treated well during their stay at Cane Hill, but the other eight all showed signs of extreme torture and deprivation. All were emaciated and facially scarred. Every single one of them was so mentally damaged that we had, so far, failed to even identify four of them.

'Some are doing better than others,' I said.

'I just don't understand *why*. Why they did that to them. And David especially.'

'We don't know,' I said, although that wasn't quite true.

There was still a lot we didn't know, and the men we had arrested were not being helpful in that regard. In interviews, Warren Merritt had spoken only to confirm his name. We knew that, a long time ago, he had been a soldier and a mercenary, and that he'd then moved into enforcement work for the city's underworld. But he'd disappeared nearly two decades ago, which was presumably the point at which he had been recruited to work for Cane. I imagined his skills and criminal connections had proved invaluable in researching sinners, following underground rumours and making connections, but beyond that, we could only guess. Either loyal to his employer to the last, or perhaps out of self-preservation, Merritt wouldn't talk to us. The five assistants arrested at the scene had been paid to do menial jobs — cooking and cleaning, for the most part — and seemed to know nothing of the wider purpose of Cane Hill.

Cane himself hadn't communicated with us at all. He simply sat in his cell, day and night, barely seeming to register his surroundings or attempts at conversation. On the occasions I'd tried to interview him, and whenever I ventured downstairs to look into his cell, he always had the exact same expression on his face. With his eyes closed, he looked completely serene, as though some deep battle within him had been completed, and now there was nothing left to say or do. The expression reminded me of something, although I couldn't think what.

And yet it was possible for us to put together part of it.

At the scene, we had found various records. There were details of anonymous financial donations Cane had made to deserving individuals over the years, along with reams of research undertaken: notes on possible offenders and accomplices; investigations into unsolved crimes. We had also found a book — a bible of a kind — apparently handwritten by Cane himself.

My fingers had tingled slightly the first time I touched it. It was old and weathered, and the black leather cover was stitched awkwardly around the different-sized pages inside: hundreds of sheets of tightly written black script. Some of the text was compressed to the extent that it was hard to make out individual letters, so that it appeared the whole page had been coloured in, whereas in other places it was more sparse. Sometimes the words were written in a regular fashion, while other sentences flowed in circles and waves, spiralling in from the outer edges of the paper to the centre, or vice versa. Some of them formed elaborate spiderwebs.

It was a work of concentrated insanity that must have taken years to compile, and I had no doubt that it had. And within it, there were clues as to the real truth behind Cane Hill.

What there wasn't, so far, was any mention of Nicholas Cane, the name the 50/50 Killer had given one time, and which had led Mercer to make the connection. So far, we had found no evidence of his existence at all. It seemed clear that he must have come from Cane Hill: the spiderwebs; the grudge against Mercer for taking his life. But who was he? He had been much younger than the Cane brother we'd arrested; was he a son? Perhaps, like Ella Matheson, he had been a child born to one of the captive sinners and raised in Heaven. We might never know. I thought of Mercer, and it pained me that he might not get the ending to his book that he wanted and needed. That even in death — even now — the 50/50 Killer remained an enigma to us.

'What about the grave?' Caroline said.

It shook me from my thoughts. 'The grave?'

'The body, I mean. The little boy we buried in place of Jamie.'

I hesitated. Strictly speaking, I shouldn't talk to her about it, especially when the results were not yet in. But then, she had visited those remains and mourned by that graveside, hadn't she? She had brought this unidentified child toys and flowers. That seemed like it should mean something.

'It's just that it's so horrible,' she continued. 'To imagine that another parent might be going through something like this right now. That their child is missing, and they don't even know where he is, or what happened to him . . .'

She trailed off, looking pained by the idea.

I chose my words carefully. 'We're still waiting for test results. I'll be honest: it *is* possible that it's the body of another missing child. But as far as we know, for all their other crimes, the Cane family never murdered children. Jamie and Ella were treated well. They were seen as innocents, without sins to wear.'

'So . . . ?'

'I'll let you know when we're sure. I promise.'

At the door, Caroline gave me that smile again, the one that was hard to read.

'It's difficult,' she said, 'but it's . . . so *good* to have him back. I prayed for it, when he went missing, but I never dared to believe it might actually happen. And when we had the body . . . Yet here he is. And however difficult it is right now, we'll work through it.'

Looking at her, I thought that, actually, I did recognise some of the emotions in her conflicted expression. That as difficult as it might be to have someone come back to you, it could sometimes be the most astonishing miracle.

★ ★ ★

Later that afternoon, the four members of our team gathered in the autopsy suite in the basement of the city hospital. Strictly speaking, three of us didn't need to be there; we could easily have waited for the official report to come through. But after everything that had happened, it felt right for us to attend.

Pete, Greg and I were standing side by side, with Simon across from us, on the other side of the gurney that had been wheeled out from the room beyond. I was close enough to feel the cold coming off it — the faintest of traces, like standing near a freezer that had been left ajar. There was a white sheet over the remains, and the items jutting against it were so small that they barely made an impression. The body might have been nothing more than a toy beneath a bed sheet.

Simon stared down at the gurney with a strange expression on his face, and I realised that I was too used to the archly raised eyebrow and the sarcasm, and that I'd never actually seen him where he did most of his work. Down here, he looked serious and respectful.

He reached out to the sheet and folded it delicately back, as though trying to untuck a blanket from someone sleeping without waking them. Fold after careful fold. The body revealed itself by increments.

By now, I had seen the crime-scene photos from when the remains had been found. I was familiar with the sight of the tiny skeleton lying on its side, curled in a peaceful pose as if it might somehow still be dreaming. In life, the remains were even smaller; an empty gurney would have weighed the same. The body was lying on its back now, some of the pale bones broken apart, its few remaining sweeps of hair dry and tense.

'So here he is,' Simon said softly.

He left the unspoken question hanging in the air for a moment. I glanced to one side, and saw that Pete and Greg were staring down at the body too. As Simon turned away to the counter behind him, the room was so quiet that all I could hear was a hum in the air: a ringing sound that was possibly only in my head.

When he turned back, he was holding the paperwork. It seemed strangely thin — a couple of sheets at most. Stupid, really, to have expected more. Not being a scientist, perhaps I'd imagined that a DNA test involved reams of paperwork, even though the end result came down to only a sentence or two.

'The test proved conclusive,' Simon said. 'Which is to say there is a correlation between the DNA of the two individuals tested, and the chances of that being coincidental are so insignificant as to be dismissible.'

He looked down at the gurney again, and smiled sadly.

'So what we have here are the remains of either Jonathan or Joseph Cane. Impossible to know, of course, which brother was which.'

I stared at the body, letting the information settle in my head. After we'd uncovered the history of Cane Hill Hospital, I'd been imagining a particular scenario: twin brothers, raised in relative isolation by strictly religious parents. We might never know the full circumstances, but we knew they'd grown up insular and warped, and ultimately intent on establishing their own version of the afterlife here on earth. Rewarding, as they saw it, the worthy, and punishing the guilty. One brother as God, the other as the Devil. One in charge of Heaven, the other of Hell. Joseph and Jonathan Cane.

But only one brother had been arrested at the

scene. There had been no trace of the other. And while Cane's handwritten bible had hinted at the truth, it wasn't until now that we could be sure. The other twin had died decades earlier, at roughly three years of age, and the surviving brother had been raised alone.

There had never been a separate God and Devil in charge at Cane Hill. There had simply been both, all at once, in the same man.

We would never know for sure what his upbringing had been like, but parts of the Cane Hill bible suggested certain things. After the death of his twin, it seemed he had been shunned and despised by his mother — that perhaps she had blamed him in some way. She had idolised the dead son, and called the other the Devil. And yet he had remained devoted to her. Throughout the entirety of the bible, there was not a single mention of his father.

She had attempted suicide, and upon her return to the property had been hospitalised on the upper floor, convinced she was dead and in Heaven. Cane had been forced to visit her, but she was no longer able to recognise him. Sometimes she thought he was the bad son, the Devil; at others that it was the good son who had come to visit her. I could hardly imagine the confusion it must have caused a child that age. The desire to be loved and accepted. The fight within him; the lifelong struggle to understand: the hated child, or the good? Who was he at heart? Which was he?

And so it came to pass that He became They.
Greg broke the silence.

'So these remains are . . . ?'

'Over sixty years old,' Simon said. 'Yes.'

'How could that happen?'

'It's not like computers, Greg, where everything is date-stamped.' For a second, Simon seemed angry, but the emotion vanished quickly. 'With skeletal remains, it's very hard to tell. Over hundreds of years, yes, of course, you can see the difference. And there are more specific tests for shorter terms, but they're not conclusive. For the most part, we have to go by circumstance, objects, clothing. And so on.'

He didn't elaborate further, and didn't need to. The body in the pit had been found dressed in the clothes Jamie Groves had been wearing when he disappeared. There had been the stuffed toy. The body had been the right age, the right ethnicity, and it had been found in a shallow grave in the woods. There had been a missing child, and there had been the need for closure. Taken together, it had been enough.

One particular passage in Cane's bible came back to me now.

And She told Them that within the heart of each individual Man the larger battle was present, just as the entirety of the tree resides in the seed. And they asked if between Them, They might therefore settle that nature in Their lifespan, and She told Them this was so.

And while I might never entirely understand Cane's motivations, I remembered the peaceful expression on the man's face now, and realised what it reminded me of. He looked like a child who had finally gone to sleep.

426

A boy and his Bear

'Are you ready?'

Sasha, calling up from downstairs. We had a long trip ahead of us, and — this was just like her — she'd been ready for at least an hour, impatient for most of that time. Always prepared. She was far more organised and efficient than I was.

'Just a minute,' I called back.

Things were much better between us now. We'd talked, and I thought she understood. This holiday had been her idea — a week away, to celebrate our engagement properly, and to escape from it all. While I had one thing I wanted to do first, the rest of the week would be ours to do as we pleased. To leave the past behind entirely, and just live in the moment, the now.

I opened the drawer in my bedside table, then lifted the pile of papers there, searching out the photograph at the bottom. I took it out and stared at it.

Lise and me. I'd taken it myself, holding the camera out at arm's length, but I couldn't remember the exact circumstances. We'd been on holiday, obviously, but not the one on which she'd drowned. It was strange: I just couldn't remember any more. There was a whole period of life on either side of this still image, and I just couldn't recall it. I didn't even know what I'd been thinking when I pressed the button and froze this single moment in time.

'Are you *not* ready?' Sasha shouted up.

'I'm *ready*.'

I put the photograph back in the drawer, the other stuff on top of it. So much wonderful stuff — all the cards and notes from Sasha especially. I had loved Lisc once; I knew that. But that was a long time ago. The photograph, recording a moment that must have been lovely at the time, went back to the bottom of the drawer, hidden away now by all the other stuff that I'd piled on top of it.

Exactly where it belonged.

★   ★   ★

The sides of the road were lined with thick trees, the branches above ending in luscious bunches of leaves, while the drive itself was powdery and dry but had the carefully raked appearance of stones in a Zen garden. The car's tyres pushed it gently down, making the compacting noise of a boot pressed slowly into snow. There was no sign of the fences behind the trees, or the fields and groves of apple trees beyond, but the sun flickered across the road, the foliage scattering the light like handfuls of bright leaves. We could have been driving through an idyllic forest — the only traffic for miles — rather than into a secure compound.

It was a world away from the drab road and

dirty clearing of Cane Hill. There were certainly far worse places that David Groves could have ended up.

Sasha took the car round a corner. Fields opened up to the sides, far and wide, and the main building revealed itself up ahead. We pulled up in the parking area close to the entrance.

'Am I waiting here?' Sasha said.

'Do you mind?'

'I have absolutely no desire to go in there.' She smiled. 'So long as we get the rest of the week together.'

'We will, don't worry.'

Inside, the floor of the reception was tiled — black and white squares, alternating, like a chess board — and polished so well that a mirror image of myself hung down below me as I approached the front desk. I might have been walking into a prestigious hotel, except that the young woman behind the desk was dressed in a pale-blue nurse's uniform, and there was only a single other door in the whole area. It was to the left of the desk, with an electronic keypad on the wall beside it.

'Hello,' I said.

The woman gave me the professional smile.

'Detective Nelson?'

'That's right.' I showed her my badge for identification. 'I have an appointment. I'm sorry. I'm a little early, I know.'

'It's fine. Bear with me, please.'

She smiled again, but checked the identification carefully, then made a brief phone call.

'He'll be right through,' she told me.

'Thank you.'

There was nowhere to sit, so I paced back and forth a little, but I didn't have long to wait. It was barely a minute before the secure door buzzed open and a man stepped through. He was short and, despite his obvious youth, dressed in an old-fashioned way: suit, shirt and waistcoat beneath a long white coat.

'Dr Gallagher?'

He shook my hand.

'Detective Nelson. Good to see you. Please follow me through.'

After a short trip through corridors that were as plush as the reception, he ushered me into a large office, closing the door behind us. The walls were lined with bookshelves, most of the titles on them academic: big, thick books. I scanned them, a small number of them bringing back vague memories from my own studies. The air smelled of wood and varnish, with an undercurrent of flowers.

'Have a seat.'

He gestured to a comfortable chair by his desk. When I sat down, Gallagher moved to the other side and took his own. The window behind him was bright white in the sun, making the doctor slightly hard to make out, almost silhouetted against it.

'Thank you for seeing me,' I said.

'Not at all. I'm grateful, to be honest; I know you've come a long way. But I'm sorry, you're going to be disappointed.'

I felt a little deflated, although not entirely surprised.

'I can't see him?'

'No. I don't think that would be wise today.'

'Okay.' I nodded. 'Well, I knew it might not happen. And I don't want to do anything that's going to . . . distress him.'

'David has suffered a break from reality. He still believes that he committed suicide two years ago, but that ultimately he passed a test God set for him. He believes he's in Heaven now. And he's happy. I'm reluctant to disturb that for the moment.'

I reached into my coat pocket, retrieving the piece of paper I'd brought with me, then unfolded it carefully on the desk between us. I'd cut it out from a newspaper a week ago. It detailed how Paul Carlisle had been charged in connection with the abduction of numerous children, and the possible murder of five. While many of his victims had not been identified and traced, early indications suggested Carlisle was not intending to contest the charges so far.

'David was a good man,' I said. 'A good policeman. His ex-partner told me that if he ever came face to face with the people who'd abducted his son, he wouldn't have taken revenge. He'd have arrested them.'

I passed the news clipping over.

'And I thought that if at some point he does get better, he might like to know that's what happened.'

Gallagher read it through.

'May I keep this?' he said. When I nodded, he folded the clipping away and placed it in the pocket of his suit jacket. 'It wouldn't be a good thing for him to see right now, I don't think. But maybe one day.'

'You say he's not well today?'

'That's one way of looking at it. Another is that he's very well indeed, given what's happened to him.' Gallagher stood up and moved over to the window, peering out. 'Come over here and look.'

I got up and joined him.

The window of his office looked out over the rear garden: a large, gently sloping expanse of grass, dotted with bright yellow dandelion stars and surrounded by apple trees. There were orderlies wandering around, here and there, their white uniforms blindingly bright in the sun. There were also patients, some meandering over the grass, with an orderly keeping pace beside them, others sitting all but alone on the handful of benches.

I scanned the grounds for a moment, until finally I saw him. David Groves was sitting alone, cross-legged on the ground, surrounded by objects, although the distance made it difficult to work out what they were and what he was doing with them. Even from here, though, it was obvious that he was talking to himself. An orderly was stationed casually nearby — but a little distance behind Groves, and not close enough to be part of the conversation.

'What's he doing?' I said.

Gallagher smiled sadly.

'He's playing with his son.'

★ ★ ★

'Catch!'

Jamie giggled as he brought his hands together, and caught the stuffed Pooh by accident rather than real design. But he caught it all the same, and that counted, so he shrieked with delight.

Hello, Pooh Bear. He gave the top of the bear's head a smacking kiss.

Groves felt an indescribable burst of love. Jamie was exactly as he remembered him. With the long blond hair that didn't quite brush his tiny shoulders, but curled up as though afraid to touch them. With the shark T-shirt and jeans, and the little red mark on his cheek that never seemed to get better or worse. With his love of life and complete lack of fear, and the way he ran about this field at full tilt — at a speed that was almost frightening — with his arms out to the sides like an aeroplane. With the way he spotted a butterfly and squatted slightly, hands on knees, and stared at it in wonder — at *everything* in wonder, in fact, because so much of the world was new to him. Because there was so much to be discovered.

Again, Daddy, again!

He passed Groves the stuffed toy. He was so excited that the words ran together:

Letsdothatagain!

And so they did.

Of course they did.

There was so much lost time to make up for. Against the backdrop of a perfect bright green field, they played with his toys, over and over, in whatever way he wanted. It was a sunny day. The

433

breeze ruffled Jamie's hair, but if he was at all cold, he never mentioned it. He was too busy. Too delighted. And there was nothing else Groves would rather be doing. He couldn't think of anything that would be more lovely than this.

Can I give you a cuddle?

'Yes,' Groves said. 'Of course you can.'

Jamie ran up and pressed himself against him. Groves hugged him back, closing his eyes, and then his son leaned away and yawned.

Are you happy now, Daddy?

'Yes,' Groves said. 'I couldn't be happier. Sleepy, little man?'

Yes, Daddy.

'You can have a nap if you want.'

Okay.

Jamie lay down on the grass, and immediately rolled on to his side. Hands clasped in front of his slightly open mouth; feet crossed at the ankles; soft blond hair swept back behind his ear. The peace of him stunned Groves. A little boy drifting off to sleep. Everything else was worthwhile; the day had been won.

And so many days to come, here in Heaven, where they had finally been reunited.

Endless possibilities.

Just for a second, it was like the sun went behind a cloud, and when Groves looked down at his son, he thought he could see something else. As though Jamie was flickering slightly. Not quite there.

But then he concentrated, and he was back.

Jamie yawned again. *Can I have a story, please?*

434

'Yes.'

Of course he could have a story. We're *all allowed stories*, Groves thought. He didn't even need a book to read from. Having read it so many times, he could do it from memory, and he did so now, as the breeze gently moved the grass.

Over time, Jamie grew still, slumbering peacefully, but Groves finished anyway. A story about how we leave things behind as time passes, but how they're always there, waiting for us to come back to them, or them to us, whenever we care to remember.

We do hope that you have enjoyed reading this large print book.

Did you know that all of our titles are available for purchase?

We publish a wide range of high quality large print books including:
Romances, Mysteries, Classics
General Fiction
Non Fiction and Westerns

Special interest titles available in large print are:
The Little Oxford Dictionary
Music Book
Song Book
Hymn Book
Service Book

Also available from us courtesy of Oxford University Press:
Young Readers' Dictionary
(large print edition)
Young Readers' Thesaurus
(large print edition)

For further information or a free brochure, please contact us at:
Ulverscroft Large Print Books Ltd.,
The Green, Bradgate Road, Anstey,
Leicester, LE7 7FU, England.
Tel: (00 44) 0116 236 4325
Fax: (00 44) 0116 234 0205

Other titles published by Ulverscroft:

THE NIGHTMARE PLACE

Steve Mosby

DI Zoe Dolan is tracking the Creeper, a stalker who's been breaking into women's homes and attacking them. The Creeper's violence is escalating and there's no pattern, no clue as to how he's getting in, and no clue as to who's next. Until Jane Webster gets a call to the helpline where she volunteers. He says he loves these women — but it's a love that ends in blood. When Jane tells the police, it should be the lead that Zoe needs — but it only pulls her further into a case that is already taking her dangerously close to the past she's never fully escaped. For Jane, Zoe and all the other young women of the city, suddenly nowhere is safe. Particularly their own bedroom in the dead of night . . .

BLACK FLOWERS

Steve Mosby

As if from nowhere, she appears, on a seaside promenade, with a black flower and a horrifying story about where she's been — which starts a chain reaction of dangerous lies that will claim more victims . . . Neil Dawson, though devastated when his father — a writer — commits suicide, knows something isn't right. And when he finds, among his father's possessions, a copy of an old novel, *The Black Flower*, Neil will be taken into a dangerous and painful investigation. Hannah Price is also mourning her father. Following his footsteps into the police force, she has a big reputation to live up to. When she's assigned to Neil's father's case, it will lead her on a journey into her own past and to the heart of a shattering secret.

STILL BLEEDING

Steve Mosby

After his wife's death, Alex Connor just wanted oblivion. Only his friend Sarah kept him going, but she's been murdered. And whilst the police have the killer, they don't have her body. The gruesome search for her drags Alex back into the land of the living — and the dead. Policeman Paul Kearney is tracking a killer who's abducting women and draining them of blood. He's drawn into a world of dark desires that people will go to great lengths to hide. Wound together by their search, if they're to save themselves and the people they love, Alex and Kearney must go to a place where normal rules don't apply — where people trade murder memorabilia, and a place where life is only the first thing you lose.

CRY FOR HELP

Steve Mosby

Dave Lewis is a man with a history. Haunted by his brother's murder when they were children, and drowning his sorrows over his lost love, Tori, he tries to leave the past behind. Dave had made a promise to Tori, which got him into trouble before, but he won't let that happen again. Detective Sam Currie is a man with a past. A shadow of grief lies over his marriage and his career. He's directed his hatred towards the man he sees as responsible, but he has other priorities right now. A killer is stalking the city, abducting girls and sending texts and emails to their families before he kills them. When Dave Lewis appears to connect both investigations, it's an opportunity Currie can't resist . . .